Crystal Heart

First paperback edition November 2021

Published by WRLMorris Publishing
Book design by Whitney Morris

ISBN 978-1-916935-00-6 (Paperback)
ISBN 978-1-916935-01-3 (Hardback)

www.wrlmorris.com

Daniel

Thanks for always believing and
giving me the strength to choose for myself

Prologue
Maggie

Maggie's heart pounded. Her limbs were shaking as she heaved for breath. Her legs ached from running. Sweat dripped down her back. As she rounded a corner, her knees buckled, and she crumpled to the ground. Her lungs burned as she sucked in cold air. With the back of her hand, she wiped the sweat from her face and took in her surroundings. Nothing but dark green leaves surrounded her. All around her were thick prickly hedges, that towered up into the sky. Every turn she'd taken looked the same as the one before. With every breath she took, it felt as if her lungs might burst. Gritting her teeth, Maggie closed her eyes and took slow breaths. She had no idea how she had ended up in this maze. It was horribly quiet, except for the disturbingly high-pitched screeches that echoed all around every few minutes. It sounded like a cross between a broken siren and a cat being strangled. She shuddered just at the thought of it. As she racked her finger through her long curls, Maggie let out a frustrated shriek. There had to be a way out of this maze.

Just an hour ago—at least she thought it had been an hour—Maggie had been walking down the high street on her way home. The sounds of traffic and the smell of car fumes had filled the air. She'd been busy thinking about what to have for dinner when everything went black. When she came to, she was covered in leaves, and everything smelled like mouldy vegetables. Before she'd been able to process where she was, that ghastly screech shook the hedges. She took off running and hadn't stopped till now.

Maggie pushed herself up and forced her legs forward.

Her limbs felt like jelly but she couldn't give up now. An exit could be just around the corner. As she came to another turn, her legs gave way, and she stumbled into a hedge. She threw her arms up over her head as thorns dug into her skin. She cried out in pain and quickly pulled herself out of the bush. Maggie slumped onto the ground, her eyes filling with tears. This wasn't working. She snorted and bit her bottom lip. Now wasn't the time to cry. Blindly running around was getting her nowhere, she had to think. First, she would deal with her wounds. Maggie lifted her injured arm to her face. Several scratches covered the length of it. They would be easily healed. She waved her other hand over her cuts and muttered the words, "Sanum quod fit." Her hand began to glow. One by one, her cuts disappeared. Being a descendant of magic beings from another world had its benefits.

Magic! Maggie slapped her forehead. Why hadn't she thought of it sooner? She'd been pretending to be human for so long it hadn't crossed her mind. Closing her eyes, she let her senses take over, and there it was—the gentle hum of magic. The area stank of it. Someone strong had created this place. She was more out of practice than she thought to have not noticed earlier.

Maggie ran her hand over the hedges and tried to push the branches apart. Nothing happened. Her forehead creased as she frowned. Never had she come across a plant she couldn't manipulate before. She narrowed her eyes at the leaves on the hedge. There was no life energy being emitted from them.

Clenching her jaw, she slammed her hands on the ground, and it began to shake. There were tremors beneath her feet, but the scenery did not falter. The ground did not crack like it should. Nor did any of the hedges move. Maggie yelled as she punched the ground. It was an illusion. How had she been so stupid? Tightening her fist, the tremors stopped. Throwing her arms in the air, light illuminated around her. As she rose to her feet, she pushed the light out. The area in front of her cracked. Maggie pulled the light back and refocused it on the crack. The illusion shattered like a glass window.

Maggie blinked a few times as if waking from a dream.

In front of her stood a forest full of evergreens. The smell of damp leaves and pine overwhelmed her. She shivered as the wind blew through the trees, rustling the leaves. Where was she? A slow clap sounded behind her. Maggie spun round.

"You really are the one," came a voice in the trees. "I was starting to think that fool had brought me the wrong girl, but you really are her heir."

Maggie searched the trees for the source of the voice. "Who's there?"

A dark figure stepped out from the trees. Maggie stumbled back, eyes wide. Shadows flowed from the figure. The Shadow Man. But that was just a story her parents had told her to frighten her as a child—a way to make sure she kept her powers hidden from the humans. He couldn't be real.

The figure walked toward her. Two black wings sprouted from the creature's back. Talons grew from its hands. Long, dark curls circled the creature's face. Shadows danced around the distinct curves of a female. The shadow man was in fact a woman. Black whisps jumped from the creature, toward Maggie. She screamed, jumping back and falling over a branch.

The dark figure cackled. "Is this it? This is all the fight I get?"

Maggie scrambled backward, trying to get her feet under her. "Who—what?"

"Disappointing. I hope the other heir is more entertaining," mused the shadow-lady's sinister voice.

Maggie's blood ran cold. They knew there was another. How could they know about her? This was all her fault. Her parents had warned her not to stay in one place too long, not to marry a human, but she had fallen in love. She'd gotten careless, too comfortable. She would not let this creature find the other heir. Maggie clenched her fists. Light radiated from her. She jumped to her feet. With all her strength, she threw a massive blast of light at the creature. A loud boom echoed through the forest. The trees in front of her lay flat. She spun round on the spot. Where had that dark figure gone? Had she defeated it? Shadow only existed in the absence of light, and she was light. Maggie was hit with a big gust of wind, and her feet flew off the ground. She screamed as she was thrown up in the air. Reaching out, Maggie called to the trees. They rapidly grew upwards, but before they could catch her, a shadow snaked round her. Maggie screamed as she was slammed into the ground. Her flesh sizzled as dark whisps dug into her skin.

"You know, earth magic is common amongst elves," the sinister voice came from above, "but light magic, now that's rare, and you have both. It's what makes you royals stand out."

Maggie wriggled on the ground. She tried to summon light, but it wouldn't come. There was a thud beside her, and a hand yanked her hair. Two big, yellow, eagle-like eyes stared her in the face.

"Now, girl," said the Shadow Lady, "tell me where I can find the other royal, and I'll make your death quick."

"Th-There is no other," stuttered Maggie. A sharp pain shot through her face as talons dug into her cheek.

"Do not lie to me. My sources tell me there is another."

Maggie winced as the talons dug deeper into her skin. Warm blood dripped down her cheek. She forced herself to stare into the shadow lady's eyes. "There is no other."

Maggie hit the ground with a thud. Dirt filled her mouth as a heavy weight pushed into her back.

"Slow deaths are always more fun."

Maggie shut her eyes. It didn't matter what this monster did to her; she would not give up the last royal. She wished she'd been given more time to teach her about magic. She hadn't even come into her powers yet. Maybe that was a good thing. It was how Maggie had been found. If no one taught her magic, she would pass as human. She would be safe.

Her daughter would be safe.

Behind the Curtain
Gregory

16 Years Later

The clickity-clack of trains rolling in and out of the station echoed off the high walls. People rushed about, hardly looking up, yet they all seemed to know where they were going. Greg took a deep breath as he tried to stop himself from pacing. Once again, he checked his watch for what felt like the hundredth time. Samson was late. He had agreed to meet him here almost twenty minutes ago. If he didn't get here soon, Samson would miss the train. Greg couldn't risk being late. The council didn't like being made to wait. He'd spent the entirety of the previous night trying to figure out what he had done wrong, but he couldn't think of anything. His father had drilled him with the rules and regulations of the council from a very young age. He'd spent his nineteen years of life trying to stay on the good side of the council. It didn't make sense for them to call on him like this.

A train screeched into the station. It was his train. He scoured the crowd for his cousin with no luck. The doors of the train whooshed open as Greg approached them. It looked like he was going to the capital on his own. Greg found a seat on the almost empty train. Who would want to go to the capital if they didn't have to? It was the last place he wanted to go, but he didn't have a choice. He looked out the window, hoping to see his cousin frantically running for the train. Hordes of people rushed by his window, none of which were Samson. Greg looked down at his hands as he fiddled with his fingers. Maybe he should get off and pretend he missed the train. Better yet, maybe he should get on another train, never to be seen again. He could go live in the north with the dwarfs. Their settlement was the farthest away from his home. They probably wouldn't have the same high expectations of him as his father. Although, his height may be a problem.

A high-pitched whistle blew, and the train shuddered forward. Greg sank into his seat. It was too late to try to run away now. Or was it? He could always hop on another train once he got to the capital. Samson hadn't made it to the station on time. There was no one to make him go to his meeting. However, he knew if he chose this course of action, he could never come back. His father would never forgive him. There had been many times when he'd thought about going against his father's wishes, but he couldn't bring himself to do it. Greg sat up straight and smoothed out his shirt. He needed to stop thinking like this. Whatever the council had in store for him, he could handle it. After all, he was the youngest person to ever pass the healing exam. He'd been told it was impossible, but he had done it. Thinking about his academic achievements didn't ease the churning in his stomach. If only he knew what they wanted. Greg jumped as someone sat down next to him. He'd been so lost in thought that he hadn't noticed Samson approach.

"Sorry I'm late," Samson said, "but I made it just in time to catch the train. I have been searching the carriages for you. They're fuller than usual."

"They are?" Greg asked. He'd only seen four other people on the train when he got on.

"Yeah. I've been the only one on this train before. No one wants to go to the capital if they don't have to. I thought for a moment that you hadn't made the train, but that was just silly of me. You're never late."

Greg pushed his fringe back. The last time he was late to something, he was six. His father hated tardiness, and he was punished accordingly. He'd never been late for anything since. He always arrived exactly when he meant to, which meant he was always early. " Did you manage to find anything out about this meeting?"

"I have no idea what the council wants to see you about." Samson leant back in his seat. "I may work for them, but I don't have the privilege of knowing what occurs in their meetings, and as you know, I spend most of my time off-site. Why did you need me here?"

This was true. Greg had all the council procedures memorised. Yet, for some reason, he'd hoped for a different answer. He sank even farther into his seat. "I don't know. I guess I'm just nervous."

Samson tilted his head as his eyebrows drew together. "Why are you nervous? You've met with the council before. Your father is a senior member. They've all been to your house."

"This is different. They were not official meetings. It's never good when they summon an outsider to a council chambers like this."

"Greg, you are not exactly an outsider. Besides you are so by the book, I don't see what the council could possibly be mad at you about. It could be something positive they wish to see you for."

"It's just extremely frustrating. I cannot think for the life of me what they could want. Good or bad."

"You'll find out once we arrive. Just sit back and enjoy the train ride. Besides, I'm sure your father wouldn't let anything bad happen to you."

Greg raised his eyebrow. "Well, you have more faith in my father than I do." Greg leant on his armrest and looked out the window. The outside world rushed by in a blur. His father cared more about keeping things hunky-dory with the council than he did about him. He might've been his father's successor, but he would've easily been passed over if he didn't live up to his expectations.

They arrived in the capital with time to spare, just as planned. Greg shuddered as they walked from the station to the council building. It had been bright and sunny when they left—

a nice spring morning—but the capital was dark and gloomy. As usual, it was overclouded with grey. Greg pulled the collar of his jacket up and tucked his hands in his pockets. The bright colours of the city always seemed dim. The darkness that loomed in the air always made Greg uneasy.

They sat in the council tearooms as Greg waited to be called on. As he sat sipping tea with Samson, he regretted being so early. He was already nervous, but with the dark shadow that loomed over the council, he felt worse than before. For some reason, today the shadowy aura seemed stronger. Trying to calm his nerves, Greg fiddled with his shirt collar and smoothed out his clothes. Just because he felt like a nervous wreck didn't mean he had to look it.

Samson patted him on the back. "Stop messing with your collar. Your shirt is fine. Neat and tidy as always, except your hair. That's what you should be messing with."

Greg patted his hair down and ran his fingers through his fringe. "What's wrong with my hair?"

"It's in desperate need of a cut, and maybe you should comb it occasionally."

Greg folded his arms. "I comb my hair."

Samson stirred his drink. "Of course you do. You and my sister are the same. It must be a healer thing. As long as it doesn't get in the way, you don't care if your hair is a mess."

Greg had taken extra time this morning to make sure he was dressed appropriately to meet with the council, but he hadn't thought about his hair. He never did. Samson's hair was shorter than his and neatly combed back. In comparison, Greg's hair looked like a messy mop. It also didn't help that he had bright red hair whereas his cousin's was mouse brown. A much neater colour. Greg flopped his hands on his lap, giving up on his appearance. "How do you work with this darkness over you all the time?" Greg asked as he pointed above them.

Samson shrugged. "Why do you think I prefer to work off-site? It's really off-putting."

"Isn't the council doing anything about it? I don't remember it being this bad as a kid. What if it spreads?"

Samson looked at the wall and fidgeted in his seat. "It

already is."

Greg's blood ran cold. How could the council have let this happen? Was there really no way for them to stop it? Before he could question Samson further, a messenger approached the table and informed him the council was ready to see him. Samson patted him on the back and wished him good luck. Greg followed the messenger down the long corridor to the main hall. He'd never been inside the official meeting chambers before. Only council members and whoever was on messenger duty were authorised to enter. It was very rare that they invited outsiders in. It had to be a matter of great importance to do so. Greg checked his shirt was straight one last time before entering the room.

The hall was much simpler than he'd expected. Plain cream walls with two big oil paintings hung on opposite sides. The only furniture in the room was a big oval table, which all the council members were sitting round. Everyone turned to look at him. He bowed. As he rose, he searched the table for his father. He spotted him on the right, but he would not meet Greg's eyes.

Lady Gabrielle stood and gave him a gentle smile. "Gregory, it is good of you to join us this morning." Greg let out a sigh of relief. She didn't seem angry, in fact she'd smiled. Lady Gabrielle was the chairwoman of the council. If she was happy, it meant the rest of them would be. "You are probably wondering why we have called you here. It is nothing to worry about. We simply want to know more about your research paper on the Great War and the elves."

Why were the council reading his paper? It was well written, and he'd gotten top marks as usual. With his grade on that paper, he now only needed twenty more credits to get his honours, but that wouldn't concern the council. "What exactly do you want to know about it?" he asked.

Lady Gabrielle interlaced her fingers. "We wanted to know how you came to your conclusion at the end of your research paper. Specifically the part about the possible location of the keeper of the Heart Crystal."

"I did a lot of research to see if there was anything more

to the story. It was something that had been bothering me for a while. I've never met an elf. No one has. They haven't been seen for years. I concluded they must have crossed the veil. Freya's heir was only a baby at the time. Maybe the elves thought she would be safer hidden amongst the humans. They're the only beings that cannot sense someone's magical aura."

"I must say, it is a very good theory. After I read your paper, I couldn't help wondering why no one else had thought of it. Which is why when the elders put you forward as the next candidate to be entrusted with the Heart Crystal, it was a unanimous vote."

Greg's eyes widened. He rubbed his ears to check he was hearing correctly. "Wait, you want me to go in search for the next crystal keeper?"

She nodded. "We want you to test your theory. We have located a tear in the veil. We are sending you to the human world. This will be no easy task. Do you accept?"

"Yes, of course."

"Good. You know how important it is that we find Freya's heir. We have lived with this darkness for far too long. We need to put an end to it."

Greg nodded. "I understand." This was what they were doing about the shadow, which meant they didn't have the power to stop it on their own.

"Very well." Lady Gabrielle flicked her wrist. "You should go prepare for your journey. You shall be given the crystal before you depart."

Greg bowed before leaving. His head spun. He'd gone to the meeting expecting the worst, but it had been the exact opposite. It was a great honour to be selected for such an important job. He felt like he was about to explode with excitement, but he kept a steady pace as he walked down the corridor. Keeping a cool outside appearance while on the inside he was leaping for joy. This was his chance to prove his capabilities. If he managed to succeed where so many had failed before, it would bring great honour. Maybe his father was more interested in what he did then he thought. He was the only person that could have shown his paper to the rest of the council. He'd never dreamed that writing that paper would lead to this. This was his chance to do something great. He was going to find the new keeper of the Heart Crystal.

Greg sat across from his father. Their carriage bounced along the bumpy pathways of the forest. He turned the crystal over in his hand. Such a simple stone, yet it held so much power, but only in the right hands. His father had barely looked at him the whole journey and had only spoken to acknowledge his existence when he entered the carriage. Greg had so many questions he wanted to ask. How had they found the tear? How had they acquired the human currency they'd given him? How were they so sure the humans on the other side spoke English? But he knew his questions would be met with disdain. His father had never been fond of questions. Greg was meant to do what he was told without ever asking why.

The carriage drew to a halt. Greg tied the crystal round his neck and looked out his window. They were no longer in the forest but atop a cliff. In the distance, he could see the ocean. They couldn't be too far away from the water nymph city. The carriage door swung open, and the footman bowed as he and his father got out.

"This way," said his father, walking to the cliffside. Greg quickly followed. His father halted on the edge. He pointed at a narrow gap between the rock. "Down there."

"Down there what?" Greg asked.

His father arched a eyebrow. "The tear is down there. No person has ever crossed it. You will be the first. We've only used it for research purposes."

"What sort of research?"

His father scowled at him. "That is not your concern. This is where we part ways. I put my reputation on the line recommending you for this job. Do not embarrass me." His father turned and walked back the way they'd come.

Greg clenched his jaw. "Goodbye to you too."

He had no idea how long he would be gone. It could be years, and all his father could say was "Do not embarrass me." He didn't know what he'd expected. His father had never been the emotional type. Maybe "Good luck, son" or some sort of well wishes. Greg shook his head. What was he thinking? He was a disappointment until he proved otherwise. He repositioned his bag on his shoulder and pushed his way through the rock. It was a tight squeeze, but he made it through into a small cave.

There was nothing inside except a small pool of water. Was that the tear? Greg dipped his toe in the pool. Nothing happened. It would've been nice if someone had given him a bit more detail on what to do. What exactly did a tear in the veil look like? Greg walked round the cave, dragging his hand across the wall. As he came back to the edge of the pool, something on the wall behind it caught his eye. He tilted his head and squinted. The wall was somehow distorted. He gasped. That was it.

Holding his bag above his head, he waded through the water to the other side. He put his hand on the back wall, and it disappeared. Greg gasped, pulling his hand back. He looked it over, then reached for the wall. Once again, his hand disappeared. A smile spread across his face. It was amazing. His hand was on the other side of the veil. Greg patted the crystal under his shirt and stepped through.

He landed with a thud. The smell of fresh cut grass invaded his nostrils. He stood, dusting himself off. All he could see for miles was grass and more grass. In the distance was what looked like rocks stacked to make a shape. This was the human world. It didn't seem too bad, but where were all the humans? Greg stepped forward. Suddenly, a high-pitched alarm went off. The grass around him rapidly grew and snaked its way round his arms and legs. He tried to fight it, but it was too strong. Out of nowhere, three men appeared.

"What is this?" Greg yelled.

The older man, who was holding a stick, stepped forward. He was average height with brown skin and short, dark, greying curls. "Tell your dark lord all the royals are long gone. We don't know how to find them. Leave the rest of us in peace."

Greg struggled against his restraints. "My what? I have no idea what you're talking about."

The man jabbed him with his stick. "You cannot fool us. Others have come looking before. Just because you've made yourself look human doesn't mean we'll fall for your master's tricks."

"Seriously, I have no idea what you're talking about. My name is Greg. I was sent by the council to find the heir to the elf throne and deliver the Heart to them."

"I knew you'd come looking for the royals. You think you can trick us by claiming the council sent you." He turned to the group behind him. "Tighten his binds, and take him to the dungeon."

The grass binds tightened around Greg as the other two men walked toward him. Why wouldn't they listen? He had barely started his search, and it had already gone wrong. On the bright side, he appeared to have found a group of elves. The two men reached to pick him up by his arms and feet. He gritted his teeth. He was not getting locked up. Greg shifted into a small bird, and the vines fell away. The men shouted. Greg hovered beside one of them. As he turned toward him, Greg transformed back. He grabbed the man's arm, flipping him over. The man yelled, and Greg flicked his wrist, trapping him with a barrier. Greg shifted into a mouse and scurried through the grass. He ran up the other man's leg. The man shouted, trying to swat him away. Greg shifted back to human form, taking the man's legs out from under him. Before he could stand, Greg flicked his wrist, trapping the man with another barrier. Greg walked toward the older man.

"You're—you're a changeling," stammered the older man, pointing his stick at Greg.

"Yes, I am," Greg said. "I don't know of this dark lord you speak of. I was sent by the council to find the elves. You're an elf, right?"

The man narrowed his eyes. "How can I be sure you are telling the truth?"

Greg pulled the crystal from round his neck and held it up for the man to see. "Because I have this."

The man's jaw dropped. "But that's—how?"

Greg tied the crystal back round his neck. "Like I said, the council sent me to deliver the Heart to its keeper."

The man lowered his stick. "My name is Daniel. I am acting leader of the elves. We have much to talk about."

A Fateful Encounter
Mellissa

creams echo around me. The ground is shaking. The ceiling has caved in. I look up at the night sky. The moon is full. A shiver shoots down my spine. A man hovers above me. I cannot see his face, but I know he's bad news. Every urge in my body tells me to run away, but I don't. He lands in front of me with a boom. The ground under his feet cracks.

"Thing's don't have to be like this," I shout.

He looks at me, his eyes dark and cold. There is no emotion in them. "You made your choice. Now you must live with it."

He runs at me with some sort of shadow sword. Swirls of light come to my aid. We both take flight, and our battle continues mid-air. So much damage. Everything is in ruins. We are evenly matched. I can't win. Dropping to the ground, I whisper to a tree. As he comes at me again, the tree begins to glow. Its branches reach out and pull him in. I whisper to the tree again. It stops glowing. He is gone, trapped inside the tree. I drop to my knees, clutching my side. There's so much blood. I don't remember getting hit.

"Then what happens?" Matt asked, clutching the edge of his seat.

I shrugged. "I usually wake up."

"Seriously? What sort of ending is that? We need to know if you make it."

"I can't help it. It's a weird dream, and I can't get back to sleep once I'm awake."

Matt put his arm round me. "And that's why you're such a grumpy beast today?"

I pushed his arm away. "I am not grumpy."

"Then why are you refusing to help me with my essay?"

"It's not my fault you left your homework till the last minute again."

Matt was always doing this—leaving his homework until the last second and coming to me for help. I, like a kind-hearted fool, always helped him. Maybe I was part of the problem, not forcing him to do it himself. I crossed my arms. "Ever think maybe I'm just tired of bailing you out?"

"Come on, Mel. This is our whole relationship. You help me with homework. I set you up on a date with one of my buddies."

"Except I don't want to date any of your buddies."

He rolled his eyes. "Can't blame me for trying to make you more social. Plus, my mates are way better than the usual nerds you date."

I narrowed my eyes at him. "I don't like your sort of socialising. Ever consider I might want to date someone with at least half a brain?" Matt liked to hang out with a bunch of meatheads. We probably wouldn't be friends if I hadn't known him before he became so popular. The art of being popular was pretending to be something you're not. Luckily, I knew the real Matt.

"How about I buy you some chocolate?" Matt asked.

"Fine, but I also want ice cream."

"Deal." He shook my hand. "Too bad our homework isn't to write a story. I would totally steal your dream for that assignment." His brow lowered as he rubbed his chin. "Hey, Mel, what do you know about the Great War?"

I tilted my head. "The what war? Like World War I or II? I thought we were doing English, not history."

He pulled a pen and paper out of his bag. "Never mind. What should I write?"

"I'm not telling you what to write. I'm just offering guidance. Anyway, I want payment up front. I can't trust you not to do a runner." I got up and walked out of the room.

Matt ran after me. "That was, like, one time, but fine, we can go to the shop first."

I pulled on my boots and jacket. "More like every time a pretty girl bats her eyelids at you."

"Not true. I am a very good friend. I can't help if the majority of your gender finds me irresistible."

I groaned. As soon as we left the house, I regretted not putting on a proper coat. The cold air pierced my skin. I stuck my hands in my pockets and pulled inward, trying to make my jacket cover more of my body. My mistake was looking at how Matt was dressed and thinking that meant it was warm. He was wearing surfer shorts and a T-shirt. He always looked like he was dressed for a trip to the beach and seemed immune to the cold.

As soon as we got to the supermarket, I headed straight to the clothing section. Matt followed. "We are in the wrong section for chocolate and ice cream," he said. "I also want sweets. Lots of sweets."

I picked up a few hats and tried them on. "I don't want ice cream anymore. I want cookies and hot chocolate. How do you stand walking around like that in this cold?"

He shrugged, leaning against a clothing rack. "I'm just hot stuff."

I shook my head. He never gave me a proper answer to that question. I didn't know why I still bothered to ask. Pulling on another hat, I frowned at myself in the mirror. It wasn't easy to find a hat that would fit over my wild curls. They pretty much had a life of their own. I pulled my hair out of the ponytail it was in. My hair fell down my back, making it easier to flatten my unruly curls and get the hat on.

"You know, it really isn't that cold," Matt said, waving his hand at me but looking off into the distance. "Just get the green one. It goes with your eyes."

"Since when does green go with brown?"

I didn't get an answer. Something else had caught his attention. I went up onto my tiptoes to see what he was looking at. Some girl around our age was eyeing Matt up. I rolled my eyes as he gave her his signature sweet smile and a slight nod of his head. The girl blushed and giggled as she ran round the corner. I threw the pink hat in my basket and put the others back, then grabbed the matching scarf and tapped Matt on the shoulder. "I've got the stuff I want. Let's get those snacks."

A big grin, completely different from the one he'd just given the girl, spread across Matt's face. It was more childish. This was the real Matt. Filling his belly was what he really cared about. As we weaved our way through people pushing trolleys, more girls ogled Matt. Wherever we went, he got a lot of attention from the opposite sex and occasionally from the same sex. I, on the other hand, would either get evil looks or treated as if I were invisible. Today, I was non-existent. I didn't understand why so many girls felt the need to throw themselves at him. I was fully aware that my best friend was well above average in the looks department. He was tall, blond with light blue eyes and well-toned, but they hardly knew him. They had no idea what sort of a person he was. I knew exactly what Matt was like—full of childlike wonder, great for a laugh but could never get anywhere on time. Matt was like the brother I never asked for but wouldn't give up now that I had him.

We turned down an aisle full of sweets. Matt's face lit up. "Now this is what I'm talking about." He rubbed his hands together as he stalked along the shelves. "Once I get this homework out of the way, I can focus on writing my letter to Santa to let him know all the sweets I want. That should have been our homework. I could've done that without your help."

"I can't believe you still write a letter to Santa," I said. Actually, I could. Matt loved the magic of Christmas, and so did I.

Someone kissed their teeth behind me. "Yes, Mellissa, he still writes to Santa, as he refuses to grow up."

I recognised the disapproving voice straight away. It was Victoria. She brushed past me. I shivered at a sudden, cold chill on the back of my neck. "What are you doing here?" I asked.

Her arms were folded, and she looked as if she'd tasted something sour. "Not that it's any of your business, but I'm getting some sweets to take to the cinema."

Victoria was Matt's twin sister. They looked almost identical. She was the kindest, loveliest person you could ever meet, if it benefitted her, and she had nothing to gain from being nice to me. She was harsh with her words, and she didn't think much of me. I used to think since I got along with her brother so well, and with them being twins, we could be friends too. I'd been completely wrong. They may have been twins, but the only thing they had in common was their birthday.

Victoria turned her nose up as she waved her hands in our general direction. "Now, could you two move along before my friends get here? You're bad for my image."

Matt glared at her. "You don't own the supermarket, Vicky. And you're the one that started talking to us. We'll take as much time as we want picking our sweets."

"You two are so childish. It's annoying. The way you act reflects badly on me. We're almost eighteen. You should start acting more grown up." She turned her gaze to me and pointed. "And you are even worse. What's with the cat-ear hat? Aren't you the oldest in our school year?"

I looked down at my basket. I didn't see what was wrong with cat ears on a hat. It was cute. I wanted to come up with a smart response, but instead, I just frowned and said, "But I like cats."

Matt stepped between me and Victoria. "You know what, Vicky? We may be childish, but at least we're comfortable with who we are. You're just a fake, too scared to show everyone the real you."

Victoria clenched her fist. For a moment, I thought she was going to hit him. "You have no idea what you're talking about. As usual, you're too stupid to realise what is going on around you." She gave Matt the most disgusted look I'd ever seen. Then she glanced my way, tilted her head back and huffed before walking away.

Matt let out a long breath once she was out of sight. "Sorry about her. I don't know why she insists on disapproving of everything. I hate how she talks to me like I'm some little kid. She seems to forget that we're twins, and she's not my older sister. Hey, Mel, are you listening?"

I was only half listening. I was used to Victoria being rude, so it didn't really bother me. Sometimes, I wished I could come up with better responses, but her opinion of me didn't matter. At that moment in time, there was something else that had captured my attention. That was the first time I saw him. I thought I was imagining things. Rabbits aren't meant to be hopping around supermarkets, yet this one was staring right at me. There was something odd about the rabbit. I couldn't take my eyes off him.

"Oh my God. It's a rabbit!" screamed a lady. Everyone in the shop turned to look, stunned.

"What are you doing in here? Get out. Now!" shouted a member of staff. He ran at the rabbit. The rabbit dodged the guy, causing him to stumble. I was confused by the crowd's overreaction to a rabbit. It wasn't exactly a vicious creature. I turned to Matt to see if he thought this was as crazy as I did, only to find him gone. I spun around. Matt was chasing the rabbit with the shop assistant. I'd never seen a rabbit move so fast. It was managing to outmanoeuvre the two people trying to catch it.

"Hey, Matt, let the rabbit be," I yelled. Both Matt and the rabbit looked up as I spoke. The rabbit circled round them and dashed toward me. I scooped the little guy up.

"Madame, are you okay?" the shop assistant said with a pant.

I shrugged. "It's only a rabbit. I'll pay for my stuff and take him out with me."

The shop assistant agreed. I paid for my shopping and left. I wrapped the rabbit snuggly in my new scarf and headed back home. As we walked Matt, kept glancing at the rabbit and frowning. He had his hands stuffed in his pockets and didn't say a word most of the walk back to my house. I didn't see what his problem was. It was just a little bunny rabbit, and he was pretty cute. Maybe he was upset that he'd been outmanoeuvred by a rabbit. It had been amusing to watch Matt and the shop employee chase the little guy around.

Just as we got to the top of the street I lived on, Matt stopped in front of me. He put his hand out. "Give me the rabbit."

I took a step back. "Why?"

"Because you don't know what he is."

"I know what a rabbit is. I'm not stupid."

Matt ran a hand though his hair. He looked like he was about to pull a chunk of it out. "That's not what I meant. I would just like the rabbit, please."

"I don't know where your sudden mood change has come from, but I'm keeping it."

"I thought you didn't like animals? You know my family has had loads of pets. Let me take it off your hands, and I'll take care of it."

"I do like animals. I just don't like keeping them as pets, but there's something different about this rabbit. Besides, he seems scared of you. You can accept that I'm keeping the rabbit, or you can keep going on like a crazy person, but I won't help you with your homework if you do."

Matt screwed his face up but seemed to accept that I wanted to keep the rabbit.

My dad's car was parked on the driveway. He was home early. I bit my lip. How was I going to get the rabbit past him? I'd hoped to get him in the house before my dad arrived. If I'd already made the rabbit comfortable, he couldn't say no to me keeping him. If I was quiet, I could sneak in and hide the little guy in my room. My dad would never have to know he was there. Then, I could bring the subject up later. Preferably when Matt wouldn't be around to offer to take him off my hands. Unfortunately, walking across the gravel that made up our low maintenance front garden was not a quiet task. I opened the door to find my dad standing in the hallway.

His face dropped as we walked in. He pointed at the creature in my arms. "Mellissa, what is that?"

"It's a rabbit. I found him hopping around the supermarket. Can I keep him? I'll look after him myself, and he won't be any hassle to you. Promise." I spoke as quickly as I possibly could. "Anyway, you're home early. Today is my turn to cook. You just go and relax while Matt and I do our homework. Then we'll make dinner. It will be a taste sensation." I hoped a change of subject would distract him. I gave my dad the biggest smile I could manage, then pushed Matt up the stairs.

"Mellissa, we will talk about this later," my dad shouted, "and nice to see you, Mathew."

"And you, Mr. Hail," Matt shouted back as I pushed him through my bedroom door. I placed the rabbit on my desk between a pile of papers and my sketchbook. Matt scowled at me. "Your dad lets you get away with practically anything. I wish I could just smile at my parents like that, and they'd let me run off."

"Yes, but I'm pretty sure you would be running off to do something you really shouldn't."

Matt pushed a pile of books to the side so he could sit in the window seat. "I think it's more like the perks of being an only child."

"Count yourself lucky. I've always wanted a sibling."

"All right then, we can swap places for a bit. I'll stay here and be an only child, and you can have my sister."

"On second thought, I'm happy with the way things are." The thought of living with Victoria did not appeal to me. "Anyway, we have homework to do."

"Yeah, we do, but where exactly are we meant to do our work in here?" Matt pointed at my desk, which was overflowing with paints, brushes and sketchbooks. I'd been working on my art coursework the night before. To an outsider, my room did look a mess, but to me, it was a well-organised mess, which is not the same as just being messy. Yes, everything was in what looked like random piles around my room, but I knew what was in each pile and could find anything I needed within seconds. Still, it was true that there wasn't room to do our homework.

"To the dining table," I proclaimed. I gave the rabbit another look before picking up my English books and laptop and heading downstairs with Matt.

After dinner, Matt went home with the best essay he'd ever written, thanks to my fantastic tutoring skills. I went back to my room to check on the rabbit. He hadn't moved. He was still on my desk, wedged between my sketchbook and water pencils. It was as if he had been waiting for me to come back. I sat at my desk and swivelled side to side. Why had I picked him up? There was something different about him. He didn't act like a normal rabbit. I'd never seen a person, let alone a rabbit, sit still for so long. I leant on my desk. There was something oddly familiar about this rabbit. He was a ginger colour with big green eyes, and he was looking at me the same way I was looking at him—like he was also trying to figure out why I was strange. Round his neck was a beautiful crystal. I'd never seen anything like it. A faint hum buzzed around my room. I spun in my chair, expecting to see a wasp, but there wasn't anything there. I shrugged and turned back to the rabbit. He was now looking down at the crystal on his collar. I didn't think rabbits wore collars, but what did I know? I had never had a pet before. With a fancy collar like that, he must've had an owner. They probably missed him. I picked up the crystal to see if it had a name on it. The room filled with rays of bright light. I jumped out of my chair, catching my feet on its legs and tumbling backward. Grabbing my desk, I pulled myself up. Where had that light come from? The rabbit jerked away from me and jumped onto my bed.

"You really are the keeper of the heart. I wasn't sure when I saw you in the shop, but the crystal just confirmed it," said the rabbit.

I opened my mouth to speak, but no sound came out. The rabbit did not just talk. I shook my head, as I rubbed my forehead. My mind was playing tricks on me. It had been a long day and I just needed to get some sleep. It was all in my imagination. Tired. Yes, that was it.

The rabbit tilted his head. "Miss Hail."

My eyes widened. He really was speaking. Unable to process any speech, I slowly backed away from the rabbit until I was against the wall.

"Miss Hail," said the rabbit again.

I looked at the small animal sat on the end of my bed, then to my bedroom door. To get out of the room, I would have to pass him. I looked out the window. Jumping would be a last resort. The rabbit hopped toward me. I screamed at the top of my voice and leaped toward the door. In my panic, I tripped over my own feet, falling face-first in a pile of clothes. Pushing my clothes out of the way, I tried to get up, only to slip back down.

My bedroom door thudded open. "Mellissa, are you all right?" my dad asked.

"I'm fine, I—well, it's just that—um…" What was I meant to say? I couldn't tell him that the rabbit was talking and had scared me half to death.

"Why are you on the floor?" He stepped over the pile of clothes and helped me up.

"It's just—" I looked back at the rabbit now sat by the window. No way my dad would believe me, and I was sure the rabbit wouldn't talk on request. "I thought the rabbit was going to hop out the window, and I fell as I tried to stop him."

"Mellissa, I thought something was really wrong. That creature is already causing problems."

"You're right, Dad. It's probably best I don't keep it. Having a pet is way too much responsibility. I'll take it to the shelter tomorrow before school."

My dad stood a little straighter. His brows narrowed as he looked down at me. "Really?"

I nodded a bit too frantically. "Really."

"Good, good. Well, shut that window for now, just to be safe." He shook his head as he walked out of my room.

I listened at my door as he walked away. Once I could no longer hear his steps, I marched across the room and grabbed the rabbit. "What are you? And how did you talk?" I turned him side to side and upside down.

"Hey, that hurts you know." He wriggled about and jumped out of my hands. I narrowed my eyes. He sounded posh. "My name is Greg, and I do not appreciate being manhandled like that." Maybe I had been a bit rough.

"Sorry, you just took me by surprise. It's not every day

that I meet a talking rabbit. How is it you can talk?" I couldn't believe I was having a conversation with a rabbit.

"I can talk the same way you can. I learned as a child. Look, Miss Hail, I'm not from around here, and I need your help."

"How can I help you? You seem like a pretty capable little rabbit. Wait, how do you know my last name?" He may have overheard Matt or my dad using my name, but they didn't tend to add *Hail* on the end. Maybe talking wasn't the only peculiar thing the rabbit could do. What if he was an evil enchanter?

"I just assumed you shared the same last name as your father," said the rabbit. I let out a nervous giggle. That made sense. I was overthinking. "Please, Miss Hail, tell me what you know about elves, leprechauns and magic?"

It seemed like an odd question, but then, the whole situation was. "They are all stuff of fairy tales." I hit my forehead with my hand. He was a talking rabbit. He was magic. That's why he wanted to know how much I knew—to see if I could help him. I jumped up and down on the spot. "This is totally wicked. You are magic. Well, a magical creature. That's what you want help with. You're not from around here, which means you're from some magic land, and you want to get back there. Right? Oh, this is so cool." I squealed with excitement. The idea of there being a whole world of magic out there was something out of the books I loved to read.

"You are partially correct. I am a magical being, and I am from a magical land, but I don't need your help getting home. I need your help to save the world."

"Wait, what?" The excitement drained from me.

The rabbit—Greg—pulled himself up onto my desk. "Miss Hail, you are the new keeper of the Heart Crystal. Do you not know what that means?"

"The what crystal? I don't have any sort of crystal. Sorry, don't have what you're looking for."

Greg put his head in his paws. "No, that's not what I mean. I have the Heart Crystal."

"Then what's the problem?"

"You are the one that needs to have it. You're the only one that can access its power and save us all."

I dropped into the window seat. "Come again?"

Greg paced along the edge of my desk. "How can this be? She knows nothing about the Heart Crystal. They said the royals went into hiding, but surely they would have kept their offspring informed of who they were."

He obviously was no longer talking to me. I leant against the window. It was cool on my back and helped ease the headache that was developing. Why hadn't I just given the rabbit to Matt when he asked for him? Then, he would've had to deal with the crazy talking beast.

"Miss Hail," said Greg

I sat up, wide-eyed. "Yep."

"It has come to my attention you know nothing about magic."

"Why would I?"

"Because you are heir to the elf throne, keeper of the Heart Crystal and our only hope. I will just have to educate you."

I bit my thumbnail. "I—um—well. Did you say *elf throne?*"

"Yes. Long ago, there was the Great War. The king of the leprechauns tried to take control of the lands using dark magic, but Queen Freya—your ancestor—stopped him."

"Did you say *leprechauns?*"

"Yes."

I laughed. "You expect me to believe leprechauns are the big bad villains of your story?"

Greg's nose twitched. "I don't see what is so funny. This was a dark time. Kadon, King of the Leprechauns, killed the Sea King and laid waste to his kingdom. He then corrupted the Moon Crystal with dark magic and used it to take control of people on the land, forcing them to fight for him."

"Wait, now there's a Moon Crystal?"

"Yes, there are three life crystals: the Moon, Sun and Heart Crystals." He put his paw to his head. "You really know nothing. This is going to be so much harder than I thought."

"So sorry I'm not up-to-date on magic rabbit stories."

"This is not some story, and I'm not a rabbit."

I stood up. "Then what are you?"

"It doesn't matter what I am. This is about what you are."

"I'm just a girl. A normal girl. I am not some heir to the whatever throne or keeper of the moonstone."

"The Heart Crystal," shouted Greg.

I pointed at him. "Don't shout at me, you creepy little rabbit."

"I'm sorry." He lowered his head. "I did not mean to offend you."

"Well, too late. I think you should go. Considering you're not really a rabbit, there's no point taking you to the animal shelter."

Greg made his way over to me. "Please, Miss Hail. Can we not start over?"

My chest tightened. He looked so cute there at my feet, looking up at me with his big green eyes. I folded my arms and closed my eyes. "No, we can't. You're confused about who I am. I'm sorry, I can't help you. You should go find someone who can."

"But Miss Hail—"

"No."

I'm not sure how long I stood there with my eyes shut, but when I opened them again, he was gone. I let out a breath I hadn't realised I was holding. I slumped onto my bed. Had that all really just happened? Talking to a rabbit. A crazy rabbit. Not much of what he said had made sense. It had all been a misunderstanding. A case of mistaken identity. The rabbit would find who he was really looking for, and I would go on with my life as before. At least, that was what I wanted to happen.

A New Approach
Gregory

reg aimlessly wandered the streets. His shoulders were hunched, with his hands stuffed in his jacket pockets. When he stumbled upon this village, he'd known it would be promising. He had discovered another tear here. This village was connected to the Novas Forest, south of the city he was from in the magic world. It was a sign that something was here. At first, he'd only discovered a pair of warlocks, but then he had found her. He had found the new keeper and succeeded where so many had failed before, and it had only taken six months. Yet, finding her had created unforeseen problems. She had no idea about magic. She didn't know what the Heart Crystal was, and she'd kicked him out before he could properly explain. Losing his temper hadn't helped. He ruffled his shaggy hair and as he let out a frustrated groan. What was he meant to do now? There was no way he could contact the council about her yet. He needed to get her to except her role as keeper of the heart crystal first.

The dark clouds that had been threatening to burst finally let loose. Greg pulled his jacket round him. Unfortunately, it seemed to rain every other day on this side of the veil. As rain drizzled down on him, he though back over his conversation with the girl. He sighed. He shouldn't have left so easily. He should have pushed harder to get her to listen, but that might've just pushed her further away. Maybe he should give the girl a bit of time to process the concept of talking rabbits and try again, or perhaps a new approach was needed.

Thunder rolled through the sky above and the rain plummeted down faster. Greg picked up his pace. For now, he needed to find some shelter.

After wandering around for hours getting soaked, Greg came across an old warehouse. The roof was leaking, and there was a draft, but it would do for the night. His clothes clung to his skin and his fingers felt like icicles. In the last six months, he'd come to appreciate the privileged life he had back home. His dad may not have been around a lot and made him jump through hoops all the time, but he had more than most and never went without. He found a dry corner sheltered from the wind to get comfortable in. With a click of his fingers, he summoned his travel bag. Summoning was one of his many specialities. He pulled his wet clothes off and changed them for dry ones. With another click of his fingers, he sent his wet clothes home. Samson repacked his bag regularly and left it in a spot he could easily summon it from. Greg smiled at the thought of his cousin. It wouldn't hurt to get a second opinion on the situation. He didn't want the council to know about Miss Hail yet, but he knew he could trust Samson. He leant against a cold wall and summoned his communis device. The small circular device appeared in his hand. With a wave of his other hand, the device activated.

"Hello," came Samson's voice. "How's the search going?"

"I found her," he replied.

"You what?" shouted Samson. Greg could imagine the look of shock on his cousin's face. "I can't believe this. After all these years, you of all people actually found the heir. Who is this person? Did you say 'her?'"

"Yes, I did say 'her,'" Greg replied. "Her name is Mellissa Hail, but the thing is, she's a human."

"A human? How is that possible?"

"Well, she appears to be mostly human. She has to have some small amount of elf blood in her. Her magical aura is very faint, but it's there. Oh, and she doesn't know about magic or the life crystals. I tried to tell her about everything, but she threw me out."

"Are you sure she's the one?"

"I am sure. The crystal really wants to be with her, but she rejected it. Who in their right mind would reject the honour of being a crystal keeper?"

"She obviously doesn't know what she's rejecting. The humans have been separated from magic for a very long time. Have you spoken to your father yet? He may be able to help."

Greg sat up at the mention of his father. "Of course I haven't, and you can't either."

"Why not?" Samson asked. "He knows more about humans than I do. He's been studying them for years."

"And all his info is well out-of-date." Greg ran his hand through his hair. "I can't tell him about her. Not yet. It would be like only doing half a job. Once she's activated the Heart Crystal, I will call him. I just need you to help me come up with a way to get her to accept the Heart."

"Couldn't you just show her your magic? Transform into something. Seeing is believing, after all."

Greg sighed as he leant against the wall again. "It's not that simple. You see, she sort of thinks I'm a talking rabbit. She doesn't know that I'm a changeling."

"Why would you do that? That is very misleading. You haven't started off very well by lying to the girl."

"I didn't mean to. And it wasn't really a lie. I just didn't correct her. She happened upon me when I was trying to sneak in and out of a place. Rabbits are nonthreatening creatures. Although, they are apparently still not wanted in shops in this world."

"It still doesn't seem right."

"She doesn't know about magic. Appearing to her as a talking rabbit actually worked in my favour. It made her more willing to listen to me. That is until I told her she was the new crystal keeper. That's when the conversation went downhill."

"Then your problem isn't getting her to believe in magic but to believe that she, personally, has magic."

"Exactly, and like you said, seeing is believing. I have no idea what sort of powers she may have, but I do know where a tear in the veil is."

"I see what you're getting at. Only higher level magic users can cross the veil, but what if she isn't a high-level magic user?"

Samson had a point. The magic he'd sensed in the girl was very faint. This plan could backfire on him if she wasn't able to cross, but she was the keeper of the Heart Crystal. There had to be more to her than he first sensed.

"She has to be a high-level user," Greg said. "Maybe her human blood is dampening her elf side."

"Even if that is so, how are you going to get her to go with you? You said she threw you out."

"That's what I need help with."

"How about you just show her your pretty face and charm her into following you?" Greg could hear the grin spreading across Samson's face.

"I don't think that would work."

"Have you finally come across a girl with enough wits not to fall for that sort of thing?"

"You know I only have girls falling over me back home because of my father's title, which means nothing to this girl. She's quite stubborn and argumentative."

Samson laughed. "I like the sound of this girl. Seriously though, try approaching her in human form."

Greg rubbed his chin. "I don't know." Why would she believe a random stranger off the street about magic? She was just as likely to reject the idea. It may freak her out even more. "Maybe I could try approaching her friend."

"What friend? You're not going to try convincing another human to do your bidding? I can't see that working well."

"There are warlocks in this village, and she happens to be friends with one of them. I don't think it's a coincidence. She was subconsciously drawn to his magic like she was me today. I'm sure he'll know about the life crystals."

"Are you sure this warlock won't see you as a threat and attack? You know how volatile they can be."

Greg rubbed his chin again, recalling what he knew of warlocks. "You have a point. He did take an instant disliking to me."

"Look, you asked for my advice, so here it is. Appear to the girl as yourself. Forget about who she's meant to be, and focus on who she is now. Approach the warlock only if the situation becomes desperate."

Greg grumbled. "I guess I can try that."

"Call me if you need any more help." Samson said his goodbyes, and the communis deactivated.

Greg lent back against the wall and shut his eyes. Come morning, he would go back to see Miss Hail as himself. He would to be patient with her and not lose his cool. No one would have thought the new crystal keeper was human. This was a good strategy because plan b could be disastrous. Samson was right about warlocks being volatile. He would probably have to defend against an attack if he approached him. Warlocks were known for their battle magic, and it could manifest in many forms. He had no way of knowing what he'd be going up against. Hopefully, it wouldn't come to that. He would win Miss Hail over, show her the veil and make a believer out of her.

After getting lost and going around in circles for hours, Greg managed to find his way back to Miss Hail's house. He paused at the end of the driveway. Maybe this wasn't a good idea. Some random guy she'd never met before, knocking on her door, would probably freak her out. She knew him as a rabbit, and that was how he'd approach her now. He could still do everything else Samson said. Once she accepted who she was, he would explain what a changeling was.

Greg transformed back into a rabbit and hopped up to the house, kicking up bits of gravel along the way. He went from window to window, but no one was in. If only he hadn't gotten lost, he would've gotten here sooner. Where could she have gone? Her light brown skin and clear complexion revealed she was young. Judging by the bright pink décor of her bedroom, the fairy lights and the paper butterflies hanging from her ceiling, she was sixteen at the most. It was a Friday. She would be at school. He had gone past a school when he was exploring the village on his arrival. That had to be where she was.

Greg shifted into a bird and flew to the school. He glided around the building a few times. It was awfully quiet for a school. He landed on the window ledge of what he believed was the school office. As soon as the lady in the office left her desk, he could look up Mellissa Hail and find out what class she was in. Hopefully, they'd also have a map in there. This place was bigger than he realised.

He was starting to think the lady was never going to leave when there was a loud ringing sound. The woman got up and walked out. He slipped into the room through the small opening in the window. He transformed back into human form. The machine on the desk looked like a giant tabular device. Greg put his hand over the screen. "Search for Mellissa Hail," he commanded. Nothing happened. He rolled his eyes. Of course, these things wouldn't run on magic. This wasn't going to be as simple a task as he originally thought. He started poking the letters on the weird board-like thing. It appeared this controlled what was on the screen. He needed to figure out how to use this thing before the woman came back.

"What do you think you are doing, young man?" asked a high-pitched voice.

Greg gulped as he turned slowly. He thought about transforming and running, but that probably wouldn't go down too well. "I was—um. I was looking for something."

"You older kids think you can do as you please. This computer is off-limits to you, just the same as any other student." She thought he was a student. Finishing school early had more benefits than he initially realised. He still looked young enough to attend high school. "I don't see what is amusing about this situation. If I see you anywhere near my office again, you will be in detention."

"Yes, madame. Sorry, I will go." Greg quickly slid out of the room.

He let out a slow breath and smirked. That had gone

well. Although, he thought they had a uniform at this school. Greg shrugged and wandered around the empty corridors. This would be a lot easier if she had a stronger magical presence for him to feel. He could always try and sense her warlock friend, or he could just go back to her house and wait.

There was another loud ringing sound, and the deserted corridors filled with students. The crystal hummed around his neck as Miss Hail walked right past him. She looked back at him, shook her head and then carried on walking. She had sensed him but hadn't recognised him in this form. She definitely had powers; she just didn't know it. He followed her down the corridor. His heart raced and sweat prickled the back of his neck. This was a bad idea. She would probably think he was some sort of crazy stalker. Greg hid behind a locker when he saw her warlock friend. He wasn't going to approach her with him around. As much as he wanted to get his job done, it was better not to rush things. For now, he would keep his distance and wait for an appropriate time.

Someone tapped his shoulder. "Young man, that is not proper school uniform," said a stern, female voice. Greg turned round to face a cross-looking woman. She was tall, almost the same height as him. Her blonde hair was tied up into a bun on top of her head. She had thick, black glasses and wore a smart dress with a blazer. She reminded him of a younger version of Lady Gabrielle. "Why do you think the uniform code doesn't apply to you?"

"Sorry, madame. I will go home now and change."

Greg went to walk away, but she stopped him. She narrowed her eyes. "My office. Now." She took hold of his shoulder and led him down the corridor. This was not good. How long before this teacher figured out he wasn't really a student here? She led him to a small room with a desk and a chair on either side of it. As she shut the door, Greg realised he'd made a mistake. How had he not sensed it before? Her magic was strong. It was that boy's fault. That warlock boy's magical presence had masked the approach of another.

The woman flicked her wrist, and a ball of fire appeared. "Who are you, and why are you following Mellissa?"

Greg instinctively put up a barrier between him and the woman. "Who am I? Who are you? Why are there so many warlocks in this village?"

The woman's eyes widened, and the fire in her hand grew. "I asked first, boy."

Greg clenched his fists. Warlocks often underestimated his kind. He could fight his way out of this, but it would cause a big commotion. The way she spoke of the girl, it was familiar. She knew her. Greg took a deep breath and lowered his barrier. "My name is Gregory Ainsworth. I was sent by the council to find the new keeper of the Heart Crystal."

The woman narrowed her eyes, fire still in hand. "You seem a little young to be entrusted with the Heart Crystal." She looked him up and down. "Ainsworth. You're a changeling, right?" Greg nodded. "Wouldn't happen to be related to Lord Steffen Ainsworth Elder Knight, would you?"

Greg stood up straighter. "He's my father."

She closed her hand, putting out the fire. "Ah, I see. That's how you got the job."

"I will have you know, I worked really hard for my position."

She walked round the desk and sat down. Clicking her fingers, she pointed at the chair across from her. "Sit down." Greg did as he was told. "My name is Catherine, and as you correctly guessed, I'm a warlock, but here, I am Mrs. Street, the guidance counsellor. So, Gregory, I am going to offer you some guidance. Stay away from Mellissa."

"What?" Greg leant forward. "I can't. Do you know who she is?"

"Of course I do. I have been watching over her since she was a baby, and I will not have some council flunky endangering her safety."

"If you know who she is, then why haven't you told her?"

"Because, her not knowing keeps her safe. If you hadn't been entrusted with the Heart Crystal, you never would've noticed her."

Greg opened his mouth to object but stopped himself.

She was right. He would have written her off as just another human if it hadn't been for the Heart Crystal. The elves said the royals had gone into hiding. What they hadn't said—hadn't known—was that they were hiding from themselves. This was why Miss Hail knew nothing about her history.

"But the darkness," said Greg, "it's spreading. We need her."

Mrs. Street interlaced her fingers. "Why did you cross the veil?"

"I told you why I came."

"They have been searching for the elf heir since long before you were born, and they've never crossed the veil. Why did you?"

"It was the only logical explanation for why no one had seen an elf. They had been unsuccessful in their search because the heir wasn't on our side of the veil."

"And you pitched this idea to the council, and they just accepted it?"

"No, I wrote an essay about it, and my father told the council about my theory." Greg waved his hand in front of his face. "What does this matter? The darkness is spreading, which can mean only one thing—Kadon is attempting to break out of his prison."

"It matters because all of this could have been avoided. My grandfather had the same theory as you."

"Really? The council said I was the first."

Mrs Street tutted as she shook her head. "Of course they did. My family has been searching for the elves just as long as the council. My ancestor was the sister of Freya's guardian, Ivan."

"The warlock who escaped the castle with Freya's daughter."

"Exactly. We've been trying to find where he went. My grandfather discovered a tear in a cave, crossed over and found a settlement of elves."

Greg leant forward. "That's the tear I used. I found the same settlement."

Mrs. Street rolled her eyes. "Of course the council knew

of that tear."

"But they haven't used it."

"Are you sure about that?"

Greg wanted to say yes but hesitated. The council only told him what they wanted him to know, but they couldn't have used it. Otherwise, they would have discovered the elves themselves.

"When my grandfather told the council what he had discovered, they laughed at him. Lord Tyson Smith said he was insane. Why would someone so important be among lowly humans?"

"I'm sorry that happened. But Tyson is no longer on the council. His son Emerson took over years ago. The whole council has changed since then." Surely she wouldn't keep Miss Hail from her destiny just because of a slight against her grandfather.

"Them not believing my grandfather isn't the problem. The problem is that when they sent him away, something followed him—a darkness that attacked the elves and hunted the royals." Mrs. Street clenched her fist as a darkness filled her eyes. "Maggie—she—I was meant to watch over her. The darkness got her. I vowed not to let the same happen to Mellissa. I tried to push Victoria and her together. Victoria could protect her if anything ever happened." She shrugged. "But she clicked better with Matt."

"That's why they went into hiding, because of this darkness?" She nodded. "This Maggie was another heir?" She nodded again, her eyes dropping to the floor. An heir she was sent to protect but lost. Greg ran his fingers through his hair. "Wait, you think that darkness was sent by the council?"

"Yes."

"You're not just protecting Miss Hail from the darkness. You're also protecting her from the council."

She looked directly at him her face blank. "I'm glad to see you understand."

Greg stared at her, open-mouthed. How could she think the council sent something to hunt down the royals? The council was many things, but they were not murderers. It was their job to protect people. They needed the heir to the elf throne. He understood Mrs. Street's concerns, but there was no point in protecting the girl anymore.

Greg pressed his fingers into the arms of his chair. "Kadon's return threatens both sides of the veil. Miss Hail is the only one capable of accessing the power needed to stop him."

"She's not a fighter. Even with the Heart Crystal, she can't go up against an evil like that."

"It may not come to that. If we act before he breaks free, all she will have to do is recast the original sealing spell."

Mrs. Street grasped the edge of the desk. She looked as if she might burn something, but she slowly released her hand, spreading her fingers. "Is the darkness really spreading?" He nodded. "But Kadon remains trapped?"

"For now, but the spreading of the darkness proves he has awakened, and his powers are growing."

Mrs. Street tapped her nails on the desk, bit them, then shuffled some papers. She got up and sat back down. She scratched the back of her neck, then tapped her nails on the desk again. "I will not stop you from approaching Mellissa, but there are conditions."

Greg raised an eyebrow. "Conditions?"

"I can sense you mean her no harm, but understand, I am trusting you and not your council. The rules are"—she pointed to her fingers as if counting—"you do not tell the council anything I have not first approved. Mellissa will need training. It is to be done on this side of the veil. When she is ready to cross the veil, it will only be to cast the sealing spell, and she will promptly return. Do not let that council try to keep her. You will also make sure no harm comes to her while she is on that side of the veil. Lastly, Mellissa must choose this of her own free will. You cannot force the crystal on her. If you do not agree to these conditions, I will set you on fire."

Her eyes darkened as a slight smile spread across her face. It made Greg want to sink into his seat. He was starting to realise this woman was crazy. "I accept your conditions, but I have one of my own."

The look she gave him made his blood run cold. "Do

you now?"

Greg sat up straighter, trying to hide his unease. "Just one. You help put me in a situation to talk to Miss Hail."

"Very well." She spun to the side and started tapping on the board connected to her oversized tabular. Her mood was so erratic it was unsettling. "I can enrol you in all the same classes as her. She is currently in art."

"Aren't I a bit old to be in the same class as a sixteen-year-old?"

"Mellissa is eighteen."

"She is?" That meant she was only a year younger than him. She didn't look it. Or it was possible he was the old bore his cousin teased him about being. Maybe that was what eighteen looked like on a child who didn't have ridiculously high expectations thrust upon them by their father.

"I know. She is adorably cute, with those gorgeous curls," said Mrs. Street, "but she is definitely eighteen, same year as my twins."

"I'm such an idiot. Her warlock friend is your son, isn't he?"

"Yes, dear. Will you be joining year thirteen art?"

Art really was not his thing. He would also rather not relive high school. "Is there any other way our paths could cross?"

"Well, she volunteers at the library on Saturday mornings."

Volunteering at a library? That sounded like heaven. That he could work with. "Perfect. Where is this library?"

Mrs. Street talked him through where the library was. She even brought up a picture of it on her tabular.

Greg got up and walked over to the door. "Thank you." He felt as if a weight had been lifted from his shoulders. He'd found something he had in common with the girl—books. This would be his way in. As he opened the door, Mrs. Street called to him.

"One more thing. Call her Mellissa, not Miss Hail. She'll think you're weird otherwise."

Shadows
Mellissa

"*T*hings don't have to be like this. There's still time to turn back. To heal the land," I shout.

A man shrouded in shadows growls. His dark eyes are locked on me. He lifts his hand. Black swirls wrap around it and form a sword. "You made your choice, Freya. Now you must live with it."

Freya? That's not my name.

He's running toward me, sword held high. I lift my arm and swirls of light defend me. I try to push him back, but he keeps coming. Cracking the rock between us, I use the earth to push myself up, taking flight. He follows suit. "Freya," he screams, "I will end you."

…but I'm Mellissa. Freya… Where have I heard that name before?

He flies at me with his sword. With a flick of my wrist, my staff appears in my hand. I use it to block his blows. He is stronger than the last time we battled. I misjudge his movements, and he plunges his sword into my stomach. I plummet to the ground. I can't win, but I can make sure he doesn't either.

I woke with a start, gasping for breath. Sweat dripped down my head. I threw back the covers and lifted my top. There was nothing there. No wound. It was just a dream. The same dream I'd had before, but not exactly. Some bits were different. It was more detailed. Almost like I was remembering a lost memory. It was all that rabbit's fault, putting crazy ideas about magic in my head. He was the one that had mentioned Freya, and I had somehow incorporated her into my dream. I needed to forget about the rabbit. He was gone now, which meant I was right. He had confused me with someone else.

I spent all morning in a daze, aimlessly sorting through returned library books. Volunteering at a library wasn't as fun as I thought it would be. I needed something to spruce up my personal statement. I loved to read. So, when the library needed volunteers, I jumped at the opportunity, but my work there involved little reading. Mostly just sorting and organising, putting books back on shelves and getting up early on Saturdays when I'd rather be in bed.

"Mellissa, could you put this pile of books back on the shelves?" Claire, the librarian, asked. She looked at her watch and frowned. "Oh, it will be time for you to head home soon. I'll sort it later."

"Don't be silly. I'll do it before I go." I took the pile of books from her. They were from the nonfiction section at the back. Balancing the books on one arm, I walked along the back shelves, placing books in their rightful spots. As I turned a corner, I bumped into the end of the bookcase, and the remaining books fell. I dropped to the floor to pick them up. Two feet were amongst the fallen books. It wasn't the bookcase I bumped into but a person.

"Sorry, let me help," said a male voice. Two hands started to pile the books back in my hands.

I angled my head so my messy curls covered my face. "No, it was all my fault. I wasn't looking where I was going. Thanks for the help." Keeping my head down, I hurried round him.

" Do you work here?" he asked.

I continued putting books on the shelf. "I'm just a volunteer."

"But you know where all the books go?"

"I guess. Is there anything in particular you're after?"

"Any books on magic?"

I froze with a book halfway on the shelf. Magic. In the nonfiction section. I flicked my hair back so I could get a sideways look at him. He was tall with red hair that looked like a mop. He was wearing jeans and polo with a smart-looking trench coat. He looked out of place. Way too posh for our small village. "There are some books about old pagan rituals in the next aisle, unless you're looking for fiction, which is near the front on the left."

"Thanks." He looked like he was going to say more but decided against it and walked away. A weird feeling overtook me, like I wanted—no, needed—to follow him. I carried on shelving the books. There was a low hum ringing in my ears. Where had he gone? I needed to know. I shoved the remaining books randomly on a shelf and hurried to the section on pagan rituals. There was no one there. Maybe he'd wanted a novel involving magic. I spun round toward the fiction and crashed into a person. I fell backward, but before I hit the floor, someone grabbed my arm and pulled me back up.

"I'm so sorry. I wasn't looking—"

"That's the second time you've walked into me." It was him. The humming was louder. It was a song that only I seemed to hear. I reached my hand out toward him but quickly dropped it, shaking my head. What the hell was I doing? "Maybe if you didn't keep covering your face with your hair, you could see better." He pushed a curl from my face. "Much better."

My face warmed, and I smacked his hand away. "I can sort my own hair thanks." I walked down the aisle away from him, running my hands over my hair.

"I'm sorry. I didn't mean to offend you."

I spun round. "What did you say?"

"I didn't mean to offend you. I'm not from around here, and things are different where I'm from." That was obvious. It was a small village. New people stood out. He walked toward me, holding his hand out. "My name's Greg, and you are?"

It couldn't be. He couldn't be called Greg as well. Greg was a relatively common name. It could just be a coincidence.

"Mellissa," I said, shaking his hand. The humming grew louder. It vibrated through the books and shelves. He was the source. No, it was the necklace round his neck. It called to me. I had to get away from him.

"Nice to meet you." I forced a smile as I backed away.

His brow lowered, and I noticed his eyes. Green like emeralds. "I've got to go. See you round." I rushed over to the counter, grabbing my coat and bag.

"Mellissa," Claire said, "I thought you had already gone."

"I was just talking to someone, but I'm off now. See you next week."

She waved as I rushed off. As I approached the door, a wave of realisation washed over me. The eyes were the same. He was the same Greg as before, but that wasn't possible. How could a rabbit and a human be the same being? My heart raced as I walked back inside. My eyes widened. Sat at the back so only I could see was a rabbit, waving. I bit my lip to hold back a scream and ran out of the library. I kept running until my legs wouldn't carry me anymore. Panting against a wall, I realised I had run to the edge of the wood. This was all so crazy. Greg wasn't a talking rabbit but a shape-shifting trickster.

"Mellissa," someone yelled. It was him. I recognised his accent. No one said the A in my name like that, it sounded more like an "R." He had followed me. My heart pounded. He had magic, and I had a bag of books. A hand touched my shoulder, and I screamed, swinging my bag round. I hit him in the side and swung again, but this time, he caught my bag. "Please, just let me explain."

"Get away from me," I shouted, yanking at my bag.

"I mean you no harm."

"Says the crazy stalker guy holding my bag ransom."

"Fine." He let go of my bag and held his hands up as if to surrender. "I just wanted to prove your magic was real."

"How does you being a creep prove anything about my magic?"

"You sensed that the rabbit and I where the same person. Only someone with magic could do that."

"No. Your eyes don't change when you shift. I knew there was something weird about your eyes as a rabbit. They were too human."

He ran his hand through his hair. "Will you just hear me out this time? Let me explain everything properly, and then if you still want rid of me, I will go."

"How did you know I would be at the library?"

"What?"

"You creep." I wagged my finger at him. "That's why you appeared to me as a rabbit. I bet you do this with all the girls. Get them to take you in as a cute little lost animal. Snoop around their house and find out what they like, then use that knowledge to try to charm them, along with your human good looks."

"You have a wild imagination. That is not—wait, you think I'm good-looking?2 He rubbed his chin. "Maybe Samson was right."

"Who the hell's Samson?" I yelled. "Another shape-shifting trickster?"

"Will you stop shouting?" Greg whispered aggressively, "I'm not a trickster. I'm a changeling, and I would explain all this if you would let me."

A man with his dog was staring at us. Not a lot of people came by the wood, except to walk their pets. This had been a stupid place to run to. I dug my nails into my bag strap. "I let you 'explain,'" I said using air quotes, "and then you'll leave me alone if I say so?" He nodded. "Very well, I will let you buy me tea and cake while you explain."

"How generous of you." He made a sweeping motion toward the road ahead. "Lead the way then, my lady."

If I managed to get back to town, maybe I could lose him. If that didn't work, if I screamed, at least there would be people round to help me. As I stepped forward, everything turned black. I swung my arm at Greg. "What are you doing?"

He took my arm, pulling me back. "This isn't me." His voice sounded as worried as mine.

Everything in front of us had disappeared into darkness but behind us the path was still normal. The darkness began to shift into four shadowy creatures. The landscape returned to normal but there was a distinct lack of light. Greg yanked my arm.

"Run." He ran, pulling me along with him, but the shadowy creatures followed.

"What are those things?" I asked.

"The darkness I was telling you about. They're a part of it."

Greg pulled me along the outside of the wood. He was too fast. My chest ached as I heaved for air. "Slow down," I yelled, but he ignored me. We ran out of path. Greg took a sharp left, and I tumbled over my feet. I hit the ground hard, scraping my knees and hitting Greg's legs with my shoulder, knocking him over. I pushed up onto all fours. One of the shadows was standing over me. Its claws were lifted above its head. As it brought its arm down, I shut my eyes, bracing for impact, but it never came.

I opened my eyes. The beast was clawing at an invisible barrier. I could just make out the edges of it. The other shadows quickly joined in trying to claw through the barrier. Greg crouched next to me with his arm out.

"Displodo," he whispered. The barrier broke apart and shot at the creatures, slicing through them. The shadows disintegrated.

Greg tugged at my arm, but I didn't budge.

"Mellissa, move," he yelled.

I was gawping at the spot where the creatures had been. Greg pulled me to my feet. I cried out as another creature appeared beside me. Greg threw me behind him. He rubbed his hands together, then pushed them out, and something sliced through the creature. I turned to run but found myself face to face with another one. I screeched as shadows wrapped around my arm. Something sliced through the shadows, and they disappeared. My feet were moving before I realised what was happening. Greg was pulling me along again. Shadow monsters kept appearing out of nowhere. Greg lifted his hand muttering under his breath, pushing the creatures back. But it was no use. They just kept coming. As one was destroyed, another appeared.

Greg lifted his free hand above his head and slid to a halt. I ran straight into his back. He muttered some words I didn't understand, and a dome appeared around us.

"There are too many for me to fight." He took hold of

both my hands. "Mellissa, you need to release some light energy to disperse them."

I pushed away from him. "I can't do that."

"Shadows only exist in the absence of light. Whatever this spell is, it has blocked the light from this area, but your magic can break it."

"I don't have any magic. Can't you make light?"

The shadow creatures clawed away at the dome. Greg held his arms wide. "Displodo."

The dome around us burst, destroying all the creatures. Greg quickly formed another dome as more creatures materialised. "Light magic is rare," he said, "but it is well known that the elf royal family all possessed it."

"But I'm not elf royalty. I don't have powers."

The dome was surrounded by creatures again. I wrapped my arms round myself. My whole body was shaking. This couldn't be happening. This was not how I imagined my day going. Even with Greg's magic, there didn't seem to be a way out. I couldn't do what he thought I could, and we were either going to die from starvation in this dome or by being ripped to shreds by those things. Neither option appealed to me.

Greg pulled his necklace off and held it out to me. "Maybe if you took the crystal, it would help activate something inside you."

"What use is some shiny stone?"

"If you would just try—"

I put my hands over my ears, wishing he'd stop talking. It was hopeless. I didn't want to die. Why had I run here of all places? Why hadn't I just gone home? If I'd let Claire sort those books, none of this would have happened. All I wanted was to be back home. I wished it with all my body. There was a burst of light. Everything went white, and I was jerked forward. It was like I was travelling through a cloud. Then, I was falling. There was a thud and then another as I slammed into something soft. I was back in my bedroom, and the creatures were gone.

I lifted my head and came face-to-face with Greg. He looked winded. "What just happened?" I asked. "How did you do that?"

"It wasn't me. I don't have the power to teleport, but you do. You said you wished you were home, and here we are."

"I did not." I hadn't realised I'd said that out loud. What else had I said in my panic without realising?

"That light came from you. I'm pretty sure if I hadn't grabbed your arm, I would've been left behind."

"You really didn't bring us here?"

"No. Now, do you mind?" His eyes widened as he tilted his head to the side. "You're compressing my lungs."

"What? Oh." My face heated. I suddenly became very aware that I was lying on top of him. He was what cushioned my landing, not one of the random piles of clothes. I pushed off him and sat on my knees, hands in lap and head low, hoping my face hadn't turned red. "Sorry. Um, thanks for softening my landing."

He sat up flicking his red hair back as he did. "You're welcome."

We looked at each other in silence for a moment. His eyes were really green. I have never met anyone with such deep green eyes. I could get lost in those eyes. My cheeks heated again, and I looked down at my hands. "What exactly where those things?" I asked.

"It was Kadon," Greg replied.

"The leprechaun king? I thought you said Freya defeated him."

He raised an eyebrow. " You were listening the other day." I narrowed my eyes at him. "Yes, the leprechaun king. Freya stopped him by sealing him away in the Tree of Time. Having Kadon inside has withered the tree, and Freya's seal is weakening. That darkness started off only covering the tree, like a cloud of misery. Then shadows began oozing out of the tree wrapping round it and has since spread to other parts of nature. I can't believe it has managed to spread to this side of the veil. He targeted you because you're the only one that can stop him from getting free."

I weaved my fingers through my hair and tugged at it. "Okay. Let's say I believe you. This big, bad leprechaun is breaking free. What exactly do you expect me to do about it?"

Greg opened his mouth to respond but froze at the sound of my dad shouting my name. "Mellissa," he shouted again. Footsteps sounded on the stairs.

I frantically waved my hands at Greg. "Change back," I whispered.

"What?"

"Turn into a rabbit."

"Why?"

"Because I would rather my dad find me in my bedroom with a rabbit than some strange boy."

He rolled his eyes but did as I asked. Twinkling lights and a gust of wind surrounded him, and when it dispersed, he was a rabbit again.

I blinked a few times. "That was weird."

My door creaked open. "Mellissa, it *is* you banging around up here. Why didn't you answer?"

"Um—I—"

"Is that the rabbit you said you were taking to the shelter. Were you trying to hide it?"

I hadn't thought this through. He thought I'd dropped the rabbit at the shelter yesterday. This was still better than him thinking I was trying to hide a boy. He folded his arms, and his eyebrows came together so they looked like one long brow. If I didn't say something soon, I would be in trouble. "Yes, well, you see, the shelter was full, so I kept him. But they have my contact details, so if space opens up or anyone comes looking for a lost rabbit, they'll call."

"The shelter was full?"

I nodded, wishing he'd believe me—not that I would believe what just came out of my mouth.

He pointed at Greg. "If that thing becomes a problem, I will happily drive out of town to the next shelter."

I picked up Greg and petted him on my lap. "I'm sure Flopsey here won't be a problem. I'm pretty sure he has an owner and won't be here long."

My dad's shoulders sagged. "Very well. It's your responsibility." He walked out, shutting my door behind him.

Greg hopped off my lap. "Why did you call me Flopsey?"

I shrugged. "It's a rabbit name."

"What's wrong with using my actual name?"

"Greg's a person name."

"Fine." He rolled his shoulders. "Can we go back to our earlier conversation?"

I got up and sat in the window seat. "It's all right. I've heard enough about magic for today."

"You said you would hear me out."

"That was before."

"Before what?"

"Before those things appeared." I waved my arms around. "Before I somehow magicked us home. Before I believed this might all be real."

"I'm sorry." His rabbit ears drooped. "I know this is a lot to take in. I wish there was another way, but you're the only one that can stop the darkness."

"How?"

"By using the Heart Crystal to recast the sealing spell. Your magic is Freya's magic."

"How many times do I have to tell you that I don't have magic? At least not that sort of magic." He really wasn't getting it. I wasn't this magical person he was looking for. Magic was definitely real. That much was true. I also may have somehow got us back here but I was sure this heir he was looking for would have better powers than magic running away. I wasn't who he wanted me to be, nor could I ever be.

Greg threw his little rabbit arms in the air. "You teleported us back here, using light magic. The exact sort of magic of the royals. What more proof do you need?"

"I don't know." I folded my arms and tilted my head upward, looking at him from the corner of my eye. "Maybe me pulling something off when you're not around. It's obvious you have powers. How do I know it wasn't you that teleported and you're not just tricking me into believing it was me"

"I did not get us back here." He pointed at me. It was weird seeing human emotions on the face of a rabbit. "You did that with your elf magic."

"You're saying I'm some sort of human elf."

"Human elf." He chuckled to himself. "I guess that's what you are, because your dad is definitely human. What about your mum? Does she have powers?"

"I wouldn't know."

"Why not? You had to get your elf blood from somewhere. Maybe if I talk to her, she can use the crystal instead of you. Then the burden doesn't have to be yours."

"My mum's dead. I was two when it happened. All I know about her is what my dad has told me, and he's never mentioned her having powers."

"I'm sorry. I didn't know."

I hugged a cushion to my chest. "How could you?"

He looked at the floor and his long ears flopped. "My mum died when I was seven. One day she was there, the next she was gone. It's been me and my father ever since."

Our eyes met across the room. My own pain reflected in his eyes. There was an unspoken understanding of how it felt to lose someone so important. He looked away first.

His bunny ears perked up as if realising something. "Your mother was Maggie."

"Yes, how did you—"

"I will leave you for now. Give you some time to think."

"Where will you go?" I asked.

"I don't know. I always find somewhere." He hopped toward the door.

"Stay."

"What did you say?"

Why was he making me repeat myself? This was already hard enough as it was. Admitting I didn't want to be alone tonight was one thing, saying I felt safer with him and his magic about was pure humiliation. I dug my nails into the cushion I was holding. "Don't go. Stay. If those things come back, I would feel better knowing I'm not alone."

He tilted his head to the side. "What about your dad?"

I shrugged. "You're a rabbit that the shelter had no space for. I hope that form is comfortable."

Frustration
Gregory

*G*reg laid looking up at the ceiling, his back aching. Mellissa had thrown a cushion and a towel in a box, calling it a bed. He had spent the last few hours twisting and turning, trying to sleep with no luck. Sleeping in that abandoned warehouse had been more comfortable than this, even with its draft. Whenever he got close to drifting off, the Heart Crystal would hum, snapping him awake. It would've been so much easier if the girl would've just taken the crystal. He let out a long breath, blowing on his long bunny ears. He had to be patient. After what happened today, he couldn't blame her for being hesitant. But surely she had to believe him now. She had teleported—a very rare power—and since their return to the house, her magical aura had skyrocketed. The glimmer of magic he'd originally sensed in her was now the strongest aura he'd come across. This was what Mrs. Street had meant about Mellissa not knowing who she was keeping her safe. There was no telling what she would be capable of doing if she tried.

The Heart Crystal hummed again. "Would you be quiet," he snapped. The crystal hummed once again. It wanted to be with Mellissa, but he couldn't force her to accept it. Greg sighed and hopped out of the box-bed. He shifted back to human form and splashed some water from the sink on his face. Mellissa had relegated him to the bathroom attached to her room. She claimed that since he wasn't really a rabbit, it would be weird staying in the same room, and she didn't want him watching her sleep. Why she thought he would watch her sleep was beyond him. If he had his way, he would be sleeping himself. He would be back home in the comforts of his own house.

Greg peeked through a crack in the door. It was quiet except for the occasional snore. He tiptoed into the room and placed the crystal on a chest of drawers. It was better off as near to Mellissa as possible. Quietly, he opened the bedroom window and shifted into a bird. He flew out and onto the roof. He shifted back and sat on the roof, taking in the landscape. The night sky was clear, the moon just a sliver up high. A gentle breeze lifted Greg's fringe off his forehead. There were no lights on in any of the houses. No one would see him up here at this time of night. He sat cross-legged on the roof and summoned his communis, reaching out to Samson. It rang out, so he tried again. It was late. Samson was likely asleep, as he should be. Just as Greg thought to give up, Samson's voice came from the device. "What time do you call this? Some of us have work in the morning," he said with a crackly voice.

"You said to call you if I needed anything," Greg said.

"Yeah, at a normal hour. Well, now that you've woke me up, what's the problem?"

"Do you know if there are any reports on the movements of the darkness?"

"There probably are, but I'm not ranked high enough to see them. Your father—"

"I can't talk to him about this."

"Fine. Well, I can tell you it hasn't spread to Novosvillas, if that's what you're worried about."

"How can that be?" Greg rubbed his chin. Novosvillas was between here and the capital. If those shadow monsters had come after Mellissa, surely the darkness had to have spread well past Novosvillas.

"I don't know," Samson said. "It has taken fifty years for the problem to get as bad as it is. I think it will take longer than six months for the evil king to break out."

"We were attacked today. Shadows in some sort of humanoid form came after Mellissa."

"As in the new keeper?" There was a hint of panic in his voice. "Where is she now?"

"I left her asleep inside."

"Gregory, when I said to charm her, I didn't mean like that."

"What—no—I didn't mean like that. I'm on watch in case those things come back. Someone has to protect her."

"Isn't that why the keepers have guardians?"

"Well, she still won't take the Heart from me, so no call has been sent out to bring her two guardians."

"A stubborn one, is she?"

"Yes, but I don't know." Greg put his head in his hand. Yes, she was infuriatingly stubborn, but there was more to it. She was frightened, and why shouldn't she be? A few days ago, she thought she was a normal human girl. Then he came along and ruined that for her. "She's scared. I probably haven't done the best job of introducing her to magic."

"Wait, did you just admit to being bad at something?"

"Very funny. I need to protect her until she can protect herself, which will be never if she won't accept the Heart Crystal. I don't know what to do, Samson."

"Neither do I. I'm sorry. I know that's not the answer you wanted. We can't force our will on people. You just have to keep talking to her and hope you get through. Or you could call your father."

"I am not calling him."

"Very well. I'll see if I can find anything out about the darkness, but there isn't much else I can do for you."

"Thanks."

"Night, Greg."

The communis stopped glowing as it deactivated. He should get some sleep, but his mind was racing. He couldn't get what happened earlier with the shadows out of his head. Greg lay back on the roof, looking up at the sky. At the end of the day, Mellissa was just a girl. Magic had threatened her life, but it had also saved her. He could show her just how wonderful magic could be. Which could make her want to learn to use her powers.

Greg woke to the sun blaring down on him. He had drifted off. It turned out the roof was a lot more comfortable than a cushion in a box. The streets were still quiet. Hopefully no one had seen him up here. He turned into a bird and flew back through Mellissa's window. Luckily, it was still open. She was sat at her desk drawing something. He shifted back again.

"Morning."

She jumped, dropping her pencil. "Where the hell have you been? I thought you said you would stay."

He picked up the fallen pencil and held it out to her. "I was up on the roof."

She looked at the pencil like it was a stick of poison. "The roof? What if someone saw you?"

"I couldn't sleep, so I went to get some fresh air and dozed off." He placed the pencil on her desk and glanced at her sketchbook. It was a drawing of the tree outside her window. "That's pretty good."

She slammed the book shut. "Don't you look at that."

"You have to show your sketches to someone. Art is one of your subjects at school, after all."

"How do you know that?"

He pushed a cushion over and sat in the window seat. "Mrs. Street told me."

"Mrs. Street as in Catherine Street, Matt's mum?"

"Yep. She's also the reason I knew you would be at the library."

"Oh, so you magicked her into helping you stalk me?" She put her hand on her forehead and the other on her hip. "It just occurred to me that I invited my stalker in."

Greg lent forward, putting his hands up. "Hey, I am not a stalker, and I didn't use magic on Mrs. Street. She helped me because she knows who you really are."

"Her son has been my best friend since, like, forever. Of course she knows who I am."

"Who you really are." Greg shook his head as he shrugged. "You know what? Forget it. I shouldn't have said anything."

She rolled her eyes. "Seriously?" She grabbed his arm

and tugged him up. "Don't sit by the window. Someone might see you."

"Of course." He bowed to her. "We wouldn't want the future elf queen to be seen with a commoner like me."

The sound of her laugh warmed his heart. It sounded genuine, not like the fake laughter he was used to from his so-called friends who liked his father's position more than him. She waved her hand at him, from head to toe. "If one of us is a commoner, it's me, Mr. I-sound-like-I-belong-at Buckingham-Palace."

"I have never heard of this palace."

"But you've heard of my best friend's mum, who you claim you didn't use your powers on. You also managed to somehow guess my mother was called Maggie and expect me not to think you're a stalker."

She sat in the spot she'd just made him move from. He swung the desk chair around to face her and sat down. "I can see why you may think this." He placed his hand over his heart. "I promise you, I did not use any magic during my encounter with Mrs. Street, but she threatened me with hers."

"Mrs. Street doesn't have magic," snapped Mellissa.

"Yes, she does. She's a warlock, and so is your friend. You have been drawn to magic your whole life without realising it."

"No, no. Just No. The Streets are not warlocks. I am not drawn to magic."

"It's what drew you to me."

Her cheeks turned red. "I was not drawn to you."

He crossed one leg over the other and leant back, swinging the chair. "If it makes you feel better, you were likely more enticed by the Heart Crystal."

"I've had enough of you." She was across the room in a flash, tugging at his arm. "You can leave now."

"What, why? I thought you would want to know more about your warlock friend."

"Well, I don't, because Matt is not a warlock, and Mrs. Street did not threaten you with magic." She put all her weight into trying to pull him out of the chair. He didn't budge. She scowled at him.

"Are you seriously kicking me out again?" Greg asked, "You still haven't let me explain things to you properly yet."

She threw her arms in the air. "I don't want to hear it."

"And what if the shadows return?"

Mellissa took a sharp intake of breath as the colour drained from her face. Greg ran his hand through his hair. A moment ago, he made her laugh, and now she was kicking him out. He had thoroughly messed up another opportunity with her. At this rate, she would never accept the Heart Crystal. She just didn't seem to like him. Maybe if she didn't associate the Heart with him, she might take it. He put his hands up in front of his chest to signal surrender. "Fine. I will go, but keep the Heart near you." He pointed at the crystal, still where he left it the night before. "If you activate it, it will protect you."

"If I keep the shiny rock, you'll leave me alone?" He nodded. Her eyes narrowed. "Deal."

Greg shifted into a bird and flew out the window. He wouldn't go too far, just in case she got herself into trouble, but for now, there wasn't much else he could do. He just had to hope she would activate the crystal of her own accord.

Warlocks
Mellissa

e run through the forest hand in hand. I'm light-headed and giddy. He turns back and smiles, making my heart flutter. He pulls me through a bush, and I gasp. Water gushes downstream and meanders through the trees. Sunlight glistens on the water's surface.

"What do you think?" he asks.

"It's beautiful," I reply, feeling like I may explode from happiness.

He holds his hand out to me. "Let's go for a swim."

I bite my lip and look at my feet. "I can't swim."

A hand gently takes hold of my chin and pushes my face up. Two beautiful grey eyes look down at me. "I'll teach you," he says.

"I don't know."

"Don't tell me you're scared of a little water."

My face heats. "It's hardly a little water."

He interlaces his fingers with mine. "How about we just sit on the edge and dip our feet in?"

I nod, letting him lead me to the water's edge. We slip our shoes off and sit down. I pull my dress up to my knees and dip my feet in. It's freezing. I jump as something touches my foot and shuffle back. Laughter sounds beside me. I punch him playfully. "It's not funny."

"It's only a eritque arcus.*"*

"A what?" I ask

"A rainbow fish, Freya."

The sound of a bell ringing shocked me awake. Chairs scrapped across the wooden floor as my classmates got up from their desks. Keeping my head down, I grabbed my stuff. I walked out of the classroom with my hair over my face, hoping no one noticed I'd fallen asleep in class. I yawned as I approached my locker. Matt was leant against it, flicking through his phone. Greg's words from yesterday ran through my head. Could Matt really be a warlock? I ruffled my hair. That was crazy; of course he wasn't. We had been best friends since we were little. I would know if he had magic. Greg had made a lot of wild claims since I'd met him. He was wrong about Matt and his family, just like he was wrong about me. Matt looked up from his phone and waved. I realised I'd stopped walking and hurried over to him.

"You didn't get any better offers for lunch then?" I asked.

"Hey, when have I ever ditched you to hang out with someone else?"

"True, you always drag me along with you, and I end up sitting there feeling awkward while you're drooled over."

"Well, I need you around to bail me out if things go south. Being drooled over is not as great as you think."

We both laughed. He had come up with a bunch of hand signals to alert me to distress. So far, I hadn't had to rescue him. I threw my books in my locker, and we headed to the common room. As we walked, Matt kept looking at me.

"What? Have I got something on my face?" I asked.

"No." He scratched the back of his neck. "It's just, there's something different about you."

"Different how?"

Matt leant toward me, narrowing his eyes. "Your aura's changed."

I frowned. "My aura?"

He nodded, scrunching up his face, as if trying to remember something. "What did you do with that rabbit?"

I took a step back, startled by the sudden change in subject. "I made him a bed out of a box and contacted the shelter to see if anyone had lost a rabbit. I haven't heard anything yet."

He looked around the common room. It was full of other students, but none of them were paying attention to us. He leant even closer to me. "The rabbit didn't do anything to you, did it?"

"What exactly would the rabbit do to me?"

"Nothing, it's just that you changed over the weekend."

"No, I didn't. I'm still me."

"Of course you are. I need to go see my mum." Before I could say anything, he darted out of the common room. I slumped in a chair by the door. Since when did Matt concern himself with my aura? He'd walked out on lunch. Matt never passed up an opportunity to eat, and he never went to see his mum during school hours. He liked to pretend she didn't work here. Something strange was going on with him, and I needed to know what it was.

I left the common room and made my way to Mrs. Street's office. The door was shut. Maybe if I could open the door a crack, I could listen to their conversation. As I leant toward the door, I hit an invisible wall and fell hard onto the floor. My blazer pocket heated. A loud hum buzzed in my ears. I pulled a napkin out of my pocket and squealed as heat bit at my fingers, dropping the item. The fabric sizzled away, revealing the crystal Greg had left me. I thought he said it would protect me, not set my pocket on fire. I prodded it with my toe, and it rolled toward the door. A bright light beamed from it and slashed through the barrier on the door. Even though it had been invisible, I knew it was gone.

I could hear arguing coming from Mrs. Street's office. It was Matt, Mrs. Street and someone else. I took off my blazer and wrapped the crystal in it. With my ear to the door, I tried to make out what was being said. Mrs. Street was telling Matt to calm down. Matt was complaining about not being told something, saying that "he shouldn't be allowed near her." I put my hand to my mouth as someone said my name, in a posh accent. I had only met one person who spoke that way—Greg. What was he doing here? I jumped up as the door opened.

Mrs. Street smiled down at me, but she couldn't hide the

shock in her eyes. "Mellissa, what are you doing here?"

"Matt—I came—you can't be…" I stammered. Mrs. Street placed her hand on my shoulder. I jumped away from her touch. My heart pounded as my eyes filled with tears. "Greg was telling the truth."

"What are you—" I didn't hear the rest of her sentence as I legged it down the corridor. Someone shouted my name. Matt, maybe, but I didn't stop—not until I crashed into someone and fell backward into a locker.

"Watch it, will you?" snapped Victoria.

I jumped to my feet and backed away from her. "Sorry, I wasn't looking where I was going."

She narrowed her eyes at me. "Mellissa, what's going on with you? Something's changed."

No, not her as well. Nothing had changed. I was still the same. They were the ones acting different. I needed to get out of there. Somewhere away from all this magic. I ran.

"Hey, don't you run away from me!" Victoria shouted.

She grabbed my arm, and I screamed. White light surrounded us, and I was jerked forward. It was happening again. I hit the cold, hard floor face-first. My head smacked the ground as something big slammed into the back of me. There was a groan as the weight rolled off me. I pushed myself up to a sitting position and rubbed my head. Seagulls squawked and water splashed. My jaw dropped; I had somehow ended up at the lake. Greg really hadn't been the one to magic us to my room.

"Oh my God," yelled a voice behind me. My eyes widened at the sight of Victoria. She was what landed on me. She pointed at me, her arm shaking. "You did not just—I mean, I have known you, like, I don't know how long, but you never… How do you suddenly have powers?"

I jumped to my feet, waving my hands in front of me. "I don't."

"Err, yes, you do. I didn't just teleport us here. How do you have such a strong magical aura?"

"I don't know what you're talking about."

"Yes, you do." She walked over to a bench by a

lamppost and pointed at it. "Come sit down and tell me everything."

I wrapped my arms around my blazer, which still had the Heart Crystal tucked in it. "Since when do you care what I have to say?"

"Sit down, Mellissa." The look she gave me sent chills down my spine.

"Okay." I sat on the bench, hands on my lap, back straight. "Well, you see, it all started when I met a rabbit." I told her about Greg—how I first met him, and then how I met him again but in a different form. This did not surprise her. Apparently, she knew all about changelings. When I finished my story, she frowned, and we sat in silence for a couple of minutes.

"Can you show me the crystal?" she asked. I nodded and unwrapped my blazer. She picked the crystal up and peered at it. "Oh my God. This is really it. Which means—" She stared at me open-mouthed.

"Well, I think we should head back." With my blazer in hand, I tried to rewrap the crystal. As I did, my skin brushed it. Lights shot out of the stone. We both jumped, and the crystal dropped to the floor. "Why didn't it do that when you touched it?" I asked.

Victoria picked the crystal up. "Because I'm not the keeper of the Heart. You are." She held it out to me.

I took a step back. "But why? Why can't you be the new keeper or Greg?"

She sat back on the bench and patted the spot next to her. I sat beside her. "It's my understanding that the crystal picks who it deems worthy. It would usually go to whoever is next in line, but if the crystal senses a darkness in someone, it could reject them."

"I don't understand why you're not worthy."

Victoria chuckled, but it wasn't a happy laugh. Her eyes wrinkled at the sides as she forced a smile. "There are lots of reasons why I'm unworthy, but Freya also bound the Heart Crystal to her bloodline. Only one of her heirs can use the heart. When Kadon corrupted the Moon Crystal, Freya didn't want the same to happen to the Heart."

"Surely I'm not the only one. Freya could have other descendants. Maybe one of them could be the keeper?"

Victoria shrugged. "The changeling, what was his name again?"

"Greg."

"Right, him. The Heart led him to you. Even if you have some distant relative out there, the Heart chose you. You need to activate it. If Kadon escapes—" She shook her head. "Just trust me when I say he's dangerous."

"Are leprechauns really that dangerous? I always thought they ran around chasing gold at the end of rainbows."

Victoria pushed her hair behind her ear. Her crystal-blue eyes locked on mine. "Leprechauns are extremely dangerous. Human folklore has gotten many things about magic wrong, and the truth about leprechauns is one of their biggest mistakes. They are fierce warriors with super strength and tough skin. Kadon is the strongest of his kind."

There was a lump in my throat, and my voice wouldn't come. This was the nicest Victoria had ever been to me. Which meant things really must be as bad as she said. Even if I was the keeper, how could someone untrained like me do anything? The crystal had made a bad decision choosing me.

"I'm scared," I croaked.

"You would be stupid not to be, but you won't be alone in this. When you activate the crystal, it will send out a call to bring you two guardians."

"It will?"

"That council did a right job in picking their messenger. That changeling is useless. Did he not explain anything?" She grabbed my blazer and wrapped the crystal back up. "Look, I need to get out of here before someone sees me with you and my reputation is ruined." My blazer was thrust back into my arms. Victoria patted my shoulder. "My mum knows all the stories about Freya and Kadon. She is the best person to ask if you have questions." She got up and walked away.

"You guys really are warlocks then?" I shouted after her.

"Yes," she said over her shoulder. A grin spread across

her face, making her eyes sparkle a frosty blue. "And you're an

♡

elf."

I threw myself on my bed, face-planting into my pillow. Going back to school was pointless. I had already missed most of my afternoon lessons, and my head was spinning. There was no way I would've been able to concentrate. The Streets were warlocks. I had weird powers, but most importantly, the Streets were warlocks! Matt, my best friend, had been hiding the truth from me for years. He had been lying our whole friendship. He should have told me. Surely he knew I could keep a secret, and that I would've thought it was totally wicked he had magic. I yelled into my pillow. Deep down, I understood this wasn't just his secret to tell. It was his family's. A family who knew who I was but didn't think to tell me. Did I even really know the Street family like I thought? They had kept me in the dark about who they really were and who I really was. Maybe if someone had told me the truth, I would've been more prepared when a talking rabbit offered me some crystal instead of being scared witless.

The crystal. It was still bundled up in my blazer on my bedside table. What had Greg said about the crystal again? If I activated it, it would protect me. I swung my legs around, pulling myself up and toward the edge of the bed. Careful not to touch it, I unwrapped the crystal. With everything that had happened recently, I could use something to protect me. I squinted at the stone. It appeared clear at first, but as I tilted my head, it changed colour depending on how the light hit it. Maybe I should touch it—activate it and just accept nothing would be the same again. Even if I didn't, things wouldn't be going back to how they were before. I couldn't forget the truths I'd learned. Things between me and Matt were going to be different no matter what. He was a warlock and had hidden it from me. My heart ached. I didn't like being mad at Matt.

A knock at my window startled me back to reality. There was another knock. I pulled myself up to see a bird pecking at the window. The bird flapped, frantically hitting the glass. I was on the other side of the room in a flash, tugging the window open. The bird flew in, bringing with it a gust of wind. I covered my eyes as twinkling lights filled my room.

"I was starting to think you weren't going to let me in," Greg said.

I opened my eyes to see him back in human form, perched on the end of my bed. He had swapped his trench coat for a hoodie and his smart shoes for trainers. He didn't look quite as out of place as before. I slammed the window shut. Why had I opened it in the first place? I should've known the bird was him. "You know, most people use the front door."

He pushed his fringe to the side. "I thought I was a rabbit the shelter had no space for. It was my understanding that rabbits on this side of the veil don't use doors."

I gritted my teeth. "What do you want?"

"I came to see if you activated the Heart Crystal."

I slumped into the window seat. "Of course you did."

"I also"—he pushed his fingers into the edge of the bed and looked at the door to the bathroom—"wanted to apologise. I haven't exactly explained things to you very well. You see, this is hard. I'm not used to this world." He glanced at me, then quickly looked away. "I've come to realise a lot of people back home only agree with me because of who my father is, but you're different. I'm sorry about everything so far. Can we start over?"

He let out a long breath when he finished speaking, then finally looked me in the eye. His green eyes shone in the light. He seemed to be trying. Maybe I hadn't been very responsive. Whenever he said something I didn't like, I'd rejected it, not allowing him to explain further. I could try too. "I guess I would be willing to listen now."

"Really?" A smile spread across his face, reaching up to his eyes, making the green in them brighter. "Um—where do I start? Where did I leave off last time?"

"Well, Victoria sort of explained some stuff to me."
"Who's Victoria?"
"Matt's sister."

"The bossy girl from the shop?" I nodded. He shrugged. "How about you ask about what still isn't clear to you."

I bit my thumbnail. There were so many questions, so much I didn't know. Though there was one thing he kept mentioning that had been bugging me. "What exactly is this veil you keep talking about?"

"The veil is what separates the human world from magic. A long time ago, humans lived amongst magical folk, but there were some who thought those without powers should serve those with."

"You mean like slaves?" He nodded. "That is just—"

"I know. Freya was a campaigner for equality for all. Kadon, on the other hand, was not. He did monstrous things to the humans. One of Freya's last acts was to create the veil to protect those without magic from those who would use their powers to mistreat them."

I gasped. "That's terrible."

To think that the only way to keep humans safe was to separate them from magic. Was the magic world really something I wanted to learn about? Were they the sort of people that deserved my help? Then again, humans had done their fair share of atrocities while separated from magic. Freya had fought for equality. There was good and bad in all races and species. I frowned as I rubbed my chin.

"Okay, so this veil is like an invisible wall separating a world of magic and the human world. How are you here? How are the Streets here, or even me?" I asked.

"I came through a tear in the veil. I assume the Streets did as well. As for you, it was my theory, Freya also separated the elves from the magic world. Her daughter at the time would have just been a baby leaving the elves without a queen to protect them. They would all be safer amongst humans."

Freya must have been powerful to do that, and I was meant to be her heir. It didn't seem possible. I shook my head. If I'd learnt anything the last few days, it was that anything was possible. "These tear things, how do you find them? You know, if the veil is invisible."

"You can sort of see them, but not really." He ran his

fingers through his bright red hair. "You know what? I'll show you." He held his hand out to me. I glared at him. "I will use the front door this time—you know, like other people do."

"You're going to show me a tear, and then we'll come straight back here?" I asked.

"If that's what you want. Unless"—he raised an eyebrow—"you want to see the other side."

My heart somersaulted. He was going to show me a tear in the veil, and on the other side was a world of magic. Who wouldn't want to see that? "Yes," I said, nodding. Without realising, I'd already stood up and was beside him. I put my hand in his and let him lead the way.

Through the Veil
Mellissa

I leant against a tree, my head in my hands. Why had I agreed to follow Greg? He'd said he was going to show me a world of magic. That should've been a major red flag, but I—like an idiot—followed him to a secluded area in the woods. I was alone with a crazy guy where it was unlikely anyone would hear my screams, and all it took was a line about magic lands.

"What are you doing?" Greg asked. "You won't be able to see the tear with your hands over your face." I dropped my hands. He was looking off into the distance, one hand stretched out in front of him, fingers spread wide. "Do you see it?"

"See what? The trees? You do realise I've lived here for most of my life and have seen this wood over a thousand times before, right?"

He raised an eyebrow at me. "You're not even trying. Come stand next to me." He beckoned me over. I dragged my feet as I walked. He put his hand on my shoulder and gently tugged me over to stand in front of him. Bending slightly, he pointed around my head. "Just there. You can see it if you squint and tilt your head."

Tilting my head, I squinted. Nothing happened, except my eyesight blurred. I pushed away from him. "I don't see anything."

"Really? Nothing happened?"

"No," I shouted out of frustration.

"The area in front of you didn't distort?"

I started to say no but stopped. He narrowed his eyes at me, and I looked at my feet.

"Mellissa," he said in an accusatory tone.

"No," I squeaked, instantly regretting how my voice sounded. Why was I such a terrible liar? Greg stepped toward me. I stepped back, putting my arm up between us. "Fine. My sight may have blurred, but that was just my eyesight going funny."

"That was the tear," he exclaimed.

A sudden wave of rage spread through me. I clenched my fists. This was ridiculous. How could this be the tear? I thought he was going to show me a gaping hole in reality. A place where two areas didn't match like someone had sewn two different places together. Instead, it was a blur.

"Do you want to cross?" Greg asked.

"Cross what?" I shouted, stamping my feet like a child throwing a tantrum. "There's nothing there. You conned me. Again."

"You're almost as temperamental as a warlock." He shrugged, walking past me. "How about I go first and prove you wrong?"

"You are such a smug—" My jaw dropped, unable to finish what I was saying, as Greg disappeared. I spun around, searching the area for him. It had to be another one of his tricks, but he was nowhere to be seen. Maybe he'd been telling the truth about the tear. Biting my lip, I inched forward with my hand out. I squealed when it disappeared and quickly pulled it back. So, the tear wasn't what I imagined, but this blur definitely led somewhere. I put my hand through and pulled it back again. I had no idea where this led. For all I knew, I could tumble into a volcano and be melted by lava. A swarm of bees could be waiting on the other side. I could fall into the ocean or be eaten by a mountain lion. I took a deep breath, shaking my hands out beside me. No, I was overthinking this. Greg had gone through. Surely he wouldn't have walked so casually into danger, unless it was all a trap for me. Although, he'd had ample opportunities to abduct me already. I just needed to take the plunge and go through.

I put my arm through again. Something grabbed me, and I screamed as I was pulled through. I slammed into Greg, who was laughing.

"What's so funny?" I yelled.

"You and your girly screams."

I pulled my arm from his grip and shoved him, but he didn't move. With my hand on his chest, I felt the muscles hidden by his jumper. He wasn't as gangly as I first thought. Putting more force behind it, I shoved him again. He moved ever so slightly and laughed even harder.

"We're going to have to work on your upper body strength." He looked me over. "We will have to come up with a proper workout schedule for you."

I threw my arms around myself. "What is that supposed to mean?"

"That you obviously haven't spent your entire life under a strict training regime."

Did he just call me fat? Because it sounded like he did. I couldn't help twisting to look at my butt. It was rather plump. This was ridiculous; I didn't care what he thought.

"What do you think?" Greg asked.

"Think of—" I forgot what I was about to say as I finally looked at my surroundings. No longer was I in the sad little wood at the edge of my village. I was standing in a giant forest. In front of us was a river like no other I had seen before. It curved gently through the forest, making no sound as the water gushed downstream. The setting sun bounced off the water in a multitude of colours. The smell of pine and damp leaves filled my nostrils. I turned on the spot. The trees were full and green, swishing gently in the breeze. Twinkling lights glimmered throughout their branches. A twig snapped under my foot, bringing me back to reality. Greg had a smirk plastered on his face.

He held his arm out to me. "Shall we explore, my lady?"

"Don't call me that."

I kept my hands firmly at my sides and walked to the water's edge. He followed, leaving a small distance between us. It took everything I had not to run like an excited child in a play park. The water was the clearest I had ever seen. Multicoloured fish glimmered beneath the surface. My eyes widened. "*Eritque arcus,*" I exclaimed.

"You have these on your side of the veil too?" Greg asked.

I bit my thumbnail. "No, I don't think so."

"But you've seen them before? Not a lot of people know what the technical name for rainbow fish is."

What was I saying? It was like my mouth was moving and words were coming out without my permission. I hadn't seen these fish before, but it felt like I had. "I feel like I've been here before, in a dream." I shook my head. I had just lucked out on the name of the fish. It was a good guess. I grabbed his arm. "I can't swim," I blurted out.

"What? Well, I didn't plan on going in the water." He put his hand over mine.

I pulled my hand away. "I don't know why I said that. I'm a great swimmer."

Greg's eyebrows pulled together as he rubbed his chin. Great, he was looking at me like I was crazy. Maybe I was. I put my hand on my forehead. It didn't feel warm, but something was wrong with me. I was remembering things that hadn't happened. Had I really dreamt them? Dreams can feel real, so why not a memory from one?

"Are you feeling okay?" Greg asked. "Maybe we should head back."

He walked back the way we'd come, and I followed. I stared at my feet as I walked. I didn't want to go back. We had barely started exploring, but for some reason, I couldn't find my voice.

Laughter chimed through the trees. My head shot up, searching for the source of the sound. More laughter flittered through the forest. There was more than one voice, and they sounded young. Without caring to see if Greg had also heard them, I twisted round and ran toward the sound. I pushed my way through branches and leaves. Something snagged my hair. I tugged it free and kept going. A bramble scratched my arm, drawing blood as I forced my way through a bush. I came out at a different part of the river. To my right was a stone bridge. On the other side of it was the source of the laughter. There were people playing in the water. I rubbed my eyes to check I was seeing clearly. They all had pale blue skin.

The bushes rustled behind me. I spun round, grabbing a stick, ready to strike whatever creature came at me. I swung as Greg stumbled out of the bush.

He stepped to the side, dodging my swing. He put his hands out in front of his chest. "Why are you attacking me?"

"I thought you were a wolf or something."

"Well, I'm not. Why did you run off?"

I pointed my stick at the water. "To see where the laughter was coming from."

He looked in the direction I pointed. "You could have said. I would've told you there was a water nymph village nearby."

"A what village?"

"Water nymph." He sounded out every syllable. I wanted to punch him. Just because I hadn't heard him properly didn't mean I was stupid. "It's what they are, like how I'm a changeling."

"I guess they have water powers?"

"Why else would they be in the river? They're teaching their young the different techniques for manipulating water. Let's get a closer look. I'm sure they won't mind." He walked toward the bridge, and I followed.

As we reached the bridge, the laughter stopped, replaced by worried whispers and big splashes. The water nymphs ran out of the river. Some older-looking nymphs had come running from the stone buildings in the distance. They appeared to be hurrying the others along.

What were they so afraid of? I looked around for what they were running from when a harsh shiver shot down my spine. My chest tightened, and I struggled to get a breath. For all the beauty of the forest, there was something dark lingering over it. It felt like something awful was trying to push its way into the wood and snuff out all the goodness.

Greg grabbed my arm. "We need to go."

He pulled me back through the bush, toward the tear. My whole body was trembling, and my legs wouldn't move the way I wanted them to. He was too fast. I could barely keep up. My heart was pounding, my breathing harsh. Greg jumped over a branch. Even though I saw it, I fell. God, I was majorly unfit. Greg pulled me up, and I threw my arms around him.

He went stiff in my arms. "What are you doing?" His voice broke at the end of the question.

"I'm trying to get us out of here." I squeezed my eyes shut and pictured my room. Now that I wanted to teleport, it wouldn't work.

"Well, it's not working. Maybe we should go back to running."

I released him, and he seemed to relax. "I can barely keep up with you. My lungs feel like they're about to explode."

"I'm not above dragging you." He took my hand and tugged me forward. Greg came to a sudden stop, throwing up a barrier. I screamed as fire exploded in front of us.

"Get away from her," yelled a voice from behind the flames. I knew that voice. A fist made contact with the barrier, and it cracked. The fire cleared, revealing a person.

"Matt," I squeaked. He was untouched by the fire. Even his clothes were fully intact. Matt punched one hand into the other and pulled a whip of fire from his hand. He whirled it around and brought it down on the barrier, shattering it. Why was he attacking us? Greg muttered something. Matt wasn't attacking us—only Greg. I just happened to be beside him.

Matt whirled the fire around again. As he brought it down, I stepped in front of Greg. "Matt, stop this!" I shouted.

Matt's eyes widened. He looked like he was trying to stop the fire but couldn't. I threw my arms up, preparing to burn. A heavy weight forced me to the ground. My nose and mouth filled with dirt. I turned my head to the side and spat it out. Greg was on top of me, with a barrier above us.

"Are you crazy?" he yelled. I wasn't sure if he was talking to me or Matt.

Greg's weight shifted, and I was pulled up by my arm. My whole front was covered in mud, and half my hair was caked in the stuff. I wiped the dirt from my face.

"Matt, what the hell?" I said.

Matt ran toward me but crashed into another barrier. He glared at Greg. "Lower this now," he said through gritted teeth.

Greg threw his arm to the side, pointing at me. "You almost burned her."

Matt clenched his fist, and his top lip curled. "I was aiming for you. Why she would protect her kidnapper is beyond me."

"He didn't kidnap me," I said. So that's why Matt came here, fire blazing. A shiver ran through me again. We needed to get out of here. I turned to Greg. "Lower the barrier."

I could tell by the look on his face that he could sense the darkness approaching too, but he also looked like he wanted to kill Matt. His better reasoning appeared to kick in as he lowered the barrier.

"We need to get—"

Greg's voice was cut off by screams. I spun around. I couldn't see anyone but us. The darkness was approaching. What if someone had gotten caught in it?

"Save us!" a voice screamed through the trees. "Your Majesty, we need you." Pleas for help echoed around me. Someone was shaking me. All I could hear were the pained cries. Where were these voices coming from? I dropped to the ground, clutching my ears.

"I can't. I'm sorry," I yelled into the forest.

Matt came into focus in front of me. His mouth was moving, but I couldn't hear him. I focused on him and tuned everything out. "What's wrong?" he shouted. "Who are you yelling at?"

"Don't you hear the screams?" My voice sounded hoarse.

Matt's brow creased. "No one's screaming."

Greg put his hand on my shoulder. "We need to get moving. The shadow is almost upon us."

Matt looked at Greg like he wanted to snap his hand off. I was pulled to my feet, my legs like jelly. Matt put his arm around me, supporting me as I ran. The screams got louder. My ears were burning, and I stumbled, falling against a tree. A jolt of energy shot through me. It was like nothing I'd felt before.

"Don't leave us. We have been waiting for you to return." It was the tree talking to me. "You can save us. You are the light in the darkness."

"I don't know how," I whispered, leaning my head against the rough bark.

"Embrace your role," the tree responded.

Matt wrapped his arm around my waist, supporting my weight, trying to get me to move again. I pulled away from him.

"I can't." I patted myself down and pulled my pockets inside out. "No. No! I'm such an idiot. I left it at home."

"Mellissa, you're scaring me," Matt said.

Greg tugged my arm as he pulled something from his pocket. "Are you looking for this?"

"The Heart Crystal," I exclaimed. "How?"

"Did you really think I would let you leave it behind?"

"How do I activate it?"

He shrugged. "It's been said the words will come to you if you're worthy."

"Well, let's hope I'm worthy." I grabbed the crystal from his hand. Sparks of light shot through the forest. The crystal burnt with heat. A vortex of wind surrounded me. I wrapped my hands around the crystal, but it didn't dull the light in the slightest. Power surged through me. My body tingled all over. My mouth began to move on its own. "Crystal Heart, I bind to thee to protect the land and keep the balance." That voice—it was mine but someone else's at the same time.

Guardians
Gregory

As soon as Mellissa took the crystal, the forest filled with light. Greg was thrown back by the storm surging around her. He slammed into a tree. White light blinded him. Gusts of wind whipped around, trying to drag him off his feet. Greg put up a barrier, but the force coming from Mellissa cut through his magic like it was nothing. He clung to the tree, trying not to be blown away. Mellissa's voice echoed through the storm. The winds died down, and Greg could see again. Mellissa was still surrounded by light, but it wasn't as blinding. Her eyes glowed green. She pushed her arms out. The Heart hovered above her hands.

"Release the light." Her voice echoed with one that wasn't hers. A pulse of light surged from Mellissa. It passed right through Greg, filling him with a warm feeling. The light spread through the forest, and the approaching darkness disappeared.

The lights receded. Mellissa's glow dulled. She stumbled forward, rubbing her head. "I have no idea what just happened."

"That was amazing," Matt's voice came from beside Greg. He hadn't realised how close they were standing. Mellissa squeaked as the Heart Crystal threw out two orbs of light. They shot up into the sky. One flew south. The other plummeted back down toward them. It whipped up Greg's hair as it sped past him. Matt yelped as the light struck him. Light surrounded him, and his eyes glazed over.

"Matt!" Mellissa screamed. She tripped over her feet as she attempted to run to him. Greg was at her side in an instant.

She pushed onto her knees, supporting herself on his arm. "What did I do to him?" Her voice croaked as her eyes filled with tears.

"You didn't do anything." Greg looked back at Matt. Lights swirled around him. "It was the crystal. I think it's deciding if he's worthy."

Mellissa's hand tightened around Greg's wrist. "Worthy of what?"

"Worthy of being your guardian."

Why would the crystal think this hot-headed fool was worthy? He was reckless and had almost harmed her in his foolish attempt at a rescue. Matt had been a part of her life for years. Maybe the fates had put them together. The lights burrowed into Matt's body, and his eyes came back into focus.

"That was intense." He slid his fingers through his hair.

Mellissa was on her feet in a flash and throwing her arms round Matt. "Are you okay? I didn't mean to. What happened?"

Matt patted her back. "I'm fine. The lights were just explaining a few things to me."

"Explaining what, exactly?" Greg asked.

Matt's jaw tensed. He pushed Mellissa behind him. "I'm her guardian now. You can leave."

Rage bubbled in Greg. He'd never met someone who could anger him so much. "You may be her guardian, but someone needs to teach her the magic to seal Kadon."

"And what makes you think you're qualified for the job?"

"I have two degrees, and I am a qualified healer. I am an expert in defensive and sealing magic and speak over fifty languages. So far, all I've seen you do is almost burn the person you're meant to protect."

Something like a growl came from Matt as his hands formed flames. Mellissa whipped round, putting one hand on his chest and reaching out with the other toward Greg. "No more fighting." Matt mumbled something under his breath as he put out his flames. Mellissa let out a long breath. "Okay, can we get out of here? We can talk about all of this craziness back at mine."

Matt grabbed her wrist, spinning her around. "You cannot be serious about letting him know where you live."

"He already knows where I live," she replied.

Matt tugged at his hair. "Mellissa, why must you make yourself such an easy target?"

Mellissa kissed her teeth. Matt wasn't only getting under Greg's skin, apparently. Hopefully Matt's dislike of him wouldn't harm the progress he'd made with Mellissa.

"Let's just get out of here," Greg said.

Mellissa nodded, heading south, back toward the tear. Matt gritted his teeth, looking like he wanted to set Greg alight. He shoved past Greg, following Mellissa. This was going to be a long night. Mellissa had finally accepted the Heart Crystal, but her newly appointed guardian was going to be a problem.

They walked back in silence. Matt kept close to Mellissa while shooting daggers with his eyes at Greg every couple of minutes. When they got back to Mellissa's house, Greg was ordered to transform. Earlier, she had moaned about him not using the front door; now she wanted him to fly through the window. Matt, of course, got to waltz in with her. Admittedly, her dad already knew the warlock; he just didn't know what he was. In order for Greg to accompany them, there would have to be some sort of explanation as to who Greg was. If her father really didn't know he had a part-elf child as Mellissa claimed, it would be a long conversation—one they didn't currently have time for. Mellissa opened her window, and Greg flew in, shifting back to human form.

"We're going to have to have a long talk about your safety," Matt said, scowling.

Mellissa rolled her eyes. "I'm pretty sure if he wanted to kill me, he would have done it by now."

The room fell into awkward silence. The only sound was the ticking of a pink butterfly clock. Matt sat in the desk chair, swinging side to side and frowning. Greg had taken up position in the window seat. Mellissa was cross-legged on the end of her bed, looking between Matt and Greg.

"Now what?" Mellissa said, finally breaking the silence.

"We start your training," Greg replied.

"There is no *we* that includes you," snapped Matt.

"Are you going to teach her sealing magic?" Greg asked.

"Yes—well, my mum will."

Greg folded his arms and leant against the window. "Your mother already told me sealing magic isn't her expertise."

Matt jumped to his feet, hands on fire. Mellissa shot between them, hands up.

"There will be no fire magic in my bedroom." With a flick of his wrists, Matt's flames went out. He sat back down, scowling at Greg.

"Since when have you had a temper?" Mellissa asked, hands on her hips, looking down at Matt.

"Since you started making terrible decisions regarding your safety," Matt replied. "Why didn't you tell me about him, anyway? I asked you about that rabbit. I knew he was a changeling."

"I don't know. Maybe if you'd told me you were a warlock and I was an elf when a weird rabbit guy approached me, you would've been the first to know."

"It's not that simple. We were forbidden to tell anyone about magic, and I had no idea about you. My mum kept that from me as well."

As much as Greg liked seeing Matt squirm, their argument wasn't getting them anywhere. They needed to start training. Mellissa needed to learn sealing magic as soon as possible. The sooner he taught her what she needed to know, the sooner she could go reinforce Kadon's seal. The world would be safe, and he could go home.

"Mathew," Mr. Hail yelled up the stairs. "Your sister is here."

The door flew open. Mellissa waved her arms at Greg. There wasn't time for him to transform. In walked a tall blonde girl. Another warlock. She looked just like Matt.

"Victoria, what are you doing here?" Matt asked, jumping in front of the girl.

Victoria slammed the door shut. She shoved Matt out of the way and marched over to Mellissa. Mellissa tensed as

Victoria grabbed her and eyed the crystal. Her eyes flickered bright.

"You activated it?"

Mellissa leant back. "Um, yeah."

Victoria threw an icy stare at Greg. "I take it you're the changeling the council sent."

"I am." Greg met her stare. Her powers were different than her brother's and stronger. She was definitely deadlier than she seemed.

"Don't tell me you're her other guardian," Victoria whined.

Why would it be so terrible if he was? So both of these warlocks were her guardians. The fates really must have been in play.

Greg nodded at Matt. "No, your brother."

"That's just as bad."

"Hey!" yelled Matt.

"Wait," Mellissa interjected, "you're telling me you two are both my guardians?"

Victoria folded her arms, sitting on the end of the bed. "Looks that way. Changeling boy, go get my bag from downstairs so I can get changed."

"I will not," Greg snapped. Who did she think she was? He was not here to run after the keeper's guardians.

"What's the point of having you then?"

"He is meant to teach me sealing magic," Mellissa answered. "Wait, why are you getting changed?"

"Well, I'm not going to sleep in my clothes."

"You want to stay here?"

"Whether I like it or not, it's my duty to protect you. You may have a lot of raw power, which I'm surprised I never noticed before, and it seems to have grown since this afternoon, but you are not experienced in using it. Also until you learn to dampen your magical aura, you can be tracked for miles. How do you think I knew when you crossed back to this side of the veil?"

Greg was impressed. Victoria seemed a lot more practical than her brother. He was hot-headed whereas she was calm and collected, if not a bit bossy.

"She has a point," he said. "Ever since you teleported us, your aura has been off the charts, and it has gotten even stronger since you activated the crystal."

Mellissa looked at them, mouth open. The day's events must have finally been getting to her. Victoria patted Mellissa's shoulder. "Trust me, we may not be friends, but I will keep you safe." She turned, clicking her fingers at her brother. "Matt, get my bag. Then, you two guys vacate the area."

"Get your own bag," Matt snapped. "And if you're staying, so am I."

"Do I not get a say in this?" Mellissa asked. "And Greg can't leave the room, at least not looking like that."

"Why not?" barked Matt.

"Because my dad thinks he's a lost rabbit I took in called Flopsey."

"Seriously, Mellissa, that talk about your safety is happening now."

Greg's pocket vibrated. It was his communis. "I need to take this. You guys argue about sleeping arrangements without me."

Before anyone could respond, Greg had shifted and was out the window. Once comfortably sat on the roof, he returned the call he'd missed. "What's up, Samson?"

"I looked into reports of the darkness spreading. You can't tell anyone about this, as I'm not actually authorised to look at these reports."

"You know I wouldn't drop you in it."

"Well, the shadow has picked up its speed of contamination. It has now spread as far as Novosvillas. However, there are new reports just in that a burst of light has stopped the shadow spreading to Novos Forest."

"That was Mellissa. Even untrained, she has already halted the shadow's progress."

"You mean you got her to cross the veil?"

"Better—she activated the crystal."

"Praise the gods. What did your father say?"

"I haven't told him yet."

"Why not? This is big news."

"I've been busy. Mellissa's newly appointed guardians don't like me."

"Her guardians have already found her? That was fast."

"Yeah, her meathead, warlock friend and his sister are her guardians. Two warlocks, Samson."

"Don't let prejudice get in the way. The Heart Crystal wouldn't have chosen them if they weren't up to the job. You should be happy you're one step closer to returning home as the hero that found the keeper."

The girl seemed capable. She was a bit forceful, but she didn't seem like she would explode in anger and set the place on fire. She seemed the sort to be calm in the face of danger, making her deadlier. His problem was with Matt. It was possible they'd just gotten off on the wrong foot. At the end of the day, they both wanted what was best for Mellissa, didn't they?

"You're right. Well, I should probably inform the council."

"Good. I will call if I hear anything else of importance."

The communis deactivated. Greg waved his hand over the device, reactivating it. He may as well get the call to his father over with. He was calling with good news. His father should be happy—maybe even proud of him for once. There wasn't anything for him to be disappointed in Greg for. Except the fact that Mellissa was an untrained magic newbie.

"You have reached the orb of Lord Steffen Ainsworth Elder Knight. His assistant will filter these messages, and if she deems it important, he may get back to you. *Beeeep*."

Greg rolled his eyes. Of course he wouldn't answer. "Hey, Anna, it's Greg. Tell my father I have succeeded in my task."

Greg deactivated the device. He wanted to add, "And tell my father he should really answer his son's phone calls instead of making him go through his assistant," but, of course, he didn't. There was no point. His father wouldn't change. Greg lay out on the roof. It was chilly, but the sky was clear. The rain seemed to have taken a break for a while. It was nice and quiet up here, better than arguing and being ridiculed by two warlocks and a human elf.

Training
Mellissa

"*Faster, Freya,*" *he yells, throwing shards of ice my way. I throw balls of energy, shattering the shards mid-air, but he is too fast. I dive to the side, dodging narrowly.*

"*Ivan, you're too fast!*" *I yell.* "*This isn't fair. You're a way more experienced fighter than me.*"

Ivan walks over and helps me up. "*Your enemies won't go easy on you, so neither will I.*"

"*What enemies? The kingdom is at peace.*"

"*A wise ruler is always ready for battle. It is at times like these, when your guard is down, that your enemies will strike.*"

I rub the side of my head. "*How did I end up with such an insane guardian? I don't recall my father's guardians making him train like this.*"

"*I'm pretty sure you weren't born when your father became the keeper of the heart. Now, let's go again.*"

He darts across the field and throws ice at me again. I release a ray of light, covering a wider area, taking out all Ivan's ice. I blast light at him, but none of my attacks hit. He's too fast and agile. No wonder the Heart chose him to protect me. I blink, and he's gone. I'm grabbed from behind, and ice is pressed into my neck. "*You got distracted. It may have only been a few seconds, but it was all that was needed.*"

I push away from him. "*You are just mean.*"

"*You are not trying hard enough.*"

"*Ivan,*" *shouts a woman walking up to us,* "*you mustn't be so hard on the queen. She is not a fighter like us. She was raised as a healer.*"

"*Oh, Tasha, you've come to save me from this brute's*

training."

She pats my shoulder. "Oh dear, no. I've come to help him." A ball of fire appears in her hand.

I woke up choking on Victoria's hair. She tied it up before bed, but with all her fidgeting, it must have come undone. I never realised that Victoria knew nothing about personal space. She walked in on me in the bathroom more than once without a care in the world. She also stripped off in front of me and proceeded to take over most of my bed during the night. Matt had sulked off to the guest room when Victoria started painting my nails last night. Even if she had *just been making the best of an awful situation*, as she claimed, I had actually had fun hanging out with her.

Greg never returned after taking his call. Maybe Matt had driven him away. Although, I doubted he would give up that easily. He probably slept on the roof again. He was weird like that. I slid out of bed and opened the window. It was light out. The sky was a pinkish colour, with dark clouds drifting this way. We had been lucky to go so long without rain. I leant out the window as far as I dared go and whispered Greg's name. No response. I said his name again, as loud as I was willing, not wanting to disturb anyone else. He might not even be up there.

"Mellissa, is that you?" came Greg's voice from above.

"You seriously slept up there again?" How on earth did he find the roof more comfortable than the box I made him? I had no idea how he didn't fall off.

"Wait a sec," he said. "I can't hear you properly."

I fell backward as a humming bird flew past my head. When I got up, Greg was standing behind me, looking slightly ruffled but pretty good for someone who'd slept on a roof. "I didn't wake you?" I asked.

He shook his head. "I was watching the sunrise. I thought you would still be asleep."

"Well, Victoria has made that a little difficult." I pointed at the mass of blonde hair in my bed.

"I see you lost the argument over sleeping arrangements."

"Maybe I should have slept on the roof. Although, isn't it cold out there?"

"The weather is pretty mild here. It will be snowing soon where I'm from. We get a good three months of snow in winter."

"Really?" I said. "That sounds amazing." He flashed a smile that made my stomach flutter. I was suddenly very aware that I was wearing cat pyjamas. I bit my bottom lip. "Do you want to go somewhere for a bit?"

"Sure."

"I'll meet you outside. Just give a minute to get changed."

I grabbed some clothes from the wardrobe and went into the bathroom. I was changed in seconds but spent at least ten minutes messing with my hair, trying to tame my curls. In the end, I gave up. It was a hopeless cause. I tiptoed down the stairs, slipped on my boots and grabbed my coat. Greg was sat on the wall at the end of our drive. He was talking into a small, circular disc.

"I already told you she is new to magic, so she doesn't know any of that stuff." He was talking about me.

"This isn't good enough," came a stern male voice from the disc. "Trust you to mess up and find a keeper that doesn't know any magic."

"Don't worry. I will teach her everything she needs to know before you meet her."

"What?" I blurted out before I could stop myself.

"Who's that?" the voice asked.

"No one. I have to go. Goodbye, Father." Greg waved his hand over the device, and it stopped glowing. He sighed, putting his head in his hand. Did he say *Father*? That was how his dad talked to him? It was such a cold and emotionless conversation. How on earth was my lack of magical knowledge Greg's fault?

"Sorry about that, but I do believe you took longer than

you said."

"Why were you talking to your dad about me?"

"How about we walk as I explain?" He gestured to the path in front of us.

"Fine."

I led the way. We walked in silence. Greg had his hands shoved in his pockets and was looking at the pavement. Other than a man walking his dog, the street was empty. The sun hadn't fully risen, so the sky was still a pink colour. There was no wind, and the air was stagnant. I was about to give up on getting an explanation when Greg started talking.

"My father is the one who put me forward for the task of searching for the new keeper, searching for you. You see, he is an elder knight and a member of the council."

"That's how you got the job?"

"Pretty much."

"Okay, but why does that mean I have to meet him?"

"You will have to travel to the Tree of Time in order to seal Kadon. The council had it moved from the ruins of Freya's castle to the capital city where they meet. They all want to meet you, not just my father."

"Can't I just do the spell from the comfort of my own home? Then, everyone will be happy, and I can stop having unexpected house guests."

"I'm afraid not. You have to make contact with the tree to cast the spell."

"Is it really necessary to meet the council?" I asked. "Can't you just show me to the tree, and I can cast the spell? Of course, you will have to show me how to do that. We can high five once we know the seal has been applied correctly, then part ways as unexpected acquaintances that exchange Christmas cards every year." I spoke as fast as I could manage without slurring my words.

Greg chuckled. "I don't blame you for being hesitant. I wouldn't want to meet the council if I were you." He looked up at the sky and frowned. "What is Christmas?"

My jaw dropped, and I must have blinked a few thousand times. Everyone knew about Christmas, even if they didn't celebrate it. I loved Christmas, but Greg was from another world. "It's a festive holiday, a celebration to spend with loved ones. There's gifts, decorations, lots of food. Oh, it's hard to explain." I shook my head, throwing my arms out. "I don't even know where we're going now."

"Well, that's great, because I've been following you."

"We should head back anyway, before Matt wakes up and thinks you've kidnapped me again."

Greg shook his head. "You have a right pair of guardians."

I linked arms with him, dragging him to the left. "Tell me about it. Come on, we need to go to the shop first."

♥

"Mellissa." My dad almost chocked on his coffee. "Did you get up before me and leave the house?"

I shrugged. "We needed milk. I wanted to go to the shop before our house guests woke up."

My dad pointed at the fur ball in my arms. "And you took the rabbit with you?"

"Of course not. I just picked him up on the way to the kitchen to get him a carrot." I gave him a big, toothy grin as I placed the milk in the fridge and plucked a carrot out. I put Greg on the floor with the carrot. He glared at me.

"Eat it," I whispered through gritted teeth.

"Since when are you and Victoria friends?" my dad asked. It had taken him long enough to ask. He'd almost fallen out of his chair last night when I told him both of the Street twins wanted to stay over.

"It's a fairly recent thing," I said, pinching a slice of his toast and sitting at the table opposite him.

He raised an eyebrow while tapping his fingers on the table. "You know, if something's wrong, you can talk to me."

I looked down at Greg. He was nibbling on the carrot, looking like the perfect pet. How could I tell my dad that the rabbit wasn't really a rabbit? He would freak out, unless he knew more about my mum than he had ever told me. He didn't speak much about her except for the occasional remark about how I looked like her. I sucked my bottom lip in.

"We are working on an art project, Victoria and I. It's about family, and I guess I don't really know how to represent Mum with my art." This was partly true. We had an art project; we just weren't working on it together. The topic of our piece was up to us. I had yet to decide. Victoria had picked family. Now that I knew the truth about the Streets, what she'd been working on made more sense.

"I'm not sure what to tell you. You are very much like your mother."

"I don't know—something significant about her, something that made her different from everyone else. Something I can paint to represent her. Victoria has painted a fire and ice scene to show how her and Matt are opposites and a golden sun for her mum to show her passion."

"A garden," my dad said. "Your mother loved her plants. She liked to make things grow."

Gardening? But that was so normal. How exactly did someone go about asking if their mum was an elf without actually asking?

"Anything else? More magical maybe?"

My dad's brow creased. He looked like he was about to say something when Matt and Victoria burst into the kitchen.

"There you are. I was so worried," Matt said.

"I told you she would be down here," snapped Victoria.

"And I told you she never gets up that early."

"Well, she did today."

The twins glared at each other.

My dad got up. "I will leave you three to get on with whatever it is teenagers do these days." He picked up his plate, placed it in the sink and left.

Matt put his hand on my forehead. "Are you feeling okay?"

I pushed his hand away. "Stop it. Sharing with Victoria made it hard to sleep."

"At least you didn't have to share a womb with her."

Victoria slammed her hand on the table. Ice spread from under her hand. "Don't make me hurt you."

I jumped up. "Ice. You have ice powers."

Victoria slumped down into a chair. "Yeah, so what?"

"It's just—I thought—I don't know."

"You thought we would have the same powers?" Victoria rolled her eyes. "Magic doesn't always work like that."

Greg hopped onto the table. "That's what your mother meant about trying to push you two together."

Victoria looked at me while pointing at Greg. "What is he talking about?"

"How should I know? He talks a lot, and I only understand about a third of it."

"When I first met Mrs. Street"—Greg nodded at the twins—"your mother explained that your ancestor was the sister of Freya's ice guardian. That's why she tried to make you befriend Mellissa."

Victoria rolled her eyes. Mrs. Street had failed at pushing her daughter into being my friend. As interesting as it was that the Streets were decedents of one of Freya's guardians, I didn't see the correlation.

"Why would that mean we needed to be friends?" I asked.

"Matt has the same powers as his mum, but Victoria's powers match those of her ancestor Ivan, Freya's guardian." He turned to Victoria. "She tried to push you into befriending Mellissa because she thought you would be her guardian one day. Little did she know, both her children would be guardians."

"She's been manipulating us this whole time," Matt said. "Our own mother, how could she do that?"

"No, I didn't mean it like that," Greg said.

"No, he's right," I said. "Why didn't she just tell us the truth?"

"Exactly." Matt almost knocked his chair over as he stood. "All this time, she knew who Mellissa really was and left her out in the open, unprotected, completely oblivious to the danger she was in."

"You're wrong," said Victoria. "She was protecting us. All of us."

Matt crossed his arms. "How so?"

"We never recognised Mellissa for what she was because she had no magic aura. Now, since she's used her powers, look how easy she is to track."

"Fine, maybe Mellissa not knowing was safer, but why not tell us?"

"The royals went into hiding for a reason. If someone came looking, we couldn't tell what we didn't know."

Matt huffed and sat back down in his chair. "Why do you know all this?"

Victoria sat up straighter. "I'm not an idiot, and Mum told me last night before I came here."

Matt glared at his sister. I wasn't sure what to make of what I'd just heard. The royals had gone into hiding. *If someone came looking…* Who else was looking for the royals? My chest tightened as I thought of the shadow creature that had attacked Greg and me. I could be tracked now that I had used my powers. Those things could find my house. Anyone around me could be put in danger.

"How can I turn my aura off?" I asked.

"You can't turn it off," replied Greg, "but you can dampen it."

"How?"

"Training."

"Well, let's start."

♡

It was decided that it was best to start training at the Streets' house. We would be away from my dad's prying eyes, and apparently, the Streets had a special barrier around their house, so they could use magic freely at home. Matt led us down a staircase I'd never seen before. A *simple glamour charm*, he had called it, to stop people from noticing the extra level. He opened a door to a massive hall. I gasped. It was the length of the house with a high ceiling. Along the far wall were racks of weapons: daggers, swords, batons and staffs—anything you could think of to cause harm. There was a punching bag, a fighting dummy and training mats. Weird symbols I'd never seen lined the walls. How could a "simple" spell hide all of this?

"I can't believe all this is under your house," I said.

Matt shrugged. "Once we stopped attending boarding school, we had to train somewhere."

"I'm guessing your boarding school wasn't really in London like you told me."

He shook his head. "It was in Magus, the warlock capital."

Victoria pulled a staff from the rack and spun it around in her hand. "What do you want to learn first?"

Greg cleared his throat. "As impressive as all this stuff is, Mellissa needs to learn sealing magic and how to dampen her aura, not play with sticks."

"This is not a stick," Victoria snarled, "but fine, you two practice boring magic." She grabbed another staff and chucked it at Matt. "I'll kick the crap out of my brother in the meantime."

I squealed as Victoria hurled herself at Matt. He only just managed to get his staff up in time to block her attack. She swished her staff through the air, bringing it down at Matt. He reacted quickly. There was a bang as the staffs collided. It was amazing watching them. I had never seen two people move so fast, but what really got me was the look on Victoria's face. She was smiling. Whenever I saw her, she usually looked like she'd tasted something sour, but in that moment, sparring with Matt, she looked happy. She was having fun.

"Mellissa," Greg said, "you ready?"

I turned to him. "Um, right, yeah."

"Okay, I guess we'll start with dampening your aura. It's a basic technique. You just need to focus on your power and pull it back into yourself."

"All right, I'll give it a go." I shut my eyes tight and tensed my body. I tried to focus, but I wasn't entirely sure what my powers felt like. How were others aware of my magic when I wasn't? They kept telling me I had this strong aura, but I sensed nothing. The banging of staffs in the background didn't help my focus.

"You are too tense," Greg said. "Push your shoulders back and try to relax." He put his hands on my shoulders. "Your magic is a part of you. You've been ignoring it for so long you probably can't tell it's there. It's like a warm ball of energy inside you that you can release on demand. Take deep breaths and focus."

His words were weirdly comforting. I took deep breaths as suggested, tuning out the sounds of the twins fighting. I focused inside me. Matt was right; I had changed. I could feel something burning inside me, like a sun ablaze in my heart. I focused on it and tugged.

"That's it," Greg said. "You're doing it."

Now that I had hold of this burning light, I couldn't believe I hadn't noticed it before. How had I managed to ignore this power inside me for so long? I opened my eyes, not sure if I'd succeeded in my task.

"Well?" I asked.

"Your aura is still a lot stronger than anyone in this room, but it's a start."

I wanted to jump and hug him but thought better of it. "What now?"

"Now I teach you the basics of sealing magic."

After hours of going over the basics of sealing magic—only stopping for lunch—I understood why Victoria referred to it as boring magic. I could see the benefits of sealing magic, but it was so involved. There were so many different parts to even the most basic sealing spell. I had to be able to form a barrier to trap the item and then latch on to the item's essence. Next I had to break through the object I was sealing the item into and stitch the object once the item was inside. The last step involved creating a different type of barrier, and lock said barrier. I wasn't sure what half of the instructions meant, just that it was hard. After spending all day on it, I hadn't managed to cast any sort of magic. I'd come close to forming a basic barrier, but then the magic fizzled away. I had started off hopeful, but now I was starting to think this was all pointless. The Heart Crystal had made a bad choice selecting me. Surely there was someone better trained for this, someone who hadn't spent their whole life without knowing they had powers. When everyone finally decided to call it a day, I was more than ready to go home.

As I went to leave, I realised I had three people trailing me. "Why are you guys following me?" I asked.

Matt and Victoria shared a look, as if speaking to each other without words. "To protect you," they said in unison. It was rare for them to do things like this, but it always freaked me out when they did.

"I will be fine. Greg taught me to dampen my aura, so I'm not as easy to track anymore, and I would really like to have my bed to myself tonight."

The twins' eyes narrowed on me, and they both frowned. I put my hand on my forehead. They obviously didn't think my request was as fair as I did.

"How are we meant to protect you if we're not with you?" Victoria asked.

"We live like ten minutes apart," I replied.

"Ten minutes is all a crazed murderer needs."

"If someone attacks me, I will teleport straight to your house."

"Of course, your unreliable ability to teleport will definitely save you. I think Matt needs to have the personal safety talk with you again."

My face warmed. She was treating me like a child. "That talk last night was not appreciated. I can take care of myself."

Victoria rolled her eyes. "Of course you can. You should at least keep the changeling."

"What? Can't he stay with you guys? You're a family of warlocks. He doesn't have to hide around your parents."

"I agree with Mellissa," Matt said. "He can't stay with her."

Victoria punched Matt's arm. "Your father already knows him as the stray rabbit you took in. All he has to do is transform back into said rabbit."

"Vicky, are you crazy?" Matt asked.

"No, but you are stupid," Victoria snapped. "The council wants her alive just as much as we do. He can be trusted for now."

"Look, I don't mind finding somewhere else," Greg said.

"No, you're going with Mellissa." Victoria put her hand up to stop him from moving. "You are the only one that can go in unnoticed."

"Do I not get a say in this?" I asked.

"No, as you don't fully understand the importance of your position." Victoria stepped in front of me with a menacing look on her face. "Either the changeling goes with you or we all do."

"I'm convinced. Come on, Greg." I grabbed his arm and tugged him out of the house. "See you two later."

"Mel, you don't have to listen to her!" Matt shouted.

I looked back as Victoria punched Matt again. She dragged him into the house, slamming the door.

"Your friends are rather strange," Greg said.

That was rich coming from the guy I had met twice, once as a rabbit and then as a person. They were all strange. We walked back to mine in silence. I was filled with dread. I couldn't explain why, but I had a bad feeling about everything.

An Unexpected Call
Gregory

Greg rummaged through the kitchen cupboards in search of something to eat. Mellissa was at school, so he had the house to himself. All this free time baffled him. He had a very strict schedule back home. He would either be working at the infirmary or furthering his studies. These were things he could not do here. It had been three weeks since he'd started training Mellissa. He was very proud of the progress she had made in such a short time, but he had become very reliant on her company and was always extremely bored when she wasn't around. He had taken up watching the projection machine in the living room and eating out of boredom.

Greg pulled out a big bag of crisps and went and sat in the living room. He looked up at the clock. It was nearly time to check in with his father. Since finding out about Mellissa, he had insisted on daily updates on her progress and kept moaning that her abilities weren't developing quickly enough. Greg had managed to find Freya's heir when so many before had failed. She had no knowledge of magic when they met, but she now knew the basic techniques needed to cast the sealing spell. She could also teleport on demand and create a barrier within seconds. The only thing he had left to teach her was how to put all the parts of the spell together. She was almost ready, but this was still not enough for his father. He was starting to think he had been wasting his life trying to gain his father's approval. He would never be happy.

Greg clicked his fingers and summoned his communis device. He may as well get this conversation over with. He could then waste his afternoon watching the projection device. Greg waved his hand over the device, and it began to glow.

"Hello, Gregory," said Lady Gabrielle.

Greg quickly sat up in his seat. "Lady Gabrielle, I didn't—I mean, I thought," he started but found himself tongue-tied. He had been expecting to speak to his father, not Lady Gabrielle.

"I realise you thought you would be talking with your father, but from now on, you will be dealing with me," she said.

"My father is all right, isn't he?" he asked. Why had this change taken place?

"Yes, he is fine. Nothing bad has occurred. There have just been a few concerns from other council members that the changelings are dominating the contact we have with the new keeper. There are fears you may be controlling her in some way."

If any of them had met Mellissa, they wouldn't be concerning themselves with such nonsense. He had absolutely no control over her. Mellissa was extremely stubborn. She had a tendency not to listen to him. The only person she listened to was Victoria. "I can assure you that is not the case."

"I realise this is nonsense, but it is simpler for me to talk to you than have tension among the council members. So, how is the girl progressing?" She was straight to the point, just like his father always was.

"She is doing well. We had a shaky start, but once she began picking up the techniques, her ability has progressed rapidly. I believe she could be ready in a matter of days. It is just a case of getting her to agree to a date to travel to the capital, which is proving difficult. She seems reluctant."

"I can understand her hesitancy. This must all be very daunting."

Greg was left temporarily speechless. If this had been his father, he would have found a way to make Mellissa's reluctance his fault. This switch to reporting to Lady Gabrielle could be very beneficial.

"Magic is still very new to her. I remember you weren't very confident when you started out, but look at you now.

Although, you were three at the time." Lady Gabrielle chuckled.

This was a way more pleasant conversation than usual. Greg relaxed back onto the sofa. "I can't imagine what she would be capable of if she had learned at three years old. She's a fast learner and powerful."

"Or, maybe she just has a good teacher," Lady Gabrielle said. Greg couldn't help but smile. "Well, I look forward to meeting her. It is good to hear your voice. You sound well. Your father never tells us how you are. He just gives us updates on the girl."

That was because his father never asked how he was. At least someone cared about him. He had known Lady Gabrielle his whole life. She and his father had been on the council for years and worked closely together. She was always very nice, but she had an authority about her that made the rest of the council listen.

Just as he was about to respond to Lady Gabrielle, Mellissa appeared out of nowhere. He almost slid off the sofa. "W-Why would you do that?" he yelled.

"Geez, Greg. Why do you keep acting like that when I teleport in?" She sat down next to him. "You should be happy that I'm improving. I didn't even fall over this time."

"Because you startle me when you appear out of nowhere without warning."

"What, like when you transform from a cute little rabbit into that"—she gestured to his whole body— "with no warning?"

"Gregory, is everything all right?" asked Lady Gabrielle. She sounded like she was trying not to laugh.

The colour drained from Mellissa's face as her eyes widened. She looked around the room and then dove behind the sofa. Greg put his hand over his face. "Yes, it's fine. Mellissa just came back early."

"I didn't realise you were talking on your glowing disc thing," Mellissa whispered from behind the sofa.

"Can I speak to her?" Lady Gabrielle asked.

Mellissa stood up, shaking her head. She made some

wild arm movements and pointed at the door before running out.

Greg shook his head. "Unfortunately, she just left."

"That was quick."

"Yes, Mellissa's teleporting has gotten really good. She pops in and out in seconds." He left out the part about her powers occasionally not working under stress and her rarely sticking the landing. He really should have congratulated her on her earlier teleport, especially as she managed to stay standing.

"It's good she is getting the hang of her powers. You two are on a first-name basis without titles?"

Greg ran his hand through his hair. Of course she would notice the informality in the way he had spoken to Mellissa. He knew it wasn't proper protocol, but he had given up, as Mellissa didn't respond to it. She hated it when he referred to her formally. However, to Lady Gabrielle, proper etiquette was still important. "They are not very formal in this world."

"Oh, I thought you might have become friends with the keeper. You are of similar age, after all."

Was he friends with Mellissa? He didn't dislike her, but could he really go so far as to say they were friends? Most of the time, it just felt like she put up with him. She was constantly going on about how annoying he was, and he found most of her behaviour odd.

"I don't know about that. She never listens to me and questions everything I do. She tries to outsmart me and calls me weird all the time."

"Sounds like she is just the sort of friend you need. Not a lot of people want to question an elder's son."

"I don't understand."

"You will. I will talk to you again tomorrow."

"Yes. Goodbye, Lady Gabrielle."

"Goodbye, Gregory."

His communis stopped glowing as it deactivated. Greg leant back in the chair. What had Lady Gabrielle meant by her last statement? He was not here to make friends. She knew that. He was dedicated to his job. He also didn't want the world to fall into chaos and neither did Mellissa. That was the only reason they were able to get along—they had a common goal. There was nothing else to it.

"Who was the woman?" Mellissa asked.

Greg jumped up. Mellissa sat on the sofa next to where he'd just been. He pointed at the door. "Why couldn't you just use the door?"

"That would involve walking from the kitchen to the hall and then here. I skipped all that, and you're always telling me to practice. So, who were you talking to?"

Greg sighed as he sat back down. "Lady Gabrielle."

"Is she your aunt?"

"No, she is the chair of the council. The council has decided that I should liaison with her from now on."

"Is she a changeling as well?"

"No, she is the warlock president."

"Sounds impressive." Mellissa grabbed the bag of crisps on the coffee table. "Seriously, Greg, you ate my crisps again. I was looking for them in the kitchen."

"Sorry, I got bored of eating carrots and lettuce. Just because I'm a vegetarian doesn't mean I only eat salad."

"Hey, don't complain when you're eating for free. You know there are noodles, pasta, beans and loads of other stuff if you cared to cook, you lazy bum."

Greg held his hands up. "Okay, sorry, I will get you some more."

"What, like the last pack you replaced?"

"Fine, I will get you two packs."

Mellissa stuck her tongue out at him, not acting her age as usual. It was no wonder he'd originally gotten her age wrong. Dressed in her school uniform with her hair in pigtails, a random loose curl at the front, she really didn't look eighteen. Greg leant on his arm. Maybe they were friends.

"What are you doing here anyway?" he asked.

"I live here."

"You know what I mean. You should still be at school."

"I have a study period, so I thought I would come see you."

"As nice as that is, shouldn't you be studying?"

"I came to see you for a reason." Mellissa pulled a notebook out of the bag she'd dropped on the floor the first time she teleported in. "What do you think of that?" She handed him the notebook.

"What is this?"

"My biology homework."

"Wouldn't it be cheating if I answered this for you?"

"I just want you to write down what you think, and then I will come up with my own answer. Come on, you said you were a healer. You should know about this stuff."

"I am a healer, but I think you are perfectly able to find the answers yourself."

"This is me finding the answers." She handed him a pen. "You know you are just dying to show off how smart you are. You never shut up when it comes to teaching me about magic. Even when I want to find the answers on my own, you're there, nattering away."

"Fine, I will help you with your homework, but you have to do your own writing."

"All right. It's not like I could hand in anything you wrote. Your handwriting is way too neat. They would know something was up."

Her homework was relatively simple for him. This was something he had covered a long time ago. It was good to see that the humans had a decent understanding of science, even if they didn't have full knowledge of the world. Where he was from, science and magic crossed over. They were nearly finished when a loud jingle came from Mellissa's bag.

"My alarm." She pulled her phone out of her bag. He had to admit, her phone was rather convenient in comparison to his communis device. It did a lot more than just make and receive calls. It was like a mini tabular and communis in one. She fumbled with her phone, almost dropping it as she turned the sound off. "Time for my next lesson." She gathered up her work and put it back in her bag. "I think I can finish this on my own. See ya later." She winked at him before disappearing.

Greg shook his head and lay back on the sofa, putting

the projection machine on. Mellissa definitely wasn't like anyone back home.

Mellissa arrived home from school that evening, announcing that their training session was cancelled. The Streets had a family thing to go to, so they wouldn't be home.

"Why can't we use their training room while they're out?" Greg asked. Mellissa was so close to mastering the sealing spell. He couldn't let her slack off in the slightest.

"Come on, Greg. Can you stop being all work for five minutes?" She sat in the window seat and leant her head on the wall. "I need a break. I've been working my butt off for weeks."

Greg sat beside her. "Fine, but there is something we need to talk about."

"What now?"

"When do you plan on travelling to the Tree of Time to actually perform the spell? I reckon you could have the spell mastered by the end of next week. I know you don't want to tell your father about magic, but he will notice your absence. It is at least a day's journey from here."

She bit her thumbnail. "Can't I just teleport there? I will be there and back in no time."

"Can you teleport somewhere you've never been before? Can you even teleport that far?"

"I don't know, but we can find out." She jumped up and held her hand out to him.

Greg raised an eyebrow. "Are you suggesting an experiment?"

"Yup, you coming?"

Greg took her hand and was tugged forward. Blinding light surrounded them. When he could see again, they were at a river. "Okay, how far away is this from your house?" he asked.

She tapped her chin and pouted. "About a mile."

"We need to record the distance more accurately."

Mellissa wriggled her nose, thinking. "I'm not really good with distances."

"Do you have a map of the area?"

"I have an app on my phone." She pulled her phone out of her jean pocket and waved it in his face.

Greg pushed the phone out of his face. "It's a start. Let's go back to yours before we continue this experiment." Greg was tugged forward again as light surrounded him. They stumbled back into Mellissa's bedroom.

Mellissa pulled up a map of the area on her phone and handed it to Greg. They determined different places to go, slowly getting farther away. To make the experiment fair, they returned to Mellissa's house to measure the distance from the same spot each time. The teleporting was going well until Mellissa tried to teleport them to the next town, and they got repulsed back. They both fell to the floor. It felt like they'd run straight into a brick wall.

"I guess there is a limit," Mellissa said, getting up off the floor.

Greg also got up and dusted himself off. "Which means teleporting to the Tree of Time is out of the question." Mellissa looked like she was about to throw up as the colour drained from her face. Travelling to the capital must be more daunting to her than he had realised. "I'm sorry this experiment didn't provide the results you wanted."

"It's all right. I just want to try one more thing." She took his hand. Greg shut his eyes as the familiar tug of Mellissa's teleporting pulled at him. When he opened them again, they were in Novos Forest.

Mellissa squeezed his hand. "Well, at least I can cross the veil."

Greg's chest tightened. She was smiling, but the shine in her eyes wasn't there. Mellissa was usually so bubbly, but that seemed to have drained from her. Greg wanted to hug her and take all her worries away. "You can take as much time as you need to decide when to travel to the Tree of Time."

Mellissa looked at her feet. "Three weeks."

"What?"

"I will go with you to the tree in three weeks, when Christmas break starts. That will give us plenty of time to practice. You overestimate my ability, thinking I'll be ready in a week."

"I think you underestimate your ability. I guess I won't complain about you not training this evening if we stick to schedule for the next three weeks."

She looked up at him with her big, brown eyes. "You don't really have a choice. I was going to leave you in the forest if you made a fuss." Then she smiled, and this time it reached her eyes. Greg's heart warmed, because that was a real smile.

Travel Plans
Mellissa

t was the last day of the school term. Everyone was looking forward to the holidays, but I wasn't. Usually, I would be jumping for joy and doing everything Christmas-related. This year, I wasn't feeling the same excitement. I had agreed to go to the magical world to reseal Kadon once the holidays started—a decision I was regretting. Greg insisted I was ready, but I wasn't as sure as him. I had picked up everything he'd taught me, and we'd been practicing the sealing spell all week, but I wasn't sure it was enough. I was also expected to meet the magic council, which made me even more nervous. They were all really important people, and I was—well, me. Greg was enough proof that I was not of their social class. They were all about protocol and regulations and proper etiquette. I couldn't even spell *etiquette* without using spell-check.

At least I'd finally come up with something to tell my dad. Well, Victoria had. She was actually really helpful when she wasn't intimidating me and completely freaking me out. I still didn't want to tell him about magic, so Victoria suggested that the art project I had told my dad we were working on involved her parents taking us to the big art gallery down south. Her parents would go and snap photos of the gallery, pretending we were with them. Meanwhile we would really be crossing the veil.

I spent the rest of the school day in a daze. While everyone else enjoyed games and slacking off normal classes, I was busy trying to stop myself from having a panic attack. I wished I could be as carefree as my fellow classmates, but I knew something they didn't. They had no idea the dangers that lurked just beyond an invisible wall. That an evil leprechaun was waiting for me to fail so he could enslave the human race. It sounded insane, but it was the truth, and no one here would ever know, except Matt and Victoria. They somehow managed to remain calm about everything. Matt seemed more concerned about Greg than the fact that the fate of the world rested in my hands. My stomach churned, and I felt like I might throw up. I'd been starting to enjoy having magic, especially teleporting, but now that the time for me to travel to the Tree of Time was so near, I wasn't feeling that joy anymore.

When the bell rang for the end of the day, I was out of that classroom in a flash. I slid out of view and teleported home. I screamed as I toppled over the coffee table in the living room.

Greg ran into the room. "Mellissa, what happened?"

I rolled over and lay on my back. "I landed badly." Greg appeared above me with his hand out. I waved it away. "I think I'm just going to lie here for a bit."

"Suit yourself," he said, sitting on the sofa. "Where are Matt and Victoria? I thought one of them always escorted you home."

That they did. At first, I hadn't minded—Matt and I spent a lot of time together anyway—but they had gotten more anal about things. I wasn't allowed to go to the bathroom alone anymore. Victoria had even stopped moaning about me hurting her reputation. They were taking their duty as my guardians very seriously. I stared at the ceiling.

"I teleported back—no escort required." He didn't need to know I had done a runner at the end of the day. "Also, my dad is working late tonight, we can just practice here."

The amount of fruit I had successfully sealed away was high, but I had a feeling sealing an apple in a melon wasn't the same as sealing a super powerful leprechaun in a tree. I needed to get as much practice in as possible. I just didn't need the twins watching over me while I did.

"Okay. Are the twins coming here?"

I sat up, slamming my hand on the floor. "I do not need

to be followed constantly! If it isn't them, it's you. I mean, at least you let me go to the bathroom alone, but can I not get a moment of peace?"

"Sorry, I just thought we were meant to be finalising our travel plans for tomorrow."

"Well, I kind of forgot about that." I laid my head on the coffee table, the fight draining out of me.

"How about I go make you a cup of tea? Will that make you feel better?"

"Yes," I grumbled.

Greg got up and left. Why was he being so nice to me when I'd snapped his head off for no reason? I needed to relax and stop worrying so much. I had been practicing for weeks, but practice in the Streets' training hall wasn't the same as the real thing. According to Greg, the magic world was polluted with Kadon's darkness. Was I really strong enough to overpower him? Regardless, snapping at the people who were trying to help me wasn't going to get me anywhere. Greg returned with a hot cup of tea and placed it on the table beside me.

"Thank you," I said, "and I'm sorry about before."

He shrugged. "I get it. You're nervous." He walked out of the room and left me alone.

I pulled my legs up to my chest and rested my arms on my knees, with my hands wrapped around my cup. The warm mug felt amazing. I breathed in the comforting smell of hot tea. My moment of peace didn't last long. Banging at the door had me on my feet. There was a crash and a snapping sound. A cold flurry swept through the living room. Victoria entered the room with a look on her face that could kill. Matt ran around her and pulled me into a bear hug.

"Don't ever disappear like that again," he said.

"What's going on?" came Greg's voice from behind Victoria. "What happened to the door?"

I pushed Matt off me and ran into the hallway. The door was in pieces. I ran back into the living room. Victoria was perched on the edge of an armchair, and Matt was lying across the sofa like they hadn't done anything wrong. "Why did you have to break the door?"

Victoria glared at me. "Someone disappeared from school and then wasn't answering the door."

"You didn't give me much time." I tugged at my hair. "How am I going to explain this to my dad?"

Matt frowned as he shrugged. Victoria admired her nails and said, "Not my problem."

"Don't worry. I can fix it," Greg said.

"You can? How?"

"With a spell."

My jaw dropped as Greg muttered some words in a weird language and the pieces of the door knit themselves back together. I ran my hand over the door. "Amazing." It was as good as new. You would never know it had been blown to pieces by a crazy ice warlock.

Greg clapped his hands together. "Well, now that everyone's here, we may as well discuss our travel plans for tomorrow." A chorus of groans sounded in the living room. I sighed, following Greg back into the room. He was right though; we might as well get it over with. "Oh, and I thought for today's practice you could seal this peg into this rock." He sat on the floor, placing a peg and rock on the coffee table.

I slipped down beside him and held my hand out toward the peg. "Disseptum." A barrier formed around the peg. I closed my fist, and the rock began to glow. "Signo que claudant abesse." The rock opened up and sucked the peg inside, resealing itself. I opened my fist, and the rock stopped glowing.

Greg lifted the rock and held it up to the light. "Very well done. I told you—you're ready."

"Except I still have to say the spell for the barrier. I've never heard you utter a word when creating a barrier."

"That will come with practice. Remember, I have been doing this a lot longer than you."

"Which is exactly why I don't think I'm ready."

"All you have to do is cast the spell as you just did. The only difference is, since Kadon is already in the tree, you have to make contact with the tree and put the barrier around that."

I leant on the coffee table. He had way too much

confidence in me. The twins joined us on the floor.

"Are we going to get on with the planning?" Matt asked.

We sat around the coffee table, finalising the plan for tomorrow. They did most of the talking while I listened. I might've been the one they all needed, but I felt like I had no say in anything that was going on. Instead, I just agreed to what they decided. It wasn't like my opinion mattered. I didn't know anything about the magic world, while they were all originally from there. Greg had a map, and they were currently deciding the best route to take. I sat playing with my hair. I was starting to wonder if my presence here was necessary. There were so many other things I could be doing right now.

"Wait, you mean your dad has a boat?" Matt said.

"It's only a riverboat," Greg replied.

Matt sat up straighter, putting his hand over his chest. "Oh, it's only a riverboat," he said with a fake posh voice. "Most normal people don't own boats."

"I'm not sorry about my background, and if it can help our journey, I will use my privilege to our advantage. Unless you wish to walk?"

Matt leant on the coffee table. "Riverboat sounds good."

Greg pointed to the river on the map. "The boat will take us to the dock in Novosvillas. Then, a sleigh will take us the rest of the way."

Victoria rolled her eyes. "Great, we're going to have to go to a changeling city first."

I sat up, my interest sparked. "Wait, did you say a sleigh?"

"Yes," Greg said, "it has been snowing all month. The snow is so deep that all normal means of transport have been suspended."

It was snowing on the other side of the veil. How was that even possible? It was cold here, but there wasn't any sign of snow. We just kept getting pummelled with rain.

"That's not good," Matt said folding his arms. "You realise if it's actually that deep, we might lose Mel in it."

"Hey!" I shouted.

"You have to admit, you are pretty tiny," Victoria said,

demonstrating how small she thought I was with her fingers.

Matt put his arm round me. "It's not all bad being small. You're cute and tiny and almost hand-luggage size."

I pushed Matt's arm away from me. "I am not that small. You are just freakishly tall."

In fact, all three of them were. Victoria was just under six feet, and the other two were well over it. I hated to say it, but compared to them, I really was tiny. This reminder of how small I was did not help with my self-confidence. I got up. "I'm going to get some snacks."

Victoria snickered. "You know, excessive eating won't make you taller, just fatter."

"Thanks for those words of wisdom," I said through gritted teeth. I walked out of the room and made my way to the kitchen. I put the kettle on to make myself tea but ended up with my head laid on the kitchen top. What had I gotten myself into? I was the weak link in this odd little group of ours. The world was doomed if I was its only hope to stop this evil.

"Mel, you all right?" asked Matt.

I looked up to see him in the doorway. "I'm fine."

"I was only joking about you being small, and I think Victoria was as well."

"I didn't realise Victoria knew how to tell a joke."

Matt walked over to me. "I know. It's surprising when she acts like a normal person. Are you sure you're all right? You've hardly said a word since we arrived."

"I don't know. I guess I'm just nervous about everything. What if I mess up and this leprechaun king gets free? The world will be in danger, and it will be all my fault."

"It would not be your fault, and you don't need to worry about all that because you've got this." He pointed at the Heart Crystal around my neck.

"How can you be so sure?" I asked.

"If you could sense the power inside you the way the rest of us can, you would also be a believer." Matt put his arm round my shoulders, giving me a squeeze.

"What if my power isn't enough?" I said, leaning on him.

"You worry too much. You won't be doing this alone. I will be with you, and my sister and Greg will be too. We sure are a weird little group—two warlocks, a changeling and a human elf. Is that all that's bothering you?"

I turned away from him. "Of course, that's all."

"No more weird dreams about a battle?"

"Why would that be worrying me? They're just dreams." I wished I hadn't told him about that dream. If I had known what I know now, I probably would've kept it to myself. The dreams had gotten clearer, they weren't as disjointed as before. They were all about Freya but in them I was Freya. It was like her life was happening to me in a dream. What was worse was that they had changed. They were now a group of repeating dreams that showed just how unlike Freya I was and just how dangerous Kadon had been. Freya was strong and confidant, whereas I was anxious and constantly overthinking everything.

"You have had more dreams then. Before, when you told me about that dream, I didn't know about your magic. I think you have been dreaming about Freya and Kadon's final battle."

"I think you're right."

"You do?"

I nodded. "After meeting Greg, the dreams became clearer. They have also changed."

"Changed how?"

"It's like I'm seeing different parts of Freya's life. Some of the dreams repeat. Mainly the more violent ones. Is this normal?"

Matt leant against the worktop, rubbing his chin. "Not really. I did some research into seers, and well, you're not one."

I grabbed his arm. "You did research on your own?"

He shrugged me off. "Hey, don't sound so surprised. My mum has a small library, and I borrowed a book or two. From what I read, seers are extremely rare and only see the future, not the past. As your dreams are all about Freya, maybe it has more to do with the Heart Crystal."

I bit my thumbnail. "What if my dreams are telling me that I can't do this?"

"Or maybe they are just preparing you for what you have to do."

I looked up at the ceiling. A part of me wanted to keep this all secret, but another part thought that was a bad idea. "Should we tell the others? Like you said, we are a team, and Greg knows a lot more about the history of the Heart than us."

"No. You especially can't tell Greg."

"Why not? I know you don't like him, but what if he can help?"

Matt looked at his feet. "It's not that I don't like him. I mean, he's not my favourite person, but that's not why you shouldn't tell him. Greg comes from a very different world than us."

"I thought you were all from the other side of the veil?"

"We are, but just like on this side, there are different social classes. He belongs to a very elite few. The name Ainsworth means something in the magic world. He has told you who his father is?"

"He said he was some knight and a member of the council, but people vote for the council members, don't they?"

"Um, no. The council is made up of leaders from the different nations. How the different leaders are chosen varies. The warlocks vote for their president, but the changelings basically have a monarchy."

"But he said his dad was a knight, not a king."

"Lord Steffen Ainsworth Elder Knight." Matt rolled his eyes. "It's just a fancy title the changelings came up with. They think it makes them sound wise, but our friend in there is basically a prince. I just don't want you revealing too much to him or getting attached and ending up hurt."

I bumped shoulders with him. "I'm a big girl, Matt. I can take care of myself. Anyway, I know I'm just a project to him, something to show off his skill and prove himself to his father. I know there are limits to any friendship I have with Greg. We can just use him for his brain."

Matt ruffled his hair. "I can't help worrying about you. You're like a younger sister to me, and as your big brother, I must look out for you. Greg's father may try and use any knowledge he has of us for his own purposes. Even Greg doesn't know that yet."

"You do realise I'm older than you, but I take your point. The politics on the other side are so confusing."

"Tell me about it. Life on this side is so much simpler. Anyway, I thought you came out here for snacks." Matt spun on his heel and opened a cupboard.

"Subtle change of subject," I said.

Matt flashed a grin over his shoulder. I sighed, opening another cupboard. We went back to the living room with crisps and drinks. As they carried on, planning around me, I couldn't help thinking about what Matt had said. Greg was basically a prince. I had blindly jumped into a friendship with Greg. For all I knew, he only put up with me because it was his duty. If Matt was right, Greg's duty to his people would always come first. Could I ever really trust him the way I trusted Matt and Victoria?

"You don't have to do this!" I shout. "It's not too late to turn back."

All eyes are on me. I'm at the gate to my kingdom, my guardians on either side of me. An army of leprechauns surrounds us, Kadon in the lead. I can't make out his features, but I know it's him. I know what is expected of me—a display of power. But if we could just talk things out… War was not what I wanted. The leprechauns outnumbered the elves, and currently, there were only three of us standing in their way.

Kadon stepped forward. "As long as you insist on stealing our human servants, we won't back down."

"How can you be so heartless? Humans are not property. I steal nothing from you. What I do is rescue slaves."

"You are a fool, Freya. Your compassion makes you weak." Kadon clicks his fingers. "Storm the gates. Take back what is ours."

His soldiers march forward. With a flick of my arm, I release a ray of light, and they stop in their tracks. Kadon snarls. A dark aura surrounds him. He charges forward, throwing me to the ground. I signal to Ivan and Tasha to stand down. I stand and face Kadon.

"This is your last chance to leave."

"Your father you are not," he says. "Time has ended on the rule of the elves."

I hold my hand out to the side and summon my staff. "Then you leave me no choice."

Kadon cackles. "I'm not afraid of you, Freya."

I lift my staff above my head, releasing a pulse that sends Kadon flying. "Maybe you should be."

The sun shone through a crack in my curtains. I rolled over, covering my head with my pillow. Today was the day. I would be meeting the magic council and attempting to reseal Kadon. My stomach churned. I had dreamt of Freya and her guardians facing down Kadon and his army of leprechauns. It had been three against an army. The fact that they had survived that encounter showed just how powerful Freya was. There was no way I could do something like that. I let out a long sigh. All I had to do was reinforce Freya's original spell. I could do this.

Groaning, I rolled over again. I didn't want to get up. All I wanted was to stay tucked up in bed, to forget about magic, heirs and leprechaun prisoners. How had this become my life? If someone had told me a couple of months ago that this was how I would be spending the first few days of my holiday, I would have laughed. Something bounced on the end of my bed.

"Rise and shine, my lady," came Greg's voice. "We have a busy day ahead of us."

I threw my pillow at the annoying rabbit on the end of my bed. "Don't call me that."

"You need to get used to it, my lady, as it's the done thing where we are going."

"I don't care what the done thing is." I dragged myself out of bed. "Now, get out while I shower."

"As you wish, my lady."

I threw another pillow at him as he hopped away.

Once dressed, I went down for breakfast but couldn't bring myself to eat. My stomach kept doing somersaults, making me feel queasy. I eventually gave up on food and decided to just get on with things. With my rucksack on my back, I grabbed Greg and stuffed him into my satchel. He protested, but it was the only way to sneak him past my dad. If I didn't hide him, my dad would want to know why I was taking the rabbit out with me. Just as I was about to leave, my dad offered to give me a lift. It would have been odd to say no. Greg would just have to suffer the constraints of my bag a bit longer.

I got in the car with Greg safely hidden away, and my dad dropped us off at Victoria and Matt's house. He spoke to their parents, and then we said our goodbyes. As I watched him drive off, there was a tightness in my chest. I hadn't been able to look him in the eye all morning. I didn't like hiding the truth from him, but this wasn't exactly an easy subject to bring up. Even if he didn't completely freak out, I didn't think he would like the idea of me going to do this on my own. I would eventually tell him everything, but that was a conversation for another day. I let Greg out of my bag, and he transformed back into his human form.

"I really hate when you carry me around in that thing. I'm not your pet." He shook out his arms and legs like I'd squished him. "You know, I could have just flown out the window and met you here."

He had a point, but I wasn't going to let him know that. "Quit moaning. It's not like I'm going to be sneaking you in and out of the house anymore after this." With that, I realised that Greg would not be coming back with us once this was over, and that I might actually miss his complaining.

"Are we ready to go?" Matt asked, throwing a big camp bag over his shoulder. I was surprised to find that he had packed more than his sister. Victoria had only packed a small backpack and had already been waiting for us when we arrived.

Mrs. Street made a fuss over us, giving everyone a hug and her children big, sloppy kisses. Mr. Street wasn't as dramatic. Both his kids got a hug, and he patted me on the back.

"Are we all ready to go?" I asked when Mrs. Street released Matt and Victoria from a big bear hug. They all nodded. "Then everyone hold on to me and don't let go. I have no idea what will happen if you do." I held my arms out, and everyone grabbed hold of me. In the shine of a bright light, I teleported us all to the wood. Then, one by one, we went through the tear in the veil to the magic forest.

Journey
Mellissa

 gasped as my foot disappeared under a layer of snow. I lifted my foot and shook the snow off it. Stepping forward, I smiled as my foot disappeared into the snow again. Greg had warned us it had been snowing here, but I hadn't expected such a drastic difference in the weather from where we just were. I pulled my hat down over my ears and wrapped my arms around myself as I shivered. The sun was shining high in the sky, but it was still freezing. I turned on the spot. The forest looked truly magical. The last time I was here, it had been after dark. Everything was brighter, and the shadow that had loomed over the forest was now non-existent.

"How is there so much snow here?" I asked. "It isn't even slightly icy back home."

"It's just like back home, where the different regions of the country have different weather," Victoria explained. "This place and our village may seem to only be separated by the veil, but we are still in a completely different place. Who's to say that if the veil came down, this place would even be next to where we live? Magic is funny like that."

I had never thought of it like that. I'd always assumed this forest and our village were next to each other, not that crossing the veil was the same as hopping on a plane to another country.

"Where is this riverboat?" Matt asked sarcastically.

Greg pointed up the river. "We will be boarding at the water nymph village up there."

Matt did a little dance. "Oh yeah. Water nymphs are

blue and mighty fine."

"You do realise that water nymphs are genderless creatures," Victoria said.

Matt's eyebrows squished together, and he tilted his head. "I thought water nymphs were all female."

"Technically, water nymphs have the potential to become either gender," Greg said, correcting them both. "Once water nymphs pair off, they decide as a couple which one of them will take on the male role and female role for reproductive purposes, but other than that, gender doesn't really matter to them."

"They can pick their gender?" I asked.

Greg nodded. "Gender is pretty fluid for many of the magic folk that originate from the ocean."

We walked toward the water nymph village. I covered my eyes as the ice covering the river reflected a stray beam of light my way. "The water is iced over. How is the boat going to get through?" I asked.

"Don't worry. The water nymphs will have it sorted," Greg replied.

I trudged behind him, kicking up snow as I went. The snow was so deep it almost reached my knees. My new winter boots were pointless as they didn't come far enough up my leg. The snow was filling up my boots and slowly soaking my leggings. This walk seemed a lot longer than I remembered, and I seemed to be the only one having a problem. Greg walked through the snow like it was a clear summer's day. Victoria was gliding across, leaving no footprints behind, and Matt was leaving puddles of water.

I turned to walk behind Matt when something in the trees caught my eye. Something fluttered between the branches. I ran over to the tree to get a closer look. Whatever creature I'd seen had disappeared into a tiny house hidden in the branches. I looked around the trees. All of them had these houses in them. Each house was made out of wood that matched the trees. They had cute little doors and windows, and roofs made from straw. What or whoever lived there must be tiny.

"Greg!" I shouted. "What are those?" I pointed at the

tiny houses in the trees.

Greg walked over and looked where I was pointing. "I thought you would know. You have loads of storybooks about them. However, your books are not very accurate."

I looked at him, confused. I had a lot of storybooks about magic from when I was little. I'd loved the idea as a little girl. Finding out I was part elf would have been a dream come true for the younger version of me.

Greg could see that I wasn't getting what he said. "They are houses of the Fay. They light the way of those lost in the forest. More commonly known as fairies."

I grabbed his arm and squeaked. "They are fairy houses! The lights I saw in the trees before were the fairies in their homes? Why didn't you tell me?" I felt like a little kid. I don't really know why I was so surprised—I was travelling with two warlocks and a changeling—but I loved fairies as a child. I still had a habit of drawing pictures of fairies on all my textbooks. It was possible all the magical creatures I had dreamt of as a child were real.

Greg shrugged. "You never asked."

How could he say that? There was so much to discover in this world. I had no idea what questions to ask.

Matt strolled over. "You know, fairies aren't always that small. They can change their size at will. Sort of like how he changes into animals." Matt linked arms with me and pulled me away, narrowing his eyes at Greg. I felt like I was missing something.

As we continued walking, Matt told me all about fairies and what they really looked like. He was loving the fact that there was something he knew more about than me. Usually, it was me helping him with schoolwork. I was the smarter one out of the two of us—on paper, at least. I was more academically inclined than Matt, but there were things Matt was good at that I wasn't. Our differences, as well as our similarities, were what made us such good friends.

The stone bridge came into view. Just beyond it was a boat. It was a lot bigger than I had imagined. It was a long, grey and white barge. There was a mast for a sail, but it was currently tied up.

"You call that 'just a riverboat?'" Matt scoffed.

"That's what it is," Greg replied, ploughing forward.

When we reached the boat, we found a group of people gathered around it. One person stood out in particular. One, because of his height, and two, because he was the only one that wasn't blue. He had short brown hair and was dressed like he was ready for work at the office instead of standing by a frozen river. He was engrossed in conversation with an older man.

"Samson?" exclaimed Greg.

The brown-haired boy turned around, a smile spreading across his face. "Greg, you're finally here." He embraced Greg, who appeared to be in shock. "You look well, though still in need of a haircut."

Greg swatted Samson's hand away as he flicked his fringe. "Samson, what are you doing here? I wasn't told you would be escorting us."

"It was rather last minute, but I managed to persuade your father to let me come meet you. Aren't you going to introduce me?"

"Yes, of course. Everyone, this is my cousin Samson." Greg ushered me forward. "Samson, this is Mellissa Hail, keeper of the Heart and heir to the elf throne, and her guardians, Mathew and Victoria Street."

Samson bowed. "It is an honour to meet you, Your Highness."

"Oh wow. He is bowing," I said. "You don't have to do that, and just Mellissa is fine."

Samson's eyes widened. "But that would be improper." He sounded just like Greg.

Matt and Victoria snickered behind me.

Greg put his hand on my arm and whispered, "Mellissa, we spoke about this."

"No, you spoke, and I tuned you out."

Greg put his head in his hands. Samson looked like he was trying to hold back a laugh.

"Is that her?" came a voice from the group gathered.

"It is. I heard him say her name," said another.

"Your Majesty," cried a chorus of voices. Then they were all on their knees.

My eyes widened. "What is happening?"

"They are bowing to their queen," Greg replied.

"I thought I was heir to the *elf* throne."

"You are. The water nymphs follow the old ways, making you their queen too."

"What? No." I shook my head. "Why aren't they standing?"

"You need to tell them to rise—something you would know if you actually listened to me."

This was crazy. I turned to the crowd and cleared my throat. "You may rise."

And they did.

A young woman stepped forward. She had long, wavy black hair and deep blue eyes. "Permission to approach?" she asked.

I looked to Greg, and he nodded. "Permission granted," I said.

"My name is Yuri, and I have been chosen by my people to assist you on your journey. It is an honour to serve you."

"That's nice." I gave her what I hoped was a believable smile, while on the inside, I was freaking out. A very big part of me wanted to run away, and the other wanted to collapse on the ground. This was too much. I hadn't expected anything like this. All this attention was unnecessary.

Greg turned his back to the crowd and tilted his head toward my ear. "She will be making sure the river stays clear of ice."

"Oh, that's what she meant." He nodded. I grabbed his arm as he went to step back. "Can we just get out of here?"

"As you wish, my lady." He turned to Samson. "Shall we get going then?"

"Of course," Samson replied. "All aboard. We shall depart immediately."

We followed Samson to the boat. The girl, Yuri, eyed Matt and Victoria with wide eyes. People bowed and reached out to me as I passed. I let out a long breath when I made it onto the boat. A man grabbed Greg's hand just before he could climb up.

"Master Ainsworth, you honour our people by bringing the keeper to us."

He put his hand over the man's. "The honour is all mine." The man nodded, releasing him, and Greg climbed aboard the boat.

I raised an eyebrow. "Master Ainsworth?" I asked.

"I told you we are more formal here," he replied.

"They are, and it's really annoying," Matt said as he leant against the railing of the boat. , "Are we going to get moving?"

"Yes, we are." Greg made a hand gesture to Samson, who nodded in response, then disappeared. After some loud bangs and thuds that made my stomach clench, the boat began to move. Yuri was at the front of the boat, waving her arms about. With each of her movements, it sounded like something was breaking. I ran to the railing Matt was leant on and looked out at the water. The ice was cracking and being pushed apart.

"Amazing," I said.

"Yeah, I know. He didn't even have to use words to order people about. His Royal Highness is really in his element here."

"That's not what I—"

"Samson and I grew up together," Greg snapped, cutting me off. "We developed our own form of nonverbal communication long ago. I am not any more royal than you are."

Matt snickered. "Yeah, right. Who are you kidding? We all know you are just some rich, privileged kid. You have no idea what it's like for us normal folk."

"You know what—" Greg paused, then said, "Doesn't matter. You're a waste of my time. I'm going to see if Samson needs help."

Matt stared in the direction Greg had gone. "Yep, always better to boss people around while standing over them."

I grabbed Matt's arm. "What's gotten into you? That

was uncalled for."

"I don't know what you're talking about."

"Yes, you do. Seriously, you say you don't hate him and then act like that. This negative energy really isn't helping my nerves. We are meant to be a team."

"I'm sorry. It's just, when I saw you two together and the way he was looking at you, it's like you're just another item to add to his display cabinet."

I blinked. That statement made him sound jealous, but I knew that couldn't be right. "What are you even talking about?"

Matt sighed as he gazed up at the sky. "It's like this—even before I became your guardian, I felt the need to protect you. You are just so naïve. You have this idealistic view of the world, but just because that's how things should be, doesn't make them so. Guys like him take advantage of people. It's in their nature. Even if he is trying to be decent, it's hard to break out of what you've been raised to do."

"Cut him some slack. He did kind of save me. We wouldn't have any transport without him, and I never would have learnt the magic I need to know. Besides, I am extremely capable, and you are constantly pushing me to make new friends."

"Yeah, well, not friends like him."

I put my hands on my hips. "I don't see you acting like this when Victoria makes a new guy friend, and I use the term 'friend' very loosely when referring to your sister."

"That's because my sister is an ice queen in every possible way. She could kick any guy's butt with her arms tied behind her back. You, on the other hand, are easy pickings."

"I am not."

Matt raised his eyebrow and tilted his head. Annoyingly, he was right. I was nowhere near as tough as Victoria, and based on what I'd seen of her magic, she was lethal. He put his arm around me. "Look, I'm sorry. I will play nice from now on. You're right; there are worse rich snobs out there than Greg."

Not quite what I had meant, but I'd take what I could get if it meant Matt would stop with the snide remarks. I needed our odd little team to get along for my own sanity.

I opened my mouth to respond when I was hit by a chorus of voices.

"Our Queen."

"You have returned to us."

"We owe you thanks."

I pushed Matt away and turned slowly on the spot. "Did you hear that?"

"Hear what?" Matt stepped toward me, but I put my arm up to stop him coming closer. My ears rang as the voices got louder. More joined in, and they began to shout.

"Your Majesty."

"The forest is where you belong."

"You must stay."

"Don't leave us."

I clutched my ears. Where were these voices coming from? Matt edged toward me. I screamed as he placed a hand on my arm. My head was ringing. I stumbled backward, turning my head side to side, searching for the voices. They kept calling to me. Matt shouted my name. I slapped his hand away to stop him from touching me. Branches suddenly shot across the boat, slamming into him.

The voices became angry. "Danger. We must protect the queen." Vines wrapped around Matt. I needed to help him, but my body wouldn't move. My head was throbbing. It was the trees. They were calling out to me and were trying to protect me. They thought Matt was a threat. I needed to stop them. Make them understand.

Fire blasted through the vines, then ice shot across the deck. The trees screamed in pain. My heart was racing. I ran to the edge of the boat and leapt in the air. Two arms grabbed me around the waist. I screamed, kicking my legs about.

"Have you lost your mind?" Victoria yelled in my ear.

"I belong in the forest!" I shouted.

She spun me around, forcing me away from the edge. "I don't know what's gotten into you, but I'm not about to let you kill yourself."

"Can't you hear the screams? The trees are in pain. They need me."

The trees surrounding the river stretched toward the boat. Branches slammed down on the deck. Vines wrapped around the boat. I tried to push Victoria away. She grabbed my arms and twisted them behind my back.

Matt appeared on his knees in front of me. "Mel, what are you going on about? Please calm down so we can help you." I could hear the worry in his voice. What was wrong with me? None of what I was doing made sense.

"Matt," shouted Greg, "you need to get through to her before she destroys the boat."

I was destroying the boat. I'd thought the attack was just the trees, but it wasn't. They were calling to me. The worry and need for help that the tree's were feeling had trigged something inside me but I hadn't meant for this to happen. Their cry for help had added to the pressure I was feeling and sent my powers haywire. I had to stop, but I didn't know how.

Matt put his hand on my cheek. "Mellissa, you feel like you have the weight of the world on your shoulders. You're scared and overwhelmed. You've been playing it cool, but inside, you are freaking out, and I'm sorry I didn't notice. I was too busy trying to protect you from the wrong thing." He glanced over his shoulder. "Something you don't need protecting from, because you are way stronger than anyone gives you credit for. I let you down, but that won't happen again. We will face whatever happens when we arrive at the Tree of Time together—you, me, Victoria and Greg. We are a team."

Tears streamed down my face. He had put into words the feelings I hadn't let myself acknowledge. "I don't know how to stop it," I croaked. "I'm not strong enough."

Matt leant his forehead against mine. "Yes, you are. You have the strongest heart of anyone. You can do anything."

Matt was suddenly yanked away from me. "No!" I screamed.

The Heart Crystal glowed. Everything seemed to slow

down. Matt was thrown by a tree branch. Victoria rose up while forming an ice wall. Greg was directing a spell in Matt's direction. The crystal floated up from round my neck and shot out a flurry of multicoloured lights. Everything around me lit up. Then, it all went dark.

Novosvillas
Gregory

reg threw a barrier up, stopping Matt from being thrown off the boat. Waves were beating up the side of the boat as tree branches crashed on the surface of the water. The boat was going to sink if he didn't do something soon, but every barrier he put up, Mellissa's magic destroyed. He had known she was powerful, but this was too much. It was like the forest had come alive.

Bright lights blinded him. Everything went silent. Greg cast a quick series of spells, temporarily patching up the boat. When he could see again, all the trees had retreated.

"Mellissa!" yelled Victoria.

Greg turned to see Mellissa passed out on the floor with a cut on her head. Victoria was shaking her, trying to wake her. He ran to her side, skidding down onto his knees.

"Sanum quod fit." Greg's hand glowed green, and he waved it over Mellissa's head. The wound began to knit itself back together.

"I guess you really are a healer," Victoria muttered.

Greg ignored the insult. The twins really had a low opinion of him. As if he would have lied about his training. Once Mellissa's head wound was healed, he checked her pulse. That was fine. He bit his lip. Something more had to be wrong with her. She had completely lost it a moment ago.

"Vulnere." Both his hands glowed yellow. He hovered them over Mellissa.

"What are you doing?" asked Matt. Greg hadn't noticed him approach. He stood over them with a worried look on his face.

"Healing her, what else?" Greg replied.

"I know that. I just don't know that spell."

"It searches for non-visible wounds." Greg's hands stopped glowing, and he clenched them into fists. Mellissa had exhausted herself with the excessive use of her magic.

"Well?" demanded Victoria.

"She's fine. Just needs to sleep it off."

There was a loud crash, and the boat tipped downward. Samson came running. "Your spells are fading. The boat is too damaged. We need to evacuate."

Greg jumped to his feet. They needed to stay on course, or they would never make it to their destination in time. He could salvage this boat.

"Matt, take Mellissa below deck and make her comfortable. She should be fine, but if her condition changes, come get me." Matt nodded, scooping Mellissa up in his arms and disappearing below deck. "Victoria, do you think you can help Yuri keep the boat afloat?"

She shrugged. "No idea, but I'll try." She grabbed Yuri and ran to the edge of the boat. In unison, they pulled their arms back and kept repeating that motion until the boat steadied itself.

"Samson, I need you to help strengthen my spells on the boat. I'm hoping the extra power will make them last longer." Samson nodded, and together they recast the repair spells, this time with more accuracy. Hopefully this fix would get them to Novosvillas.

"How long until we reach Novosvillas?" Victoria groaned. "My arms are getting tired."

"Not much longer," Greg replied. "Once we get past that mound of trees, you will be able to see the port."

"Then what?" she asked. "We are way behind schedule, and Mellissa still hasn't woken up."

This was the exact question he had been asking himself

a couple of hours ago and then practically screamed at Samson when he had asked what was wrong. He had instantly regretted his outburst. It wasn't Samson's fault but he was the only person onboard who would understand his worry. Greg knew once his father found out about the delay he wouldn't be pleased and there would be some sort of punishment to follow. Luckily, after discussing things with his cousin, he had calmed down and they had decided on how to proceed next.

"Samson is currently contacting the council to tell them we are running late. There is no way we are going to make it to the capital today. I figured we could stay overnight in Novosvillas. That should allow plenty of time for Mellissa to recover."

"Seriously, you want us to stay in a changeling city?"

Greg put his head in his hands. Did she not hear herself? She sounded prejudice and snobby. Novosvillas was a beautifully city—full of culture and knowledge. She should be grateful to stay in such a place.

"Oh, miss, Novosvillas is a beautiful city," Yuri said, "so full of life, and it has the most magnificent library."

Greg smirked. "Thank you, Yuri."

"You're welcome, Master Ainsworth. I assist many boats along the river and always look forward to the ones that go to Novosvillas."

Victoria rolled her eyes and muttered something under her breath.

"What was that?" Greg asked.

Victoria glared at him. "It's cold."

"Well, maybe you should wear the cloak I gave you." He pointed at a dark blue bundle at her feet, knowing that wasn't what she'd muttered. "It's lined with fleece."

She looked him up and down. "And look as stupid as you do? No thanks."

Samson stumbled onto the deck. "Err, Greg, your father wishes to speak with you."

"What? You were meant to call Lady Gabrielle."

"I did. I explained everything, and she was very understanding, but not long after the call ended, Uncle

Steffen—I mean, Lord Ainsworth—called. He doesn't sound happy."

"He never is."

"I left my communis in my cabin. Thought you might want some privacy." Samson mouthed *"Sorry!"* as he walked past.

Greg hurried down to Samson's cabin. Why had he thought he could avoid his father's wrath? Once again, he would be a disappointment. The fact that he had found the new keeper, taught her sealing magic and gotten her halfway to the Tree of Time would all be forgotten. He was behind schedule and embarrassing his father. He took a deep breath and pushed the door open. The communis glowed on a small table. Greg picked the device up and sat on Samson's bunk.

"Hello, Father. I understand you wish to speak with me."

"Gregory, what took you so long?" snapped his father. "Don't you know I'm an important person and my time is valuable?"

"It's a wonder you took the time to call me then."

"Don't get smart with me, boy. You have brought shame to the family, and there is nothing more important than protecting our family name."

Greg was glad his father couldn't see him as he rolled his eyes. "And how exactly have I shamed the family?"

"You are running late. You know how I feel about tardiness. You have also damaged my boat and injured the keeper. Worst of all, I had to hear all this from Gabrielle."

Greg clenched his jaw. How dare he throw an accusation like that at him. There was no way he would injure Mellissa. In fact, he had healed her. How quick his father was to blame him for everything. He must have twisted Samson's message. Technically, what happened was all because of Mellissa, but she hadn't meant it. Greg wanted to scream at his father, but that would achieve nothing. He counted to five while taking deep breaths, carefully considering his response.

"The delay could not be helped. Things happened beyond my control. Mellissa had a mishap with her powers.

That is all."

"You were meant to teach her to control her powers. Another task you have failed at."

"I did my best, Father, but no one has a full understanding of elf magic as they've been missing from our world for so long."

"Even so, I expect you to report these problems directly to me, not Gabrielle."

"I was just following protocol, Father. Is that not what you've always taught me to do? It was agreed that I would discuss all things concerning Mellissa with Lady Gabrielle."

"Those pesky fools on the council getting in my way," growled his father.

Their conversation was interrupted by a knock at the door. Samson walked in. "We are coming into port."

Greg nodded. "Sorry, Father, I have to go. I need to make sure your boat doesn't suffer any more damage at the port."

"Well, at least you made it to Novosvillas. You can all stay at the house. Anna will be there to greet you."

"Won't you be there?"

"Of course not. I'm in the capital, organising things with the council. Why on earth would I be in Novosvillas?"

Greg sighed. Novosvillas was the city his father was meant to oversee and where their home was but of course his father wouldn't be there. Preparing for Mellissa's arrival in the capital was more important. His father had never been the sentimental type. The fact that he hadn't seen his son in months didn't matter, but a small part of Greg had hoped he would have been there to greet him. "Very well, Father. Sorry to disappoint you, but thank you for your generosity and allowing everyone to stay at the house."

"Don't think that apology will get you out of disciplinary action when you finally make it to the capital, and that includes your cousin."

The device stopped glowing as his father hung up on him. He chucked the communis at Samson and made his way back up top. Samson followed.

"Why do I have a disciplinary?" he asked.

"Because you reported to Lady Gabrielle."

"But that's what we were meant to do."

"My father is just in a mood. The council won't approve it."

Since Greg had been below deck, the dark of the night had really set in. There was a cold chill in the air. As Yuri pulled them into port, Greg admired the twinkling lights of the city. Snow covered the ground and all the rooftops. In the distance, the clock tower stood tall. A smile spread across Greg's face. He was home.

Rest
Mellissa

he market bustles with life. There is an array of fruits and vegetables on display. I pick out a pair of juicy-looking plums and pay the stallholder. I hand one to my companion. He frowns, his grey eyes narrowing on the fruit.

"Is something wrong?" I ask.

He shakes his head, as if waking from a dream. "No, just thinking how much this place has changed."

I take a bite of my plum. It's the sweetest plum I've ever tasted. "In what way?"

"There are just so many humans."

"It was all part of my father's plan to integrate them into our society, to live in harmony."

"But why? They have no magic, no purpose."

I take a step back. "Every being has a purpose."

"What use is a human if not as a servant?"

"They have many skills. They think differently than us and are very creative. It was a human that designed our streetlights."

He frowned. "But they are still run by magic."

"Yes, but they found a way to make it work. Humans are great builders and bakers. They make the best sweet bread."

"Sweet bread?"

"Yes," I exclaim, "you must try some."

"Must I?"

I take his hand and run to the human bakery, dragging him behind me. I buy a basket full of sweet bread and hand him a roll. He sniffs it before taking a bite.

"Okay, I guess the human sweet bread is good."

I awoke on something hard with no memory of how I got here. The last thing I remembered was talking with Matt by the railing of the boat. My head was throbbing, and my mouth was dry. Everything was quiet and still. Where was everyone? I rolled over and hit the floor with a thud. What I'd been laid on was not very wide. I groaned as I dragged myself off the floor and slowly made my way above deck.

It was dark out. How long had I slept? Stars twinkled above, and the moon was just a sliver in the sky. I shivered at the frosty wind. The boat was tied to a wooden post in line with a bunch of others. We docked, and it seemed everyone had left. Wrapping my arms around my body, I wandered around the boat. They couldn't have all gone. I let out a sigh of relief as I spotted two figures still on board. They were both wearing dark blue robes and stood looking toward the water. I caught a glimmer of blond hair under a hood and red under the other. "Matt!" I shouted. "Greg!"

They both turned. "You're awake." They said in unison.

"Yep." I ran my hands up and down my arms. "Can one of you tell me what happened?"

Matt shrugged. "You, like, totally went crazy for a moment and knocked yourself out."

My jaw dropped. *"I did what?"* is what I tried to ask but instead I made a series of weird squeaks.

"That's the really, really simplified version," Greg said. "You must be cold. I'll go get you a cloak."

"Nah, it's all right," Matt said. "She can have mine. I always run warmer than most." He took his cloak off and chucked it over my head. "I was only wearing it because it made me look like an adventurer."

I pulled the cloak down and readjusted it on my shoulders. "Thanks. What's the more detailed version of what happened?"

Greg gestured off the boat. "Let's join the others, and I'll explain on the way."

I nodded, hugging the cloak tighter to my body. Greg

led the way off the boat. We crunched through snow that appeared to have fallen recently. As Greg explained what happened, with Matt chiming in every so often, images flashed through my mind. I cringed at the memories: trying to jump off the boat, calling on the trees to attack, screaming and flailing about. Matt had been right about me going crazy. The farther away we got from the dock, the more densely populated the place became. We walked past house after house, all varying in size.

"I'm sorry about everything," I said. "And your dad's boat. I will figure out how to fix that."

Greg shrugged. "There's no need. I've already hired a guy to fix it. It will be good as new in no time."

Matt put his arm around me. "Don't worry about what happened. We all have magic mishaps—usually as toddlers, but you're late to the party."

I could have died of shame. Basically, according to Matt, I'd had a tantrum like a toddler and almost sunk the boat. I hid my face under the big hood of the cloak, hoping neither of them would notice how embarrassed I was. We turned a corner to a crowded street. So far, our walk had been quiet. Hardly anyone had been about, but not here. This part of the city was bustling with people.

Greg pulled his hood lower and tugged at mine. "Both of you stay close. Wouldn't want to lose each other in the crowd."

The street was lit by bright floating orbs. They were like lampposts but without the posts. We passed row after row of shops and restaurants and bars packed with people. There was what looked like a library and a big clock tower in the centre of everything. This was just like a big city back home, except everyone seemed to be staring.

"Where exactly are we?" I asked.

"Novosvillas," Matt replied. "Changeling territory. I think it's their biggest city." He turned to Greg. "Is that right?"

Greg nodded, but his eyes didn't move from the path ahead. He'd picked up the pace, and Matt was practically dragging me to make sure we kept up.

"This place seems to have some decent nightlife," Matt

said, side-eyeing all the pretty girls we passed. "Once I drop you off at the house, I might come back out."

"I can give you a list of all the best places to go," Greg said, his gaze still straight ahead.

"What do you mean? You're not coming with me? You would be the perfect wingman."

"Someone needs to keep an eye on Mellissa, and your sister has already managed to convince Samson to take her around town."

"Of course she has. Tell your cousin to be careful around my sister. She's toxic."

Greg smiled. "Will do."

I must have hit my head hard when I lost consciousness. That actually sounded like a friendly conversation. Matt and Greg were getting along. I had to make the most of this.

"You know, I'm not a baby. I don't need a sitter. You two go out and have fun."

They both looked at each other and laughed. "Notice how she didn't offer to come out with us?" Matt said. "So antisocial, this one."

"Cut her some slack," Greg said. "It's tiring work destroying boats."

"But she got to nap for the rest of the boat ride!"

I was stunned into silence. They were making fun of me. I missed when they'd hated each other. The streets grew quieter. We were out of the centre and back in a residential area. The houses on this side of town were massive. All the houses had long walkways and gated entrances. We kept walking eventually stopping at one of the gates. This house was surrounded by a wall. The gate was silver with bars with animals, such as cats, monkeys and birds, climbing them. There was an intercom on the wall next to the gate. Greg pressed it. A women's voice answered.

"Who is it?"

"It's me," Greg said into the device. There was a beep, and the gate opened. I followed Greg down the long path, staring at the beautiful gardens. They seemed to go on forever. There were all sorts of plants—some I'd never seen before. The house itself was magnificent. It was like those old manor houses in historical movies. A fountain sat in the middle of the path. As we walked around, I gazed at my reflection in the water.

"Wow, this place is awesome," Matt said. "I can't believe you live here."

"Wait, this is your house?" I asked.

"Technically, it's my father's," replied Greg.

When we reached the house, a woman stood in the doorway. She was an older woman. She had grey hair and wore a black suit. She took Greg in her arms. "Master Gregory, you're back. When your ID card was swiped and you were nowhere in sight, I was so worried. Samson explained everything, but still." She ushered us all inside. "Quick, get inside where it's warm."

"You don't need to worry about me, Anna," Greg said.

We stepped into a large foyer. There was a massive staircase in the centre that split off into two. I wished I hadn't let Greg stay at my house. Compared to him, I lived like a tramp.

"Oh, you have been gone for so long." Anna squished Greg in a hug. "I'm glad you're back. It hasn't been the same without you." She released Greg from her grip and gasped, putting her hand over her mouth as she laid eyes on me. "Is this her?"

"Yes. Anna, this is Mellissa Hail, keeper of the Heart Crystal. Mellissa, this is Anna. She is my father's assistant. Everything would fall apart without her."

I held out my hand to shake hers. "Nice to meet you."

She took my hand and bowed. "It's an honour." She clasped my hands. "My child, you are freezing. Go warm yourself by the fire, and I will bring you something to eat."

She took our cloaks and ushered us into a room on the right, shutting us in. This room was enormous. There was a curving sofa in the middle of the room positioned in front of a blazing fire. On either side of the sofa were two matching armchairs. Just one of those armchairs would have taken up half of my living room. Matt plonked himself down in one of them, putting his feet up on the coffee table.

"Awesome," he said, looking around the room. "I could get used to this."

I sat on the sofa at the end closest to Matt. Greg sat at the other end of the sofa. "Are you all right?" he asked. I nodded. All this fancy stuff was making my head spin. Matt had said Greg was practically a prince, but I hadn't thought about what that would look like in reality. Greg really was from a different world than us.

Anna came back in with trays of food hovering in front of her. She placed one down in front of each of us. "Eat up. Once you are finished, I will show you your rooms. The other guests have already settled in. Of course, Gregory, you will find your room as you left it." She curtsied and left the room with a smile that filled her face.

I picked up my tray. I had no idea what it was. It looked like some sort of stew and smelled amazing. I guzzled it down. I hadn't realised how hungry I was until I started eating. The door swung open, and in strutted Victoria, wearing a short, tight red dress and strappy heals. She struck a pose in the middle of the room.

"How do I look? Amazing, right?"

"Like you're going to freeze to death if you leave the house," I said.

"I'm an ice warlock. The cold doesn't bother me."

"Those shoes are not suitable for walking in the snow," Greg said.

Victoria stamped her feet. "Well, you two aren't exactly fashionable. Matt, what do you think?"

He shrugged. "What they said."

"Wow," came a voice from the doorway. Yuri stood with her mouth open, staring at Victoria. She was also dressed to go out but not in anything as tight or revealing as Victoria. "You look amazing, Miss Victoria."

Victoria put her hands on her hips. "Now that is how you pay a compliment. Now, where is Samson? He promised to show me all the best places."

"He is in the dayroom," replied Yuri.

"Why does this house have so many rooms?" Victoria marched to the door. "Oh, Mellissa, are you coming with? I have a dress you can borrow."

"Um, thanks, but I'm going to stay in. Unlike you, the cold really bothers me."

She tossed her hair over her shoulder. "Suit yourself." She strutted off. Yuri bowed to all three of us separately before following.

I stared at the empty doorway. "Wait a minute." I turned to Matt. "Did Victoria just ask me to go out with her?"

He nodded. "Yeah, she did. Strange. I'm not sure what's come over her."

"Probably just the lack of better options," said Greg.

"Harsh, but good point," I said. Still, it'd been nice of her to offer. Maybe Victoria wasn't as cold as I thought. She had given me some pretty good advice not so long ago, and she'd stopped me from jumping off the boat earlier. Apparently, there were many layers to her. I'd just not looked deep enough to see what was beneath her icy surface before.

The next day, I awoke refreshed. My room was amazing. The bed was a huge vintage four-poster. There was an en-suite bathroom with a clawfoot bathtub, which I had a long soak in the night before. Anna had brought me a heated bathrobe. She was the best assistant ever. Then I curled up in bed and slept like a baby. Even my weird dreams hadn't bothered me. Once I was dressed, I skipped down the stairs. After searching five rooms, I found Greg at a table in the kitchen.

"Morning," I said, taking a seat opposite him. "Where is everyone?"

"Still in bed. Want tea?" He got up and grabbed some mugs out of a cupboard, making the tea before I actually answered.

"I'm guessing they got in late," I said.

"You didn't hear the ruckus they made when they came

in last night?" I shook my head. "Lucky you." He handed me a hot cup of tea and sat back down with one of his own. "Victoria and Yuri decided to go swimming in the fountain. When I finally got them out and in the house, I discovered Matt walking around naked. When I told him to go back to his room, he challenged me to a dance off. I wish I could burn the memory from my mind."

I almost choked on my tea as I burst into laughter. "Yeah, Matt has a thing about nakedness when he's had a drink. He becomes some sort of a nudist."

"You've seen him naked too?"

"Who hasn't? He ran across the school car park butt naked last year. Apparently, I challenged him, which I really don't remember doing."

"Wait, did you also run across this car park?"

"God, no. I'm not an idiot." We both laughed. My ears twitched at the sound of a beep. A few seconds later, there was another one.

Greg perked up as if he could sense something. "Hey, there's this bakery that does the best pastries. I've missed it. I think we should go pick some up for breakfast." He was up in a flash. Taking my arm, he led us to the front door. He shoved my boots in my hands. As I was putting them on, a cloak was wrapped around my shoulders.

"Why the sudden rush?"

"Oh, no reason." He'd pulled on snow boots and a winter coat. He opened the front door. "Shall we?"

I took the arm he held out to me, and we left the house. Just as we reached the fountain, there was a loud bang from inside. I heard a cry and then another and another. The others were waking up, and they didn't sound happy.

I tugged at Greg's arm. "What did you do?"

"I may have rigged a magical wake-up call for the others. I needed to make sure they got up in time to be ready for when the sleigh arrives."

"That's why you rushed me out of the house. They are going to think I was in on it."

The front door flew open. Victoria was still in her dress

from the night before, but now, it was covered in blue and green paint. Her teeth were gritted, and her fists were clenched. Greg grabbed my hands. "I suggest you teleport."

"Where?" I asked.

"Anywhere from our walk last night."

I pictured the route we took last night and teleported.

Confession
Gregory

reg was pulled through white light and thrown out into the snow. He hit the ground with a thud, and Mellissa smacked into his back. She rolled off him, and he turned so he was looking up at the grey sky. They both lay in the snow for a couple of minutes. People stared and whispered behind their hands as they walked by the pair. They must have looked odd. "Sorry," Greg said, finally breaking the silence. "It is possible I was annoyed with them for their antics last night when I set up the alarm, but I should have told you what I'd done."

She sat up and glared down at him. "Yes, you should have. It is freezing out here, and I'm covered in snow. These pastries better be good, unless that was another lie."

Greg got up, shaking snow from his body. "That was definitely the truth, but whether we get them all depends on where you teleported us to."

Snow splattered on the side of his face. Mellissa got to her feet and threw another handful of snow at him.

"Hey! What was that for?"

"For being super annoying," she shouted.

"I said I was sorry." Mellissa's eyes narrowed. She picked up a ball of snow. Greg put both his palms up to signal surrender. "All right, I will make sure you get those pastries."

She dropped the snow and tucked her hands under her cloak. "Good," she said, pouting. "Where is this bakery?"

Greg looked around. She had brought them to the clock tower. Made sense—it was probably the most memorable thing they had passed last night. Luckily, it wasn't too far from their destination.

"This way," he said, walking in the direction of the bakery.

At first, Mellissa didn't say a word. She was obviously annoyed, but rows of shops eventually broke her. Every so often, something would catch her eye. She would gasp, tug at his arm, then ask a million questions about what the shop sold. It slowed their journey, and more people gawked at them, but it was better than awkward silence.

They smelled the bakery before they saw it. The smell of freshly baked pastries sailed down the street. Mellissa perked up and skipped off ahead of him. The smell warmed Greg's soul. It was an old comfort that he had missed. When Greg made it inside, Mellissa was already eyeing all the items on display.

"You didn't tell me they did pastry sculptures." She pointed at a bunch of animal shaped pastries.

"It must have slipped my mind." Greg walked over to the counter. "Let me guess—you want a cat one."

She skipped over to his side. "No, I want a rabbit." She pointed at pastries sculpted to look like rabbits on their back legs holding a carrot.

"As you wish, my lady."

"Don't start with that again."

They brought enough pastries for everyone. Once outside the shop, Mellissa took a big bite out of her rabbit. "Oh, this really is the best pastry ever. It is so buttery and flaky."

"Glad you like it. We should head back. Do you think you could teleport us? Wouldn't want the others' pastries to get cold."

"Yeah, sure," she said, walking over to the quill shop. Greg sighed. She hadn't heard a word he said. He walked over to her. She had one hand on the window and was gazing at all the quills on display. "I didn't know there were so many different types of quills."

"Yeah, but it's all a con. It's the different nibs that affect the style of writing, not the handle."

She pointed at a large, white quill. "That says it's made from the wing of a Pegasus. Is that true?"

"Yes, it is. They are hard to find, since the Pegasus like to live in secluded areas and tend to shy away from people." She looked up at him, her big brown eyes full of wonder. Greg's heart melted a little. Everything here was so new to her. It was like seeing his home in a whole new light.

"Oh my Gods," came a shrill voice. "Greg, is that you?" A tall blonde ran at him and threw her arms round him, almost knocking him over. "I heard about your mission, but I didn't know you were back." The hug lasted way longer than Greg was comfortable with. When she finally let go, Greg's throat tightened as he recognised the girl's face. The last time he'd seen her, her hair was chestnut brown. She must have dyed it while he was gone.

"Hey, Lucy," he said, trying to sound cool. "Good to see you. Well, I was just on my way home, we'll see you around." He grabbed Mellissa's hand and walked away.

"Wait." Lucy stepped into his path. She stroked his arm and fluttered her eyelashes. "I heard you found the new keeper. Do you think you could get me an introduction?"

"Fine." Greg gestured to Mellissa. "This is Lady Mellissa Hail, keeper of the Heart Crystal and heir to the elf throne. Like I said, good to see you, but we were just leaving."

Lucy curled her lip and pointed down at Mellissa. "Wait, that's her? You're joking right? I mean she's so—"

"So what?" snapped Greg. "She is exactly who I said she is. You asked for an introduction. You got one. Now we are leaving." He pulled Mellissa around Lucy and marched off.

"I'm sorry, Your Majesty. I didn't mean it. If you want, I can do your makeup," Lucy shouted after them.

Greg kept walking. He should have known better than to bring Mellissa out. Of course someone would recognise them. Why did it have to be Lucy, though? She was shallow. The only things that mattered to her were appearance and status. How he had ever dated someone like that was beyond him. She had a good family name, and good connections were the sort of thing his father expected. Wow, was his life messed up. Well, at least it was before.

"Greg," shouted Mellissa. "Will you slow down?" Greg

stopped on the spot. Mellissa was panting. "Thank you."

He hadn't realised how fast he was going, and he'd been dragging Mellissa along, forcing her to run to keep up. "Sorry."

"It's all right. Who exactly was that?"

"Just some girl I know."

Her eyebrow arched. "An ex?" He turned way. "I will take that as a yes. So what if she was trying to use your past relationship to her advantage. She is your ex for a reason. Don't let her get to you."

"I don't care about that. People are always trying to use me for my father's influence. It's what she said about you that bothered me."

"About me?" Mellissa took Greg's hand. "Look, I have come to accept that I'm not what your people are going to expect. By your people, I mean the rich elite. Ultimately, it doesn't matter as long as I get my job done. Right?"

Greg nodded. "Right."

Mellissa's hand tightened in his. "If I let it affect me, I will just freak out again like I did on the boat, and I can't do that again." The ground began to shake. "Just because I'm not this proper glam princess doesn't mean I'm not royalty, because I am, whether I like it or not." Everything around them began to shake. Shop signs tumbled over and window displays fell over. The glasses and plates shook off the tables outside a café smashing as they hit the floor. People cowered under tables and ran away. "I have come here to help—to do the right thing— but ever since we left the water nymphs, everyone has been staring and looking down at me. And only God knows what you really think of me. How on earth did you put up with staying in my house? I mean, you're practically royalty yourself."

This earthquake was definitely another new power of Mellissa's, and Greg had to stop it before she did any real damage. He clasped her shoulders. "I'm sorry, Mellissa. I never thought about how all of this would affect you when I brought you here. I am not royalty the way you are. My family may be wealthy, but money isn't everything. You are so much more than a crystal and a title. You have the biggest heart of anyone I have ever met, and that trumps everyone's opinion, including Lucy."

Mellissa buried her head in his chest, wrapping her arms around his waist. Greg stroked her hair, making soothing noises. As her breathing slowed, the shaking stopped. Mellissa's hold on him loosened. "I'm sorry. I didn't mean to."

"I know," Greg replied.

"I didn't even know I could do that."

"Look, let's get back, and we can figure out what happened later."

Mellissa nodded. Greg felt like the air was sucked out of him as she teleported them back home. Mellissa screamed as they crashed into the coffee table, splitting it in half. Her landings definitely needed work.

"Well, that's one way to make an entrance," said Matt. "Good thing that table wasn't glass." He was on the sofa with Yuri.

Yuri jumped to her feet. "Are you both all right?" She took Mellissa's arm, helping her to her feet. Once Mellissa was out of the way, Greg swept his feet around and jumped up.

Victoria and Samson came running in. "What happened?" they asked in unison.

Victoria's eyes narrowed on Greg. "You're back."

Greg held up the bag. "We bought pastries."

Victoria's blue eyes sparkled as she snatched the bag from him. "This isn't over, Flopsey."

Mellissa slid next to him. "Did you notice they were paired off in different rooms?"

"Yuck, we interrupted something, didn't we?"

Mellissa giggled as she nodded. "Yep."

The sound of her laugh brought a smile to his face.

The Council
Mellissa

I stood staring at myself in the full-length mirror in the guest room. Victoria was right; I had zero fashion sense. It didn't usually bother me. I lived for comfort, I always wore jeans or leggings, but today, that didn't seem to fit the dress code—not that anyone had given me a strict dress code. I just felt my leggings and black star jumper were not appropriate for meeting the council, especially after seeing what Victoria and Yuri were wearing. Victoria looked like she was dressed for a winter wedding, and Yuri had on some sort of ceremonial robes. Although, Matt was still wearing shorts.

At least Victoria had tamed my curls. I had no idea how she did it, but she came in with Yuri, waved a whole lot of hair products around and somehow wrapped my hair to the side, leaving a few stray curls to frame my face. There was a knock on my door.

"Come in," I shouted.

In walked Greg. "The sleigh's here, but first, I wanted to give you this." He dangled a silver chain in front of me.

I examined the chain. "You got this for me?"

"What are friends for? And in case you haven't noticed, I can afford things on this side of the veil." I scrunched up my face. People didn't usually do nice things out of the goodness of their hearts. Instead, there was always a catch. Greg took my hand and placed the chain in my palm. "It's for the Heart Crystal. I thought it would be sturdier than the string you currently have it on. Oh, and one more thing." Greg rummaged through his jacket pockets and pulled out the Pegasus quill I had been admiring in the shop window.

"Okay, now I know something's up. No one is this generous just because."

Greg shrugged. "Just think of it as me paying you back for all the food you snuck me and the crisps I stole."

"These are hardly a packet of crisps. It's too much."

"I'm the one that came into your life and turned it upside down. It's the least I could do. Now, come on. The council awaits."

I shuddered at the mention the council. "Is it really necessary for me to meet them?"

Greg took the Heart Crystal and chain from me. He removed the crystal from the string and put it on the chain. "Just be your lovely, cynical self, and I'm sure you will get along with the council fine." He handed the Heart Crystal back to me.

"I am not cynical."

"Your first instinct when presented with a gift was to question my motives." Greg smiled at my inability to come up with a response. He was right as usual. He was rarely wrong, which was annoying. He shrugged. "It's not necessarily a bad thing. It may serve you well in the long run. Seriously though, you don't need to worry about the council. Remember, they need you, and if that doesn't help, quills made from the feather of a Pegasus bring good fortune." He tickled the end of my nose with the feather.

I swatted his hand away. "You're just making that up."

"No, I'm not."

I took the quill and twirled it round. It was even prettier than I remembered. "This isn't a trick?"

"Of course not. I thought a future queen deserved a good quill." Greg turned to leave.

"Wait," I said. As Greg turned to face me, I threw my arms around him. "I'm sorry. I'm not good at receiving gifts."

"Oh, I couldn't tell."

I punched his arm. "Shut up. I'm trying to say thank you."

"Well, you're welcome. Now, come on. The others are

waiting."

There were two enclosed sleighs waiting outside. They looked like something straight out of a fairy tale. The sleighs had high sides and were dark blue with gold edges. Gold drapes covered the windows, and the silver runners shone in the daylight. The driver sat up front, dressed in a tailored jacket and matching hat. The only thing missing were the horses to pull us along. Samson, Yuri and Greg got in the sleigh at the front. Matt, Victoria and I got in the other. I sat next to Matt and looked out the front window. "How do these things move?"

Victoria looked at me like I'd asked the stupidest question ever. "They run on magic."

The door slammed shut, and we slid forward. We made our way back through the city. Everything went by in a blur. The sleighs were a lot faster than I'd expected. Then again, I had expected horses. As we left city limits, a lump formed in my throat. There really was no going back now. We would be in the capital soon, meeting the council. I had no idea what they expected of me. I should have dressed nicer. What if they were expecting someone more regal? The council was going to be deeply disappointed when they met me.

"Hey, Mel," whispered Matt, taking my hand. "Don't worry so much. It's all going to be all right."

"I'm fine. I'm not worried."

Matt raised his eyebrow at me, tilting his head. "Mel, I've known you long enough to recognise when you're thinking yourself into a panic. Just relax. Enjoy the ride. You've got this."

"But what if I don't?"

"I believe in you. Just be yourself, and it will be all right."

I laid my head on Matt's shoulder and tried to relax for the remainder of the journey.

"We're here," Victoria said.

I sat up and looked out the window. It was already dark outside. We were approaching a great white wall and a set of golden gates. The gates opened, and we went through. The golden gates closed behind us, and a shiver shot down my back at the strength of the dark presence here. Behind the wall was a city full of people. The place hummed with the hustle and bustle of city life. It was not what I expected. I thought we would arrive at a building full of council people, with a tree in the back garden.

"I can't remember the last time we came to the capital," Matt said, looking out the window. "It sure has gone downhill."

Of course, we hadn't arrived at the council yet, but the capital city. There was an odd mixture of run-down buildings and wonderfully kept ones. All the big buildings were made from white stone. Everything else looked to be made from standard building materials. Floating balls of light lined the paths, giving the city a beautiful glow. I could hear water flowing nearby but couldn't see the source. We headed into the centre of the city, toward what looked like a giant cathedral. The closer to the city's centre, the better maintained everything was, but there was a darkness overshadowing it all. As we got nearer to the cathedral, I noticed people set up in campsites. They appeared to be gathering for some sort of event. It must have been freezing staying in a tent in this snow. They must've been dedicated to their cause. I was still cold, even wrapped in my fleece-lined cloak.

The sleigh stopped moving. The driver opened the door for us, and we all got out. We were right in front of the cathedral. It looked even more magnificent up close. A wide flight of stone steps led up to the building. Four columns lined the front, with a pointed archway covering the main entrance. In the centre of the building was a giant, circular stained glass window. Down the sides were rectangular stained glass windows. An array of sculptures lined the front of the building, and a mosaic border ran across the middle. Judging by their gasps, Matt and Victoria were just as impressed at the sight of the building as I was.

"Everyone, follow me," Samson said.

He led us up the stairs and inside. I gazed at the stunning interior. Pillars lined the long corridor we walked through, encasing either a stained glass window or artwork. We stopped at a desk. Samson spoke to the man behind it briefly, and then the man left. He returned in seconds and nodded us through a pair of big wooden doors. The ceiling above the entrance was extremely high but got lower as we walked through another pointed archway.

Even the furniture looked like pieces of art. We passed tables that looked handcrafted with beautiful patterns carved into them. I held my hands close to my chest. I didn't want to touch anything for fear of ruining it. We followed Samson down another corridor. At the end was another pair of big wooden doors. He pushed them open, and we stepped into a huge room. Around the edge of the room were a couple of fancy-looking sofas with a swirl pattern. On the walls hung two giant oil paintings of different landscapes. In the centre of the room was an oval-shaped table full of people, and all eyes were on us.

Samson stepped forward and bowed. "Ladies and gentlemen of the council, I would like to present to you, Master Gregory Ainsworth. He has returned from the other side of the veil with a special guest."

This was the council. Maybe they weren't as scary as I had thought. They were all middle-aged or older, dressed in white robes. The fabric had a shine to it, and a glimmer of gold thread lined the edges.

Greg stepped forward and also bowed. "I have returned from the mission you sent me on, with Lady Mellissa Hail— who hails from the human world—heir to the elf throne and the keeper of the Heart Crystal."

All these introductions were excessive. Surely they already knew who we were. Victoria grabbed my arm and pushed me forward. I had obviously missed my cue. Everyone was staring at me, and I had no idea what to say. I wanted to melt into the ground.

"You are the human elf girl," said a man with short

white hair and a white beard.

"She looks rather young," said a woman with dark hair.

"Her age is insignificant," the man replied, "as long as she has the power to do what is necessary. Come, my child. Sit." He gestured for me to sit in a chair near him. "And your guardians too." He gave me a gentle smile.

Matt and Victoria walked over to the table with me, practically holding me up. I sat down with them standing guard behind me.

The man turned to Greg. "You have done well, Gregory, but we are not in need of your services at the moment. You and Samson are dismissed. Take the water nymph with you and see she gets paid."

"Very well, Father—I mean, sir." Greg bowed.

He left with Samson, shutting the doors behind them. This man next to me was Greg's dad. I looked at him, blinking a couple hundred times. That was such a cold greeting. He hadn't seen his son in months. I couldn't believe he had just dismissed him like that. There had been no emotion in the way they spoke to one another. It was all business. My dad would've been overjoyed to see me if I had been away for so long.

"I am Lord Steffen, and it is a pleasure to meet you." By the way he looked at me, I think he was expecting me to say something, but I was lost for words, so he carried on talking. "Gregory has informed you of what is needed of you?"

I nodded. "Yes." My voice came out as a squeak. I needed to get my act together. I cleared my throat. "I need to reseal Kadon."

A stern-looking woman stood up at the other end of the table. Her greying brown hair was tied up in a tight bun. She looked like your stereotypical, strict head teacher. Everyone in the room turned to her when she spoke. "It is of great importance that you are able to do this. We understand that you are not very familiar with the magical world, but Gregory informed us that you were successful in learning sealing magic."

I sank down into my chair, feeling out of place. "Yes."

"That is good to hear," said the stern woman. "I hate to

put you on the spot, but do you think you could take a look at the tree now? Time is becoming scarce."

"Um, sure." I bit my lip. Maybe this was good. The sooner I did the spell, the sooner I could get away from here and go back home.

Steffen got up. "This way." He showed me to a side door. I followed him, holding on to Matt and Victoria tightly.

"This is fantastic. Finally, Kadon's dark presence will no longer be looming over us," came a man's voice behind us.

I clutched on to my guardians' arms even tighter. Matt gave me an encouraging smile. Victoria rolled her eyes at me but let me keep hold of her arm. The other council members followed. We walked through another big room to another door, which led to a small garden. I walked outside and was hit by a dark shadow. It made me feel sick. In the centre of the garden was a dying tree, and dark shadows pulsated from it. This was the Tree of Time. Having Kadon inside was killing it. I tensed and took slow breaths. I needed to stay calm and not let the pressure get to me. I could do this. I had Victoria and Matt with me. What could go wrong?

"Hey, Mel, you okay?" Matt asked. "Because you're crushing my arm."

I didn't answer. I was too busy staring at the tree covered in shadows. I had never felt a force like this before.

"Do you think you can seal it?" asked a water nymph.

"I only asked her to look," came the stern woman's voice, but I couldn't see her. My vision began to blur. All I could see was darkness.

"Why wait?" said a different voice.

"Go on. Do it now," said another, and then there was another voice and another. They were all pushing me to perform the spell now, but I couldn't. Kadon's darkness was too strong; it was overwhelming me. It made my skin crawl. I didn't want to let anybody down, but the more they pleaded with me, the worse I felt. My heart was racing, and I couldn't breathe.

"Just do the spell," I told myself, but the incantation wouldn't come. Everything I'd learned had vanished.

"Sorry, I can't do it," I shouted, pushing my way past them and running away.

"Mellissa, wait!" Matt yelled, but it was too late; all the pressure had gotten to me. I was in flight mode. I ran as fast as I could. Shutting my eyes, I pictured myself back home and teleported, only to be repulsed back. I fell face-first on the hard marble floor. I couldn't get myself home. I was too far away. My heart was still racing, and my whole body was shaking. I needed to calm down.

I balled my hands on the floor and pushed myself up. I went through another archway, finding myself outside again but in a different spot. There was a water fountain with a statue at its centre. I read the plaque on it. It was a statue of Queen Freya. I looked up at her. How could I live up to her greatness? I sat on the edge of the fountain, staring at my reflection in the water. I had made a fool of myself, but I needed to go back. I smacked my reflection, causing the water to ripple. This wasn't fair. Why did this have to be my responsibility? I sighed. Even though it was hard, I couldn't turn my back on this.

"Mel!" Matt shouted, jogging over to me. He was out of breath. "Man, you can run fast when you go into major freak-out mode. I lost you for a bit, but I'm glad I found you."

"Matt, I'm so sorry." I clutched the ledge I was sat on. "I don't know what came over me. Everyone was talking at the same time, putting pressure on me, and I couldn't remember the incantation. I panicked. I'm so glad you're here." Matt sat down next to me, and I leant my head on his shoulder. "I'm sorry."

He patted my back. "It's all right. They were really pushy. I just needed to know you were okay."

"What must all the council members think of me?" I covered my face with my hands. "I must look like a right idiot."

Matt put his arm round me and squeezed my shoulder. "Don't worry about it. I left Vicky to deal with them."

That didn't make me feel any better. I wished I could handle pressure better. If it had been up to Victoria, she wouldn't have crumbled so easily. She would have taken charge of the situation, and Kadon would have probably been resealed by now. Everyone would be happy and rejoicing in her success. She might have been stuck up, really harsh and rude at times, but she did have some good qualities—qualities I wished I had.

"You couldn't remember the sealing spell?" Matt asked. I nodded. "Unfortunately, sealing magic isn't really my thing. Maybe we should find Greg. He could refresh your memory."

"But I don't know where he is," I said. "I don't even know where we are."

"Why don't you just teleport to him?"

"Because, like I already said, I don't know where he is." Matt stared at me. I could tell by the look on his face that he didn't understand why this mattered, so I explained further. "Well, first, I have to picture where I want to go, so if I don't know where he is, I can't picture it in my head, and second, I don't know this place. I've never teleported somewhere I haven't been before."

"Basically, what you're saying is that you have to know where you're going. How about instead of picturing the place you want to go, you think about the person you want to see. So when you teleport, picture materialising in front of Greg."

"That's actually a good idea and worth a try." I closed my eyes to test his theory. Then, I opened them again, quickly grabbing Matt's hand, not wanting to leave him behind. I did just as Matt suggested and pictured teleporting in front of Greg, visualising his face, his hair, his know-it-all tone and captivating eyes.

I screamed as I fell backward and was greeted by a surprised shout from another person. It was Yuri, and beside her was Samson, looking just as startled. Greg was the only one unfazed by our entrance. Matt laughed behind me.

I got up. "I am so sorry. I didn't mean to startle you."

"Where did you guys come from?" Samson asked, picking up the chair I assumed I knocked over with my landing.

"Mellissa," said Greg. "Why aren't you with the council?"

I spun round and gave him a fake grin. "Long story—"

"Not really," Matt said. "Dude, you should have seen

it." Matt put his hand on Greg's shoulder. "Mel had a crazy moment back there and went into major meltdown mode. For someone that shies away from any sort of physical activity, she sure can run when she wants to. Don't get me wrong, those council guys were proper pushy, like…" Matt explained everything while not really explaining anything at all—except for the fact that I was a crazy person.

"Gee thanks, Matt." I made a face at him. "It's not as bad as he makes it sound. I think. Anyway, what actually happened was…" I went on to tell Greg, Samson and Yuri what happened. Once finished, I realised it *was* as bad as Matt had made it sound.

"I'm sorry they put you on the spot like that. They are not usually that pushy. They are just desperate for this to be over," Greg said. "How about we go over the spell again? You can do this. You just cracked under pressure."

Maybe I could turn this around. "Thanks for understanding."

He was completely right. I had performed the spell before during practice. I was just suffering a case of performance anxiety. Greg went over the incantation with me again and then a second time when I insisted. In the meantime, Matt took Greg's place in the card game we had interrupted. At least one of us was having fun.

"Are you going to go back and talk to the council members?" Greg asked. "Maybe you could suggest waiting till morning, when Kadon's power isn't as strong."

"Only if you come with me," I said, holding out my hand.

"But I was dismissed. I can't just walk into a council meeting."

I crossed my arms. "I'm not going then."

"Hey, as future queen, doesn't she have some sort of authority over you?" Matt asked without turning his gaze away from the cards in his hand.

"Well, technically, I guess she sort of does," Greg replied.

"I wish I had known that when you were bossing me

about during our magic lessons." I smiled smugly, putting my hand out to him again. "Well then, with whatever authority I have, I order you to come with me."

"It doesn't quite work like that, but fine, I will come." He took hold of my hand.

"And you, Matt," I said, holding out my other hand. He threw his cards down on the table and hurried over, taking my other hand. I teleported us back into the council room where we had started out.

"What is with you and landing on tables?" Matt shouted.

"I didn't do it on purpose," I replied more quietly than him. We had landed in the centre of the oval table all the council members were sat around.

"At least you didn't break this one."

"What on earth is the meaning of this?" cried a member of the council.

"It was all her," Matt said, pointing at me. He was quick to throw blame on me.

I widened my eyes and gritted my teeth. Greg apologised to the council members for our unconventional arrival while bowing. He led us off the table and went on to explain how I had gone to him for assistance.

"It is good of you to return, Mellissa. Are you ready to proceed now?" Steffen asked.

"Yes. I mean…" I started. I was annoyed that my words were not coming as easily as I had hoped. "I'm sorry for running off like that with no warning. I totally freaked, but I found Greg. I had a memory lapse, so we went over the spell. I was thinking that maybe, like, Kadon's presence is, like, really wow at the moment." I spoke fast, slurring my words, explaining things just as badly as Matt had to Greg—maybe more so. They all looked at me like I was speaking another language. I hung my head.

Greg stepped forward. "Basically, what Mellissa is trying to say is that she will perform the sealing spell in the morning, when Kadon's presence isn't as strong. It is well known the moon crystals power is at it's peak at night. This will also give me more time to go over the spell with her." Why hadn't I been able to say something like that? Instead, I'd rambled and added to their bad impression of me.

"This is ridiculous," cried a water nymph. "We have camps of people all over the city on guard for if Kadon escapes. We've waited long enough. We need to get this done."

"I know we are all anxious," Steffen said, "but is it not better that it is done correctly than rushed?"

"Yes, we wouldn't want the girl to make a mistake," said another councilman.

They were talking about me like I wasn't even there, making me feel worse in the process. The discussion was dominated by six council members, who had a golden broach pinned to their robes. I assumed this meant they had higher roles on the council. Greg had mentioned something about his dad being a senior member.

"Very well, you shall perform the spell after sunrise," said the stern-faced woman from earlier. Her robes were more regal than the others. I assumed from this, and by the way she spoke, that she was in charge of the assembly. "We shall meet again in the morning, and there will be no running off this time. As you are here, Gregory, you can show the keeper and her guardians to their temporary quarters."

"As you wish, Lady Gabrielle." Greg bowed to her and then led us out of the room. That was Lady Gabrielle? But she had seemed so nice on Greg's phone call.

Victoria rejoined us. As soon as we were out of the council's earshot, she began insulting me. She was not happy about being left with the council members to answer all their questions and attempt to reassure them that I wasn't completely insane, which she had found difficult to do as she wasn't completely convinced herself. I apologised and told her it wouldn't happen again.

We arrived at our sleeping quarters. They were pretty fancy, like the rest of the building. Victoria's face lit up when she saw the four-poster bed. As Greg was showing the other two where everything was and what amenities were available, I peered out in the corridor and made sure we were all alone. Once satisfied, I shut the door. "Guys, we need to go seal Kadon now."

The Seal
Mellissa

hey all stopped in their tracks and stared at me like I had just sprouted wings. No one said a word.

"We need to go and seal Kadon," I repeated.

"What happened to waiting till morning?" Victoria asked. "I've had enough of your crazy mood swings."

"I have been thinking—"

"It's never good when you say that," Matt said.

"Hey, hear me out. I was thinking about what happened earlier. You guys were right. It's not that I don't know the spell; I just cracked under pressure. All those council members watching me was the problem. Also, that water nymph was right—the sooner we get this done, the better. I think now is the best time to act, while everyone thinks we're in bed. I can do this with you guys as my backup, but only you guys."

They looked at me. All that filled the silence was the clock ticking on the wall. I knew the council thought I was crazy, but hopefully my team hadn't lost faith in me. Victoria had a point—I was all over the place, and my decisions lately hadn't been the best, but I was sure this time. Now was the time to act. Without the overbearing presence of the council, I could do this.

Victoria rolled her eyes as she walked toward me. "Annoyingly, your logic makes sense."

Matt took hold of my arm. "If it's what you want to do, I'm in, so let's get teleporting."

Victoria took my other arm.

"You're all crazy," Greg said with his arms folded.

"That is hardly news," I replied. "Are you coming?"

"I'm not one of your guardians."

"Since when has that stopped you from saving me?"

The side of his mouth twitched, as if holding back a smile, as he came to join us. Holding onto everyone, I teleported us back to the garden, where the Tree of Time stood at its centre.

Instantly, we were hit by a dark shadow. I couldn't see what was in front of me. The dark energy had grown significantly in only a few hours. Strong winds blew us back. Shadows whipped around the courtyard. I screamed as one caught my hand, sending a burning sensation through my body. A barrier appeared around us. Greg stood with his arms stretched out.

"Kadon must have sensed your presence earlier and is putting everything he has into escaping," yelled Greg over the swirling sound of the wind.

This was my fault. I had taken too long to get here. Kadon was about to escape. Cracks began to appear in the barrier. "Mellissa, a little help," yelled Greg. "I can only hold this on my own for so long."

I shook my arms out. Now wasn't the time for beating myself up; I had to act. I threw my arms up and reinforced the barrier, just how Greg had shown me in the past. We pushed our way through the darkness. As we approached the tree, the barrier began to crack again.

"The barrier won't hold much longer," I shouted.

"Just be ready to grab that tree and start the spell," Matt yelled. "We'll protect you."

Victoria and Matt stood on either side of me, hands out, ready to strike. As the barrier cracked, heat erupted at my left, and ice exploded from the right. I lunged forward, placing my hand on the tree. The coldness of the tree sent a shock wave through my body. As I began the spell, a circle of light appeared around my hand and at my feet. It swirled around, forming shapes I'd never seen before. This wasn't at all like what happened in practice. I was halfway through the spell when something curled up my outstretched arm. I screamed as a shadow burned my skin. I was yanked away from the tree and thrown to the ground. Pain surged through me. I had to keep going. Using my good arm, I pushed myself up.

"Look out!" yelled Matt.

I cried out in agony as I was shoved to the ground again, landing on my burned arm. Matt's body covered mine, then suddenly, he was gone. I scrambled to my feet. A giant shadow hand was dragging Matt into the tree. I froze on the spot. A creature was emerging from the tree. Ice flew through the air. The creature was knocked back into the tree. Victoria jumped over me, throwing more ice, freezing the tree. The shadow disappeared, and Matt fell to the ground. Victoria went running toward him, but the ice shattered. The shadow hand returned, slapping Victoria across the courtyard. It grabbed hold of Matt again. I couldn't let it take Matt. I screamed in frustration, and a pulse of light shot out of the Heart Crystal. The creature withdrew from the light. The shadows stopped whirling and came hurling at me all at once. Greg ran to my side and threw up a barrier, but it wasn't enough. As it shattered, we were both thrown to the ground. My head smacked hard on a rock. My ears buzzed, and my vision blurred. The only thing that fazed this thing was my light. I had to do something. My hands began to heat. I pushed myself up and ran at the tree.

"Let him go," I shouted. Focusing all my energy at the tree, I fired rays of light. Matt fell to the ground as the shadow whimpered back. I released a pulse of bright light into the sky. It lit up the entire city. The shadow retreated back into the tree.

Grabbing hold of a part of the tree with both hands, I began reciting the sealing incantation. "Disseptum." A circle appeared beneath my feet again, and the same circle was mirrored on the tree. "Signo que claudant abesse." I could feel the crystal, illuminated with power, floating in front of me. The magic circle beneath me started to pulse and shift shape. My entire body glowed. Light spread all over the tree. The spell was working. The light dispersed, and everything was calm.

I let out a sigh of relief. My heart was still pounding. I had never been so scared in my life. I had no idea how, but I had done it. My throat clogged as I recalled the hits Matt and

Victoria had taken. They were the reason I had managed to pull this off. I turned around quickly, shouting their names. Matt was still on the ground, with Greg knelt beside him. Greg's hands glowed as he ran them over Matt's head. I ran to his side.

"Don't worry. He is all right," Greg said.

"What about Victoria?" I asked, frantically looking around the courtyard.

"I'm fine, just a few bruises." Victoria walked toward us with a hand on her shoulder as she rolled her neck. "Matt got the worst of it, but Flopsey here is pretty good at healing magic. I guess he has his uses." There was a slight hint of worry in her voice. When it came down to it, she did care about her brother.

Greg turned round to look at her. "That is not my name, and I would like it if you didn't continue to use that ridiculous rabbit name."

She shrugged. "Whatever, Flopsey." She slumped down on the other side of Matt. With her legs crossed, she looked at her nails.

I knelt beside Greg. "I have no idea how she does it, but she managed to not use my name for a whole year once."

I took hold of Matt's hand. He was breathing, which was always a good sign. A healer I was not. I was just going to have to trust that Greg knew what he was doing. He muttered some words I didn't understand, and his hands went from yellow to green. He waved them over Matt, and the cuts on his body began to disappear. Useful had been an understatement. Even though I knew Greg had healed me back on the boat, I hadn't been awake to witness it. Healing magic was amazing.

Greg leant back. "All his wounds are healed. He will just need some rest to fully recover."

I looked up at the sky. Small flakes of light sprinkled over us as the ray of light I had shone over the city dispersed. I put my hand out and caught some of the small specks of light. They felt warm on my skin. I had no idea how I had managed to produce all that energy.

Greg put his hand on my shoulder. "Let me see your arm."

In the heat of things, I'd forgotten about my injured arm. I showed him my burns.

He took hold of my arm with one hand and hovered the other over my wound. "Sanum quod fit." His hand glowed green, and my wound disappeared.

I turned my freshly healed arm over. There were no marks left from the burn. "Amazing." I was hit by a sudden memory. "Hey, I don't remember those shadows that attacked us back home burning."

Greg looked up at the sky. "Maybe they weren't as strong. Anyway, you don't need to worry about that now. You did it. You should be proud."

I was proud, but there was also another feeling bugging me. I couldn't quite put my finger on what it was. Things never would have gotten this bad if I hadn't freaked out earlier and just cast the spell. Matt was injured all because I couldn't handle the pressure. Yes, I had achieved what I thought was impossible, but my friends had gotten hurt along the way.

"I do believe I've earned a long soak in that magnificent bathtub," Victoria said.

She definitely had. She was magnificent. Not once did I see her hesitate, and she had come to Matt's rescue in an instant. I had been too scared to move. She was a true warrior.

"What on earth happened here?" asked a stern voice, making me jump. We all turned in the direction of the voice. I gulped. It was Lady Gabrielle. Behind her was a bunch of other people. All the commotion must have caught their attention. All the lights were now on in the building. We appeared to have woken everyone up. "I will ask one more time. What is going on here?"

"Lady Gabrielle," Greg said, getting up and bowing to her. "We are sorry to wake you all at this hour, but after meeting with the council, Mellissa decided that maybe it wasn't best to wait. We came out here to assist while she performed the sealing spell."

"You mean she has done it? Kadon is sealed?" Lady Gabrielle asked. The shocked tone in her voice was not appreciated. Then again, I hadn't made the best first impression.

"Yes, madame, it is done. Mellissa has resealed Kadon in the Tree of Time."

Everyone seemed to perk up, suddenly realising that Kadon's dark shadow was gone. They talked amongst themselves. From what I could hear, they seemed happy.

"This is wonderful news, but what happened to him?" Lady Gabrielle pointed at Matt on the ground.

"I'm afraid that things were not quite as simple as initially anticipated, and he was injured. However, I have checked him over and healed his injuries," Greg said.

"Very well. You two over there, get him across to the infirmary so he can sleep it off." Lady Gabrielle waved at two bystanders.

They bowed to her and hurriedly did as she requested. From out of nowhere, they produced a stretcher and moved Matt onto it and carried him inside. I wanted to follow, but as I stood, I was swarmed by people. They were all so excited and asked questions about what happened. I answered the best I could, but for some reason, I wasn't feeling well.

"Enough. Everyone give the girl some room to breathe." Lady Gabrielle cleared a route through all the people so we could go back inside "Let us all go inside. She can tell us the tale of what occurred here and how she has saved us all."

Her tone had completely changed. No longer was she looking down at me, unimpressed. I knew I was not what they'd expected, and my earlier stunt, running off, hadn't helped her opinion of me. However, everyone was now looking up to me and were overjoyed by my presence. It was strange. I hated being the centre of attention like this, but thankfully, I wasn't completely lost for words as I was before.

Everyone headed inside. As I walked, my body suddenly grew weak, and everything was blurry. I felt light-headed and I heard someone shout my name as everything went black.

Unexpected Conversations
Gregory

Greg's chest tightened as he saw Mellissa crumble before him. He quickly leant forward and grabbed her. He managed to catch her just before she hit the ground. Victoria screamed Mellissa's name, but she was out cold.

"What's wrong with her?" Victoria shouted, kneeling in front of him. "She was fine just a moment ago. She was talking with us like normal."

This was the first time since meeting her that he had seen Victoria look truly frightened. As much as she went about dismissing Mellissa and intimidating her, she seemed to be genuinely concerned. This went beyond her duty as her guardian. She was more concerned than when he was healing her brother. Maybe it was because Mellissa's reaction had been delayed. Whereas, she had seen what had happened to Matt. His condition made sense, so it must have been easier to manage her worry. Victoria's worry mimicked exactly what he was feeling, but he couldn't let that show. He was a healer, and he had to do his job.

"What is your evaluation?" Lady Gabrielle asked.

Greg waved his hand over Mellissa head. "Magic exhaustion."

"She is going to be all right then?" Victoria asked.

"Yes," Greg said. "She used more magic than her body is used to. She will sleep for a while, but she should recover on her own."

Lady Gabrielle gestured two people over. "Take the keeper to her quarters where she will be more comfortable."

With a click of their fingers, a stretcher was produced. Greg helped them move Mellissa onto it and watched as they took her away. Victoria followed them. Greg wanted to go with her, but Lady Gabrielle put her hand on his shoulder. She then turned to everyone. "Nothing to see here. Everyone back to your rooms." She waved her arms at them, and they all did as she said.

Greg stayed where he was as everyone left. Once the corridor was empty, Lady Gabrielle gestured for him to follow her. He did as he was told. She led him to her office and pointed at a chair.

"Take a seat, Gregory."

Greg sat in the chair. "What is this all about? I thought you would be happy."

"I am happy, but I am also concerned," she said, walking over to a cabinet. She opened one of the drawers and started flicking through some papers.

"Concerned? I know it looks bad, but Mellissa will be fine and so will Matt." He hoped he managed to keep the worry out of his voice.

Lady Gabrielle picked out a couple of papers from the pile and went and sat at her desk. "That's not what I mean. I trust in your ability as a healer."

"Oh, thank you. What is concerning you then?"

"I am concerned about Lady Mellissa's future. She has great power, just like you said, but she is not ready."

"I don't understand. She has completed the task we asked of her."

Lady Gabrielle interlaced her fingers. "You cannot repeat what I am about to tell you. Only the council knows about this, but I believe you are in the best position to help her. After you went to show the keeper her quarters, the council continued to discuss matters. There is an overwhelming number that do not wish to let the girl leave now that she is here."

Greg leant forward in his seat. "What?"

"They wish to reinstate the elf monarchy. They want to make her queen, whether she likes it or not."

He shouldn't have been surprised. Of course they would want her to become queen. However, it would be nothing but a PR stunt—something to make the people happy and hopefully encourage them to overlook the real problems. One thing was for sure: Mellissa wouldn't like it, and she wouldn't be as easy to keep here as they thought.

"You can't let the council do that. She knows the responsibly she has as the keeper of the Heart Crystal. She has already proved she will help us when needed, but you can't force her into a life she doesn't want. That would be bad for all parties. Do they really want to turn Mellissa against them?"

Lady Gabrielle's whole body seemed to relax. "I am so happy you responded like that. You have grown so much in your absence. You are looking at the big picture and the effects a decision like this could have on the people involved."

Greg would've liked to think he was considering all those involved, but really, his main concern was Mellissa. He may not have gone looking to make friends when he left, but he couldn't deny that was what happened. He'd gotten to know Mellissa and knew this wouldn't make her happy. Greg knew what it was like living under the scrutiny of the council. He wouldn't let that happen to her.

Lady Gabrielle pushed the papers across her desk. "I happen to agree with you."

"You do?"

"Yes. I feel the only reason certain members are so eager for her to become queen now is so they can manipulate her lack of knowledge of this world. That is why I want you to fill out this form." She handed him the papers. "I will be putting it forward to the council that the girl return home and continue to learn about magic there. When she feels ready, she can then return to this world and take up her position as queen."

Greg looked at the form. "What does me filling out this form got to do with your motion?"

"I want you to apply to go back with her, to continue teaching her. You cannot tell me you did not enjoy your time in the human world. I believe Lady Mellissa is as good an influence on you as you are on her." Greg wasn't sure what to say. Lady Gabrielle took his hands in hers. "Just think about it. Although, if you want your father onside, I suggest you exaggerate the situation. Make him think Mellissa needs extra training even more than she does. Now, I think you should go get some rest. It is very late."

Greg got up. "I will definitely think about it."

"Oh, and one more thing before you go."

"What is it?"

"What is Lady Mellissa's favourite colour?"

"Why do you need to know that?"

"I think a celebration is in order. Kadon has been resealed. The girl deserves a party in her honour before she leaves."

"It's pink." Greg shook his head. "Wait, why do I know that?"

"Good night, Gregory." She gave him a wave as he left.

Greg made his way back to his room. On this stay, he was lucky enough to be able to stay with Samson, meaning he wouldn't have to explain himself to his father. He hoped Samson would be asleep when he got back, but he was not. He wanted to know all about what happened when Mellissa had sealed Kadon. Instead of getting rest, he ended up telling his cousin everything that had happened, while trying to not overthink what Lady Gabrielle had suggested to him.

Greg woke bright and early as usual. He got himself ready for the day, but just as he was about to leave the room, he paused at the door. He may be back in the magic world, but for some reason, he wasn't sure what to do with himself. What was he leaving this room to do? Greg lay back on his bed and looked up at the ceiling. Now that Kadon was sealed, he didn't have a purpose anymore. He'd thought that when he returned, he would be happy. His dad would be proud of his achievements, and he would go back to his old life. So what was this he was feeling? Maybe this wasn't what he wanted anymore. Had it ever been what he wanted? He had spent so long trying to live up to his father's expectations that he hadn't realised that everything he had done was not truly what he had wanted, but what was expected of him. Lady Gabrielle had given him the option to do something else. He hadn't considered returning to the human world. He hadn't thought it was a possibility, but maybe that was what he should do.

"Greg, are you actually going to do anything today?" Samson asked, standing in the doorway.

"I thought you were on messenger duty for the council," Greg replied.

"I am, but I came to check on you after I found out no one had seen you all morning. It is nearly seven o'clock, and you haven't left this room."

Greg shot up. "Did you say seven?" Samson nodded. "Then it is late enough to go check on her." Greg walked past his cousin and headed down the corridor.

"What is significant about seven o'clock?" Samson asked, following him.

"Mellissa is not a morning person like us. She would actually consider seven early."

"Seven o'clock early? That's insane."

"I know, but you get used to the odd human behaviour after a while."

Samson put his hand on Greg's shoulder. "Are you all right?"

"Why wouldn't I be?"

"I don't know. You just seem different."

"Different isn't always bad."

"I guess not."

Greg patted Samson's arm. "Don't worry about me. I'm fine. Now, you go back to your council duties, and I will do my job as a healer and check up on a patient."

Samson smirked while raising an eyebrow. "But are you just checking on a patient?"

"Of course." Greg flashed a smile at Samson and ran down the corridor. He skidded around the corner, narrowly missing a member of staff. He didn't stop until he reached Mellissa's room.

Greg knocked on the door. He heard fast-moving footsteps, and the door swung open. He was greeted by a glare from Victoria. "It is about time you got here." She grabbed his arm and dragged him through the sitting room and into one of the bedrooms. She pointed at Mellissa asleep in the bed. "Why isn't she awake yet?"

"She hasn't stirred at all?" Greg asked.

"No, she hasn't twitched all night. You're a healer. Do something."

Greg walked over to the bed and checked Mellissa's pulse. He waved his hand over her head while whispering a healing spell. There was no response. There wasn't anything medically wrong with her. Greg turned back to Victoria. "Her condition hasn't changed. She just needs more time to recover."

"I have depleted my magic before, and it didn't take me this long to recover," Victoria said. "Are you sure you know what you're doing? Maybe I should get another healer to check."

"Magic depletion and magic exhaustion are not the same thing," Greg replied. "Magic depletion is when you use up all your magic. It varies from person to person, but we all have our limits. Magic exhaustion is different and is less common. It happens when you use magic you are physically not ready to."

"How would she have been able to pull off those techniques if she wasn't ready?"

"Because I fast-tracked her training. The way you and I learnt magic is not the way I taught Mellissa. We learned lower level spells first, which allowed our bodies to adjust slowly to the use of magic. I went straight to higher level techniques when teaching Mellissa because it was what was necessary at the time."

Victoria clenched her fist. "This is your fault." For a moment, he thought she meant to hit him. He knew he could block any attack she threw at him, but he wasn't sure he should.

"I know. I didn't think about the consequences at the time."

Victoria unclenched her fist, but her jaw was still tensed. "I guess it isn't really your fault. Time wasn't on our side, and she picked it up so quickly none of us thought it would affect her negatively. You're still an idiot though."

That was almost Victoria being nice, until she added that insult on the end. He didn't blame her for being mad at him. She was just worried about Mellissa, but there wasn't anything he could do.

"I am going to go check on your brother now," Greg said.

"He was fine last time I checked." Victoria put her finger on her chin. "Can being hit on the head change the way you talk?"

"Sometimes people can slur words and have difficulty expressing themselves, but that is only if they are not treated straight away. I healed Matt quickly after he got hurt. He shouldn't have any lasting damage."

"It is nothing like that. He just doesn't sound like himself."

"I'm sure it will pass. I will check myself."

Victoria rolled her eyes. "Whatever."

Greg left and headed to the infirmary across the street. Once inside, he could barely move. The infirmary was overrun with people, but none of them seemed injured. He pushed his way through the crowd to the front desk. "What's going on?" he asked the woman behind the desk.

Without looking up from her tabular screen, she replied, "They all want to meet the keeper's guardian, who risked his life to help save us all from Kadon."

"I guess I won't be getting in that room anytime soon."

"Nope. You will have to get in line with all the other groupies."

"I am not a groupie. I was the first responder last night."

"Oh." The woman looked up at him. "Hey, aren't you that elder's son?"

"I'm Lord Ainsworth's son."

The woman's eyes widened. "I'm sorry. You didn't say. Of course you can go in ahead of the others."

"No, that's quite all right. I just wanted to know Matt was okay."

"Of course. He is absolutely fine. He has been awake for hours and is seeing people in small groups and giving out autographs."

Of course he was. It sounded like Matt's newfound fame had already gone to his head. "Thank you for your help." Greg pushed his way back through the crowd and out of the infirmary. The massive crowd was ridiculous. The people were like sheep flocking to Matt. They really needed to move along. If someone actually needed help, they wouldn't be able to get through. Maybe he should go talk to Lady Gabrielle about this.

"Greg, there you are!" shouted Samson, running over from the council building.

"Samson, I told you I was fine. You really shouldn't keep leaving your post to check on me."

"I am here with a message for you. Your father would like to see you in the tearooms."

Greg looked back at the infirmary. It was something he could also bring up with his father. That was if he was able to get a word in after they had discussed whatever it was he'd called on him for. Greg walked back to the council building with Samson. "What sort of mood was my father in when he gave you this message?"

"He seemed all right. He was in a better mood than Miss Victoria. She answered the door to the keeper's quarters when I went looking for you. She doesn't seem overly fond of you and referred to you as Flopsey—whatever that means."

Greg put his hand on his head. "It is a rabbit reference. I am sorry you had to suffer her."

Samson sighed and tilted his head. "It's fine. She is rather feisty, but she is awfully pretty."

Greg raised an eyebrow. "Do you like her?"

"I hardly know her, but she holds herself with such confidence. It is something to be admired."

Greg held back a laugh. "If you say so."

He gave Samson a big grin before wandering off to the tearooms. Even if he wouldn't admit it, Samson definitely had a crush on Victoria. The smile on his face faded as he arrived at his destination. It was a public area, so his father couldn't have called him here to have a go at him. Samson said he was in a better mood than Victoria, but she had been rather unhappy when he'd seen her. A step up from that was still not happy. Greg pulled at his shirt to make sure it was straight and pushed his fringe back. A haircut was seriously overdue now. He headed to his father's table.

"Father, I heard you wanted to see me."

"You heard correct. Now sit." His father pointed at the chair opposite him. "I ordered you a pot of tea."

Greg sat. "Thank you, Father."

"Is there anything else you would like?" Steffen asked.

Something to eat would have been nice, but he knew his father was just trying to butter him up before revealing what he wanted. "What is it you wanted to see me about?"

Steffen poured them both a cup of tea. "Straight to the point, I see. Very well. I wanted to speak with you about the girl."

Of course that was what he wanted. Everyone was interested in Mellissa. She had a great power and no allegiance to anyone. It scared them. They all wanted it for themselves and needed to find a way to get her on their side. This was where he came in. He would hear his father out. What Lady Gabrielle wanted for her wasn't bad. Maybe his father would think in a similar way.

"What do you want to know about Mellissa?" Greg asked.

"For starters, why do you think it is all right not to follow protocol when it comes to *Miss Hail?*" This was how he should refer to her, according to proper etiquette.

"Mellissa is not from our world and does not understand our ways. I believed getting her onside was more important than following protocol."

"Well, now that you are home, you shall go back to following the rules and regulations of the council, with no deviation. The council plans on giving the girl her crown. She is to become queen. From now on, she shall be Lady Mellissa to you."

Greg tried to stop himself, but he couldn't help laughing.

His father scowled at him. "This is not a laughing matter."

"I am sorry, Father, but I do not believe *Lady Mellissa* will respond well to that." He made sure to emphasize her name the same way his father had.

"That is why I want you to convince her to stay. You have built a relationship with the girl. She trusts you. Make her see that it is in her best interest to stay here."

He didn't like how informal his relationship was with Mellissa, but at the same time, he wanted him to exploit said relationship. Greg took a sip of tea and tried to stop any emotion showing on his face. "Why are you so insistent she stay here?"

"She is the keeper of the Heart Crystal. We have searched years for her. We cannot just let her leave. We need her power."

"I think we should let her go."

Steffen leant forward and put his arm on the table. "You think what?"

"We should let her go home. She is not ready for all of this. If we try and make her stay, she will just disappear on us, and trust me, she is very good at disappearing. If we give her time, she will return on her own."

"How can you be so sure she will come back?"

"Because Mellissa likes to help people." His father shot him a disapproving look. "I'm sorry—*Lady* Mellissa. In time, she will come to realise that, with her powers, she can help more people on this side of the veil."

"Does this mean you will not convince her to stay?"

"I will not."

Steffen looked him up and down. "You have never disobeyed an order before."

"You have never asked me to manipulate a friend before."

"I did not send you to the human world to make friends. You were meant to cement the changelings' position with the new keeper. I thought I had trained you better than this."

"I don't recall cementing the changeling's position as part of my briefing when I was sent to the human world."

"I thought you were smart enough to realise it was a secondary mission for our people. It was why I agreed to put you forward for the task when Emerson suggested it."

Greg's heart sank. His father had never put him forward as a candidate to find the new keeper. He had taken comfort thinking his father had been paying at least a tiny bit of attention to him but it had been Emerson all along. Greg pushed his shoulders back sitting up straight. "I don't see how being Mellissa's friend harms our position."

"It has already harmed our position as you are not willing to do what is necessary."

"No, Father. We just don't agree on what is actually necessary. Mellissa is more than just a crystal; she is a person as well. Maybe if you treat her like one, she won't run scared of us. If this is all you wanted me for, I will be going."

Greg stood to leave but his father grabbed his arm. "Don't let a few months in the human world ruin years of training."

"Don't let a difference of opinion ruin the appearance of a nice father-son chat." Greg gestured to the room full of people. His father's choice of venue actually worked in his favour. Steffen let go of his arm. "I will speak to you later, Father. I have some paperwork I need to see to."

Greg left the tearooms and went straight back to his room. He pulled out the forms Lady Gabrielle had given him and started filling them in. His father may not have meant to, but he'd given him the push he needed. He knew his father meant well, but his point of view was skewed. Hopefully after Lady Gabrielle made her motion, he would see things differently. He was more likely to listen to her than Greg. Even if his father didn't come around, he wasn't going to change his mind. He was going to do what he thought was right, not what his father wanted anymore.

The Ball
Mellissa

I hide behind a pillar, staring out at all the ball goers. My cheeks are sore from smiling too much. I have been paraded around for hours, meeting all sorts of lords and ladies, but I have yet to lay eyes on the prince I met earlier. Our encounter was brief, but for some reason, I can't get him out of my mind. At least I now have a moment to myself.

"Princess Freya." I jump at the sound of my name. My solitude hadn't lasted long. I turn, and my heart skitters. It's him. The prince from before. He bows, and I am entranced by his stunning grey eyes. "Why are you hiding?" he asks. "I thought this ball was to celebrate your sixteenth birthday."

"It is. It's just—" I pause.

"Just what?"

"Well, I don't know anyone here, and there is hardly anyone my age. It does not really feel like a party for me."

He smiles, and my heart flutters. "I understand. It feels more like an opportunity for our parents to show us off to one another. It's the only reason my father brought me—so he can parade around his heir."

I laugh. "Exactly."

"Well, you know what? I think we should make the most of it. While they do all the boring chitchat, we should have fun."

"And how do you suggest we do that?"

"How about we start with a dance?" He bows, holding out his hand. I place my hand in his. His touch sends tingles up my arm. He

leads me onto the dance floor.

I woke up feeling groggy, my head pounding. I sat up in bed, rubbing the side of my face. How did I get here? The last thing I could remember was being swarmed by people asking questions I didn't have answers for.

Victoria walked in the room. "Thank God, you're awake."

"What happened?" I asked, rubbing my head.

She sat on the edge of my bed. "You passed out. Apparently, it was a delayed reaction from using so much power."

"Great, just as everyone's starting to think better of me, I go and faint." I hid my face behind my hands. "I'm never going to give a good impression."

Victoria waved her hand at me. "Nobody cares about that. They are all super grateful for what you did. In fact, they are planning a ball in your honour once you recover. How are you feeling? I'm up for getting my party on."

I slumped my arms beside my body. "Exhausted. I feel like I haven't slept in days."

"Seriously? You've been asleep for over twenty-four hours."

"What? You mean I have missed a whole day?"

"Pretty much, but don't worry. I had a great time while you were asleep. They are extremely grateful to your guardians as well. I had a tour of the city and went to some great shops. I got some really cute dresses and a great one for the ball. We will have to sort something out for you as well, as the heir to the elf throne can't look like that." She gestured at me.

"What's wrong with how I look?"

"What isn't? But don't worry, it's fixable. I will go tell everyone you're awake. It's the early hours of the morning, but these weirdos will be up. Then we can party posh people style tonight." She got up and walked toward the door.

"Wait!" I yelled after her. "How's Matt doing?" The image of Matt being taken away on a stretcher flashed through

my mind. That had been a whole twenty-four hours ago.

"He's fine. He is being really annoying as usual."

My whole body relaxed. I went to get up, but Victoria came running back over to me. "What are you doing?"

"Coming with you. I think I've spent enough time in bed."

"No, you still look pretty rough. How about you go relax in that nice, big bath. When I come back, I will make you look all pretty."

I didn't appreciate her comments on my appearance, but a bath did sound good. "Fine."

Victoria walked off with a bounce in her step. At least my guardians were enjoying themselves while I wasted my time sleeping. I went and ran myself a bath. I watched as the tub filled with water. I still couldn't get over the fact that I'd slept through an entire day. Resting my head on the cool edge of the tub, I shut my eyes. Images of my dream ran through my head. I had dreamt of a ball. Maybe it was a coincidence. It was possible I had overheard Victoria talking about the ball in my sleep and my imagination had taken over, but I hadn't dreamt about a ball for me. It had been a celebration of a birthday. It was a ball for Freya's sixteenth birthday. What if all these strange dreams weren't really dreams at all, but something else? Like maybe the Heart Crystal was trying to tell me something— but what? What was significant about Freya meeting a prince at the ball? This prince had been in some of my other dreams. I pressed my finger to the side of my head, trying to remember what this prince looked like.

"Mellissa," shouted a voice. "What are you doing?"

I looked up to see Greg turning the taps off to the bath. The tub had overflowed, and the bathroom was full of water. How had I not noticed? My legs were soaked and so was the front of my hair. Greg took both my hands and pulled me up. "Are you okay?" he asked. He looked down at me, his eyes full of worry.

"I-I don't know," I said.

Greg wrapped a towel round me and led me back into the main room. I sat on the bed. I leant on the headboard as

Greg recited some healing spells. He sat beside me, clasping my hand between both of his. "You appear to be perfectly healthy, so what happened?"

I had no idea what had happened. Somehow, I had completely zoned out. A light caught my eye on the bedside table. The Heart Crystal. I picked it up. "Greg, can the crystal communicate?"

"Yes. It told me where to find you."

"It talked to you?"

"No, it didn't talk as such. It was more like a hum, but I knew what it meant. Why do you ask?"

"No reason."

Greg opened his mouth to talk but was interrupted by a knock on the door. I went to get up. Greg laid a hand on my shoulder, stopping me. "I'll get it."

He opened the door, and in walked Yuri with a tray of food. "Miss Victoria sent me up with this. She said you may be hungry." She placed the tray on the bedside cabinet. I swung my legs around to the side. There was a bowl of fruit, two croissants and a pot of tea. My tummy rumbled.

"Thank you, Yuri." I took a massive bite out of a croissant and poured myself a cup of tea.

She bowed. "Miss Victoria said she has something to pick up and will be back soon." Yuri walked toward the door, looking round the room.

"Yuri, is everything all right?" I asked

"Yes, of course. I was just wondering where Matt was. I visited him in the infirmary, but he treated me like I was just another of his fans."

My chest tightened, and I almost dropped my tea. "I haven't seen Matt."

Greg put his hand on Yuri's shoulder. "I'm sure it is nothing, just his newfound fame going to his head. Once everything calms down, I'm sure he will be back to his old self."

What was Greg talking about? Since when was Matt famous? More importantly, where was he? Victoria seemed to have been checking on me regularly while I was asleep. Greg had come the instant Victoria had informed people I was awake, but Matt was nowhere to be seen.

"You are probably right, Master Ainsworth," Yuri said.

"Greg is fine," Greg replied. "Will you be at the ball later?"

"Of course, I wouldn't miss it." Yuri bowed before leaving. Greg shut the door behind her.

My heart hurt. What was going on with Matt? I was worried about his injuries, but by the sounds of it, he was all fixed up with no concern for my well-being.

Greg sat next to me. "Don't worry about Matt. He probably just got swept away by all the attention."

"Even so, he is meant to be my best friend, so where is he? Victoria was here, and you're here, so why isn't he?"

"I don't know. Look, why don't you eat up, and then I'll take you for a tour of the city. How does that sound?"

I knew he was trying to distract me. It wouldn't stop me

from being upset about Matt, but a tour did sound good. There was probably so much to see in this city.

"Sounds good."

Once I finished my food, I splashed through the mess I'd made in the bathroom and had a quick freshen up. I put on my boots and cloak and followed Greg down to the main entrance. We had only taken a few steps outside when we were swarmed by people.

"There she is!" someone shouted.

"It's her. It's her."

"Your Majesty."

I froze on the spot. Where had all these people come from? Was this what Greg had meant about Matt's newfound fame. It was awful. Greg pulled me back inside. A few members of staff rushed to the doors, making sure they were shut and locked.

"What on earth was that?" I asked.

"Your new fans," Greg replied. "We could try one of the other exits."

"Master Gregory, the building is surrounded," said a member of staff. "Extra guards have been called for."

"I guess I'm trapped in here." At least my prison was nice. There were worse places I could have been trapped, and at least I wasn't alone.

Greg took my hand. "Come on. I have an idea."

He led me through a maze of corridors and up flight after flight of stairs. His idea seemed to consist of exhausting me. The seemingly never-ending stairs finally led to a big wooden door. We walked out onto the roof.

"We can't tour the city, but you can get a pretty good view of it up here," Greg said.

The cold air pricked my cheeks. Blue sky stretched above us. We made our way to the edge of the roof. There was a metal railing going all the way around. I took in a sharp breath. The view was stunning. I could see for miles. The city buzzed with life beneath us. "This is more than pretty good."

"And do you feel that?"

"What?"

"The darkness is gone."

He was right. The horrible presence that had made me feel sick was gone. The air was clear, and I could breathe easy. No wonder these people were so happy. I squeezed Greg's hand. "Thank you for bringing me here."

"This is also a good place to talk about things that are bothering you," he said.

"I don't know what you mean."

"Why did you ask if the crystal can communicate?"

I looked at the floor. "It doesn't matter."

"Mellissa, let me help you."

Matt had told me to keep my dreams a secret, especially from Greg, but where was he now? I thought I'd figured something out about the dreams, and the only other person that knew about them was nowhere to be seen.

"Okay, this might sound crazy, but I think the Heart Crystal is trying to tell me something in my dreams by showing me things in Freya's life. I was having this recurring dream about a flying guy, a tree and being stabbed. I thought it was a nightmare, but then I met you, and Freya's fight with Kadon sounded just like my dream. Then my dreams changed, but they were still all about Freya."

Greg looked into the distance. "Some say the Heart Crystal takes an imprint of every keeper and records everything that happens around it. I don't know if that's true, but if it is, I don't see why it wouldn't be able to pass those recordings on. But you said you were having these dreams before you met me?"

"Yes, but I can't say for how long. Do you think it's possible that from the moment you crossed the veil, the crystal began calling out to me, but the only way it could communicate with me was when my conscious mind was asleep?"

"Anything's possible when it comes to a life crystal. There is still so much we don't know about them. No one has met a crystal keeper in thousands of years—until you." He gave me a smile that made my heart flutter. I hadn't realised how much I would miss all his explanations about magic until that moment. Greg patted my shoulder. "Maybe it's something we can look into when we get you home, along with all the other training I have planned for you."

I shook my head. "What do you mean training? I thought—"

"You thought because you're all the talk on this side of the veil that you didn't have to train anymore?"

"No, it's just…You're coming back with us?"

"That's not a problem, is it?"

I squealed as I threw my arms around his neck, almost knocking him over. I could have burst with excitement.

"Well, don't you two look comfortable." Victoria stood in the doorway, eyebrow raised.

We both jumped. "Victoria, you scared me half to death," I said.

She folded her arms. "I assume Her Royal Highness is fit and healthy."

Greg nodded. "She is fully recovered."

"Great. Now back to our room so I can turn this mess into a princess." She grabbed my arm and pulled me away from

Greg.

I tried to free my arm. "Hey, don't I get a say in this?"

Victoria tightened her grip and pulled me through the door. "Oh, come on. You will see him at the ball."

I caught Greg's eye from the door. *"Help me,"* I mouthed.

"Have fun you two, and I'll see you later," Greg said.

"Traitor," I shouted.

He winked as I was pulled away. Victoria didn't let go of me until we were back in our room.

"I assume you didn't have that bath," Victoria said. I shook my head. She marched into the bathroom. "What the hell happened in here? You know what? I don't need to know." After some loud banging, I heard water running in the bathroom. There were a few more bangs, then Victoria popped her head round the door. "Come on, then."

I walked into the bathroom and was shocked into silence. The room sparkled. There was no evidence that I had ever flooded the place. The tub was filled with bubbles and what looked like lavender. A cold shiver shot threw me as Victoria started to pulled my clothes off. I grabbed my top back. "I can undress myself."

"Well, you were just standing there, and I thought maybe you'd watched one to many of those shows with queens and princesses with personal handmaidens."

"I was just amazed at how you fixed all the mess."

"I have some magical skills other than freezing things. Now, get in the bath already."

"Are you not leaving?"

She rolled her eyes. "You are such a prude. How about I go get the fancy shampoo I bought from some witch today while you hide yourself under the bubbles."

Victoria walked out. I quickly finished getting undressed and submerged myself in the water. The warm bath felt so good. I stretched my body out in the tub and laid my head on the edge of the bath. Victoria came back in carrying a bunch of toiletries. As she laid things out, she nattered away about how amazing the party preparations looked. She walked over with two bottles and poured them on my head.

"What is that?" I asked.

"It's a special formula to make you hair super soft, add shine and give your curls a nice bounce." Victoria massaged the stuff through my hair. It felt really nice having someone wash my hair for me, and I began to relax.

Once I was clean, Victoria grabbed me a bathrobe out of a cupboard. I wrapped myself up with it. Victoria plopped a towel on my head and dragged me out of the bathroom. She sat me down at the dressing table, where she had laid out loads of different hair products and makeup. Victoria had a field day playing with my hair. I lost count of all the different products she used on my head. My hair was tugged about, pulled up, down and all over the place. Finally, Victoria wrapped my hair up on the top of my head in a bun, leaving a few curls hanging loose around my face. She did my makeup and then pulled a big box out of the wardrobe. Inside was a beautiful, dark green gown with a satin train that looked like it had stars woven into it.

"What do you think? According to Flopsey, dark green is the colour of elf royalty."

I ran my hand over the dress. The fabric was smooth. "It's stunning. I can't wear that. It's way too nice."

"You can, and you will. Do not make me have to force you into this dress."

No way was I going to get into a fight with Victoria, so I slipped the dress on. I hadn't realised how exposed my back would be by the U-shaped cut out, but the dress felt amazing. The fabric glided over my body. The straps were held together by two gold hoops at the top. It fit like a glove. How had she managed to get a dress so exact to my size?

"Oh, it looks even better on," Victoria said. "I have such amazing taste. It hugs your curves perfectly. Oh, I almost forgot the shoes." She ran over to the wardrobe and pulled out a bag. How much shopping had she done, and where had the money come from? "I know you can't walk in heels, so I got you some cute sandals." She pulled a pair of gold strappy sandals out and handed them to me.

"Thanks," I said.

"No problem. Now, it's my turn to get ready." She grabbed a few things off the dresser and went into the bathroom. Of course she got privacy when it was her turn to get ready. I looked in the mirror. Victoria had done a really good job. I hardly recognised myself. The dress was something I never would have chosen, but it was beautiful.

Victoria put her arm round me. "Don't we look gorgeous?"

"How?" I asked. "I mean, when? You look amazing, but you just went in there."

She was wearing a full face of makeup. Her long, blonde hair had been artfully twisted around to the side and rested on her left shoulder. She wore a black dress that sparkled like the night sky. The front reached her knees, but the back was floor-length. I felt like an ugly duckling next to her.

"I've had practice getting ready quick. We look so good. Everyone is going to want to dance with us," she said.

"Dance! You never said there would be dancing."

"It's a ball, Mellissa. Of course, there will be dancing. I didn't think I would have to tell you that."

"Victoria, you know I can't dance."

"True." She held her hands out. "Come here. We have time. I'll give you a quick lesson."

I scrunched up my face. She knew too well how bad I was at dancing. She had made fun of me about it plenty of times, but now she was offering help. I took her hands. "Fine."

Victoria pulled me toward her. "Okay, stand up straight, shoulders back. One hand on my shoulder and the other in mine." She put my hands in position. "Your partner should have their hand on your lower back, but if it wanders too low, feel free to knee them in the groin. Now, try to keep looking at your partner. If you really can't stand looking at them, then over their shoulder—or in your case, at the shoulder. Just don't look at your feet or the floor. Usually the male leads, so all you have to do is follow. As I lean forward, you go back. Ready?" I nodded. Victoria moved, and I head-butted her shoulder as she kicked my shin.

"You were meant to move," she shouted, "not stand there like a statue." She scowled at me. "Let's try again, and this time move your feet."

We went over the basic steps a few times. Victoria kept moaning. Apparently, I was too stiff. After a few mishaps, we managed to do one full turn of the room. It would have to do. I just hoped no one asked me to dance. There was a knock at the door. Victoria answered it.

"Samson," she said.

He bowed. "I have come to escort Lady Mellissa Hail and her guardians to the ball."

"Time to go, Mellissa," Victoria called.

"What about Matt?"

"I don't know. I couldn't find him earlier, so I gave up. I'm sure he will have made his own way to the ball."

Victoria linked arms with me, and we followed Samson. Even Victoria didn't know what Matt was doing. His absence was really starting to worry me. We made our way downstairs. Samson led us to a pair of giant double doors. He opened them, and the room went silent. All eyes were on me. I froze on the spot. Victoria dragged me into the room.

Samson stepped forward. "I present to you, Lady Mellissa Hail, keeper of the Heart Crystal, and her guardian, Miss Victoria Street."

Samson had this whole announcing thing down pretty well. His voice was loud, clear and carried far. The whole room bowed to us. My face heated. As they all rose, a man in a smart black suit stepped away from the crowd. It was Lord Steffen.

He greeted us and led us both through the room. As we walked, people kept putting their hands out to touch me, praising me. I smiled awkwardly and tried to stay calm. If Victoria wasn't holding on to me so tightly, I probably would have run back to our room. Lord Steffen led me over to what looked like the head table and left me next to Lady Gabrielle. No longer was she in her robes. Instead, she wore a long black dress that showed off her feminine figure. She seemed more relaxed than before, but still intimidating. Lord Steffen then led Victoria to the end of the table, where Matt stood. My whole body went tense. I didn't want her to leave me. Lady Gabrielle tapped a champagne flute in her hand. Everyone went silent and turned their attention to her.

"We are all here to honour the great accomplishment of Lady Mellissa Hail, keeper of the Heart Crystal, and her guardians." She gestured her glass toward me and then to Matt and Victoria. "We can rejoice in the knowledge that Kadon has been resealed, and his darkness shall no longer be plaguing us. Let us celebrate the fact that the Heart Crystal has been reactivated and shall bring peace to the land. A toast to the future elf queen."

Everyone raised their glasses and toasted me—the future elf queen. I gulped and forced a smile. Lady Gabrielle gestured for me to sit. Once I was sat, everyone followed suit. This was all so weird. I had never been to an event like this, and it was all based around me.

Trays of food were brought out and drinks passed round. The smell of freshly roasted chicken struck me, causing my tummy to rumble. I fiddled with a napkin. I needed to push my worries to the side. For now, I would enjoy the meal. After all, the whole purpose of this banquet was to honour me, and I hadn't eaten since this morning. The meal was amazing, tender chicken, crisp roast potatoes, sweet carrots and parsnip, smothered in a sweet gravy. Lady Gabrielle didn't press me with hard questions. She mainly asked simple things about my family and what it was like on the other side of the veil—all things I could easily answer. She wasn't as scary as I'd originally thought.

Once the meal was over, Lady Gabrielle led me to another room that had a dance floor and music playing. There was a dessert table full of different sweet treats. There was ice cream, cookies, cakes and jellies. A chocolate fountain was at the centre of the table. Everything looked really tasty. This room was decorated with pink and white streamers. Pink balloons floated above us. Lady Gabrielle went around, introducing me to all the council members and then to all her staff. Lots of people had questions for me and wanted to thank me once again. I went around with a smile plastered on my face and answered their questions the best I could, accepting their thanks. I don't think my version of events was quite as exciting as they were hoping, but nonetheless, they were still happy to hear my story.

I slid away the first chance I got and rubbed the sides of my jaw. After hours of forcing a smile, my jaw ached. I searched for my guardians. Spotting Matt, I practically ran across the ballroom.

"Matt, I'm so glad you're okay." I squished him with a hug. He stiffened in my arms, patting my back awkwardly.

"And I am also delighted you are in good health, Mellissa," he replied sounding really formal.

"Why are you talking like that?"

"Whatever do you mean? I always talk like this. Anyway, I have some adoring fans over there waiting for me." He pointed at a group of girls. "I must dash. There are so many girls that want to dance with me and so little time."

He swayed off, leaving me on my own. Even the way he walked seemed off. I had been so worried about him, and he just gave me the brush-off. I guess I was only his friend and took a back seat to all the girls that were throwing themselves at him. He was just as popular with the ladies here as back home—maybe more so—and I appeared to be just as much of a loner. The room was full of people chattering away in small groups. Couples twirled on the dance floor. I didn't recognise any of the music playing. It was mostly instrumental. I felt so out of place. There wasn't a familiar face to be seen.

"Matt has been acting like that ever since he woke up," Victoria said, startling me. "His head has tripled in size due to his new fan group. They think he is so amazing for putting himself on the line to protect you." She folded her arms over her chest and curled her top lip. She obviously didn't think he deserved the attention he was getting.

"I guess that explains him being distant," I said. "He is trying to impress all the girls."

"That's no excuse. Besides, what he did wasn't that great. He spent most of the fight being beaten up. You are the one that actually saved us." She looked over in Matt's direction and rolled her eyes. He was happily flirting with a group of girls.

"I don't know about that. It was more of a team effort." I curled a stray piece of hair round my finger.

"Anyway, we need to find you a dance partner," Victoria said, twitching her eyebrow at me. "You deserve to have a little fun tonight."

"What?" My hand shot to my heart. "You know I am a terrible dancer. Our little lesson didn't exactly go well."

"That is true." She tapped her finger on her chin. "I'm sure I can still find a way to hook you up."

"I don't need hooking up."

"Speaking of—" Victoria jabbed me in the side and nodded toward Greg, who was walking over to us. "I must say, he cleans up pretty well. He looks much better in a suit than I expected. What do you think?"

My whole face was on fire. I tilted my head, but I didn't have enough hair free to cover my face. I prayed my cheeks hadn't gone red, but she was right. Greg wore a black suit and tie. His hair had been styled so his fringe wasn't in his face. The smile he gave me as our eyes met made my heart flutter. Victoria wriggled her eyebrows, and the corner of her mouth curled into a smirk.

"What are you two doing stood in a corner like this?" Greg asked.

"Nothing," I replied, looking at Victoria's shoulder.

"Trying to find Mellissa a dance partner," Victoria said.

"Victoria!" I exclaimed. "I said no. I don't dance."

"Well, that should be easy enough," Greg said, completing ignoring my objection. He stood next to Victoria and scanned the room. "There are plenty of people that would dance with her. Any preferences?"

"Just keep her away from that pervy dwarf, and no snooty witches." Victoria pointed at a couple of men in the room. "I don't need to kill anyone on her behalf tonight."

"There is no need to worry about Hogan. Mellissa is too short for his liking. He likes the tall ones, and not all witches are snooty."

"I guess that would explain why he kept drooling at my legs. All the witches I have met here are snooty, especially the one that claimed to be the son of a lord. I don't care who his father is; he's still twice my age and stuck up."

"You must be referring to Lee. I will have to agree with you about him. However, I don't think Mellissa will encounter the same problems as you. She has a status you don't. I'm not saying it's right but her title will force them to be more respectful toward her."

"I want to smack you for that status remark, but I'm afraid you're right. This room is full of privileged snobs, but still there must be someone decent about for her." Victoria raised her eyebrows and looked him up and down. I'm not sure if Greg noticed, but I did.

"Will you two stop?" I pushed my way in between them. "Do you not understand what *no* means? I'm not dancing with anyone." My words were aimed more at Victoria. Once again, I was ignored.

Victoria took my hand. "You know what? None of these snobs are good enough for your first dance of the ball, so you will dance with me."

"What?"

I was pulled onto the dance floor before I could make any more objections. Victoria threw me into a spin. Just as I was about to fall over, she took hold of both my hands. We stepped from side to side, and Victoria spun me again. She took hold of one of my hands and walked around me. With a hand on either side of me, she shimmied down, shaping my body with her hands. Slowly, people began to stare. I felt flushed. I wanted the ground to swallow me whole. Victoria twirled us around the dance floor, ending the dance by dipping me and lifting one of my legs over her shoulder. There was a round of applause.

Victoria curtsied. "That should get us some attention."

"I didn't want any attention," I said through gritted teeth. Victoria shrugged as I marched off the dance floor. I slipped behind a pillar, hoping to hide from any unwanted attention Victoria's actions may have brought.

"Lady Mellissa." I jumped at the sound of my name.

A man in a purple dinner jacket bowed to me. "I am Master Lee, son of Lord Grayson." He had pale skin and dark hair. His eyes were brown and looked like they were trying to bore into me.

"You're a witch," I said. The one Victoria had mentioned not liking.

He nodded. "That was quite an interesting dance there between you and your guardian. You two aren't involved, are you?"

"What? No, of course not."

"Oh good, good. I was wondering then—"

Oh God no. He was going to ask me to dance. This was all Victoria's fault. She knew I had two left feet. That dance had basically been her throwing me around. She also knew how awkward I was with strangers. I needed a way out of this situation. "Well, I was just about to get a drink. Dancing is thirsty work." I was going to have to have a serious talk about boundaries with my guardian.

His lips curled into what I think was meant to be a smile. "That it is."

I shuddered, taking a step back.

"Mellissa." I turned at the sound of Greg's voice. "Here's that drink you asked for," he said, handing me a glass.

I could have hugged him. "Thanks," I said.

Lee's eyes narrowed on Greg. "Gregory."

"Lee," Greg said. "How are things? It's been a while."

"Things are fantastic. Our city is prospering. Anyway, I was about to ask Lady Mellissa here something before you interrupted."

Greg feigned surprise. "I didn't realise. How rude of me to fulfil the lady's request of a drink."

Lee scowled. Turning to me, he forced a smile. My eyes widened. He still planned to ask. I downed my drink and grabbed Greg's arm. "Greg, dance with me." They both looked shocked.

I pushed my glass at Lee and pulled Greg toward the dance floor. "I thought you didn't dance," Greg said.

"I don't, but I also don't know how to say no. Better you than him, and at least you know you have a useless dance partner."

He spun me around, positioning my hands the same way Victoria had in our lesson earlier. "I wouldn't say useless, just untrained. I taught you magic, and I will teach you this."

"Okay, but you can't complain if I step on your feet."

"I promise you, I won't be complaining."

With a gentle push, we began to move. He kept to his word. I lost count of how many times I stepped on his toes, but he didn't complain once. Just like Victoria, he kept telling me to stop looking at my feet and not to be so stiff. It was no surprise to see Victoria on the dance floor, her partner changing regularly. I didn't leave Greg's side, in fear of Lee or someone else approaching me.

Victoria winked at me over the shoulder of one of her dance partners. Matt didn't seem to notice me or his sister on the dance floor. He danced with girl after girl, not giving them a second glance once their turn was over. How could they be okay with the way he was treating them? He didn't show any of them any real attention, yet they still kept flocking to him.

Greg went to get us drinks while I went outside for some fresh air. I found myself back at the fountain I discovered after freaking out and getting lost. Glittering lights floated in the water. There was a nice, refreshing breeze. The pressure that had been holding me down over the last few days drifted away on the wind. I looked at my reflection in the water. My dress was amazing. It really did make me look royal.

The click-clack of footsteps sounded behind me. I turned, expecting to see Greg but saw his father approaching me instead. There really wasn't much of a family resemblance. His eyes were brown, not emerald green like Greg's. He was at least four inches shorter than his son. I suppose his white hair could have been red once upon a time. I tilted my head. Samson actually looked more like him. They must be related on his father's side.

"Hello, Lady Mellissa," Lord Steffen said, bowing his head to me.

"Just Mellissa is fine," I said, wrapping one arm round myself.

"Mellissa it is, then. I understand that you plan on heading back to the human world tomorrow."

"Yes, that is the plan. I promised my dad I would be back for Christmas Eve."

"Yes, Gregory explained that Christmas is some sort of important celebration to the humans. Do you have any plans for when you will return?"

Returning? I thought this was a one-time trip. Coming back hadn't seemed like an option. I had planned to go back home and carry on like before.

Could I carry on like before?

"I'm sorry, I haven't really got any plans. I hadn't thought past coming here and sealing Kadon. I guess if I'm needed, I will come back."

"Lady Mellissa, you are the heir to the elf throne. You will always be needed here."

"I know I'm the heir to the throne, but I don't really think I'm queen material."

"Gregory did mention your lack of confidence. You've achieved so much already. I think with a little more training—as suggested by my son—you will be a wonderful queen."

"Greg said I lack confidence? What else did he say?"

"The council has decided that you are not ready to take the throne yet and need more training. You also need your confidence boosting and to be taught proper etiquette. Gregory agreed with this ruling. He has already been training with you, so we think it best he continue. I hope to see you back here again soon." Lord Steffen gave me a nod and wished me a good night before walking back inside.

I tugged at my loose curls and stared down at my reflection in the fountain. My face painted in makeup and a ridiculously beautiful dress didn't hide the truth. I didn't belong here, and they all knew it. I was not one of them. Greg was always telling me how he believed in me, but that didn't seem to be the case after what his father just told me. How could he agree with that ruling? I had managed to pull off magic that he hadn't even taught me when sealing Kadon. He had some nerve pretending to be my friend, when really I was just a tool for him to further his political profile.

Matt had warned me about this. He had said not to trust Greg. I had known all he really wanted to do was impress his father, but I somehow lost sight of that. Who exactly did the council members think they were, discussing my future? They thought I could be trained to be something I wasn't, but I couldn't—no, I wouldn't—change myself for them. They had no say in my life. I wasn't even sure I wanted to be queen, and it was not a decision someone else would make for me, especially not a group of people who hardly knew me. I wanted to go home, but I knew I would be repulsed back again. I cursed the limited distance I could teleport.

"Mellissa, are you all right?" asked Greg, two drinks in hand. I almost fell forward as I hadn't heard his footsteps on the stone. "Was that my father I just saw?"

I flung my arm at him, almost knocking a drink out of his hand. "What do you care if I'm all right? You act like you're concerned, but really, it's all an act. I am just a little project for you to impress your father with. You know what? I don't even want to talk to you anymore. In fact, I'm done for tonight."

"What are you talking about?" he asked, but I didn't answer. I teleported myself back to my room upstairs.

I slumped face-first onto the bed. Why was I so mad? It wasn't like I had known Greg for long but I had trusted him. It was nice for a moment to think I could have more than just Matt as a friend. I had liked the little new friendship group the four of us had made. But that was all falling apart. Matt was acting weird and giving me the cold shoulder. As nice as it was to be getting along with Victoria, I didn't think it would last after returning home. And Greg—I didn't know what Greg was to me.

I couldn't wait to go home and for everything to go back to normal. Matt would go back to being my best friend. Victoria would go back to just about acknowledging my existence, and Greg would not be there. He would stay here. As future queen, did I not have some sort of power to fire him as my magic teacher? I could refuse to let him teach me.

I stuck my head up as I heard a knock at the door. I instinctively went to answer it but stopped as I put my hand on the handle. I wasn't in the mood for company. Hopefully if I ignored them, they would go away. There was another knock. I started to walk back to bed. They knocked again.

"Mellissa, I know you're in there." I froze on the spot. It was Greg. "I don't know what my father said to you, but I can explain."

"I don't want to talk to you," I shouted back at the door. There went my plan to ignore him and pretend I wasn't in. I heard the door handle go, and Greg walked in.

"Does that thing not lock?" I yelled.

"Well, yes, but you didn't lock it."

"I will make sure I remember to lock it just as soon as you leave." I tried to push him back out of the room.

He darted round me. "What are you doing?"

"Trying to get rid of you." I pulled at his arm, but he didn't budge. I threw my arms down beside me and stormed over to the other side of the room. "Well, you can forget about coming back to the human world with us. I don't care if the council has approved it."

"But you were happy about me returning with you earlier."

"That was before, but then your dad said—"

Greg stepped forward, pointing at me. "You cannot listen to anything he says. He's just mad I didn't agree with his plans."

"Well, that's not what he said," I shouted. "He told me about the council's ruling and how you agreed with them. You know, how my skills are lacking and I have no confidence. What sort of friend does that?"

"What council ruling?" Greg asked. "Mellissa, I really don't know what you are talking about."

I pointed at him. "You expect me to believe you don't know? Your father said because of what you told him, he doesn't think I am ready and wants you to continue training me. The real reason you are returning to the human world is because your father ordered it, not because you wanted to."

"Well, my father sure changed his tune. He didn't want to let you go home before."

"Wait, what? Since when wasn't I going home?"

Greg ran his hand through his hair. "Forget I said that."

I grabbed hold of his arm. "Tell me, or I will teleport you to—I don't know—the middle of a volcano."

"You do realise you will also end up in said volcano."

"Fine, to like, the edge, and I will push you in."

Greg laughed. "Do you need me to go get one of your guardians, so they can threaten me for you?"

"Don't laugh at me." I stomped my foot and folded my arms. "Just tell me, please."

"It's not fair when you pout at me like that," he said, sitting on the end of the bed. My arms fell beside me. I hadn't realised I was pouting. "I will tell you, but you can't tell anyone about this, because I am not meant to know."

"I won't even tell my guardians." I crossed my heart with my finger, skipping across the room to sit next to him.

"There were certain council members that wanted you to stay here and become queen. Lady Gabrielle thought it was better you go home and make up your own mind. She asked me to put in a request and make out that your ability was worse than it was to sway the members that were on the fence to her view. I didn't mean any of what I wrote."

"Really?" He nodded. I found myself pouting again. "That council has some cheek, making decisions about me like that." Although, it was nice to know Lady Gabrielle had rigged the situation to give me a choice in the matter. I was terrified of her, but she was definitely nicer than I'd thought.

"Well, it is what they do. Sometimes, it is like they forget the decisions they make actually affect real-life people."

"I do not envy you having to work for them."

"I don't actually work for them. I just have to live with one of them. I work at the infirmary in Novosvillas. Although, I will eventually be expected to take my father's place. Hence why he is so strict about me knowing the council's ways. If you become queen, you will also have a place on the council."

"Really? I don't want to be on the council. I don't really like being around the council members as it is."

"To be honest, I don't know if I really want to either, but it's not something I need to worry about for a long time."

"Won't you miss your home if you come back with me? I mean, you only just got back after being gone for months, and you're just going to leave again."

"I did miss this place at first, but I have come to realise there is a lot for me to learn in the human world. There is still so much I have yet to discover. I was so busy searching for you, and then training you, that I didn't really take notice of how amazing that place was."

"You sound like me when I was thinking about coming to this place."

"Well, what is normal for you is completely bizarre to me, and it probably works the other way around."

"You are pretty odd."

"Well, shall we go back to the party? It would be rude for you to just disappear." He got up and held his hand out to me.

"I will go back for a little while, but then I'm coming back here soon. I'm getting tired." I took his hand, and he pulled me up.

"How can you be tired after sleeping for a whole day?"

"Hey, spending all day in bed is exhausting. I'm sorry for getting so mad at you. I should've just asked you about it."

"It's all right. My father has a way of leaving out key bits of information," he replied. "Shall we go then, my lady?"

I felt myself blush. I nodded in response and teleported us back to the party, where no one had noticed our absence.

Homebound
Mellissa

y mother wraps her arms round me.

"Thank goodness you are here, Freya."

"How is he?" I ask, my voice nothing but a whisper.

"Not good. Come, dear. He has been asking for you."

She takes my hand and takes me up to my father's chambers. Pausing at the door, she clasps both my hands to her chest. "I warn you, he has deteriorated a lot since you left on your tour of the country."

I nod. "Understood."

She opens the door and gestures for me to go in. I look to see if she will come too, but she shakes her head. I walk across the room to my father's bedside. My heart feels like it has shattered. There lies a pale, gaunt man. His eyes are sunken, and his bones jut out. I hardly recognise my own father.

"Freya," he croaks, reaching out to me.

I take his hand. "Yes, Father, it's me."

"There is something I must give you." He tries to get out of bed.

I shoot forward, putting my hand on his chest. "Father, don't stress yourself. This can wait. You need to rest."

He takes both my hands. "My sweet girl, I believe my time is coming to an end."

Tears threaten to fall, but I don't let them. "That can't be. The elves are the creators of healing magic. There must be a healer somewhere that can do something."

"All magic has its limits, and all life must come to an end."

"No, I won't believe it. You are the king and the keeper of the Heart Crystal. You are the strongest person I know."

My father wipes away the tears I can no longer hold back. "And you are the strongest person I know. I wanted to do this properly, but I have become too weak." He pulls the Heart Crystal from around his neck. "Heart Crystal, I release you from our bind and place you with a new keeper."

The room fills with light. He takes my hand and places the crystal in it. "No," I whisper.

"You must. I believe in you, Freya. You can continue my work to make this world a better place." He rests back on his pillows, taking staggered breaths. "Now, you must bind with it. If you are worthy, the words will come."

The crystal glowed in my hand. It felt warm like a heartbeat. Words came into my head, almost like a whisper. "Crystal Heart, I bind to thee to protect the land and keep the balance." My voice boomed through the room with the echo of another. Lights shot around the room, creating a strong gust. Two lights separated from the rest and shot out the window. The lights disappeared, and the room fell silent.

"Father, I did it." There was no response. "Father." I grabbed his arm. He didn't move. He looked like he was sleeping, but he was no longer breathing. "No!" I screamed, dropping to my knees, tears

streaming.

"Mellissa." Someone was shaking me. "Mellissa." My heart hurt. I felt like I was about to burst from the pain. "Mellissa, wake up," they shouted. I opened my eyes. Victoria was beside me, shaking me. My sight blurred as I choked on my tears.

"What the hell is wrong with you?"

"The king. Freya's dad. It felt so real, like I was there with her."

Victoria grasped my shoulders. "Mellissa, it was just a dream."

"No, it was a memory. Freya's memory."

Victoria's brows drew together as she took a step back. "What are you talking about?"

Once I was able to pull myself together, I told her all

about my dreams. She sat on the end of my bed listening intently, occasionally giving a slight nod of her head. "these dreams, she said, You believe they are coming from the Heart Crystal?" I nodded. "And Matt knows about them, and Greg." I nodded again. She jumped off the bed and threw her arms in the air. "And no one thought to tell me?"

"It's not like that. Matt told me not to tell anyone."

"Since when has Matt been the master of good ideas?" she yelled. "And you told Greg!"

"That was only recently, and I sort of just blurted it out."

She wagged her finger in my face. "I am your best guardian. You do not keep things from me. Do you understand?"

"Yes, I'm sorry."

She sat back on the bed, scowling at me. "Did you ever think that maybe the crystal is just trying to get you to understand what happened before and show you how it got here, with you?"

"Maybe." I bit my bottom lip. I had no idea why the crystal was giving me these dreams, but it was trying to tell me something. I just didn't know what. All the memories had been so different. Some were nice, some scary and others completely heart breaking. There didn't seem to be any link other than Freya.

Victoria slapped my legs under the cover, making me jump. "Well, we better start getting ready for the journey home, and I want to be the first to know about any more weird dreams."

I nodded. She skipped off into the bathroom, and within seconds, I heard water running.

Home. My heart felt lighter. We were going home.

Victoria and I stood outside by the sleigh, waiting on the others. The hustle and bustle of the city roared around us. People occasionally stopped to stare or point at us, but mostly, they left us alone. Greg and Yuri had gone looking for Matt. No one had seen him after he disappeared from the ball last night. I stayed to help Victoria stuff all her extra bags in the sleigh. The girl sure could shop, especially when it was someone else's money she was spending. We had one sleigh this time. Greg would sit in the back with us, and Yuri would sit up front with the driver. We would be taking the sleigh all the way to the veil this time. No chance for me to ruin any boats, and apparently, it would actually be quicker. Why we hadn't done this in the first place, I had no idea.

Victoria leant on the sleigh, looking up at the sky. "Well, it seems we have time to spare as my idiot brother has not turned up."

"I guess," I said.

"We have time for you to tell me where you and Flopsey disappeared to last night."

"Wait, what?"

"Did you think I wouldn't notice your absence? I'm your guardian. It is my job to notice these things, so tell me everything." She looked down at me with a menacing smile. I'm not sure what she thought I had to tell, but I had nothing to hide, and I had no problem telling her what happened.

When I finished telling her about the misunderstanding between Greg and me, she looked disappointed. Victoria crossed her arms and tilted her head toward me. "Do you really expect me to believe you just talked?"

"Well, it's what happened."

She handed me a small glass bottle of pink liquid. "Well, I guess I got you this made for nothing."

I held the bottle up to the light. "What is this?"

"A contraceptive potion."

"A what? Why would I need that?"

"Because it's better than any human contraception." She pointed at her fingers in turn as she listed off benefits. "It takes effect straight away, lasts six months, doesn't have any unwanted side effects, works for both genders and tastes like raspberries."

I stuffed the bottle into one of my bags on the sleigh.

"They are all great reasons to switch from the pill to this stuff, but what I meant is: why would I need it now?"

She shrugged. "Well, when you disappeared, I thought maybe you and Flopsey—"

"What! No," I shouted. "Why would you think that? Greg is my friend. Friends don't do that."

"If you say so."

My face was on fire. Why would that be the conclusion she came to? That was likely what Matt had been up to, but I wasn't like Matt. Greg may be attractive, but I wouldn't ruin our friendship with a one-night stand. I didn't understand why she cared about this. Although, it was nice of her to get me the potion. It seemed to be her way of looking out for me. I looked up at the sky.

"We just spoke about the council rudely trying to decide my fate and Greg coming back with us. Nothing else. So sorry I didn't record our conversation to replay for you," I said.

She rolled her eyes. "You don't have to be embarrassed. I know you're not a virgin."

"How do you know that? Matt doesn't even know."

"Oh, he knows. He just doesn't want to acknowledge it. He likes to believe you're still too innocent. Pretty rich when you think of how many girls he's been with. He still occasionally lectures me about safe sex and how I can say no. Trust me, I say no plenty." Victoria raised an eyebrow. "Wait, you mean you and Matt never?"

I gagged. My stomach churned, and I thought I might be sick. "God, no. That is just disgusting." At least Greg was just a friend, but Matt was like family. How could she even suggest it?

Victoria bent over laughing. "You are the first girl to ever look like they are about to throw up at the thought of being with my brother."

"Glad you find this so funny." I folded my arms over my chest and frowned.

She patted my shoulder. "I'm sorry. I never understood why your friendship lasted after the first years of high school and kind of assumed friends with benefits at first. Although, I think I understand better now."

"Well, thanks for that disturbing imagery. I'm going to check that I've remembered to pack everything." I walked around the side of the sleigh to get away from this conversation and bumped into Matt.

"When did you get here?" I asked, taking a step back.

"What do you mean? I have been here the whole time." My eyes went wide. I hoped he hadn't heard our entire conversation.

"You were right here the whole time we were loading the sleigh? I never heard you approach."

"Yes, I was. You obviously aren't very observant," he replied.

How dare he talk to me like that? If he had been here the whole time, he could have helped us load the sleigh. Greg and Yuri had been searching pointlessly. And he must've heard what Victoria said.

"Where have you been?" Victoria yelled, marching around the sleigh.

"I have been around. Anyway, where is that changeling and water nymph?" he asked, looking at his nails. "We really should be on our way."

Victoria kissed her teeth. "They are off looking for you."

Matt turned away from Victoria and shoved his bag in my face. "Here, be a good little girl and put my things in the sleigh."

"She will do nothing of the sort, you rude cretin." Victoria grabbed the bag off me and threw it back at him.

Matt sighed, looking down his nose at us. "Whoever thought it was a good idea to put women in positions of power needs a good beating."

"What did you say?" yelled Victoria. I was just as shocked as she was.

"Well, I'm ready to leave now." Matt waved his hand at me. "Mellissa, go fetch Gregory and what's-her-face. You can teleport them."

I gritted my teeth. What had gotten into him? He was being so rude—not to mention cold, demanding and sexist. It was like he'd adopted Victoria's harshness and taken it to a whole new level. I teleported to get Greg, not because Matt told me to, but because if I didn't leave, I might just hit him. I managed to teleport right in front of Greg. Unfortunately, he wasn't looking and knocked me over. One of the few times I landed well, and I still ended up on my butt.

"Mellissa, you should be more careful about where you teleport," he said, helping me up.

I dusted myself off. "Matt has turned up out of nowhere, so you can stop searching for the idiot. I think he is hung over and taking his bad mood out on everyone else. Where's Yuri?"

"She went that way." He pointed down a corridor.

We hurried in the direction he pointed, finding her searching in a staff canteen. If Matt had been acting like himself, this would have been a good guess of where he might have been. Holding on to the both of them, I teleported us to the sleigh.

"Good, you are back," Victoria said. "Now, let's go. The sooner we leave, the sooner I can get away from him." Victoria glared at Matt.

He stuck his nose up at her and got in the sleigh. Yuri went up front, while the rest of us got in the back. The sleigh jolted forward with a gentle whoosh sound. We were on our way home.

Matt sat slouched over with his arms crossed. "I don't see why we need to take this stupid sleigh back to the human world. Couldn't you just teleport us there? It would be a lot quicker."

"Why are you always asking stupid questions?" snapped Victoria. I wasn't sure what had happened in the short time I was gone, but she was really wound up.

"It's okay, Victoria. I don't mind explaining again," I said, trying to calm the situation.

"Just because you don't mind doesn't make it okay. He should know why," she replied, giving Matt the evil eye.

"Matt, I can't teleport us there simply because it's too far. I can only teleport a certain distance. If I tried to teleport us home, we would just be repulsed back," I explained.

He huffed. "You could just do multiple teleports till we

got there."

"You actually expect her to use that much magic just to get us home a bit quicker?" Victoria said. "What is wrong with you? She was out cold for a whole day. How can you ask that of her so soon? You are being even more of an idiot than usual."

He shrugged and looked out the window. It was nice that Victoria had defended me—something I never thought would happen. It was like the two of them had switched roles. Matt really wasn't acting like himself. He had dark circles under his eyes like he had hardly slept. The way he rested his head against the window, looked like he had had a long night. However, being hung over and tired was no excuse for his bad attitude.

We spent the rest of the journey in silence until we eventually reached the tear in the veil. It had taken us most of the day to get back, and it was dark out. We got out of the sleigh and all waved to the driver as he drove off, except Matt. He still had his arms folded and was looking in the opposite direction. We said goodbye to Yuri and thanked her for her help. Matt did nothing but scowl.

I took hold of everyone. "We should be close enough to teleport now."

We landed outside Matt and Victoria's house and were pummelled by rain. Already, I missed the snow. We ran into the house. Next time, I would aim for inside the house. We were greeted by Mr. and Mrs. Street, who wanted to know all about our trip. Victoria and I told them everything that happened, while Matt sat silently in the corner, looking miserable. After a few refreshments, I teleported with Greg back to my house.

Everything was exactly the same as when we left. My dad hadn't even touched Greg's rabbit bed that I'd left in the hall. I threw my stuff down in my room and face-planted on my bed. It was nice to be home again and back in my own room. I had only been gone a few days, but it felt like a lot longer. Everything was dealt with for now, and I could chill out and be a normal girl again—at least for a little while.

Greg popped his head around the door. "Hey, I thought you said you were going to show me where this flat is my father found for me."

I rolled to the edge of my bed and sat up. "I did say that, but you shouldn't have let me come home first because now I don't want to leave."

"Don't worry about it. I will find it myself." Greg walked away.

"Wait," I shouted. Rain drops hammered against the glass of the window. I couldn't leave him to aimlessly wander around the village. It was likely I knew where this flat was. I could teleport him there and be back in bed in a couple of minutes.

"What's wrong?" he asked, reappearing in the doorway.

"I will take you there. Wouldn't want you getting lost, never to be seen again. What's the address?"

He handed me a piece of paper. I looked down at it and cringed. I definitely knew this place. You would have thought the council could have afforded something a bit nicer. I took his hand and teleported us under a tree opposite a block of flats. I had gotten us as close as possible without risking someone seeing us appear out of thin air. Even under the shelter of the tree, we were getting hit by rain.

"Are you sure you want to stay there? It's like, the worst place to live in town."

Greg shrugged. "The picture in the advertisement looked all right, and I haven't really got anywhere else to go."

"They always do," I muttered.

Greg walked across the road. I thought about just going back to the warmth of my dry house. I sighed as I ran after him.

I looked at the numbers on the building. "Seriously, you're on the top floor."

"Why don't you go back home where it is dry? I will be fine on my own from this point." Greg put his arm around me, nudging me toward the building and swapping places with me, sheltering me from the rain.

"Are you sure? I mean, shouldn't there be someone here to meet you and give you keys and stuff?"

"They said they would leave the keys under the doormat."

"Really? Who does that?"

"These people, obviously. Seriously, Mellissa, I will be fine. I will see you bright and early tomorrow morning for a whole day of lessons, as you insist on having three days to yourself for this Christmas thing."

"I am not agreeing to that," I said. "I now know what 'bright and early' really means to you."

"Fine, seven o'clock then."

"I was thinking more like after lunch, so like, half one-ish."

"You are going to have to start earlier than that to make up for the three days you want off."

"One o'clock."

"Eight."

"No, that is still too early."

"Nine o'clock, and I will buy you lunch."

I pushed my hair back. Nine o'clock was still too early, but I did like free food. "Half nine and you buy me lunch."

"Deal," he said, putting his hand out to me. We shook on it, and I teleported home.

"Mellissa," came my dad's voice. He walked out into the hallway. He went to hug me and then stopped. "You're soaked."

"Well, it is raining." I had only been out in the rain a few minutes, but I was wet through. My jeans stuck to my thighs and weighed a ton.

"You should have called. I would have picked you up."

"I thought you would still be at work."

"Why don't you get changed, then you can tell me all about your trip. I will order a takeaway for dinner. I haven't had time to go shopping."

I wasn't sure what I could tell him about my trip, but I was sure I could come up with something. "Sounds good. I noticed that we are sort of lacking in Christmas stuff." I waved my arms to gesture at the whole house. "You know, just because I'm not here doesn't mean you can't put up the decorations.”

“Well, since you weren’t here, I have been working late, so I haven’t had time. But because of that, I can now have New Year’s off to spend with you.”

“That’s great, Dad. I can’t remember the last time you didn’t work New Year’s.”

“I was thinking we could have a party this year. You can invite Matt and Victoria.”

My heart sank at the mention of the twins. As much as Victoria loved a good party, I wasn’t sure our newfound friendship extended to this side of the veil. I forced a smile, trying to not show what I was feeling. “That sounds great. Hey, could I invite another friend as well?”

“You have another friend to invite?”

“Don’t sound so shocked. I can make friends. I just usually choose not to.”

“Invite whoever you want.” My dad chuckled as he walked back into the living room. I ran upstairs. I put on a nice, dry pair of pyjamas and threw my wet clothes in the wash. I spent the rest of the evening watching a film with my dad and eating Chinese food. Things felt almost normal again.

That night, I went to sleep in my own bed, happy that things were going back to somewhat normal. I knew I couldn’t be completely normal again, but for now I was happy with how things were. As I closed my eyes, I saw a light come out of the Heart Crystal. I sat up to look at it, but it was inactive. I assumed it must have been a trick of the light. I put it back down on my bedside table and slowly drifted off to sleep.

I woke to rain hammering against my bedroom window. As cold as it was on the other side of the veil, I was missing the snow. It was way better than this downpour. I rolled over and looked at the clock on my bedside table. I jumped out of bed. It was already half nine. I ran to the bathroom and got myself dressed. I was going to lose my free lunch if I didn’t get there on time. I ran through the house, picking up my things, some of which I didn't really need, but it all got stuffed in my bag anyway. I opened the front door to rain bouncing off the gravel outside. What was I doing? I could just teleport there. I closed the door. There was no need for me to get soaked. I shut my eyes and thought about where I wanted to go.

I screamed as I slipped on something and fell on the floor. I wrinkled my nose as I was struck by the smell of damp.

"You're late," Greg said without looking up from what he was reading.

I got up and rubbed my side. "I overslept. I haven't even had breakfast yet."

"Who hasn't had breakfast by ten o'clock?"

"Me. I was too busy trying to get here on time so you wouldn't moan at me."

"Well, you failed. I don't understand how someone with your powers can ever be late."

I went to argue, but I found myself distracted by the conditions of my surroundings. I turned on the spot. This place was even more run-down inside than it was outside. It didn't look like it had ever been cleaned, and all the furniture was worn out. I had thought the smell of damp was because of the rain, but it was just this place's general odour. The cupboards on the wall were wonky, with doors hanging off, and only half the tiles in the tiny kitchen were still attached to the wall. The only decent thing in the room was the table Greg sat at. "Seriously, like what is up with this place? I can't believe you actually slept here last night."

"Yes, this place is not quite as advertised, but it will do."

I was gobsmacked. Considering he came from such a privileged background, he was taking this all really well. I would have freaked out the moment I opened the door. I screamed and jumped on a chair as I saw a creature run across the floor. "Was that a rat?"

"Oh, so you noticed Bill?" Greg put his book down on the table. "It is all right. We came to an understanding last night about our living arrangements."

"You named the rat."

"No, he told me his name."

"You speak rat?"

"I can speak to most animals when transformed."

That was actually an interesting fact. I would have been more impressed if I wasn't freaking out. I screamed again as a spider landed on my shoulder. I smacked it off as I jumped off the chair to get away from its web. I screamed as I saw the rat again and jumped back on the chair. I crouched down with my hands over my head.

"Will you stop screaming?" Greg asked.

"I can't help it. How can you be so chilled about this? That spider was the size of my fist."

"Your fist is quite small, and it is better than nothing. At least I have a roof over my head."

"A roof that's letting the rain in." I pointed to all the spots water was seeping through. "I can't take this anymore. We are going."

Greg laughed and didn't move from his seat.

"This is not funny," I shouted.

"It really is. You should see your face. I can't believe a little rat freaked you out this much."

"You are so mean," I said, standing up. "I'll just go without you."

"Wait." Greg got up, holding my arm. "Don't think you are getting out of training that easily."

I screamed as I saw that Bill had friends. I jumped forward, throwing my arms around Greg, and teleported home. Once again, I screamed as I fell backward. Greg grabbed hold of the banister and quickly pulled me toward him. I wrapped my arms around him and tensed my body. I had teleported us to the top of the stairs, and that could have gone really wrong.

"I should probably aim better next time," I said, looking at the bottom of the stairs.

"Yes, that would be a good idea," he said. "You could really hurt yourself. Your landings aren't great in the first place."

"Hey," I said, looking up at him. He was already looking down at me, and I was suddenly very aware of how close we currently were. I stepped back and turned. "Well, I will be going downstairs. We can figure out what we're doing in the kitchen."

I walked down the stairs, and Greg followed me out to the kitchen. I started rummaging through the cupboards for something to eat. There really wasn't much to choose from.

Greg sat at the table. "What are you doing?"

"Getting myself breakfast. What magic are we going to work on now?" I asked. "I mean, am I free to learn anything I want now?"

"Pretty much, but I am also here to teach you about council procedures and the customs of my world. You need to know about all the different species you are potentially responsible for."

"Oh, so like, no pressure."

"I said *potentially*. It will ultimately be your choice to take up the position of queen."

"Can I learn fire or ice magic then?"

"I can't teach you that. Battle magic is generally something you are born with, similar to a changeling's ability to shift or like your power to teleport. You have it or you don't."

"I can't learn battle magic then?" That was a bummer. Matt and Victoria's powers were really cool. "What can I learn then?"

"Spell casting, healing, defensive magic and potion making," Greg replied, "but I do believe that you have some sort of battle magic in you already."

I finally found something edible in the cupboards. I pulled out a fork and sat opposite Greg. "What do you mean? I can't shoot fireballs."

"The light energy you produced when sealing Kadon— that is a form of battle magic. It's a rare form, but from what I read, it is common amongst elf royalty. You also have plant magic. Most elves were experts in plant magic, and your display with the trees confirms it. Then, there is your teleporting and the time you shook the ground. You already know how to form a barrier thanks to the sealing spell, but we can expand on that—wait, are you eating cake for breakfast?"

I pointed my fork at him. "Technically, it's brunch, and

there was nothing else to eat. My dad didn't have time to go shopping while I was gone. I should probably go do some for him. Maybe we should cut this lesson short so I can go to the shop. I also need to get Christmas stuff."

"I haven't even started teaching you anything."

"I beg to differ. I have learnt that battle magic is something you are born with and not something you can be taught."

Greg leant one arm on the table. "Mellissa, we agreed you would spend today learning in exchange for having Christmas off."

"Come on, relax a little. We don't have any sort of deadline anymore. We can take our time with my training."

"There is taking things slow, and then there is not even starting."

"Fine. We can work till twelve, then we break for lunch, and we can go shopping at the same time. We can carry on in the afternoon. What ability are we going to look at first?"

Greg sat up straight and put his hands together on the table. "Plant magic. I have a few books on the subject." He waved his arm, and the table filled up with books. We obviously had different definitions for the word *few*. "We will also need a plant to play with."

I went and got one of the plants on the window ledge and placed it on the table. "Now what?"

"Well, you can either try communicating with it, or you can try to make it grow. Just try not to let it go crazy like in the forest."

I narrowed my eyes at him. He wasn't going to let me forget about that mishap anytime soon. I put my hands around the plant pot. When I communicated with the trees, they had been like voices in my head. I didn't actually know how I triggered it. "I have no idea how to do either of those things."

"You need to focus on the magic within you, then latch on to the life energy in the plant and imagine it growing. The process is similar to when you latched on to the object you wished to seal something in."

I felt ridiculous trying to talk to a plant. He made it

sound so easy. Shutting my eyes, I focused on the magic inside me. It felt like a burning sun within me. Opening my eyes, I held my hand up to the plant and tried to latch on to its energy. Light shot from my hand, and I screamed as the plant caught fire. Greg jumped to his feet, flicking his wrist. A barrier formed around the fire, and it slowly dwindled.

"Maybe we should be working on your light magic then."

"This is hopeless," I said, lying across two of the kitchen table chairs.

"Don't be like that. You performed magic."

"But that wasn't what I was trying to do."

"You just need to focus. Learn to distinguish how your different abilities feel," Greg said. "Maybe you should read some of these books on plant magic yourself."

I put my arm over my face. "Or maybe I don't have the natural ability to do plant magic. What happened in the forest may have just been a fluke."

"I highly doubt that." Greg knelt beside me. "When you used your powers, you were feeling strong emotions, but depending on the emotion, the power you displayed changed."

"Right, like when the first time I teleported I was scared?"

"Exactly, and on the boat, you were anxious. When you shook the ground, you were angry."

"And when I used light magic, I was scared again, but not for myself, for Matt."

Greg stood while taking my hands, forcing me up. "Yes, but you can't rely on those emotions to trigger your power. I have an idea."

"What?" I asked.

"We are going to meditate."

We cleared space in the living room and sat on the floor cross-legged. Greg went through some relaxation techniques with me. At first, I felt ridiculous, but after a while, I closed my eyes, shutting everything out except the sound of his voice, and it really relaxed me. "Good," Greg said. "Now that you are relaxed, look within, at your magic. What does it feel like?"

"A burning sun." I felt his hands on mine. He turned them around so my palms were facing up. My palms were warm.

"That's your light magic. What else do you feel?"

"I don't know. It's just the sun. There's nothing else."

"Take deep breaths and focus on your magic. Are you sure there is nothing else?"

I did as he said. He was right. There was more. "There's a beat, like a drum, and something hard on the surface."

"Good, focus on that."

I focused on the beat. It was a constant *patter-pat-pat*. I let the beat fill me and tapped it out on my knee. Greg gasped. I opened my eyes. The plants on the window ledge had come to life. I gaped at them as they grew. I moved my arm left and right, and the plants followed. I could feel them, their life force like little heartbeats, drumming to the same beat as me.

"I told you the forest wasn't a one-off."

I dropped my arm, and the plants stopped moving. "It was a one-off because it won't happen again. I don't want to lose control like that ever again."

"And that's why we practice. Now that you know how to access this power, we can work on your ability to manipulate plants, then work our way up to making things grow from scratch."

"Aren't you getting a bit ahead of yourself? I think we should have a snack break." I was starving. I hadn't realised how hungry meditation could make you.

"But we've only just made some progress."

I glanced up at the clock. "Seriously, is that the time? No wonder I'm hungry. It's already past one. It's defo time for a break." I got up and stretched. We'd been sat on the floor for ages.

Greg also got up. "But Mellissa—"

"No, we agreed to have a break at midday, and you owe me lunch."

"I don't owe you anything. You didn't show up on time."

I poked him in the chest. "What? How could you play

me like that? It was the whole reason I got up this morning."

"You only got up because of the promise of food and not the excitement to learn something new."

"Well, yeah."

Greg put his head in his hands. "I'm starting to see why you and Matt are such good friends."

I didn't get what his problem was. It was the school holidays. It was meant to be two weeks of getting up late and pretty much doing whatever I wanted. Instead, I was stuck with him bossing me about. Maybe I should go back to the magic world and become queen, then I would be bossing him about. There was no deadline on me learning any of this stuff. He needed to learn to relax.

I pulled at his arm. "Look, I promise to stop complaining and try even harder after I've had something to eat. Oh, and been shopping. I really need to get some food in this house."

Greg looked down at me. "Fine."

"Yes!" I shouted, running out of the living room and pulling Greg along behind me.

"Why must you drag me?" he asked.

"Because you don't know how to move with excitement." I grabbed a coat and was still running as I teleported us into town.

Act of Kindness
Gregory

reg stepped back as he looked at the garland he'd just hung. He had no idea how he had ended up doing this. They were meant to spend the whole day on magic lessons, yet somehow Mellissa had gotten him to help her put these ridiculous things all around her house.

"What are these decorations for exactly?" he asked.

"Christmas," she replied, balancing on a chair, trying to put up another strand of garland on the other side of the room. If she wasn't careful, she would fall off, which was highly likely. She was probably the clumsiest person he had ever met.

Greg walked over and took it off her, placing it effortlessly where she'd struggled to reach. "Yes, I know that, but what purpose do they serve?"

"To make the place look festive. Surely you have special occasions you celebrate in the magic world."

"Well, we have the coming of winter festival, but we don't decorate our homes. We just light up the city. There are also the solstices."

"I bet Novosvillas looks amazing all lit up."

Greg smiled. "Yes, it does." He looked down at the floor as his smile faded. He had missed this year's festival as he'd been in the human world searching for the keeper of the Heart Crystal. It was one of the few times his father's position as elder was fun. He always got the best view of the lights. It was something he actually enjoyed doing with his father each year.

When he had left this time, his father still hadn't been

happy with him for disagreeing with him. He had discovered that his father voted in favour of Lady Gabrielle's proposal for Mellissa to go back home, but that didn't seem to change his father's disappointment in him. Greg shook his head. He was done seeking his father's approval. He was doing what he thought was right from now on. Although, putting up Christmas decorations had not been on his agenda for the day.

"Mellissa, we should be getting back to learning magic," Greg said. "We have wasted enough time with shopping."

"I'm not finished yet. Besides, I don't count lunch and that shopping trip as a break, since you spent the whole time explaining council regulations and quizzing me."

"Well, you need to learn about that stuff, as well as developing your powers."

"Yes, you have told me that at least three times today, but right now, I would like to do something that doesn't involve me having to think too much."

He'd been trying to make the most of the time they had, but she kept trying to waste it. Mellissa climbed onto the coffee table and leant on the fireplace as she tried to hang something above it. Her struggle was fairly amusing. Greg walked over and took the string of lights off her.

"You really need to stop balancing on furniture like that before you hurt yourself. Besides, there is a better way for you to do it."

She folded her arms. "And how's that?"

"Magic." Greg flicked his wrist, creating a small horizontal barrier. He stepped onto it, then created another, slightly higher than the other, putting one foot on it. "It's just a variation on the barrier I have taught you."

She walked around the barriers. "How is this safer than balancing on furniture? At that angle, I can barely see the barrier."

"But you can feel the magic. Just give it a try. It's exactly the same spell, just angle it differently."

"Fine." She flicked her wrist. "Disseptum." A barrier formed in front of her at an angle. She pouted as her shoulders slumped. "I can't exactly walk on a slope."

"No, but you can slide down it." Mellissa glared at him. Greg laughed, jumping from his steps. "All you have to do is flick your wrist at a slight angle." He took her wrist, showing her the direction she should move.

"Disseptum." With a slight change in angle, she flicked her wrist. The barrier appeared horizontally. She stepped on it, casting the spell again and again until she was high enough to reach the ceiling. Greg passed her the fairy lights, and she hung them up. She ran down a couple of steps, then jumped into Greg's arms with a squeal. "Okay, that is a cool trick to know."

"A little warning before you jump next time, please." She stuck her tongue out at him. "Well, next we can work on you not having to say the spell out loud."

She flicked his nose. "No, we are going to decorate the tree."

Mellissa ran out of the room and returned with two more bags of decorations and dropped them beside an artificial tree in front of the window. Greg looked up at it. It almost reached the ceiling. "I still don't understand the purpose of the tree."

"Well, Christmas is all about giving gifts to the people you care about, and that's where we put them until we give them out."

As usual, her answers didn't really explain anything. He was starting to think she didn't actually know the answers herself. She just blindly followed the customs she'd been taught. She had probably never questioned them. He couldn't really blame her. He had spent a long time blindly following his father's example without question. At least she appeared to be doing this all because she actually wanted to and enjoyed it.

Mellissa's head popped out from behind the Christmas tree. "You know what? I will take you to the library next week, and you can look up the origins of all our Christmas traditions if you want. I know I don't quite have the answers you want. I don't question things as much as you do."

"I would like that." She was more insightful than he gave her credit for. He had been reluctant to share anything about himself when they'd met. He hadn't deemed it as necessary. Yet somehow, it was almost like she knew what he was thinking.

The bright lights of a car shone through the front window. Mellissa looked outside. "My dad's back early."

"I guess that's my cue to go." Annoyingly, she had succeeded in getting out of more magic practice. Why was it so hard to keep her on track?

"Well, actually, I may have already let my dad know I was going to have a friend over."

"You did what?" he asked. "I thought you wanted to keep magic away from your dad."

"I'm not going to tell him you're a changeling," she said, looking at him like he was an idiot. "You are just my friend who needs somewhere stay."

"I do not. I have a place to live. It may not be up to your standards, but it is just fine."

"Living with that much damp is a health risk. In case you haven't noticed, it's been raining all day, and there are holes in the roof of that place. Also, let's not forget the rats. You should be happy I am being so nice, especially considering I know how annoying you are."

"What is your problem with Bill?" Greg asked.

"Stop talking about that rat like it's a person!"

"Mellissa," came Mr. Hail's voice, "why are you shouting?"

Mellissa leapt across the room to stand in the doorway. She blocked her father's path into the living room. She gave him a massive grin. "Nothing is wrong, Dad. You're home early."

"There wasn't much to do today, so I left early," he replied. "Which twin is over today?"

"Neither." She stepped back, letting her dad walk in the room. His face dropped as he saw Greg. "This is Greg—you know, the friend I told you about. Because Matt is not my only friend, you know."

Mr. Hail rubbed his chin. "When you said you were having a friend stay, I thought you meant Victoria."

"Hey, I never said that," Mellissa said. "And you can't

change your mind now. He is practically a homeless person."

"What do you mean *homeless*?" Mr. Hail asked, shocked. "Where are your parents?"

"I am not homeless. I have a place to live," Greg replied. "It was nice to meet you, Mr. Hail. I don't want to be a bother to anyone, so I will just go."

"Greg, do not move," Mellissa demanded, putting her arm up in front of him. He froze on the spot. And she called *him* bossy. She turned to her father. "Dad, can we talk in the hall for a moment?"

Mr. Hail followed his daughter out of the room. Greg couldn't hear what they were saying, but he was sure he was the topic of discussion. He didn't understand why she was being so persistent about this. He thought she would be happy to be rid of him, as she was always complaining how annoying he was. Although, the rats had really freaked her out. They weren't the sort of thing that bothered him. However, she did have a point about the roof and damp. It would be nice to stay somewhere warm and dry again. That flat didn't even have heat. How had his father managed to get him somewhere so horrible to live? Maybe he had done it on purpose. This was his punishment for not agreeing with his plan for Mellissa.

Mellissa and Mr. Hail walked back in the room. Mr. Hail walked over to him and clasped his shoulder. "Mellissa has explained everything. You can stay in the guest room until you find somewhere new. How could your father leave the country and let you live like that?"

Mellissa waved her hands at him from behind her dad and mouthed, *"Just go with it!"* What had she told him exactly? "You really don't have to," Greg replied. "I wouldn't want to be in your way. Bill and I have come to an agreement on our living arrangements."

"Who is Bill?" Mr. Hail asked.

"Bill is one of the rats," Mellissa said. "I told you, he thinks it's normal to have a family of rats as roommates."

Mr. Hail patted Greg's shoulder. "I insist. I couldn't in good conscience let you go back there."

"Thank you, Mr. Hail."

"Well, I am going to put on some dinner. Mellissa can show you to the guest room and explain the rules we agreed on." Mr. Hail gave Greg a sympathetic smile and left the room. This was the first time he had met him properly. Her father had no reason to show him any sort of concern, but he had. Greg wasn't used to people doing things simply out of the kindness of their heart.

"Your dad is really nice, but what exactly did you tell him?" Greg asked.

Mellissa shrugged. "I told him everything that's wrong with your place. He, unlike you, understands that rats are not good flatmates, and no heating can lead to health issues. Come on, I will show you the guest room."

Greg followed her up the stairs. "Since when does my health concern you?"

"Since I met you. I don't want to catch a nasty disease from you. You could be dying from the plague, and you'd still insist on being up bright and early for my training."

"I am not that bad."

Mellissa stopped at the door farthest from the stairs. "Well, this will be your room for now. I would give you a tour of the house, but you know where everything is, as you've already secretly been living here. The main rules you need to know are that we stay out of each other's room after hours and you are to help with stuff around the house." She gasped, and her hand shot to her mouth. "Oh, no. We need to come up with a story for how we met."

"How about you just tell your dad the truth about magic?"

"Let me think about that." Mellissa put her finger over her mouth and then pointed at him. "No."

"Fine. We met at the library."

Mellissa eyes sparkled. "That's a great idea. We can go get your stuff later, if you want."

"It's fine. I should be able to summon it from here."

"Cool, can you show me how you do it?" He nodded. She grabbed his arm. "Oh crap, I should tell my dad you're a vegetarian."

She ran downstairs. He would never understand her train of thought. Greg went into the guest room and looked around. This was probably the only room he hadn't been in. It had a simple layout. There was a double bed against the back wall, with a bedside cabinet on both sides. The butterfly bedding and curtains were obviously chosen by Mellissa. A wardrobe stood next to the window, which looked out onto the back garden. He had to admit, it was a lot nicer here. There was only so much magic could do to make his other place decent. The floor was covered by a soft carpet rather than the rubbery one back at that flat. To top it off, there was heating.

The Eve of Christmas
Mellissa

The smell of my dad cooking breakfast drifted up the stairs. I opened my curtains. It was nice to see it wasn't raining again. Although, the dark clouds in the sky suggested the dry spell wouldn't last. Hopefully, it would last long enough for me to go shopping with my dad. He had arranged a late start at work, and we would get everything we needed for the next day. We did this every year on Christmas Eve. It was just the two of us, so our Christmas dinner didn't need much planning. I skipped downstairs to the kitchen.

"Morning, sweetie," my dad said, filling a plate with food. It was no surprise that Greg was already up and sat at the table eating. I really didn't know how he functioned getting up so early every day.

"Morning, Mellissa. I understand that today is the eve of Christmas. Are there any traditions that go with this day?" Greg asked.

"Well, this morning, my dad and I are going shopping, but then in the afternoon, I will open your mind to all things Christmas. We will make cookies and cakes, go carol-singing and see the singing elves. Matt and I usually go see whatever Christmas film they have out. Oh, and decorating gingerbread houses is a must."

My dad joined us at the table with a plate of food for himself and one for me. "I am sure he will be all Christmas-ed out once you and Matt are done with him."

"Matt will be around today?" Greg asked. "We haven't seen him in a couple of days."

I looked down at my plate. I hadn't seen Matt since we had got back from the magic world. At least Victoria had rung to check on me. She had said Matt had had the flu since we returned and was locked away in his room ignoring everyone. But that didn't explain why he hadn't responded to any of my texts. I had texted him last night to remind him about today, and again, he hadn't replied. I just hoped he was feeling better and would turn up.

"Um, yeah. He should be," I said. "We do this stuff every year."

"Are you sure you will be all right here on your own while we go out?" Dad asked Greg.

"He will be fine," I said. "He will probably spend the time reading, as learning new things is such fun."

"You say that like it is a bad thing." Greg got up from the table. "Thanks for the food, Mr. Hail. You are a wonderful cook. I see where Mellissa gets her cooking ability from." Greg left the room.

My dad glared at me from across the table. I wasn't sure what I had done wrong. "When exactly did you cook for that boy?" he asked, pointing in the direction Greg had just gone.

I stuffed a load of food in my mouth to give me time to think. This was meant to be the first time Greg had been here. He shouldn't have eaten anything I'd cooked before.

"At a cooking class." It was the first thing that popped into my head. "You remember, right? The one I went to with Matt. He thought it might be a good way to pick up girls who were able to cook. It just so happened Greg was also part of that class. Yeah, that's what happened." I smiled awkwardly at my dad. I don't think he believed me. I didn't believe me. I should have just said Greg had been around before while he was working. He worked late often enough. Lying to my dad was something I didn't do often, so I was far from good at it.

I finished my food and ran away. I barged into the guest room. Greg was sat on the bed but jumped up as I stormed in the room. "You almost got me caught in a lie," I said, jabbing my finger in his face.

Greg pushed my hand to the side. "What are you talking

about?"

"You haven't been here before, remember? I haven't been secretly feeding you for weeks, and you don't know whether I can cook or not."

"Sorry about that. I didn't think." He sat back down. "However, you do realise I'm not the one forcing you to lie to your dad. It was your choice not to tell him about magic."

He was right. The decision not to tell my dad the truth had nothing to do with Greg. It had been my choice. I was too scared to tell him the truth. I had no idea how he would react or if he would believe me.

"It's not the easiest subject to bring up. What am I meant to say? *Hey, Dad, did you know mum's side of the family were elves, and oh, my friend here can turn into a rabbit.* He'd think I'd lost my mind."

"I will happily help you explain everything to him, if you want. I can actually demonstrate my ability to turn into a rabbit or any other animal, as there are lots of animals I can change into."

It was a nice offer, but I wasn't ready to have the "magic is real" conversation with my dad. "I will get back to you when I'm ready to talk to my dad, and I know you don't only transform into a rabbit." I walked off to get ready to go out.

I headed into the house and put all the shopping away. As expected, Greg was in the living room reading. I looked at the clock. It was already past one. Matt should have already been here. He was probably just running late. It wouldn't hurt to start without him. I grabbed Greg's book out of his hands.

"Hey, what are you doing?" he asked.

I pointed to the door. "To the kitchen. These cookies aren't going to make themselves."

"I thought you were doing all that stuff with Matt. I was going to observe, so I could learn about your customs."

"Well, he's not here yet, so I'll have to make do with you as my assistant. If we don't start now, we won't fit everything in." I pulled at Greg's arm. I almost fell backward when he got up.

"Fine, but you do realise I don't bake."

"Like never?" I asked. He shook his head. "Well, don't worry. I'll be doing all the hard stuff."

I ran to the kitchen and pulled out all the ingredients needed. Greg lagged behind me and leant on the counter when he finally made it to the kitchen. This was exactly what I'd meant about him not moving with excitement. I picked up a handful of flour and flicked it at him.

"Hey!" he shouted. "What was that for?"

"I only want happy faces in my kitchen," I said. "At least pretend to be excited."

"You know what? You're crazy."

"Old news much?" I handed him a mixing bowl, and I got out another one for myself. I measured out ingredients while telling Greg what to do. I'd made this recipe so many times before, I knew it off the top of my head.

The first batch of cookies cooled on the side, and I put the second lot in the oven. That was when it dawned on me that Matt still hadn't shown up. He was more than a little late now. I went and checked my phone to see if he had messaged me. Nothing.

"Is something wrong?" Greg asked.

"It's just, Matt is really late. I'm just going to ring him to check he's all right." I tapped on Matt's name. It went straight to voice mail. I tried again only to have the same thing happen. This wasn't like Matt. He was permanently attached to his phone. If he didn't answer a call, he would usually call back within seconds. What if something bad had happened to him?

"I'll be right back." I disappeared in a burst of bright light. I looked up at the house I'd materialised in front of and knocked on the door. Victoria answered.

"Mellissa, what are you doing here?" she asked.

"Is Matt here?" I asked.

She tilted her head sideways and lifted her top lip. "He left ages ago. I assumed to meet you."

"Well we never actually made any plans but he usually

is round by midday to start making cookies. You don't think something's wrong? I haven't heard from him since we got back."

"Really?" she asked, sounding surprised. "He left really early this morning, seeming to miraculously recover from the flu."

I looked down at the ground. "Maybe he doesn't want to see me but doesn't know how to tell me. I'll just get going then."

I turned to leave, but Victoria reached out and put her hand on my shoulder. "Mellissa, I'm sure that is not the case. He was really ill. After you dropped us off the other day, he deteriorated fast. He looked awful and didn't leave his room for two days." She sighed and shrugged. "As for today, I don't know. He is probably just hanging out with some of the guys from school. You know what an idiot he turns into when he hangs around those douchebags."

I gave her a small smile, even though smiling was the last thing I felt like doing. "Yeah, sure."

"Don't worry. I'll let him know what a terrible person he is when he gets home. Even I know about the stupidly childish things you two always do on Christmas Eve."

"Thanks," I said before teleporting back home.

As I materialised in the kitchen, I was hit by a cloud of smoke and the high-pitched ringing of the smoke alarms. Greg was frantically running water over a tray of burnt cookies.

"What the hell, Greg?"

Greg jumped and turned round with a startled look on his face. "I don't know what happened. They just went up in smoke. You left without much warning, and I told you I didn't know what I was doing."

I climbed on the kitchen worktop and opened both windows to let the smoke out. "How the hell do you burn cookies this badly?"

"Your oven doesn't work on magic energy."

"Of course it doesn't work on magic energy!" I snapped, jumping off the worktop.

"I told you I couldn't bake."

"How hard is it to take some cookies out of the oven before they burn to a crisp?"

"I said I was sorry. One batch of burnt cookies isn't the end of the word."

I sat at the kitchen table, my head in my hands. The cookies weren't even what I was mad about. Yes, it was annoying, but it was easily fixed. Where was Matt? We did the same thing every year. How could he just ditch me like this? I thought everything would go back to normal on this side of the veil, but it hadn't. I had to face it: things weren't going to be the same anymore. I had these new powers and loads of responsibility thrust upon me. But why should that change my friendship with Matt? He had been ill according to Victoria but that didn't explain today.

"Mellissa, where's Matt?" Greg asked. "I thought when you disappeared that might have been where you were going."

Why did he have to ask that? I didn't really want to talk about it. However, it wasn't a subject I could avoid. It was quite apparent he wasn't going to show up. I sat up and leant back in my chair. "I don't know where he is and neither does Victoria. He appears to have gotten a better offer for how to spend the day but didn't bother to tell me. You know what? I don't care. He can do what he wants."

"If you don't care, why are you so upset?"

"I am not upset," I shouted, standing up and slamming my hands on the table. "I am angry. How dare he just toss me aside like yesterday's news? I have been nothing but a good friend to him since, like, forever. He could have at least sent me a text."

"Maybe he just forgot," Greg suggested. "I am sure there is a reasonable explanation. Just give him a chance to explain."

"No!" I yelled, throwing my arms in the air and pacing the length of the room. "You don't just forget a tradition you do every year, and I texted him last night. Also, how do you expect me to let him explain when he won't answer my calls? He obviously doesn't care."

"I know for a fact that Matt cares about you. It has been

very apparent from the moment I met him."

"Well, he's got a funny way of showing it. He has been off with me ever since we came back from the magic world. In fact, it was after I woke up from sleeping all day."

"Did you ever think it's me he has a problem with and not you?" Greg asked as he leant against the kitchen worktop.

I stopped pacing. "What makes you think that?" I couldn't think of anything Greg could have done to offend Matt. Last time I checked, they were getting along, and he was also the only person Matt hadn't insulted on the way home.

"It was quite obvious he didn't like me when we met. He threatened me with fire, just like his mother."

I turned away from him and burst out laughing. My anger dissipated as I thought of Matt threatening Greg. The image was comical.

"Why is that so funny?"

I cleared my throat. "I'm sorry. It's not funny to threaten someone. It's just, I can't imagine it."

"Really? After everything we've been through, you can't imagine it? Matt was extremely worried about your safety."

My smile slowly faded. I looked down at the floor. Matt may have been concerned about me back then, but he wasn't now. I just wished I knew what I had done wrong, then maybe I could fix things. I squealed as I was hit by a dust cloud of flour.

"What the hell, Greg?"

He shrugged at me with a smirk on his face. "Only happy faces in the kitchen, remember? It's your rule. I'm only enforcing it." I went to grab the bag of flour, but he picked it up before me. "You can't retaliate. I'm not frowning at the floor like you."

"It doesn't apply the other way around," I yelled. "Now, give me the flour." I tried to take the bag out of his hand, but he lifted it out of my reach. I had appreciated our height difference when he was helping me put up the Christmas decorations, but now, it was extremely frustrating. He was finding this way too amusing. I jumped up, trying to take the bag from him, but knocked it out of his grasp instead. I dropped to the floor to try to catch it, but I wasn't fast enough. The bag bust as it hit the ground, sending flour flying all over the room. I slumped down on the floor. "Now, look what you've done." I gestured to the mess of a kitchen.

Greg sat beside me. "This is just as much your fault."

"You know what? I blame Matt. None of this would've happened if he had just turned up."

"Why is today so important? I thought the important day was tomorrow." I wrapped my finger in a loose curl. I wasn't sure how to answer. "You don't have to tell me if you don't want to."

"No, it's fine," I said, leaning against a cupboard. "You're right. Tomorrow is the main day. But you see, I don't really have any family other than my dad, and he works a lot. So, I spend a lot of time alone. Matt is like the sibling every only child wants. He's the one that came up with all the stuff we do on Christmas Eve just so I wouldn't spend it alone. When he didn't show up, it hurt."

"I can understand that."

That was right. Greg's dad was probably away from home a lot more than mine, meaning being left alone was something we had in common. However, we weren't alone now. We had each other. I picked up a handful of flour off the floor and threw it at Greg.

"Hey!" he yelled. "No retaliation, remember?"

"I never agreed to that." I gathered up another handful of flour, but before I could throw it, Greg dropped two handfuls over my head. I shrieked, throwing my handful.

Greg laughed. "You have really bad aim."

"Well, maybe if I didn't have flour in my eyes…"

"I can help with that." Greg leant over and wiped the flour from my face.

I shivered and slid closer to Greg. I wanted to curl up in his lap and forget about my worries. Biting my lip, I shook my head. What was I thinking?

Greg interlaced his fingers with mine. "Hey, are you okay?"

I looked up at him, and our eyes met. His eyes

shimmered. I really could've lost myself in his stare. I leant forward.

"Mellissa." We both jumped to our feet at the sound of my name. Victoria was in the kitchen doorway, eyebrows raised. "Do I even want to know what you two were doing?"

I dusted myself off. "Baking mishap. What are you doing here? Wait, how did you get in? You better not have broken the door down again."

"You left the door unlocked this time."

Of course, I had left the door unlocked for Matt, but he hadn't bothered to show up. "That still doesn't explain why you're here. You could've just called to check up on me."

"After I realised Matt had stood you up, I thought I'd take you to this party I'm going to. You know, to cheer you up, but I see someone already beat me to it."

"Oh," I said. She nodded behind me. I turned and looked at Greg, who was also covered in flour. "Oh, no—I mean, yeah—no. Wait, what?"

Victoria rolled her eyes. "Do you want to come to this party or what? I suppose Flopsey can come too."

"Okay. I'll have to get changed," I said, regaining my composure.

"Of course. Go get a shower, and I'll pick you an outfit." I nodded. She looked Greg up and down. "It's a fairly casual party. I assume you can sort yourself out."

I followed Victoria up to my room, leaving Greg to do his own thing. Victoria threw her coat onto my bed. I raised an eyebrow. "I thought this was a casual party," I said.

She was wearing a tight-fitting red dress with lacy sleeves. It came to the middle of her thighs, showing off her long legs.

"It is." She spun round. "This is my casual party dress." Victoria went over to my wardrobe and flicked through my clothes, making faces at everything. I went into my bathroom and left her to it.

When I returned, she'd laid a simple black dress on the bed and a pair of ankle boots. I slipped the dress on. Victoria dragged me to my desk. She spun me around in the chair while messing with my hair. She dried it and rubbed some hair lotion in. Then she braided my hair, leaving the ends free to hang over my shoulder. Spinning the chair around so I was facing her, she pulled a few curls loose to hang on the other side of my face.

She frowned. "I suppose it will do. I can't believe you don't own any heels."

"They hurt my feet," I said.

"You will never get used to them if you don't try." Victoria grabbed her coat off my bed. "Come on. Let's go."

I followed her downstairs. She shouted for Greg, and he walked out of the kitchen. He was flour-free, in a fresh pair of jeans and a dark shirt. Victoria told me where the party was—some club in town. Kit Harrington was one of the most popular guys at our school. Apparently his parents had spent a fortune renting the place out for this party of his. A party I had known nothing about until Victoria told me. My chest tightened. What if Matt was there? He was popular enough to be invited, and instead of telling me about it, he had ditched me. I shook my head. It didn't matter if he was. I would ignore him like he'd ignored me and enjoy myself with the people that hadn't ditched me. I took both their hands and teleported.

Loud music blasted all around me. Flashing lights darted around the dance floor. I was probably the only one not dancing or at the bar. Instead, I sat at a table in the corner, stirring my drink. It was a cocktail of some sort that Victoria had picked. She had roped me into going to the bar earlier, as I was actually legally allowed to buy drinks, and she wasn't. I had no idea what to get myself, so I just got two of what she wanted. I had been back to the bar a few times on her behalf, but this was only my second drink. It was some fruity cocktail and was actually really nice, but I just wasn't feeling it.

Victoria, of course, was on the dance floor. It was hard to see her through the crowd, but occasionally, I would catch a glimpse of her glossy blonde hair and red dress. Greg had left me to go to the bathroom and never made it back. A group of giggling girls had him corned—the sort that always seemed to be drawn to Matt. I sure knew how to pick friends. Basically, they were all way more attractive than me and knew how to carry a conversation. At least they seemed to be having fun. I glanced over at Greg. One of the girls was stroking his arm, while another laid her hand on his shoulder. I gritted my teeth. Maybe I should just head home. This wasn't my sort of thing. I would find Victoria and tell her thanks for bringing me, but I was going. Wouldn't want her to realise I had left without telling her and go all crazy guardian on me. I downed my drink and got up, walking straight into Greg.

"Hey," he said, taking my hand. "No more sitting in the corner. Let's dance."

"What?"

He pulled me onto the dance floor, spinning me around. I looked back at the group of girls he had been talking to. They were all glaring at me. When he pulled me back to him, I wrapped my arms around his neck. Standing on my tiptoes, I whispered in his ear.

"You're using me to get away from those girls."

"They are very pushy," he said into my ear, "and wouldn't take no for an answer, till I told them I was here with you."

"So, you lied."

"No, I am here with you. Victoria would never have invited me if it weren't for you."

"Not true."

He raised an eyebrow. It was completely true. Victoria only invited me because she felt sorry for me. The problem was, we didn't really like the same sorts of things. Although, since Greg had dragged me onto the dance floor, I was having more fun. The music changed, and the crowd cheered and jumped about, separating me from Greg. I tried to make my way back to him but couldn't. Arms flew about, and I was elbowed and shoved. I wriggled my way out of the crowd. It would be easier to stand off to the side and let him find me. Someone grabbed my wrist.

"Greg, I—" My words caught in my throat. It wasn't

Greg. A tall, muscular man looked down at me with dark grey eyes. He had long, black hair tied in a ponytail.

"Are you here alone?" he asked.

"No, I'm not." I tried to pull my wrist free, but his grip was like iron.

He growled, dragging me out of the back.

"Let go of me. Help!" I shouted, but no one could hear me over the loud music. I was tossed through a door and landed on wet concrete. It had been raining while we were inside. I got to my feet and ran. Someone grabbed me, throwing me to the ground. I felt a knee press into my back.

"I know you like to play with your prey, but remember what the boss said about her powers. We don't want her getting away."

I was pulled up by my hair, and then those grey eyes were staring at me again. "I suppose you're right."

I shivered. "What do you want with me?"

"Not you as such. The master wants your power, and who are we to deny that to him?"

I threw my hands in his face, releasing light. He cried out in pain, and his grip on my hair loosened. Before I could think, the other one grabbed my arm, twisting it around behind me. He pulled my other arm, forcing my hands together. "Knock her out."

The big guy marched over. I'd burned his face. "With pleasure." He drew back his fist. I shut my eyes, waiting for an explosion of pain. It never came. Instead, I felt an icy wind surround me. My arms were released, and I tumbled forward.

"Mellissa, teleport now!" Victoria yelled, firing ice at both men. I didn't move. I wanted to run, but my legs wouldn't work. "Mellissa!" Victoria screamed. She spun around, shooting ice shards as one of the guys ran at me. I shook myself. I needed to get out of there, but I wasn't going to leave Victoria behind to fight alone.

As I went to grab her hand, I was hit hard in the side. Everything went sideways as I crashed into the ground. A woman had come out of nowhere and taken me down. I struggled on the ground under her grip. She was very strong. I could hardly move. Victoria ran toward me but was grabbed by one of the men. She spun round, freezing his arm and smashing it with a swift kick. The man yelled, clasping what was left of his arm. Victoria had her own battle to fight; I needed to get myself out of this. I tried to summon light energy, but it wasn't working. Why hadn't I teleported away when Victoria had said? I had been too scared to move at first, and now that fear was about to get me killed.

An icy mist covered the area. It must've been Victoria's doing. This was my chance. I teleported across the alley. It was enough to put the woman off balance. I kicked up and tried to run, but the woman moved with speed like I'd never seen before. Before I knew what was happening, I hit the pavement. With her knees across my chest and arms, she leant forward, digging her claws into my arm. I cried out in pain.

"Quit your struggling, elf. I wouldn't want to accidentally kill you." She raised her hand, and her claws grew in length. I screamed as her hand came down to cut me. A burst of light struck her from the Heart Crystal around my neck. I scrambled to my feet and began to run, but she grabbed my foot, causing me to fall back down. I kicked at her with my free foot, forcing her to let go. Then I teleported out of her reach, but I didn't go far.

Victoria was a better fighter than me, but I couldn't leave her there to fight three assailants on her own. However, this mist of hers didn't make it easy to find her. Finally, I spotted Victoria in the mist and ran toward her, but something caught hold of my hair and pulled me back. It was the woman again. She dragged me toward her and smacked me into the hard pavement. A metallic taste filled my mouth as my bottom lip split open. She stamped her foot on my chest and lifted her hand to strike me again. I shut my eyes and teleported. I hit the pavement behind her and rolled up to my feet. I took a deep breath and focused on the magic within me. The woman spun around and went to slash me. Her movements were almost as quick as my teleporting. I put my hands together and released a ray of light. She went flying back. Unfortunately, she was apparently extremely strong and got up like my attack was nothing. She ran at me just as a tiger jumped out of the mist and bit down on her arm, throwing her back into the mist and out of my sight. I shuffled backward. My mouth went dry. All I could hear were roars and the occasional scream.

The mist cleared. Victoria stood next to the tiger, surrounded by three ice statues. The tiger stepped forward and shifted into Greg. I ran into his arms, burying my face in his chest, and burst into tears. Greg clutched my shoulders and held me at arm's length.

"Are you hurt?" he asked. I shook my head. He wiped my tears and looked me up and down. He put his finger on my cut lip. I winced. "Don't worry. It's easily healed."

"We need to get out of here," Victoria said. "I don't know how long they'll stay frozen."

"Who—what are they?"

"Leprechauns. Now, we have to go." She took my hand.

Holding tightly to her and Greg, I teleported.

Regroup
Gregory

They sat around the kitchen table back at Mellissa's. Greg had healed the cut on her lip and the scratches on her arm. Other than that, she hadn't suffered any other injuries. Mellissa slowly sipped the cup of tea he'd made her. Greg's own drink remained untouched, and Victoria had turned hers to ice in silent anger.

"What were those leprechauns doing on this side of the veil?" snapped Victoria, breaking the silence.

"I don't know," Greg replied. "Their magic wasn't that strong. They were more brute strength than anything. They shouldn't have been able to cross."

"And why attack now? They have been living on the edge of society without a peep for years now."

"Yes, but there were no elves around to direct their hate toward."

"What have the elves ever done to them?"

"Nothing. It's our people that pushed them to the edge of society, the original council who refused them representation and brought about their poverty."

Victoria threw her arm to the side. "Exactly."

"But Freya sealing Kadon and her death created a power void. A void that our ancestors filled by forming the council. If it wasn't for Freya's actions the council wouldn't exist."

"Freya did what was right. Kadon would have destroyed the world," Victoria said. "And by what you have said, they should hate all magical beings *except* the elves. None of this has anything to do with Mellissa."

"I know none of it has anything to do with her, but it's about what she represents."

"And what's that, peace and love?"

"The person who got rid of the last great ruler who demanded respect for the leprechauns."

Victoria gagged. "Kadon, a great ruler? You have got to be kidding me. He was a monster."

"I know that, and you know that, but you have to account for other biases and tunnel vision."

"I do not! I will go find this group of leprechauns and crush them."

Greg rubbed his chin. "I don't understand how they could cross the veil with such low levels of magic."

"Maybe it was their master." Mellissa's voice sounded like a squeak.

They both turned to look at her. "What master?" asked Victoria.

"The leprechauns said something about their master wanting my power. It's why they wanted me alive. Otherwise—" She dropped her head.

"This complicates things," Greg said. "This isn't a simple hate crime anymore. Whoever this master is, he has to be strong to bring others through the veil with him."

"But if he is so strong, why didn't he just come for Mellissa himself?" asked Victoria.

"I don't know. I need to talk to the council."

Greg got up to leave, but Mellissa grabbed his hand. She looked up at him, her big eyes full of fear. Greg sat back down. "We can all talk to the council." He clicked his fingers and summoned his communis. He placed the small disc in the centre of the table and waved his hand over it while thinking of Lady Gabrielle. She answered after the first ring.

"Greg, is everything all right?"

"Yes, fine—well, not really. Three leprechauns tried to abduct Mellissa."

"What? Is she all right?" There was worry in her voice.

"Yes, Victoria turned them all to ice."

"She must be very strong to take on three high-level magic users on her own. Especially considering the brute strength of leprechauns."

"That's the thing—they weren't high-level magic users. They shouldn't have been able to cross the veil."

"This is very disturbing news. I thought you and the keeper would be safe in the human world. Maybe you should all come back here where I can assign guards to you."

"No!" exclaimed Mellissa.

"Lady Mellissa?" Lady Gabrielle sounded surprised.

"I'm sorry," Mellissa said, "but I can't leave my dad, and this is my home."

"I understand, but your safety is what concerns me."

"Victoria is perfectly capable of keeping me safe."

"This is a one-off incident at the moment," Greg said. "We need more information before making decisions, like how they got here and who sent them. For now, I will cast some protection spells around the house, and Mellissa is always with one of her guardians when out."

"Very well," Lady Gabrielle replied. "I will look into this matter myself. Do not go anywhere alone. Watch each other's backs."

"Yes, Lady Gabrielle." Greg ended the call and sent the device back upstairs. Hopefully, Lady Gabrielle would be able to get answers for them. This attack made no sense. Greg clenched his fist. If he hadn't lost Mellissa in that club, they never would've got their hands on her. If he was a better teacher, she would've been able to better defend herself.

Victoria got up. "Right, I will go grab some stuff from home and let my parents know I'm staying here."

"What? No," Mellissa said. "It's Christmas tomorrow. You should be with your family."

"This is important." Victoria sighed. "They will understand."

Mellissa took Victoria's hand. "I would feel terrible if you missed Christmas with your family. I'll be fine with the protection spells Greg is putting up."

Victoria pushed her fringe to the side. "Fine, but if there

is any danger, you teleport without hesitating."

Mellissa nodded.

The front door banged shut. "Mellissa," Mr. Hail yelled. "Sorry I'm so late, but I brought Chinese."

He walked into the kitchen, briefcase in one hand and a white carrier bag in the other. The smell of sweet sauce wafted across the room. Mellissa got up and took the white bag from him and placed it on the kitchen counter.

He put his briefcase down. "Hello, Victoria. I didn't realise you would be here. Where's your brother?"

Mellissa slammed a pile of plates down on the kitchen counter, making them all jump.

"He caught a tummy bug," Victoria said.

"Oh, I hope he feels better soon. Will you be staying for a late dinner?"

"I was just going. I'll see you guys later. Mellissa, remember what I said."

Mellissa didn't look away from the plates she was tightly gripping. Greg got up from the table. "I'll walk you out." Greg followed Victoria out of the house. "Will you help me with the protection spells before you go? The extra power will strengthen the spell."

"Wouldn't Mellissa's power be better to strengthen the spell?"

"I don't want her magical aura anywhere near this. It's very distinctive, and I don't want them tracking her."

"Makes sense. Let's get this over with then."

The two of them made their way around the house, chanting five different protection spells. The combination of their magic made for a strong spell. The magic was even better than when he worked with Samson. Hopefully, it would be enough to keep any unwanted visitors out. He waved as Victoria left and went back inside. Mellissa and her dad were already at the table eating. There was a plate of food left for him. Mr. Hail tried to make conversation, but Mellissa only gave one-word answers. They spent the rest of the evening in awkward silence.

When Greg finally went up to bed, he found himself

lying awake, staring at the ceiling. He kept going over the evening's events in his head and what would have happened if Victoria hadn't intervened when she did. They would have taken Mellissa, and it would have been all his fault for not training her properly. He had to get back on track with her lessons. More importantly, he needed to teach her how to effectively defend herself. He needed to be stricter and stop letting her procrastinate. Maybe he should re-enlist the Streets. Victoria was a trained fighter, and she had a way of making Mellissa stay on track. Greg sighed, putting his arm over his head. He had been such an idiot. Maybe his father had been right—he was letting his relationship with Mellissa affect his judgement.

The door creaked open. "Greg," whispered Mellissa.

He sat up. "What's wrong?" He heard the door click shut. She didn't say anything. He could just about see her silhouette in the dark by the door. "Mellissa?"

"I—I couldn't sleep."

"Neither could I."

"It's just, I can't get what happened out of my head. I'm such an idiot." She was talking fast. "And I'm sorry. I should take training more seriously. If I listened more, I wouldn't be so useless, and I wouldn't constantly have to be saved."

Greg marched across the room and pulled her into his arms. "You are not useless, and you have nothing to be sorry for."

She laid her head on his chest and dug her fingers into his back. "But if you and Victoria hadn't been there—"

"But we were. If I hadn't lost you on the dance floor—"

She looked up at him. Her eyes shimmered in the dark. "But that wasn't your fault."

"And none of what happened was yours." They stood in silence for a moment. Greg could feel Mellissa's heart beating against him. The hairs on the back of his neck stood up, and he shivered. He never wanted to let her go.

Mellissa put her hand on his chest and stepped back. "Greg, tell me about council procedures and regulations."

"Why would you want me to tell you that?"

"Because neither of us can sleep, and it's so boring. I'm sure it will send us both off in no time."

Greg awoke nice and early as always. It was still dark out. Everything was silent except for the tiny snores of Mellissa. She had been right. Once he started talking protocol, it hadn't taken long for her to drift off. Greg rolled onto his side. She looked so peaceful. His arm had gone numb where she rested on it. He gently tugged it from under her and shook it until the feeling returned. He could have lain like that for hours, but he needed to get her back to her own room. Gently shaking her shoulder, he whispered her name.

She rolled away from him. "Go away, Greg. I'm not training till the sun's up." What happened to her saying she should have listened to him more?

He tried again. "Mellissa, you need to go back to your room. I'm pretty sure you're breaking your dad's rules."

She turned to look at him. "What?" She rubbed her eyes and pushed herself up on her elbows. Her eyes widened. "Oh crap. What time is it?"

Greg picked his watch up off the bedside table. "Five."

"Seriously, is that it?" She lay back down. If she didn't care, then neither did he. Greg went to lie back down when she shot up, pushing his shoulder. "Oh my God! It's Christmas!"

She ran out of the room. Greg heard a few doors bang, then Mr. Hail yell, "Mellissa, aren't you getting too old for this?"

"Never," Mellissa shouted.

Greg got up and almost collided with Mellissa as she ran back into his room. She grabbed his hand and pulled him out of the room. Mr. Hail was in his bedroom doorway shaking his head. Mellissa led him to the kitchen. She handed him bars of chocolate and milk and pulled out a bunch of pans, placing them on the stove.

"What are you doing?" Greg asked.

"Making the ultimate hot chocolate." Mellissa ran about

the kitchen, pulling items from cupboards and the fridge. Mr. Hail walked in, and Mellissa handed him a load of stuff. "My dad makes the best pancakes. You're gonna love 'em."

Mr. Hail began mixing some stuff in a bowl, and Mellissa took the chocolate from Greg and broke it up, placing it in a glass bowl sat on top of a pan of simmering water.

Greg leant over her. "Now what are you doing?"

She pushed him toward the table. "You know what? You just sit down as we don't want breakfast burnt."

"I burnt one batch of cookies."

She narrowed her eyes at him. "Stay away from the cooking."

Greg did as he was told. After a while, the smell of melted chocolate filled the kitchen. Once Mellissa was done, Mr. Hail took over use of the stove. He put a pan on the stove, and it began to sizzle. Mellissa skipped over and handed Greg a mug of hot chocolate. He took a sip. It was sickly sweet. He could see why she liked it.

After eating a massive pile of pancakes, they retired to the living room, where they exchanged gifts. Mellissa seemed overjoyed with a pair of earrings her dad gave her. Greg didn't get what the point was. Surely you didn't need some winter celebration to give gifts to those you cared about. And although breakfast had been nice, he didn't understand its significance either. Maybe he would never understand human customs, but he could at least appreciate that they were important to them. Mellissa sat next to him and handed him a box.

"What's this?"

"A present."

"But I didn't get you anything."

She rolled her eyes. "That's not how this works. It's nothing special—just a notebook and a pen so you can see how us normal people write. Besides, I'm pretty sure you already got me a quill and this chain." She pulled the Heart Crystal out from under her top.

Mr. Hail arched his eyebrow. "I wondered where that necklace came from."

Mellissa jumped up. "Here, Dad. Open your other

present." She handed him a box.

He gave her a suspicious look but didn't question her further. Greg turned his gift over and opened it. It was a notebook and a pen. Like she said, it was nothing special, but it put a smile on his face. Christmas was weird.

Whispers
Mellissa

scream as I'm grabbed from behind. My arms are pulled together. They think that means I can't summon light, but they are wrong. I surround myself in light. My attacker yells and backs away. I spin around, throwing my arm out, shooting vines and binding my attacker. I stand over him. He is a young leprechaun.

"Who are you?" I demand.

He spits at me. "I do not answer to you."

"Freya." Ivan comes running to me, followed by a group of guards. He clasps my shoulders. "Are you all right? Why didn't you call for help?"

"I am fine. I have things under control."

The guards surround the boy. "What shall we do with him?" asks one of the guards.

"Take him to the dungeons. I will question him later," replies Ivan.

"The time of the elves is coming to an end," yells the boy as he is dragged away.

A darkness falls over Ivan's face as he grips his sword at his side. I place my hand on his arm. "Ivan, he is just a boy."

"A boy that tried to kill you."

"But failed."

"Freya, as your guardian, I insist you call for help the instant danger arises."

"I thought the point of your crazy training was so I didn't have to."

"It is. It's just—" His shoulders droop as he looks at the ground.

I take his hand. "I appreciate your concern, but I can take care of myself. Believe in me and your training."
He squeezes my hand and nods.

I was rudely awoken by a very annoying rabbit bouncing on my bed. Light shimmered through the gap in my curtain. At least he'd waited for sunrise, but I wasn't getting up. Rolling over, I kicked him off. "Go away."

My cover was pulled off, sending a cold blast over my skin. Greg had hold of it, back in human form. "We need to train."

I grabbed the other end of my quilt and pulled. "How dare you? That was pure evil." I fell backward as he let go.

"Seriously, Mellissa, have you forgotten what happened only a couple of days ago?"

A shiver ran through my body. I had not forgotten. How could I? "No."

"Good, then get dressed and meet me downstairs so we can go to the Streets."

He walked out, leaving me on my bed with my quilt piled on top of me. Throwing my quilt to the side, I got up. I went to the bathroom and got in the shower. Even with the hot water running over me, I felt a cold chill. There was a darkness. Maybe it was just my fear of the leprechauns playing tricks on my mind. Lady Gabrielle was looking into the movements of the leprechauns, but we hadn't heard anything from her. I needed to be better prepared if they tried to kidnap me again. At least they wanted me alive—for now, anyway.

I got out of the shower and dressed in comfy leggings and an oversized T-shirt—an outfit I didn't mind getting ruined by magic. When I entered the kitchen, Greg handed me a bowl of cereal and a glass of juice. "Eat up."

I downed the juice and sat at the table, eating my cereal. "Do we have to go to the Streets'? It's cold out."

"You can teleport, Mellissa."

"Right. What about my dad?"

"I'm pretty sure I heard him leave for work already."

Of course, the only time my dad got off this time of year was Christmas Day. This wasn't what was really bothering me anyway. I didn't want to run into Matt. I wasn't ready for the excuses he had for why he'd ditched me the other day.

"Why don't you want to go to the Streets'? Victoria will be waiting for us."

Victoria, not Matt. "No reason," I said, putting my empty bowl in the sink. I took his hand. "Shall we go?" He nodded, and I teleported directly to the training hall.

"It's about time you got here," Victoria said. She threw a staff at me, grabbed another and twirled it around. "The aim of the game is to stay standing."

"What, no warm-up?"

"This is the warm-up." She ran at me. I yelled, running in the opposite direction. She caught me in no time and swung her staff at my legs, knocking me flat on my face. Greg helped me up. "Don't help her. She didn't even try," yelled Victoria.

Greg shrugged. "At least she didn't stand still."

"I would hardly call that progress."

"Well, we should train her for a few hours, then you can play again."

"Fine." She snatched the staff off me and placed them back on the stand. She pulled a lever, and the ground shook. Targets rose up from the floor.

"Target practice. I'll demonstrate." She curled her fingers, and an ice cloud appeared around her hand. Throwing her arms out, she took out the first row of targets with a quick succession of ice shards. Greg pressed a button, and the next row moved forward. "Your turn." She stepped to the side and pushed me into place. I could do this. Focusing on the burning ball of power inside me, I formed a ball of light in my hand. I threw it at a target and completely missed, hitting the back wall. I tried again with the same result. It took me six goes to brush the side of a target.

"Wow, your aim sucks," said Victoria. She took my arm. "You need to be more confident in your movements. Also, don't look at the target. Look just past it." She demonstrated how amazing she was at this again, then stepped aside for me to try. We kept going until I finally hit all the targets. I may not have knocked all the targets clean off their stands like Victoria, but I had hit them.

"Next, we will work on your barriers," Greg said. "We know you can cast the spell, but remember, you can trap people inside barriers as well as protect yourself with them." I nodded. "Your task is to make it from one end of the hall to the other without getting hit. I'll demonstrate." He went and stood at the far end of the hall. "Victoria, try and hit me."

A devilish grin appeared on her face. "There will be no try. Three, two, one." Victoria fired off a reel of ice blasts. Greg ran, and I lost sight of him in the mist of ice. Victoria stamped her foot, and the mist cleared. Greg didn't have a shred of ice on him.

"Your turn," he said.

"I didn't exactly see what you did because of the mist," I said.

"Get to the other side of the wall before I turn you into an icicle," Victoria snapped.

"Fine." I shuffled to the start point.

"Three, two, one."

I ran, and Victoria fired at me. I threw up a barrier. The ice hit, and it shattered. More ice flew at me, and I was knocked to the ground. I groaned at the pain. Victoria pointed at the start point. I pushed myself up, and we started over. She counted down again, and I ran. I made it halfway across before she knocked me over again. We did the drill over and over, but I never made it any farther than halfway.

I lay on the floor, looking up at the high ceiling. Victoria had just knocked me down again. My whole body ached. I was sure I had bruises all over. Greg sat beside me. "Time for a break. Victoria has gone upstairs to get some food."

"How did you do it?"

He smiled. "I put a barrier around her. Of course, she broke out, but it bought me time to form a more solid barrier to protect myself." I sat up, staring at him, open-mouthed. "I did tell you barriers could be used to trap others."

That's true, but I hadn't seen his demonstration properly because of the mist. They had done that on purpose. At least, Victoria had. "You two are such cheaters."

"Your enemies won't play fair, so neither should we."

Victoria returned with a tray of food. There was a variety of sandwiches, packets of crisps, a bowl of fruit and some chocolate. She sat on the other side of me, putting the tray down. "My mum insisted on the fruit. Something about balancing out all the junk food."

As we ate, I thought of Matt. I had been nervous about seeing him, but he didn't appear to be in. Hadn't Victoria told him what happened at the club? Surely, as my guardian, he should be here to help me train. It was obvious he didn't care about our friendship anymore, but still, he should've been taking his duty as my guardian more seriously. "Victoria, where's Matt?" I asked.

She looked down and frowned. "I have no idea where he is. He walked out yesterday with no explanation and hasn't been back."

"Why didn't you say anything? Something has got to be wrong for him to act like this."

"You had enough to worry about. My dad has gone looking for him." Her brow creased as she played with her food. "It's a good thing I didn't stay at yours the other night. Mum was really upset when Matt missed Christmas."

I bit my thumbnail. How could Matt do this to his family? It wasn't just me he was ignoring. "Is it possible some magic is to blame?" I asked.

Victoria shrugged. "Possibly. I've been wondering"— she turned to Greg—"is it possible that when Matt was hit by those shadows, they infected him somehow?"

"I don't know," Greg said. "Shadow magic is outlawed, so I don't know much about it. I would have to check him over to see if he was under a spell."

If Victoria was starting to worry about Matt, something was definitely up. I had this terrible feeling something was wrong. I could feel it in the pit of my stomach but had no idea what to do.

Victoria clapped her hands. "Right, more target practice."

And just like that, the topic of Matt was dropped. The targets were set up just like before. We spent the rest of the afternoon trying to improve my aim. By the end of the day, I was finally hitting all the targets. I was still out of Victoria's league. She had such grace and speed. It would take me years before I was half as good as her, but at least I had made progress. I was exhausted by the time I teleported home. Greg headed straight upstairs, and I sat in the kitchen, head on the table. Every part of my body hurt. I had never done so much physical activity in one day.

The door clicked open. "Mellissa," said my dad. "When did you get back? I didn't hear you come in."

I sat up. "Not been in long."

He filled up the kettle. "Where have you and Greg been?"

"Just hanging out with Victoria."

He frowned. "Hmm. You've been spending a lot of time with Victoria and not Matt."

"Yup. No Matt, but lots of Victoria."

My dad placed a cup of tea in front of me. I hadn't asked for it, but it was exactly what I needed. He put his hand on my shoulder. "Is everything all right?"

I nodded. "Of course. Thanks for the tea."

Greg walked in. "Hi, Mr. Hail."

"Hello, Greg." He handed him a cup of tea as well.

Greg looked down at the cup. "Thanks."

"Well, you know where I am if you want to talk," my dad told me. He left with his own cup of tea.

Greg sat beside me and handed me a small vial of purple liquid. "Put a drop of this in a bath, and all those aches and pains from training should go away."

I held the bottle up to the light. It looked like a tiny bottle of shower gel. "Really?"

"Trust me. It works wonders."

After dinner, I ran myself a bath, ready to give the bottle of purple stuff a try. I put a drop in the bath, and the water turned bright purple. I slipped into the bath and instantly felt better. This stuff really worked.

When I got out, I found a pile of books on my desk. There was a note from Greg saying to read them as we would be working on plant magic and hand-to-hand combat tomorrow. Tomorrow was going to be another long day. I picked the first book off the pile and read until I fell asleep.

The next morning was very similar to the day before. Greg woke me up. I got showered and dressed, had breakfast and teleported to the Streets'. Victoria greeted me by throwing a staff at me and attacking me. I lasted all of ten seconds before I hit the floor. Greg pulled me up. "Better than yesterday."

Victoria snatched the staff from me. "Barely."

"You know, maybe if you guys taught me how to fight with one of those, I would do better."

"She has a point," Greg said, looking at Victoria.

"First, we see how well she throws a punch," replied Victoria. I was getting sick of these two making decisions for me.

"Why does that matter?" I asked. "I'm pretty sure fighting with my fists isn't going to help me against a leprechaun with superhuman strength."

"Your magic is just an extension of your body," explained Victoria. "If you don't know how to use both properly, you won't be any good in a fight. In a real fight, your opponent isn't going to stand still like the targets."

"I guess that makes sense."

"Good. Now, try to hit me." She took a wide stance and gestured me forward.

"You want me to fight you? Can't I fight Greg instead?"

She nodded. "Sure, go for it."

"Really?"

A wicked grin spread across her face. "Do you really think he will be any easier to beat than me?"

Of course he wouldn't. He had been training since he

was a child, just like her. Knowing what his father was like, his training had probably been a lot stricter than hers. I really hadn't thought this through. "No, but I think he's less likely to kill me."

"What sort of guardian would I be if I killed you?" she said. "Now, go on. Hit him."

I walked over to Greg, fists clenched. He was just standing there and hadn't uttered a word. "I can't do it."

"It's all right. Just hit me," Greg said.

"This seems wrong."

"Is this how you plan to defend yourself against a leprechaun attack?" Greg replied.

"No, but you're not a leprechaun."

"Then pretend I am and try to hit me. It's all right. You'll probably miss."

I gritted my teeth. He was so arrogant. I was stood right in front of him. There was no space for him to dodge an attack. I clenched my fist and swung. With the slightest of movements, he dodged the hit. I grumbled and swung at him again. I missed.

"How?" I yelled.

"You keep aiming where I am, not where I'm going."

"That doesn't even make sense."

Victoria laughed from the sideline. "At least she knows how to throw a punch. She just can't land one on a moving person."

Greg gave me some pointers, and I tried again. I threw punch after punch. No matter what technique I used, I couldn't touch him. He told me to hit him, but then he kept moving.

"Would you please stay still?" I shouted.

"Why would I do that? An attacker isn't going to stand around and make things easy for you."

"Well, how else am I going to learn?" I threw another punch at him, but he dodged. I quickly followed up with another punch and made contact. I grabbed my hand back and held it close to my chest. I bit my lip to stop myself from crying out in pain. I had finally managed to land a hit but ended up hurting myself. That would teach me for lashing out in anger.

"Are you all right?" he asked.

I turned away from him, nursing my hand. "I'm just fine."

"Come on. Let me see. I know you hurt yourself. I felt it."

I turned and scowled at him, but I showed him my hand. He turned my hand over and played with my fingers. "Good news—you just bruised it."

I snatched my hand back. "How is that good news?"

"Well, it could have been broken. It is a well-known fact that female bones are more fragile than men's."

I knew, on average, men generally had more muscle mass than women, but I didn't know that. I threw my arms up. "Well, I'm screwed then. I'm pretty sure a leprechaun is made of tougher stuff than you."

Victoria walked over to us. "No, you just need to be more precise when you hit. Target weaker parts of the body, like the nose, throat, abdomen or groin. Also, you're small, which means you have a lower centre of gravity. Take his feet out from under him, and he will take longer to regain balance than you."

"You could have also just poked me in the eye," said Greg.

"Oh yeah, eyes are a good one," Victoria said. "Anyway, you two go play with plants while I pick which weapons to train you with."

She walked over to the rack of weapons. Greg walked over to a table full of plants. I ran my hand over the leaves of one of the plants. "You two have done a lot of talking behind my back, I see."

"No, we haven't. We've just planned the best way to help you improve your powers." He pushed the leafy plant closer to me. "You are going to practice making plants grow."

I cupped the plant in my hands and let out a long breath. This was all too much. There was so much to learn, and we had no idea when I might be attacked again. I could have ages to learn this stuff, but then again, I could be attacked again tonight. To make things worse, Matt still hadn't turned up.

Mrs. Street had joined her husband in searching for him, yet these two just wanted to keep pushing forward. I felt helpless. How could I help Matt, when I couldn't even protect myself? How was I meant to learn what they'd spent their whole lives doing in a couple of days? I didn't want to be weak anymore, but I didn't know how to be strong.

"We will help you, Our Queen," said a voice in my head.

"Will you?"

"Of course."

"Then grow."

The plants flew out of their pots, growing rapidly. Vines grabbed Greg, throwing him in the air. More vines shot across the hall, wrapping up Victoria. The plants kept growing, filling the room. They recoiled as Victoria shot ice at them. I turned in her direction, and the plants doubled in number, slamming her against the wall. Leaves cocooned her.

"Mellissa," Greg shouted. I looked up. He was pinned to the ceiling by foliage.

I shut my eyes. "Return." I pulled the plants back to me, and they returned to their original size.

"I don't think she needs to practice plant magic," said Victoria.

I had just wanted to prove I was good at something—that I wasn't useless—but I'd almost hurt them both. "I'm sorry." I wrapped my arms around myself and teleported.

I materialised in Novos Forest. Snowflakes glistened in the sun as they fell. I hugged myself tightly; it was freezing. The smell of pine and fresh snow filled the air. I trudged through the snow toward the river. I had no idea why I'd come here. It had been the first place that had popped into my head when I had wanted to escape. It would take Greg and Victoria longer to find me on this side of the veil.

I sat on a log, looking out at the river. It was still frozen. The ice sparkled as fresh flakes of snow landed on it. A twig snapped behind me, and I was on my feet in an instant.

"How nice of you to come to us," said a gruff voice. "The master will be pleased he doesn't have to use up his power to send us across the veil." Two leprechauns emerged from the bushes.

My blood ran cold. I was such an idiot. I put myself in danger coming here alone—but I wasn't alone.

"That's right, Your Majesty," said the trees. Throwing my arm up, the branches of the trees shot at the leprechauns, winding around them. They both yelled as they were pulled off the ground. I took the opportunity to get out of there and teleported home.

I crumbled to the floor of my living room. My heart was pounding. Had that really just happened?

"Mellissa." Greg pulled me off the floor. I flopped into him. "Where were you? We were worried."

"Is that her?" shouted Victoria. She marched into the room and wagged her finger at me. "Don't you ever run off like that again."

"I'm sorry. I'm so stupid. I just wanted a break, but I shouldn't have gone there."

"Gone where?" she asked.

"Novos Forest. Two leprechauns were there. I think they were waiting for their master so they could cross the veil."

"What?!" they said in unison.

"How did you get away?" Victoria asked.

I slumped into the sofa. "I used the trees and teleported. I am so stupid."

Greg sat beside me and stroked my hair. "No, you're not. You used your powers to get away."

"Yes, you are stupid for leaving," said Victoria, "but your escape was smart. Try to be Smart Mellissa more often."

I looked from Greg to Victoria. "What were you both doing here?"

"We were about to perform a tracking spell," replied Greg.

"You can do that?"

"Yes. We needed something of yours, so we came here."

"Right," Victoria said. "Now that I know where you are, I'm going to head home." She pointed at me. "Do not leave the house. The protection spells around it will keep you safe. I will talk to my mum about putting extra ones around our house for training tomorrow."

"Okay," I said. Victoria left, slamming the door behind her. She must be mad at me. I couldn't blame her. I had acted rashly and put myself in danger. "Now what?" I asked.

"More reading. Your plant magic is good, but your control could be better."

"Seriously?" I shouted. "You still want me to train?"

"You just said the leprechauns were trying to get back here again. Do you not care about your safety?"

"Of course I do, but what about my sanity? You are driving me crazy."

"Sorry I'm trying to keep you alive," he shouted.

"I'm just your job, Gregory. Don't pretend you care." I stamped up the stairs and into my room, slamming the door behind me. I threw myself on my bed. I tried to sleep, but I couldn't. I was too angry. He was so annoying. Why did he have to push me so much? I yelled into my pillow. It wasn't Greg I was mad at. Not really. It was myself. He was just trying to help me—they both were—and I was a rubbish student.

After staring at the ceiling for what felt like forever, there was a knock on my door. "Go away, Greg," I said.

He didn't listen and came into the room. "Mellissa, we don't have to do any reading. Can we just talk?"

I sat up. "What's the point? Nothing you can say is going to change the fact that this is all hopeless. There is no amount of training that will have me ready to fight anytime soon."

"Not true," he said. "You managed to escape today."

"What if they keep coming? They mentioned their master again. We have no idea what he wants, and I assume since we haven't heard from Lady Gabrielle, she hasn't found anything out."

"I know it's scary, but Victoria and I are here to help you."

I jumped up and started pacing the room. "Why is it down to you two to keep me safe? I know Victoria is my guardian, but you don't see Matt hanging around to protect me.

This duty stuff obviously isn't that important. And you—why do you even care what happens to me?" I stopped walking and stared out the window. "Why is Matt doing this? Everything is falling apart."

Greg stood beside me. "Everything is not falling apart. Things just seem that way because so much is happening at once. As for Matt, I really can't say why he is acting this way, but magic could be the reason. Once his parents find him. I can assess him for any magical damage and hopefully heal him." His shoulders dropped. "In the meantime, I just want you to stay safe."

"Why does my safety matter so much?"

"Because you are my friend, and I care what happens to you."

"Are we friends, Greg?" *Or was it just because I was the keeper of the Heart?* I never asked him before because I was afraid of the answer. As much as I kept referring to Greg as just a friend, I couldn't deny that things felt different with him. Even with everything in chaos, he made me believe it would all be okay. It would kill me if I really was just a project to him.

"Of course, we are friends," Greg said. "What makes you think we're not?"

"It's just something Matt said to me a while back. He told me you're basically a prince and any knowledge you have of me, your father will use for personal gain." I sighed. "I mean I get it. You have a responsibility to your people. It's just— sometimes things between us feel real but other times I worry it's just an act. A really convincing act."

Greg grabbed my shoulders and spun me to face him. "Melissa, you have to know that isn't true. I would never let my father influence me in that way. Everything between us is real. I will never leave you. When you're in danger—I don't know— it's like the world stops turning until I know you're safe."

I leant my head against his chest. His heart was beating fast.

"I know," I whispered. Why was I so insecure all the time? He hadn't told me anything I didn't already know but I had let that annoying voice of doubt get to me. It had felt nice to hear it out loud and the way he struggled to put it all into words was something I could relate to. I felt safe around Greg. I clutched hold of his shirt, went up onto my tiptoes and kissed him.

Greg's whole body went rigid. What was I doing? I went to pull away, but as I did, it was like what had happened registered with him. With one arm around my waist and the other on the back of my head, he pulled me closer and returned my kiss. His lips were soft and gentle. I wanted more. There was a burning fire of want inside me that I hadn't noticed before. I ran my fingers along his shirt, popping the buttons. Pushing my lips harder to his, I ran my tongue along his bottom lip and moaned as he opened his mouth and our tongues intertwined. I ran my fingers through his hair, pulling him closer, not wanting there to be an inch of space between us. He tugged at my top, and I pushed him onto the bed. I climbed on top of him. He pulled me close, kissing me more fiercely, his hands wandering over my body.

"Mellissa!"

The sound of my dad's shouting from downstairs killed the moment and panic set in.

Tracker Spells
Gregory

reg walked down the street, hands in pockets. His head was spinning. It was still early morning. The streets were empty, except for the occasional person walking a dog and the odd car. The sun hadn't fully risen yet, and there was a slight chill in the air, but it was nothing compared to the coldness back home. He just needed some fresh air and some time to think. Even after spending all night going over what happened, he still wasn't sure what to make of it.

It had been completely unexpected. Mellissa had kissed him so suddenly. He shouldn't have let that happen. It wasn't proper. He was meant to be teaching her magic and preparing her to become queen. That was all; there shouldn't be anything else. She was just upset. That was it. He had just been reassuring her and that was why it happened. She had just needed that human contact to feel better. Nothing else to it.

Then why hadn't he stopped it sooner? Greg shook his head. This wasn't the time for that. There was a reason he had left so early.

Greg stopped under a tree and looked around. This should be a good spot. It was quiet, and there was no one around to see him. He pulled a pair of earphones out of his pocket. Apparently, these tiny things could be used to listen to music, but more importantly, they belonged to Matt. A lot of things Mellissa and Victoria had been saying about Matt recently had bothered him, so Greg had come up with a plan. From his other pocket, he pulled out a small glass bottle. To those that didn't know any better, they would have thought it was simply a bottle of sand, but it was more than that. Greg popped open the bottle and sprinkled its contents over the earphones.

"Lost item, find your way back to the one you belong," whispered Greg. The earphones began to glow and hovered above his hand. He watched them, waiting to see which direction they would lead him in. Matt's odd behaviour was the cause of a lot of Mellissa's self-doubt and worry. Finding out what was going on with him could solve a few things. However, the earphones didn't appear to be going anywhere. Greg frowned. It didn't usually take this long for the spell to work. The glow slowly disappeared, and the earphones dropped back down into his hand. Greg repeated the process. The same thing happened again. Why wasn't this working? Greg clenched his fist to stop himself from throwing the earphones.

Greg leant against the tree. The spell should have worked. He needed it to work. It was the only way he could think to help Mellissa. She wouldn't be feeling so insecure if Matt would just do his duty as her guardian. Where had he disappeared to? He didn't even seem like the same person anymore. Greg ruffled his hair. It wasn't him it was bothering, it was Mellissa, and she was the only reason he cared about Matt.

Solving the mystery of why Matt wasn't around wouldn't solve the problem he and Mellissa had. He had gotten too close to her and lines had been crossed. But was it even really a problem? Of course it was. The council would frown upon it. He had overstepped. She was the heir to the elf thrown. She was someone important. He was just the son of an elder knight. He had convinced himself he cared about Mellissa's safety the same way Victoria did but that had never been true. His feelings toward her had been growing gradually, he hadn't noticed the change at first. She was like no one he had ever met before. She made him laugh; she was quirky and fun to be around. But he had pushed all his feelings down as he wasn't meant to fall for her. She had been right when she said his duty came first. He had been putting his duty first, but that was before she kissed him. When she kissed him, it was like that all went out the window. He had just instinctively kissed her back, but then it had turned into something more. It had just felt right. If her dad hadn't come back when he did, snapping them back in to reality. She had quickly teleported downstairs, acting like they had been in different rooms the whole time. He shook his head. Now wasn't the time to be thinking about this. He needed to figure out why this spell wasn't working.

Greg held the earphones in front of him. Maybe he had been mistaken in thinking these where Matt's. Even if that was so, the spell should have led him back to Mellissa. Dread filled Greg's body. There was one other reason a tracking spell wouldn't work—if the owner was deceased. Matt had to be alive. Victoria had seen him before he had wandered off. Greg put the items back in his pocket and started running. He ran up the pathway to a house with a red door. He hoped he had the right place. All these houses looked the same, and he had never been here without Mellissa. He knocked on the door.

Mrs. Street answered. Her hand shot to her cheek. "Oh, it's you. Where's Mellissa?" She bit her thumbnail and looked behind him.

"She's still at home behind a bunch of protection spells. I'm here to see Victoria. Is she in?"

"Oh." Her forehead creased as she frowned. "I'll get her." She disappeared, leaving Greg on the doorstep. A minute later, Victoria appeared.

"What are you doing here?" she asked with a frown. "Where's Mellissa?"

"She's at home. We need to talk about your brother."

"Well he's not here and I would rather not upset my mother more by discussing it."

"But it is upsetting Mellissa and I need your help."

She put her hand up in front of him. "Look, my mum is a lot more upset than she appears. My dad has travelled to the magic world to ask for help after his fifth tracking spell failed."

Greg pushed his fringe to the side. Of course they would have already tried a tracking spell. It's the most basic technique for finding a missing person. Victoria slapped his shoulder. "Wait, you didn't leave Mellissa on her own, did you?"

"She's at home with her dad. He is working from home. She promised she wouldn't leave the house."

"And you believed her?" Victoria shouted, throwing her arm in his direction. "You're an idiot. That girl can't stay still."

"Will you just hear me out for a second? I have an idea for locating your brother."

Victoria crossed her arms and curled her top lip. "I'm listening, but this better be good."

"Look, Mellissa doesn't even know I'm here. She thinks I'm looking at a new place to live. I am trying to find your brother, but as you know the tracking spell won't work."

She rolled her eyes. "Of course you would be performing your own spells. You still haven't explained why you're here."

Greg gritted his teeth. "I came here because blood magic creates a much stronger spell."

"And can be extremely dangerous."

"How else do you suggest we find Matt? The sort of spell we will be casting holds very little risk. Are you not even a little bit concerned by his weird behaviour?"

She looked away from him, clenching her fists, and started tapping her foot. He shouldn't have said that. Of course she was concerned. She constantly insulted and complained about her brother, but that was just her way of covering up her feelings. Victoria sighed as she dropped her arms at her sides. "Fine, I will help you, but why didn't you just tell Mellissa the truth? Her magic is stronger than ours."

"I didn't want to get her hopes up," Greg replied. "She is too emotionally attached."

"And you're not? What exactly is your relationship with Mellissa?"

Greg suddenly felt hot. She couldn't know what happened. "What is that supposed to mean?"

A smirk spread across Victoria's face. "Nothing." He didn't like the way she said that. She waved her hand at him. "Come in so we can do this stupid spell."

Victoria led Greg through the house into a small sitting room. She went over to a drawer and pulled a folded piece of paper out. She handed it to Greg. "This map should be big enough. I can't see him having travelled any farther on his own."

Greg unfolded the map and laid it out on the table. He really hoped this worked. He got the small bottle he'd used earlier and sprinkled some of the dust on the map. "I will need some of your blood."

"Yeah, I know." Victoria produced a needle and pricked her finger. She held her hand over the map and squeezed a couple of drops of blood onto it. "Blood to blood, heart to heart, find my missing loved one, so we can be reunited."

They both looked at the map, but nothing happened. The blood that was meant to show where Matt was didn't move. Something was very wrong. Blood magic was the strongest form of spell casting.

"Why isn't it working?" asked Victoria, panicked.

"Maybe the map isn't big enough. Let's try this one instead." Greg flicked his wrist and produced his own map.

"What would Matt be doing in the magic world?"

"I don't know, but there's a tear in this village, so it's worth a try." Victoria rolled up her sleeves. They repeated the spell using his map instead. The blood quickly shifted from where it fell on the map. The blood travelled across the map. When the blood started circling one spot, it had found who it was looking for.

"What is he doing at the council building?" Greg asked.

"I have no idea, but I think we are going to need Mellissa's teleporting if we want to find out."

"Agreed." Greg folded the map and followed Victoria out of the room.

She grabbed a coat, and they left the house. They walked to Mellissa's house in silence. None of this made sense. Greg couldn't think of any reason Matt would be at the council building. How had he gotten there? Travelling to the capital was not a short journey from here. Mellissa was the only person he knew that could make it there so quickly.

Greg knocked on the door, and Mr. Hail answered. He smiled at Greg. "You're back. What was the flat like? Any better than the last one?"

Greg put his hand on his head. Of course Mellissa had told him that's where he had gone. "It looks promising."

"Hi, Mr. Hail," Victoria said, pushing in front of Greg. "Is Mellissa upstairs?"

"Oh, Victoria, I didn't see you there." Mr. Hail pointed behind him. "Yes, she is up in her bedroom."

"Thanks," she said, running up the stairs.

Greg walked into the house and shut the door.

"She seems in a hurry," Mr. Hail said.

Victoria came hurtling down the stairs. "She's gone."

"What? She was up there a moment ago," Mr. Hail said.

He shouldn't have left her here alone. What had he been thinking? The truth was, he hadn't been thinking. Victoria grabbed the collar of Greg's shirt and lifted her fist, ready to punch him.

Mr. Hail gasped. "Victoria."

Victoria's eyes shone with power, and she tensed her jaw. "You were meant to watch over her. I should turn you into a human icicle and smash your limbs one by one."

Greg looked her straight in the eye. "Fighting with me is a waste of time. We need to find Mellissa. You can throw as much ice at me as you want later."

She let go of him. He put his hand on the door handle. Victoria grabbed his arm. "You are going nowhere. I will find her myself."

"Will one of you tell me what is going on?" asked Mr. Hail. "Victoria, this behaviour is so unlike you."

"There isn't time for me to explain. I need to find Mellissa before she gets herself into trouble again. Stay here, Flopsey. She might come back on her own. Call me if she reappears."

"Victoria, wait—" Greg said, but she wasn't listening. She pushed him out of the way and stormed out of the house. Maybe he should stay put. Mellissa could reappear here like nothing had happened. She could've just popped to the shop. He hoped they were overreacting, and if they were, maybe he could confirm it. A tracking spell would do the trick. He still had some dust left. He could find her in no time.

"What on earth was that all about?" Mr. Hail asked. "Why is it so important she finds Mellissa? She isn't in trouble, is she? Should we go with her?"

Greg ran his hand through his hair. He wasn't sure how to answer Mr. Hail's questions without revealing too much. "It's hard to explain. I think a talk with your daughter is long overdue."

The Fire Nymph
Mellissa

I walked along the lake. Loud quacks echoed to the left of me. A bunch of ducks swam toward me, probably expecting me to feed them. I looked around the area. There wasn't another person in sight. In summer, loads of people came here, but in winter, only dog walkers and dedicated runners ventured out to the lake. I wandered over to a bench shaped like a fish and checked the time on my phone. I was a little early but I had been too excited to stay put any longer. Matt had finally reached out to me. I wasn't sure why he had wanted to meet here but hopefully this meant things could start to go back to normal.

I looked out at the water. A light breeze rippled the surface. I had promised Greg I wouldn't leave the house, but some things were more important. I needed to know Matt was all right. Besides, I wasn't sure Greg was coming back. I don't know what I was thinking when I kissed him. I had been caught up in the moment. He had said things between us were real but I obviously misinterpreted what he meant. He had just meant in terms of being friends. I had really messed things up as he couldn't get away from me any quicker. I wasn't stupid. There is no way he just suddenly had a flat to go view, especially that early in the morning, and he never let me out of a training session that easy. I would probably get home and find Victoria waiting to tell me Greg had gone home, leaving her to train me. I had made things really awkward, and that would be the simplest way to solve things.

I checked my phone again. Matt was hopeless at getting anywhere on time. He'd better show up. This meeting was his idea, after all. I looked up at the clear blue sky. Maybe I should have phoned Victoria, she had also been worried about Matt. So had their parents.

"Mellissa!" someone shouted. I didn't recognise the voice. I turned to see Matt walking toward me. His voice didn't sound right. The smile he gave me made me shiver. It seemed to lack any emotion. "Shall we walk by the lake? I'm sure you have questions," he said.

"Yeah, like what the hell have you been up to?" I said, trying not to sound too aggressive.

We walked along the edge of the lake. "Yes, I realise you must have been really down without your friend recently."

Was this his weird way of telling me he didn't think of me as a friend anymore? If it was, why didn't he just say that and get it over with? Matt stopped walking and stared into the distance.

"The lake looks restless."

"Freya couldn't swim," I said.

"I know, and what is your relationship with the water?"

"Matt, you know I'm—" A force shoved me forward. I hit the railing hard. Spinning around, I gasped. A leprechaun towered over me. He grabbed me and threw me over the railing. The freezing water consumed my body. It felt like pinpricks on my skin. I tried to kick and swim to the surface, but something was pulling me down. My lungs burned as they longed for air. I reached forward, trying to swim up and out, but the water felt like it had turned to jelly and was solidifying. No matter how hard I tried, I couldn't move through the water. Everything above me was a blur as I sank farther down.

A hand grabbed my arm and pulled me up to the surface. I gasped, taking in as much air as possible. The water was back to normal, and I could move again. My rescuer was already out of the water, surrounded by fire. Matt was facing off against two leprechauns. I pulled myself up on the railing and climbed over. I landed on my knees and coughed up water. My clothes stuck to my body, and my hair was dripping. Two leprechauns ran toward me but were pushed back by a wall of fire. I had to get up. Shivering, I forced myself up and ran toward the fight. If I could grab Matt, I could get us out of here.

I screamed as someone grabbed my arm, twisting it around and forcing me to my knees. It was another leprechaun. He was taller than the other two and skinny, but he was still super strong. I teleported, but the leprechaun held on tight, teleporting with me.

"That won't work, elf," he whispered into my ear. "As long as I have hold of you, you can't escape."

I reached for my phone. We were outnumbered. If I could just get a message to Victoria… I was swiping through my contacts when another leprechaun snatched the phone out of my hand. She lifted it to her face and sniffed it. She threw it down and stamped on it.

"She was trying to contact someone. We should just kill her."

The skinny guy yanked me away from her. "The master needs her alive to take her power, then he will kill her."

They argued over the orders of their master. Apparently, my dead body was better than not capturing me. I closed my eyes to focus my magic. I had to trust Matt could handle the other two. I would get myself out of this mess. Throwing my free arm up, I shot a blinding burst of light upward. They jumped back from the light, and the skinny guy let go of me. Before I had time to think, the woman grabbed my arm, spinning me around, and slammed me to the ground. She stamped on my chest, leaving me breathless. I screamed as she slammed her foot on my arm, causing it to crack. This leprechaun was quick, super strong and ruthless.

"I told you we should just kill her. These elves are tricky," she growled, pulling back her hand. As she did this, the nails on her hands grew into long, sharp claws. My whole body went numb. This was it. They were going to kill me. Victoria wasn't here to save me this time. Even after all that training, I was still useless. Where was Matt? Had the other two taken him down? Tears were falling down my cheeks.

A flurry of fire blasts came flying at the two leprechauns. It was Matt. He had come to save me. The blasts kept coming. The skinny guy went down first. The woman stood her ground against the fire. A small person, engulfed in flames, came running at her, throwing a flaming kick. It wasn't Matt. He quickly followed up by firing a wheel of flames at the leprechauns.

He skidded to a halt beside me. His dark blue eyes were ablaze with magic. He held his hand out to me. "Quickly, Your Majesty, come with me."

I wasn't sure if I could trust this person, but he had just stopped the leprechauns. I took his hand. He pulled me up, and we started to run. He was around my height, with black spiky hair. "It is my understanding that Your Majesty can teleport. I suggest you get yourself to safety," shouted the stranger.

I searched the area for Matt, but he was nowhere to be seen. "I can't leave without Matt."

"There is no one else in the area but you, me and five leprechauns."

"No, that doesn't make sense. There should also be a warlock." The stranger pushed me aside as something sharp shot through the air. My arm throbbed with pain.

"It is you they want. Get yourself to safety." He ran toward the regrouped leprechauns, hands ablaze.

"What about you?" I shouted. I may have just met him, but he'd saved me. I couldn't let him fight alone.

"Don't worry about me. I am your guardian. I am here to protect you," he yelled.

A coldness spread through my core. I couldn't have heard him correctly. What he said wasn't possible. I already had two guardians—unless something had happened to Matt. He'd disappeared. The stranger had said there were five leprechauns, but I had only seen four. What if the missing leprechaun had taken Matt?

The Heart Crystal heated around my neck as it pulsated with power. I ran toward the leprechauns, firing light blasts at them. I knew my life was in danger, but I didn't care. I forgot all about the pain in my arm. I sent a giant ray of light energy, knocking the whole group down, destroying a bench and lamppost at the same time. Standing over the skinny guy, with an energy ball in my hand, I screamed at him, "Where's Matt?"

He put his arms up over his body and claimed to have no idea what I was talking about. I fired a ball of light at his chest. "Don't make me ask again."

I was too focused on trying to get information out of the skinny leprechaun that I wasn't paying attention to the others. One of the muscled guys grabbed me by my hair and spun me round. He clutched my neck and started to squeeze. I tried to wiggle free and blasted him with light energy, but he kept squeezing. I gasped for breath. My surroundings started to blur.

A blaze of fire struck the guy in the back, and I fell to the ground as he dropped me. The stranger who claimed to be my guardian had come to my rescue again. He threw a flaming punch at the guy and swept a blaze of fire at him, taking his feet out from under him. The leprechaun fell to the ground with a thud. This time, the stranger picked me up. He put me over his shoulder and ran.

"Your Majesty, I demand that you teleport to safety right now," he shouted.

"But what about Matt? I need to know where he is." Tears streamed down my face.

"I do not know what happened to this Matt person you speak of. What I do know is that your life is in danger, and it is my duty to protect you. I cannot do that if you won't cooperate. Now, you need to teleport."

I didn't want to leave without knowing where Matt was, but if I stayed here any longer, I was just going to get myself killed. I shut my eyes and teleported.

We crash-landed in the hallway of my house. I rolled across the floor and hit the bottom of the stairs. I screamed for Greg. He had to be here. He was who I'd thought of when I teleported. I hadn't expected to come home.

Greg came running out of the living room. He dropped to his knees beside me and cupped my face with his hands. "What happened? You're ice cold."

"It doesn't matter. I need to find Matt." I tried to get up, only to fall back down. I had managed to hurt my leg without realising it. My heart almost stopped when I saw my dad in the living room doorway, hand on his head, mouth wide open.

Greg shook my shoulders. "Mellissa, what happened? You promised not to leave the house."

"Greg, we need to find Matt!" I yelled, trying to get up again.

Greg caught me as I fell this time. "You are in no condition to go anywhere."

"Will someone please tell me what is going on?" said my dad, both hands on his head.

"The leprechauns, they have Matt," I cried, clutching Greg's arm. The look on his face did not help my current panic.

"Mellissa, you just appeared out of nowhere, and now you're going on about leprechauns. We need to get you to the hospital. I'll go get the car," Dad said.

"Dad, no," I shouted. "I don't need a hospital, just Greg."

"Your Majesty, where are we?" asked the stranger I'd teleported with, getting up off the ground.

"Who are you?" Greg asked, quickly putting up a barrier between us and the guy who had saved me.

"Master Gregory, I did not realise the queen was bringing us to you," said the stranger. He dropped down on his knee, bowing to Greg.

"Greg, it's okay. This guy saved me. I wouldn't have made it back without him." I leant my head on his shoulder as everything blurred. "We need to find Matt."

"I need to heal you. We need to get you somewhere I can examine you better." He scooped me up in his arms and took me into the living room. "Mr. Hail, can you get some blankets?"

My dad nodded and walked out of the room, seemingly in a daze. Why was no one listening to me? I was fine. It was more important we found Matt.

Greg sat me on the sofa and summoned his medical kit. My rescuer tried to approach, but there was still a barrier around us. Greg narrowed his eyes at him. The stranger went and stood against the wall farthest from us. My dad came back with a pile of blankets. Greg wrapped one around my shoulder. It was soft and fluffy. I hadn't realised how badly I was shivering.

"I need you to lie down," Greg said.

With a huff, I stretched across the sofa. Annoyingly, he was right. I needed to be healed. I would be of no use to Matt in my current state. Greg cut into the leg of my jeans. There was a giant slash along my leg. "Sanum quod fit." Greg's hands glowed green. He hovered them over my wound, and the skin knit itself back together. My dad's jaw dropped. I had a lot of explaining to do.

Greg turned to the stranger who had saved me. "All right, then. Who are you, and how do you know who Mellissa and I are?"

"I am Harkura of the Tonoe River water nymph tribe." The stranger bowed. "Stories of you and the queen have been travelling among the water nymphs for days now. It is an honour to meet you both. I will do my best to protect the queen in my new role as her guardian."

"What? Mellissa already has two guardians." Greg examined my broken arm. I grimaced every time he moved it. He pulled the coffee table closer to the sofa, placed my arm on it and got out a bunch of multicoloured stones. He placed five stones under my arm and another five on top of it, whispering another incantation. The stones began to glow.

"All I know is, a few days ago, a light appeared to me and led me here. I knew it was calling me here to protect the queen, to become her guardian," Harkura explained.

"That's what Victoria and Matt said happened to them," I said, sitting up. "How is that possible? We need to find Matt. He is my guardian, not you, and if you're a water nymph, why aren't you blue?"

"Mellissa, stay still. Your arm is broken in three places. This may take a while. You need to let the healing stones do their job." Greg put his arm out and made me lie back down. "She isn't blue due to a simple glamour charm, and what makes you think she's replacing Matt?"

"Because he has fire powers like Matt. He saved me with some crazy fire karate. Also, why are you calling him she?"

"I don't know. I just assumed Harkura was female, and that is very interesting. You're a water nymph with fire powers?" Greg asked, turning toward Harkura.

"Yes, I am a bit of an oddity amongst my people," Harkura replied.

"I am sorry to ask this, but what is your chosen gender?"

"I am still undecided. I don't mind which gender you refer to me as."

I clenched the fist of my good hand. "This doesn't really matter right now. We have to find Matt," I said and tried to get up again.

"Lie down. You are in no shape to go anywhere." Greg forced me to lie back down.

"Why can't you just do what you did with my leg? That was a lot quicker. I don't have time for this."

"That was only a flesh wound. Your arm is broken, and it will take longer to heal." Greg turned to my dad. "Mr. Hail, could you please contact Victoria and let her know she no longer needs to search for Mellissa?"

My dad shook his head. "Um, yeah. I can do that. I will call her, and then I want an explanation, Mellissa. You will have time while your arm heals, by the sound of it."

I looked up at the ceiling, wondering what I would tell him. I guess I had no choice but to have the "magic is real" talk now.

Greg poked me in the side. I slapped his hand away. "That hurts you know."

"Sorry. I was just trying to see if anything else is broken. Luckily, it's just a bruise, which is easy to heal."

I put my other arm over my head. "This is ridiculous. Why am I so mashed up, but Harkura doesn't have a scratch on him?"

"As you put it, he knows crazy fire karate, and you have only just started learning to fight."

"Sorry I'm not an expert fighter after a couple of lessons."

"I don't expect you to be, but you could have teleported yourself to safety sooner. How many times do I need to tell you to think of your safety first?"

"Well, where were you? You left me on my own, and I got a call from Matt. What else was I going to do?"

Greg put his head in his hands as he sat back on the floor. He had some nerve being annoyed at me. He'd just buggered off, and I hadn't just left for the sake of it. I had gone to make sure my friend was all right—a friend who was also my guardian, so I didn't see the problem. However, I now had no idea where he was. God knows what those leprechauns had done to Matt.

"I'm sorry." Greg stroked my cheek. "You're still freezing." He placed two more blankets over me.

My dad came back into the room and told us that Victoria was on her way. I guess now was as a good as any to have the talk. He sat in the armchair across from me, and I told him everything. I started at the beginning, telling him how I really met Greg. He wasn't impressed with how I smuggled him into the house disguised as a rabbit. Considering I was telling him about leprechauns, elves and warlocks, he took it all pretty well. When I was done, he wouldn't look me in the eye. He looked up at the ceiling and then out the window while rubbing his face. He sighed and turned to me, leaning his head to the side.

"There is something I need to tell you about your mother," he said. "You see, your mother had these powers. She could manipulate plant life and shake the earth. Your mother was an elf."

My jaw dropped. He'd known about my mum being an elf all this time and had said nothing. He'd told me so many stories about her, yet somehow, he had managed to leave that key detail out. I went to sit up again, but Greg grabbed my shoulder to stop me. I clenched my fist. I took a sharp intake of breath and looked at the ceiling. "What—how—I mean, why didn't you tell me this before?"

"I never thought something like this would happen to you. I had no idea your mother was a descendant of some queen." My dad put his hand to his head again. "Your mother said something about you not having a strong magical presence as a baby. You never displayed any abilities over plants. I thought maybe you were more human than elf. With your mother not here to tell you herself, I didn't really know what to say."

"Well, obviously, I have powers. I don't know why they took so long to manifest. Although, Greg did say something about my magic signature being off when we met." My dad and I both turned to Greg. If anyone could explain this to us, it was him.

Greg put his hands up. "I already told you, I don't know. You are the first human elf I have met. Although, I'm sure you're not the only one. There is a whole village of them. I'm sure they're not all purely elfish."

"There's a what? So you're keeping things from me too?"

"It never came up. We can talk about it later."

"I am sorry I didn't tell you sooner," Dad said.

I shut my eyes, scared I might cry. "I am also sorry for not telling you that I met a talking rabbit. You have to admit, it sounds crazy."

It felt like a weight had been lifted. I hadn't realised how much keeping my magic secret had been weighing on me. Maybe if he'd informed me about my mother's abilities, I wouldn't have lied in the first place, but now wasn't the time to be upset about that. Matt was still missing. I needed to know where he was. These stupid healing stones were taking too long.

I almost fell off the sofa as Victoria burst in, bringing a cold flurry with her. Her fists were clenched, and she was scowling. I hoped she hadn't knocked the front door down again. She marched past my dad and Harkura, only to run into the barrier Greg still had around the two of us.

"What is with this barrier?" she shouted, hitting it with some ice. "You spineless little changeling. This is all your fault. You never should have trusted her to stay put." She threw some more ice at the barrier. "I never should have trusted you to keep her safe." The barrier cracked with her next blast.

"It's not his fault." I needed to make this clear before

she broke through the barrier and killed Greg. "I'm the one that broke my promise. I went to meet Matt, so I thought it would be all right."

"Don't get me started on you," she shouted, pointing at me. "I don't know which one of you is stupider. Do you not care about your own safety, and what's with the water nymph?" She pointed at Harkura while still glaring at Greg. How was it that both of them instantly knew Harkura was a water nymph? If I hadn't been told, I never would have known.

"Hello, madame," Harkura said, bowing to Victoria. "I am Harkura of the Tonoe River water nymph tribe. I am Her Majesty's new guardian. It is a pleasure to meet you." Harkura put out his hand to shake hers, but she ignored him.

Victoria's jaw dropped. Her look of anger turned to one of shock. "What do you mean?" She looked at me. "Matt is your other guardian. Something's wrong. Wait, you said you were meeting Matt?"

"Yes. He rang me not long after Greg left."

She turned to Greg. "You haven't told her, have you?"

I looked at Victoria and then Greg. "Haven't told me what?"

"I was waiting till all your wounds were healed, as you are in no shape to go anywhere," Greg said.

"Will one of you just tell me what is going on?"

Greg took a deep breath. "Fine. I didn't really go to view a flat."

"Yeah, I know that. I'm not a complete idiot. Just because Victoria says I am, doesn't make it true."

"Then why did you—" Greg shook his head. "Never mind. I went to find out what Matt was doing. I cast a tracking spell, but it didn't work."

"So, he came to me," Victoria said. "Using my blood, we tracked Matt to the council building in the capital city."

"How is that possible?" I asked. "There is no way he could make that journey in a day. Are you sure the spell was correct?" If that was where he was, there was no way he could've made it to the river to meet me today. They had to have made a mistake.

"The spell was done correctly," Greg said, "and there is no spell stronger than one cast with blood."

"It doesn't make sense." I sat up, knocking the healing stones off my arm. I winced as pain shot through my arm, but I didn't care. Greg tried to make me lie back down, but I resisted. "Matt has no reason to be there. If you can use your blood to track Matt, do it again. Show me."

"Okay, I will do it," Victoria said. "Greg, do you have that map?"

Greg flicked his wrist and produced a map. He handed it to Victoria and also gave her a small glass bottle out of his pocket. Victoria laid the map out on the floor and sprinkled some sand from the bottle onto it. She then cut her finger and chanted some words. I didn't catch all of them, but it was something to do with blood and finding a lost loved one. I watched as the blood moved across the map. It stopped at the council building.

Victoria pointed at the map. "He is still there. Mellissa, blood magic doesn't lie."

I shook my head. "I will believe it when I see it for myself." I shut my eyes and attempted teleportation to the capital. I screamed as I was rebuffed and fell on my broken arm.

Greg picked me up off the floor and rearranged the stones on my arm. "You can't teleport that far."

"Then I'll do multiple teleports." He stroked my cheek. I clasped his hand. "Greg, please. I need to know what's going on."

"Mellissa, you haven't healed properly. You're just going to make your arm worse."

There was a sharp prick on my arm. A cold shiver shot up my arm, and I suddenly felt light-headed. "What did you do to me?" I grabbed his shirt, trying to pull myself up. Everything was becoming a blur.

"Don't fight it. It's just a sedative to help with the pain while you heal."

I tried to talk, but the words wouldn't come. How could he do this to me? I'd trusted him. I fell against Greg as I passed out.

Fractured
Mellissa

I was tucked up in bed with no memory of how I'd gotten there. I looked out the window. It was now dark out. The sky was clear, giving me the perfect view of the moon. It shone brightly in the darkness. My body felt stiff as I pushed myself up. I shook my head. I needed to focus. What had I been doing before I'd fallen asleep?

Matt.

Leprechauns had attacked us this morning, and he had disappeared. My legs gave way as I clambered out of bed. My bedroom door flew open.

"You're awake," Victoria said. She pulled me to my feet and forced me back on my bed.

"What's happening? Where's Matt?"

"Still in the capital, according to the tracking spell."

A tracking spell? Blood magic. Victoria had done a spell, but if he was in the capital, how had he gotten there from the lake so quick? I had tried to find out, but Greg put me to sleep. I hadn't just drifted off. That's why everything was so hazy. "Where's Greg?" I asked.

"Talking with Lady Gabrielle. From what I overheard, things aren't good. All the known leprechaun villages have been abandoned. They seem to be congregating in the forest. There is talk of a new leader bringing them together. The council fear an attack is imminent."

"But surely they would be outnumbered. Why start a fight they can't win?"

Victoria looked down at me with sad eyes. "I believe that's why this leader of theirs wants you alive—so he can steal your power. Assuming he knows how to use your magic, he would be difficult to stop, even with an army."

"This is so messed up."

"Flopsey is still talking with Lady Gabrielle. She may have a solution. He is also asking her about Matt, so try not to worry too much. I will go get you some food. You must be starving."

I nodded. The look of pity on her face as she left almost broke me. There was something she wasn't telling me, or at least something she suspected that she didn't want to share with me. How had this become my life? Every time I thought I'd discovered my new normal, everything fell apart. If the leprechauns didn't get my power, would they still attack? That woman had said my dead body was better than no capture. They were going to attack no matter what. My magic would just be a bonus, and if they couldn't have it, they wanted me out of the way. I looked at my palms. Was my magic really that powerful?

"Mellissa," my dad shouted from downstairs, making me jump. I thought Victoria was coming back with food, but he must've had other ideas. I dragged myself up and walked out of my room. I almost fell over my feet. Walking toward me was Matt. I felt like a weight had been lifted off my shoulders at the sight of him.

I ran to him and hugged him. "Matt, where have you been? I was so worried."

"I'm sorry about this morning," he said, looking down at me. His gaze was cold and empty. The usual light in his eyes was gone. "I'm glad you are all right. I was captured by leprechauns, but I managed to escape."

I put my hand over my mouth. "Oh my God. Are you all right? Greg can heal any wounds."

"I am just fine now that I have found you." Matt gave me a smile, but it didn't have any warmth in it. The way he was speaking wasn't like him at all. Something was wrong. I could feel it deep in my heart.

"Come on. I was just about to get some food," I said, turning to walk downstairs. I screamed as something dragged me back and threw me into the wall. I hit the floor with a thud.

Matt laughed. "I realised I made a mistake approaching you this morning."

I looked up to see Matt with what looked like a ball of shadows in his hand. "Matt, what is going on?"

"I should have waited for moonlight. Now, my power will exceed that of you and your guardians."

He threw the shadow ball at me. I threw my arms in front of me, forming a barrier. The shadows dissolved it. Before I had time to blink, Matt lifted his arm, and a dark sphere formed around me. I punched and kicked at it, but it was solid, like a wall. Matt slowly walked toward me with a smirk on his face. He turned his wrist, and the ball began to fill with water.

This couldn't be happening. Matt had just attacked me. He was my best friend. Nothing made sense. I blasted light energy at the sphere, but my magic had no effect on it. My blood ran cold. Water gushed around me. If I didn't get out soon, I would be immersed in seconds.

"Once you are close to death, your power will be mine to take."

The smile on Matt's face faded as a barrier appeared around him. Barrier after barrier formed around Matt. After at least twelve barriers were around him, Matt was pulled away from me. Greg ran to me and put his hands on the sphere. My head was only just above the water now. I couldn't stand anymore. I wasn't sure how long I could hold my breath.

"Mellissa, you need to get yourself out of there," Greg shouted. "The magic he is using is of a higher level than mine."

I tried to form an energy blast, but it faded as the sphere completely filled. It was like time slowed. I threw my arms around, trying to blast my way out, but my magic wasn't working. This couldn't be it for me. Greg hit the sphere from the outside. He was shouting at me, but I couldn't hear him anymore. I couldn't hold my breath for much longer.

A flurry of dark shadows appeared behind Greg. I tried to shout, only to have my mouth fill with water. It felt like pinpricks as it went down, and my lungs burned. Shadows wrapped around Greg and pulled him toward Matt. How had he managed to get out of so many barriers so quickly? This magic wasn't Matt's. It was something darker. I had to save myself. I couldn't just give up. My life wasn't the only one in danger. I shut my eyes and released a blast of light energy.

I hit the floor and gasped for air. I didn't have time to think. I released another blast of light, breaking through the shadows. I dived at Greg and teleported. We landed on the floor in the living room. I rolled onto my back, sucking in big breaths.

Greg got up and walked over to the door. "Mellissa, you need to teleport somewhere farther away."

I sat up. "I can't just go. What about the others?" I put my hand on my chest. My throat stung with every breath I took. It felt like my heart was about to break. "Matt attacked me. Why would he do that?"

Greg walked back over to me. He knelt in front of me and put his hand on my cheek. "That's not Matt. Your safety is all that matters now. You need to teleport away."

Greg was almost as soaked as I was. We both jumped up at the sound of a scream and a crash. It sounded like there was a fight going on just outside this room. I ran out of the room to see Harkura being thrown down the hall and through the kitchen door. Matt went to walk toward Harkura, but Victoria stepped in his path. "Matt, what are you doing?"

"You really are all so stupid," he replied. "I assume that one is the little elf's new guardian. I will kill you two, and then there will be no one left to protect her."

A dark shadow surrounded Matt. He lifted his hand and threw a shadow ball at Victoria. She swiftly froze his attack. The ball of ice fell to the floor and shattered. They both fired off another attack. They were siblings; they shouldn't be fighting. Everything that was going on was almost a blur. It was as if my brain didn't want to process what was happening. Their fight moved to the kitchen.

This person may look like Matt, but he was not the same person. Everything about him was so cold, and the magic he was using was so dark. I had sensed something wasn't right about him, but I'd pretended everything was fine. I hadn't wanted to believe something was wrong. I had wanted things to go back to normal so much that I'd ignored my gut feeling in hopes of making that happen.

I went to join the fight but froze on the spot. My dad lay on the bottom of the stairs. I ran over to him and knelt beside him. "Dad." I rolled him over, but he was not responsive. My eyes began to fill with tears. Greg appeared beside me. He laid my dad flat out on the floor and started chanting. Matt had done this. At least, his look-alike had. I stood up with my fists clenched and teleported to the kitchen.

The room was completely destroyed, but no one was inside. There was a massive hole in the side of the house that led to the garden. I ran through it and put my hands over my mouth.

Matt smirked. "Good of you to join us, elf-ling. Now, if you are a good little girl, I will let you exchange your life for your guardians." He had both Harkura and Victoria wrapped in shadows.

"Mellissa, get out of here now," Victoria yelled, struggling against her restraints.

"Quiet, you," snarled Matt. He tightened his grip on her and wrapped a shadow around her mouth. "Now, what will it be—your life or your guardians'?"

There really wasn't any choice to make. The answer was obvious. I stepped forward. "Let them go, and you can have me."

"Mellissa, no." Greg grabbed my arm and pulled me back.

"Nobody asked for your input!" Matt yelled, releasing a ray of darkness, blasting Greg away from me.

"Greg!" I screamed. I went to run to him, but I stopped myself. I couldn't trade my life for Victoria's. Whoever this person was, he didn't care about anyone here. I had no guarantee he wouldn't hurt them once he was rid of me. I turned to face Matt when a flurry of fireballs hit him. Harkura had somehow gotten free. He dived at Matt with his body engulfed in flames. This was my chance. I ducked down and put my hand on the ground.

Matt sent Harkura flying across the garden with a blast of water. He trapped him in a sphere like I'd been trapped in. Matt turned back to me, but Harkura had provided all the time I needed. Just as Matt was about to throw an attack, vines shot up from the ground and wrapped themselves around him. Matt blasted the vines with shadows. I stood up, lifting my arms, wrapping them tighter and tighter. It didn't matter how many vines he broke; I could just make more. I released a ray of light at Victoria, freeing her. She went straight into attack mode. She grabbed his leg and froze him, leaving only his head free.

I tightened the vines. Now that he was a human popsicle, I could easily break him. "Now, tell me what you did with Matt."

He rolled his eyes. "I haven't done anything with him. It was all you, elf-ling."

"Liar," Victoria shouted. "Mellissa would never do anything to hurt Matt."

The imposter snickered. "I haven't harmed the warlock boy in any way. All I did was swap places with him and donned this glamour spell."

"No, that isn't possible," I said.

"Oh, but it is," he said in a singsong tone. "Your changeling friend over there figured it out the moment he saw me. I guess he is the only one in this little group that has any sort of a brain. You were too late when you came to the Tree of Time, but I must thank you. My escape went unnoticed because of you, and I was able to rebuild my strength."

I looked over to Greg, but he turned away from me. My arms fell beside me. He'd already known but hadn't cared to share it with me. I put my hand over my chest. My heart felt like it was about to burst. My legs almost gave way. I hadn't sealed Kadon. I'd sealed Matt instead, which meant that the person standing in front of me was Kadon himself.

The crystal began to glow. This was Kadon we were dealing with. He had the Moon Crystal locked away inside him. His power equalled mine, and he knew how to use it better than I did. This was all an act and he'd let us restrain him. I needed to act fast. I lifted my arm, but with a simple tilt of his head, Kadon released a giant pulse of dark energy, knocking us all to the ground and freeing himself.

I got up as fast as I could and released a burst of light. He dispersed it with one hand. I went to throw an energy ball, but he ran at me with super speed and grabbed my hand. He forced me to my knees. He looked down at me with cold eyes. "I'm going to enjoy putting an end to Freya's line."

He bent down and wrapped his hand around my neck, lifting me off the ground. This was the second time someone had tried to strangle me today. I kicked at him. My struggle only made him laugh. Kadon was hit by an ice blast. Rings of light appeared around his wrists.

"A binding spell, really?" He dropped me, bent his knees and jumped high into the air.

My jaw dropped. My eyes widened as I looked up at Kadon. He was flying. I hadn't realised that sort of magic was possible. But I had. The Heart Crystal had warned me in a dream. This confrontation was what my dreams were meant to prepare me for. Kadon clicked his fingers, trapping Greg and Victoria in dark spheres just like Harkura.

"I really have no need for this glamour spell anymore. None of you will live long enough to warn anyone about me." Kadon waved his arm over his body, and his appearance changed. He no longer looked like Matt. He was now a tall, grey creature with long, silver hair that was braided and tied into a ponytail. His grey eyes cut through me. I'd seen those eyes before. "You are all such nuisances," he snarled. "I hope you're happy, elf-ling. If you had come willingly, I might have spared your friends." He lifted his arms and shadows swirled around them.

I clutched my sides. My presence was putting everyone in danger. Their association with me was going to get them killed. I took a sharp intake of breath and threw my arms down. I wasn't going to let him hurt anyone else. I ran at Kadon and blasted light energy at the ground, throwing myself into the air. I reached out and grabbed his leg. As soon as I made contact, I teleported.

We landed with a thud in the middle of the Novos

Forest. As usual, my landing was terrible, but this actually helped for a change. I was used to my bad landings, but Kadon was not. I used this to my advantage. While he was still dazed by the teleportation, I rolled away from him, shooting a bright ray of light, temporarily blinding him. I used this opportunity to teleport back home. I landed in the garden and fell flat on my face.

Everyone was still trapped in the dark spheres. Removing Kadon didn't get rid of his magic. I got up and put my hands round the Heart Crystal. I took a deep breath and pushed my hands outward, producing a wave of light. The dark spheres disappeared. Victoria ran over to me. She took hold of my shoulders.

"Don't ever do that again," Victoria shouted. "You scared me to death when you teleported away with him like that." I could see the worry on her face, but there was something else. Pain. She was upset, and it was all my doing. I was such a failure.

"I'm sorry. I had to do something. I couldn't let him hurt anyone else." I paused. My wet clothes stuck to my body. I wrapped my arms round myself. How could she be concerned for me after everything that had just happened? Matt was trapped, and it was all my fault. I breathed unevenly as I burst into tears. "Victoria, I'm so sorry. I don't know what to do. I will find a way to fix this. I will get Matt back."

"Mellissa, this is not your fault. Kadon is the one to blame," she said. "He is the one that trapped my brother and tricked us. I'm the one that should have noticed. I knew something was wrong but ignored it. What sort of sister am I to not have realised he was an imposter all this time?" Her voice broke, and her eyes were tearing. I'd never seen her like this. She always hid her emotions with insults.

"Your Majesty, perhaps you should rest," Harkura said. "This is the second time you have been attacked today."

"No, we have to get out of here," Greg said.

I looked over at Greg. "How is my dad?"

"He's fine. I left him resting in the living room," he replied. "Look, it isn't safe here anymore. Although, I don't understand why Kadon waited this long to attack you at home."

"He didn't know where I lived before," I said. He may have looked like Matt, but he didn't know what Matt did. It was my own fault that he'd found me. "I lost my phone this morning when I was attacked. He can now find me wherever I go."

"Now he has something to cast a tracking spell with," Greg said, nodding. He put his hand on his chin. He appeared to be thinking. However, I wasn't about to stick around to hear his thoughts on the topic. I couldn't let them know what I was about to do as they would only try to stop me. I took a step back to make sure no one was making contact with me and teleported.

I rolled down a hill on arrival. Pain shot through my side. I pushed myself up to see I was at the edge of Novosvillas. I teleported two more times, arriving at the Tree of Time. As usual, I landed on my butt. My heart sank as I looked up at the tree. The last time I was here, we had been celebrating. Little did I know, that all that time, my best friend was the one trapped in this tree.

I scrambled to my feet and placed my hand on the tree. "Matt, I'm so sorry, but I'm going to get you out of there." I shut my eyes, focusing on the energy inside me. I summoned a massive amount of light and fired it at the tree. It didn't even make a scratch. I tried again and again, throwing energy blast after energy blast. Why wasn't this working? It was my magic that had sealed him. Surely I should be able to break the spell. I screamed as I collapsed to the ground, letting out a giant pulse of light. Tears rolled down my cheeks. I put my hand on the tree and pictured Matt—the real Matt. My best friend. I teleported, only to be repulsed back by the tree. I screamed again, blasting the tree. Nothing I did had any effect.

What was the point of all the training I had done? I had learnt nothing that could help me now. Everyone kept telling me about all this power I was meant to have, but all I seemed to do was nearly get myself killed and put others in danger. I wiped away my tears. There was still one thing I hadn't tried. I put my hand on the tree and tried to communicate with it. I didn't get any response. I punched the tree, cutting my hand. I looked at my bleeding hand. I deserved to be hurt after what I'd done. My world had come crashing down around me. I'd thought I could be more than what I was. I was wrong. I believed I was helping people, but all I did was make things worse. Kadon was free, and because of me, he had managed to work on his plans in secret, getting ahead of everyone. I collapsed against the tree, sobbing.

"Lady Mellissa, what is going on?" came a voice. I turned to see Lord Steffen and a few others. "Why are you attacking the tree?"

I wiped my hand over my face and dragged myself up. "It's Matt. He's the one in the tree, not Kadon. This is all my fault. I have to get him out of there."

"But you cannot. Only a power greater than the magic used can break the seal. It is not only your magic at work, but that of the tree itself. It's why the original seal held for so long." Lord Steffen put his hand on his chin. He gestured to the others who had come out with him. "This is bad. We must prepare for an attack from Kadon. You over there, go alert the other council members. Kadon has escaped. All nations must prepare for battle."

"There has to be another way to release Matt. Kadon broke the seal." I looked up at him, hopeful he would know what to do. He was Greg's dad after all. Greg had to get his know-it-all attitude from somewhere.

"Yes, but it took Kadon thousands of years to break free, and all magic weakens over time."

"You mean Matt will stay trapped for thousands of years?" That was not what I wanted to hear. My eyes filled with tears again.

"Maybe you should go rest, my dear. You look like you have been though a lot this evening," Lord Steffen suggested.

"No, I will not rest," I screamed, throwing my arms in the air. "There has to be a way. I just have to find it."

I teleported away, landing in a muddy field. I teleported again, landed on a rock and slipped down, cutting my knee.

One more teleport should get me home. I had to believe there was a way to save Matt. Greg was the smartest person I knew. He had to know something his dad didn't, and he owed me. I teleported home and landed at the end of the garden. Bright lights shot into the sky. *Boom.*

My heart almost stopped as I jumped to the side. My neighbours where setting off fireworks. I placed my hand over my heart. They did this every year on the lead-up to the new year. I usually loved to watch the free firework display; however, watching them now, I felt nothing—no excitement or joy. I wasn't even angry anymore. I just felt numb as I looked up at the sky. My throat was dry, and my eyes stung. A loud bang echoed around me, but I didn't flinch this time. I stood there motionless, not knowing what to do next.

Victoria came running out of the house. "Mellissa, I'm so glad you are back. I was so worried." She grabbed my arm and bent down to my eye level. "What happened? Where did you go?"

I opened my mouth to talk, but nothing came out. My chest felt tight, and my throat was sore. She gave me a comforting pat. I shrugged it away. I didn't deserve to be comforted.

"I can't," I said, "Lord Steffen said—why can't I fix this? I'm to blame."

Victoria put both her hands on my shoulders and bent down to meet my gaze. "I'm not sure what Lord Steffen said to you, but this is definitely not your fault. This is Kadon's doing, and he is going to pay for what he's done. Let's go inside."

Victoria took my hand and attempted to lead me inside. I pulled away from her. "No, I can't. I need to do something." My head was spinning. I needed to think of something. I needed Greg's help, but he had known. He knew something was wrong but didn't tell me. Could I really trust him now? My eyes started to well up. I couldn't be mad at Greg. This was my fault. If I wasn't so careless, I could have figured things out sooner. Some keeper of the Heart I was turning out to be. Victoria let go of me and headed back toward the house. I shut my eyes and felt the wind on my face. My whole body was shaking.

A hand rested on my shoulder. I opened my eyes to see Greg. I went to talk, but the words wouldn't come. I was so mad at him, but at the same time, I wasn't. I buried my face in his shirt and hugged him. "I don't know what to do."

Greg leant back so we were looking at one another. He wiped away the tears rolling down my cheeks and tilted his head. "I'm sorry. I don't have any answers for you at the moment. For now, you need to go get some rest."

"No," I said, pushing him away from me. "Will everyone stop telling me to rest? I need you to help figure out how to save Matt."

"I understand you're upset—"

"No, you don't. Matt was my friend, and I let this happen. This is all my fault."

"None of this is your fault. I will help you find a way to save Matt, but first, you need to rest. You have used a lot of magic this evening."

"What does it matter? Your dad told me I can't break my own spell."

"My father doesn't know everything. We will figure this out, but you have to allow yourself time to recover."

I looked at the ground. I was exhausted, and my whole body ached. My stupid human body needed to catch up with all of my magic usage. My eyes were sore from all the crying. My legs felt like jelly. I wasn't sure how I was still standing. I took Greg's hand and let him walk me back to the house. Victoria was by the door with her arms crossed.

Greg healed the cuts on my hand and knee before leaving me to get some sleep. I pulled off my mud-soaked clothes and replaced them with dry pyjamas. Their softness didn't feel right against my skin. I curled up in a ball and drifted off.

I woke up in a sweat, my heart racing. I lay still and patted myself down. It had all been a dream, and I was still in one piece. I had dreamt of Matt. He had merged with the tree and told me I was a failure. Everything was my fault. Kadon appeared out of nowhere and captured Greg and Victoria. I tried to save them, but I couldn't. Kadon had me beat and was about to make the final blow when I'd woken up.

My bed felt hard for some reason. I put my hand down beside me. Instead of feeling my soft sheets, it was damp and cold. I sat up and shivered. My eyes widened. In front of me was a tree, and another stood beside me. I looked around. I'd somehow woken up in the forest. Had I teleported in my sleep? That seemed to be the only explanation. I'd managed to bring my quilt with me. I bundled it up and teleported back to my bedroom.

I couldn't get back to sleep after that. I lay in bed, staring up at the ceiling, thinking about everything that had happened and what I could have done to change things. No matter how much I thought about it, I couldn't change the past. I was also worried about where I might wake up next if I went back to sleep. I wasn't sure if I should tell anyone about what happened. I didn't need them obsessing over my powers when there were more important things to be thinking about. Plus, it was the first time it'd happened. It could just be a one-off.

I had to focus on what was happening now. I wouldn't stop until I found a way to free Matt. I also had to be ready for Kadon if he attacked again. We had barely survived our last encounter with him. I had no idea what his plans were or when he would be back, but I knew he wanted revenge, and that would involve killing me.

I went to see if Greg was awake. I figured he would have some books with ideas on how to save Matt. As I went to knock on his door, I heard him talking to someone. I opened the door a crack to see who was in there with him. I peeked inside, but there was no one there. Instead, he was on the bed talking to his glowing circular communication thing. He seemed to be arguing with someone. I could just about hear what he was saying. There was more than one voice on the other end. The council. They wanted him to bring me to their headquarters right away. Greg was arguing against their decision. I really didn't want to go back there, but with everything that had happened, I knew I would have to face them soon. I shut the door and headed downstairs. I could look at books later. My dad was already up.

"How are you feeling this morning?" he asked.

"Like someone stomped on my chest, but better than last night."

My dad hugged me. "Victoria explained everything to me. I'm sorry about Matt. I'm here if you need me."

"Thanks, Dad."

I followed him into the kitchen. My jaw dropped. The kitchen was back to normal. The massive hole in the side of the house was gone, and everything was back in its place. There was no evidence of yesterday's fight. My dad smiled at me. "Greg fixed it all with a spell. His magic just saved me a massive bill fixing the place."

I sat at the table, and my dad made us breakfast. Harkura came in from outside, bowing to me and wishing us a good morning. I told him he didn't have to be so formal, but he insisted it wasn't right that a commoner like himself refer to me by only my first name. Harkura had set up a tent in our garden as he didn't want to stay in the house. Being outside meant he would be alerted first if there was an attack.

"Harkura, do you know any other types of magic?" I asked. Hopefully, he might know something that could help free Matt.

He shook his head. "As a water nymph with fire abilities, I wasn't able to take part in most magic lessons taught, as they were all water-based. I learnt everything I know from a warlock who lived near my village."

He went on to tell us more about his village and upbringing. It was interesting listening to Harkura and just the distraction I needed. He hadn't had it easy being the only wielder of fire magic amongst a village built for those with water magic. He wasn't sure where his powers came from. It was assumed that some distant relative in his family must not have been a water nymph.

Greg came downstairs to join us after what seemed like

hours talking with the council. He didn't look like he had good news. I was right. He informed us that the council had demanded my presence in order to prepare for Kadon's next attack. He'd tried to convince them to wait, but they insisted on having me there now. I really didn't want to go. The thought of going back again just reminded me of how I'd failed Matt. In addition, I didn't really believe I could stand up to Kadon's power. But I had to try, didn't I? It was my responsibility as the keeper of the Heart Crystal. So, I agreed to go.

Harkura said he would go wherever I went, as it was his duty to protect me. He took his duty as a guardian very seriously, even more so than Victoria. I called Victoria to see if she would come with us. Of course, she agreed. She had gone home last night to talk to her parents. I didn't think I could ever face them again. Mr. and Mrs. Street had always been so nice to me, and I had taken their son from them. I wouldn't blame them if they hated me for the rest of their lives. I went upstairs to prepare myself to go back to the magic world.

I found myself staring out the window. I didn't feel like myself. My whole body was tense. My heart was heavy, weighing me down. So much was expected from me. I didn't even have time to get over losing Matt. I hadn't had any time to try finding a solution to the problem. So much had changed in my life in such a short amount of time. It was all too much. I just wanted to curl up in my bed and hide away from the world.

There was a knock on my door. It was Greg. Everything had changed when I met him. He informed me that Victoria had arrived and everyone was ready to leave. I followed him downstairs where the others were waiting. They all grabbed hold of me, and I teleported us to Novosvillas.

"Wait, is this Novosvillas?" Greg asked. "This is the farthest you've ever teleported. Your powers are growing significantly."

"Yeah, well, obviously not enough." I rolled my eyes at him. "I can get us to the council in two more teleports."

"Are you sure you're okay?" Greg asked.

How could he ask such a stupid question? Of course, I wasn't okay. How could I be with everything that had just happened? Kadon was free because of me, and my best friend was trapped. I felt like I was about to explode.

"No, I'm not okay," I shouted. "Why would I be? I know I said I would do this, but I just can't. How can you expect me to go back and help them again? The last time I did that, I lost Matt. This time, it could be Victoria, and they will just keep taking people from me until I have no one."

"Mellissa, calm down. Nothing is going to happen to me," Victoria said, putting her hand out.

I shook my head. "Matt told me everything would be all right, but it wasn't. I don't want you or Harkura to risk your lives being my guardians."

"Your Majesty, it is an honour to be your guardian," Harkura said. "I know we have only just met, but I truly believe in your ability as queen."

"I know you mean well, Harkura, but I am no queen. I'm just a human girl thrown into a world of magic. I have no idea what I am doing."

"Mellissa, I know you're upset about Matt, but you can't let that hold you back," Greg said, putting his hand on my shoulder. "We need you. You are the only one that could possibly stand up to Kadon."

"No!" I screamed, hitting his arm away. "I am not doing this. This is not my problem; it's yours. Why should I ruin my life to help you? This is a problem of the magic world, and I'm not from here, so it isn't my responsibility."

"Do you really think this is just a problem for the magic world? Once Kadon is done getting his revenge on us, do you truly believe that he won't come after the humans? Kadon still hates humans. He will go after them too, and you along with them." I could tell by Greg's tone he was annoyed with me. "Even if you try to deny it, you can't change your ancestry."

"I am done listening to you, Greg. Listening to you is what got me into this mess in the first place. I wish we had never met!" I yelled, throwing my arm to the side.

The ground shook, and a massive crack appeared. Cries of passers-by echoed as they stumbled. I looked down at my hand, wide-eyed. Had I just done that? Both Harkura and

Victoria looked shocked at my outburst. Greg looked like I'd just slapped him in the face. I turned away and teleported home, leaving them all in the middle of Novosvillas.

Regrets
Gregory

reg took a deep breath to keep himself composed. His body was tense, and his jaw was sore from forcing himself to keep a straight face. All those months ago, when he had first been called to meet with the council, he'd been so nervous. He'd thought he had been given a great honour. The second time he'd been in this room, he had been so proud of himself. He had brought them the keeper of the Heart Crystal and finally achieved something significant. However, right now, as he stood listening to the council, he felt no pride. He was not nervous. He was annoyed. He stood with his hands behind his back so no one could see his clenched fists. It was all he could do to keep his annoyance from showing.

"How could you come back here without her?" asked Lord Ping.

Lord Ping was the leader of the fairies, and he was not the first person to ask that question. Greg had already explained what happened, but they didn't seem to be getting it.

"As I have already said, she refused to come," Greg replied.

"You should have made her come," Lord Ping snapped.

"Please, tell me, how I am meant to get a teleporter to go somewhere against their will?"

"You could have overpowered her."

"There isn't anyone in this room that could overpower her. Is that not the reason you want her here to begin with?"

Lord Ping curled his mouth and lowered his brow. "Do not forget who you are addressing, boy."

Greg gritted his teeth. He hadn't forgotten who he was

talking to. He just couldn't believe that the people that were meant to be leading the world of magic were being so petty. They were scared, which was understandable—they would be stupid not to be—but going over why Mellissa hadn't returned with him was a waste of time. This was time they should be spending coming up with a plan to stop Kadon.

"We should send someone else to go collect the girl," suggested Chancellor Den. "We entrusted too much responsibility to someone so young."

"It doesn't matter who you send; she won't come," Greg said. "She needs time to get over what's happened to her friend. She will come around. Mellissa won't let Kadon destroy the world."

"This is a council matter, and we did not ask your opinion," snapped Ping.

"I believe your judgement is impaired, Gregory," Den said.

"I am thinking very clearly, thank you."

"You are too emotionally involved," Den said. "You overstepped in the position you were given. You have blurred the line between colleagues and friends, which never ends well. We cannot trust your opinion on the matter any longer."

Lady Gabrielle put her hand up, and the two fairies stopped talking. Everyone at the table turned to look at her. "Gregory's opinion is the only one that matters. He is the only one of us that actually knows the girl. If we want her on our side, we must act with compassion and be considerate of what she is feeling right now. Trying to force her here will only push her further away."

Lord Ping frowned but didn't say anything. Den put his finger to his mouth. "Perhaps you are right. The girl is a teleporter, after all. We wouldn't be able to make her stay even if we somehow managed to get her here."

Greg wanted to shout but held his tongue. That was exactly what he'd said. Why did it take Lady Gabrielle saying it for them to finally get it?

"Are you certain Mellissa will return in time?" Lady Gabrielle asked.

"She will be here when we need her," Greg replied.

"Thank you, Gregory. You are dismissed."

Greg bowed and left the room. That had been the biggest waste of four hours. He understood their initial shock of him returning alone, but the meeting shouldn't have taken that long. He'd repeated himself so many times he had lost count. Although, his father had been uncommonly quiet. He had expected him to question him along the same lines as Lord Ping, yet he'd hardly said a word.

Greg went to the tearooms. He got himself a drink and sat at a table. There wasn't much else he could do right now. This was a council matter, after all, and his opinion wasn't wanted. He wasn't sure if he would be staying here or if he would be sent back to Novosvillas. He hoped to just be sent home. He'd had enough of the council, and he hadn't been properly home in a long time. It was overdue. That decision would ultimately be up to his father, but did he have to listen? He was an adult.

He didn't have to listen to any of them. Greg stirred his drink. Yet, that was exactly what he had done, and by doing so, he had messed up big-time. If he hadn't done everything the way the council wanted, maybe Mellissa wouldn't have gotten to the Tree of Time too late. He should have listened when she said she didn't want to meet with them. After spending four hours going around in circles, he could understand why Mellissa had freaked out when she first met them. He couldn't believe he hadn't realised how pushy they all were before. They acted like children when things didn't go the way they wanted.

Greg jumped as he felt a hand on his shoulder. "Is it all right if I join you?" his father asked.

"Of course," Greg said. "Has the council come to a decision, then?"

Steffen walked round the table and sat down. "Yes, it has."

"Will we be returning home?"

"No. Novosvillas is to be evacuated. All of our soldiers have been called to the capital, so there will be no one left to protect the city. Our people will go to one of the other two changeling cities. The fairy and warlock armies will also be making their way here."

"Is it really a good idea for us all to gather in one place?"

"Kadon is too strong. We must throw everything we have at him if we wish to stand a chance against him. Which means combining all our armies here."

Greg looked down at the table. He really hoped this conversation wasn't about to take the turn he thought it was. "And what would you have me do?"

"Nothing. I just want to spend some time with my son. I have hardly seen you over the past few months." His father gave him a weary smile. "I will get you another drink and one of those cream cakes you like."

Steffen got up and walked over to the counter. Greg leant on his arm. Something was wrong. His father didn't seem like himself. Maybe being on the cusp of a war was getting to him. It took the world falling into chaos for his father to want to spend time with him. Steffen returned with a tray of drinks. He sat down and placed a slice of cake in front of Greg.

"When you were little, whenever I brought you here, that cake was all you would eat."

"That's only because you let me get away with it. Anna was very strict about letting me eat sweet things."

"Yes, my assistant probably looked after you more than she should have. It was never meant to be part of her job. I should have been around more."

"I have no complaints about my childhood. I always had everything I needed. There is no need to feel bad."

"Hard times are coming. I am allowed to wish I had been around more when you were growing up. I realise I have spent most of my time pushing you, but I don't think I have ever told you how proud I am of you."

Greg's jaw dropped. "You are?"

"Of course I am. I'm sorry that I didn't make that clear to you. You have achieved so much at such a young age. I just wanted to push you to be the best you could be, but I realise that maybe I didn't go about it in the best way. I pushed you away instead of taking you under my wing."

Greg tilted his head. "Thank you." This was surreal. Greg had worked so long to get his father to be proud of him. However, he never expected him to apologise for anything. His father had always been too proud to even consider that he may have been wrong about something.

Steffen leant forward and put his hands together. "Now, about Miss Hail."

Greg slumped back. It had all been too good to be true. He'd just been buttering him up so he could force his agenda upon him. "Father, there isn't anything else I can tell you that I haven't already told the council."

"That is not what I meant." Steffen looked at his hands and took a deep breath. He looked back up at Greg. "You are not to blame for what happened with her. I should have listened when you said she wasn't ready. I pushed you into coming back, and I may have caused a problem for you."

"It's fine. I didn't really belong there anyway."

"Do you remember that cliffside I used to take you to on your birthday to see the fireworks?" Greg nodded. His birthday was on summer solstice, and there were always festivities. He'd loved it when his dad showed him that spot on the cliff. It was their own private viewing area, and you could see the whole city from up there. "I never did understand why you used to get so excited about it all. When this is all over, I think you should take Miss Hail there. Someone like her will appreciate it a lot more than I ever could."

Greg looked down at his hands. "I am not exactly on speaking terms with her."

Mellissa probably would love it there, but he was the last person she would want to go with. He didn't know how everything had gone so wrong between them. He wasn't sure how he could fix things—that was if there was a relationship left to fix. Maybe when it came down to it, they were just too different. They were from different worlds after all.

"I don't know what happened between the two of you, but you are right—she will come back here. However, I don't think it will just be because we need her. She will come because of you. When she does return, you shouldn't hold anything back." Steffen chuckled to himself. "I will be honest with you, Lady Gabrielle had to point this out to me. I feel so silly for not seeing it myself."

"What are you talking about?"

"I think you know. I understand if you don't want to talk to me about it. I never was around for all that stuff with girls and what not." Steffen got up. "I have a few things to get sorted, but I will see you later. I'll buy you dinner if I can."

"That would be nice," Greg said.

Steffen nodded at him and walked away.

Greg watched as his father left the tearooms. Had that whole conversation really just happened? He turned back and looked at his uneaten cake. He smiled as he picked up a fork.

Then a feeling of dread shot through him. That conversation had been weird, almost like his father was trying to make up for lost time because he didn't have much left. Was there something he hadn't told him? Were things worse than the council had let on? Greg shook his head. He couldn't think like that. He had to believe everything was going to work out. He believed in Mellissa. She may hate him right now, but she wouldn't let this world plunge into chaos. He was the only one here that had seen Kadon's power. He was extremely powerful, but it hadn't been the first time he'd sensed power like that. Mellissa's power was just as fierce. She would be able to stop him.

A Heavy Heart
Mellissa

ou can't do this," a male voice shouts at me. I swallow the lump in my throat. "I thought you would understand."

"Understand what?" A pair of grey eyes tear through me. "Now that you are going to be queen, you think you are too good for me?"

"That is not true. You know we don't work. We both have a duty to our people, and our beliefs are just too different."

"You elves think you're better than the rest of us."

"That is not true. You know my vision has always been for us to live as one people—not separated by race, but as the people of the land."

He laughs. "You are delusional, Freya."

"The elves and humans already live in harmony. Why not the rest of us?"

"You keep your human pets, because that's all they are."

"No, they are not. They are people like you and me."

"Don't insult me. You are a fool, Freya. I can't believe I loved someone so naïve."

"You have no heart. You don't know how to love, Kadon."

Kadon steps from the shadows. Darkness glimmering in his eyes. "I will show you how misguided you are. One day, your world will come crashing down."

"Is that a threat?"

"A promise." He marches out of the room.

I stare at the spot he was standing. How had I never realised what he really was before? I had been blinded by love, but I was blind no more.

I was shocked from sleep. Freya and Kadon had been together. The prince at the ball, the boy by the river and at the market—they had all been Kadon. The crystal had been trying to get me to understand their history. His hate for Freya ran so much deeper than her simply stopping him from enslaving humans. This fight was personal for him.

I ran to the guest room, but it was empty. Greg was gone. How could I forget? I had left him in Novosvillas eight days ago. Harkura had come to me that evening and informed me that Greg had carried on to the council alone. I had been so awful to him. Yet, he was the first person I wanted to tell about my dream. Surely we could use this knowledge to our advantage, but there was no "we," not anymore. I slunk back to my room and got ready for school.

The Christmas holidays were over. Harkura would walk me to school and pick me up to make sure I was safe. Victoria would guard me during the day. We hadn't talked about what happened in Novosvillas. In fact, we barely spoke at all. I went from class to class, barely listening, feeling numb inside. I missed Matt. It was hard without him. Lord Steffen had told me I couldn't break the spell, but I didn't let that stop me.

Every evening, I would go home and read Greg's books. He'd left a ton behind. I would find a way to save Matt on my own. My skills had already grown significantly by practicing the different incantations and spells from out of the books. No help required. I didn't need Greg. From now on, I would teach myself. I was determined to find something I could use. However, nothing I had learnt so far helped with freeing Matt. I also hadn't heard from Greg since our argument. I regretted everything I had said to him. I kept telling myself I didn't need his help, but it wasn't really a matter of need but want. It was strange how he had become such a big part of my life. I didn't like how we left things. I wanted to see him.

Once again, when the school day was over, I sat in the corner of the living room surrounded by books, practising spells. I was still in the corner when my dad got in that evening. The last week, he'd pretty much left me to it. He would poke his head in, see that I was practising magic, and leave. However, this evening, he came and sat in one of the armchairs. He put his hands together and leant forward, placing his arms on his knees. "Mellissa, we need to talk."

I glanced at him over the book I was reading. "What is it, Dad?"

"You haven't been yourself the last few days. You spend all your free time in that corner looking at those books. I am worried about you."

"I'm fine. Just busy. Someone has to find a way to free Matt."

My dad looked up at the ceiling and shuffled his feet. "Sweetie, what are you going to do if there isn't a way?"

I slammed the book down. "Failure isn't an option. It was my hesitation that got Matt trapped. I will never stop looking for a solution."

My dad rubbed his hands together. He was fidgety this evening. "And what about Greg?"

"What about him?"

"What does he think of what you're doing?"

"I don't know, and I don't care." I didn't understand why my dad was bothered about what Greg thought. I didn't need his opinion on any of this. He had chosen to leave. Although, thinking about it, he may not have had much of a choice. On the other hand, I may have given him a push.

"You mean you haven't spoken to him since he went home?" my dad asked.

"No. Why would I?"

"I thought he was your friend and that he was helping you with all this magic stuff. Do those books not belong to him?"

I tightened my grip on the book in my hands. "Yes, they do. It's just—well, we may not have parted on good terms."

"I know you're upset about Matt, but you shouldn't push your other friends away."

Why did he instantly think it was me that was the

problem? I wasn't pushing anyone away. I hung my head. That was a lie. I was definitely pushing them away. I hardly spoke to Victoria during the day at school. I tried to keep Harkura at a distance, since I didn't want to get to know and care about my new guardian. If I did, it would only hurt more if I lost him too. I regretted everything I had said to Greg, but I hadn't attempted to apologise because he was better off without me in his life. I was a danger to everyone around me. I had doomed my best friend, and I didn't want to end up hurting anyone else I cared about.

I looked up at my dad. "I don't mean to push them away. I just don't know what to do."

My dad sat back in the chair. "Tell me what the problem is, and I might be able to help. I may not know magic, but I know how people work."

"They want me to stand and fight, but I said no. I refused to go back to the magic world, and I left Greg to return on his own."

"They want you to what?" my dad exclaimed. "How can they expect you to fight? You are just a child."

"Dad, I'm eighteen. I'm not a child anymore." I pulled the crystal from round my neck and dangled it in front of him. "You see, this is what is known as a life crystal. It has great power. It was created by the gods to bring balance to the worlds, and I am the only one that can use it. There are two other life crystals, and Kadon has one of them."

"Kadon. He's the evil leprechaun that blew up my house?" I nodded. He put his hand on his chin. "I guess I can understand why they need you then, but that's a lot of responsibility to put on one person."

"It doesn't matter anyway. I ran away from my duty. It's not that I don't want to help. It's just I'm not the strong warrior they need."

My dad leant forward and put his hand on my shoulder. "Mellissa, you are stronger than you realise. Strength is a funny thing. We all think of it as brute force, but that isn't always the case. You have a strong mind, Mellissa. You are extremely stubborn when you want to be. You also have a strong heart.

You're scared of caring for people because of Matt, but don't be. I believe both of those things can amplify your magic."

"I thought you said you didn't know about magic?"

"Your mother may have taught me a thing or two."

"I just don't know what to do. I don't know how to fix things."

"Just say you're sorry. I am sure he will forgive you." My dad patted me on the head and gave me a gentle smile. "As much as I'd like to keep you hidden away from this fight, I don't think I could if I tried. I believe you will know what to do when the time comes. I have faith in you, sweetie."

He got up and left the room. I went back to reading my book, but I was finding it hard to concentrate. My dad had gotten me thinking about Greg again. Maybe I should just apologise and get it over with. However, I had no way to contact him. I could get to the capital in a couple of teleports. Who's to say that's where he still was? He might not even want to see me. I shook my head and covered my face with my hands.

It would be easier to slowly start chatting to Victoria again. That relationship would be easier to fix. I decided to go for a bath to try and relax. Maybe I was just overthinking everything.

I'd just gotten in the bath when Victoria burst into the bathroom. "What are you doing?" I yelled.

"Get dressed now. It's an emergency," she said, grabbing a towel and holding it up to me. By the look on her face, I knew she meant business. I took the towel and got out of the bath.

"What's going on?" I asked, following her back to my room.

She grabbed some clothes out of my wardrobe and threw them at me. "I just got word that Kadon is attacking the magic council. We have to go now."

I took a sharp intake of breath and grabbed hold of my arm to stop it from shaking. "Why is that my problem?" I hoped the fear I was feeling wasn't showing on my face.

"I thought if I gave you time, you would come to your

senses. You need to get yourself together now. This is not like you at all. What happened to the childish, caring, stupidly courageous person I knew? I know you're upset about Matt, and so am I, but he would be ashamed of you for not helping," she said.

She was right. I was too busy feeling sorry for myself to look at the big picture. I had to get myself out of this funk. People's lives were in danger, and I was the only one that could help.

"You're right. I am stupid, but I was never courageous. It's not that I don't want to help. I'm just so scared of losing someone else."

"You cannot let fear get the best of you," she said. "Doing nothing will have the same result. Who do you think contacted me?"

I gasped. "Greg."

I threw on some clothes and ran downstairs. I pulled on my boots, my heart beating rapidly, and shouted for Harkura. Holding my guardians' hands, I teleported the three of us directly to council headquarters.

The Price of Hesitation
Mellissa

I jumped to my feet. I was instantly hit by the sound of screams. Crashes and bangs went off all around us. I choked on the dust and could hardly see with all the smoke. The beautiful council building was in ruins. It looked like it had been hit by a bomb, but the dust hadn't settled yet. People were running all over the place. The leprechauns were attacking at random and destroying anything and anyone that was still standing. I didn't know what to do first. Victoria and Harkura, however, went straight into action, blasting any leprechauns they came across. Victoria ordered me to stay behind them and let them deal with the henchmen. I had to save my magical energy to fight Kadon once we found him. I did as she said. Flurries of many different types of magic were being thrown around. I didn't recognise half the techniques. Soldiers from all the different nations had been called to fight. We fought our way through the battlefield. Just as we were about to be hit by crossfire, I grabbed both Victoria and Harkura and teleported us away from the fight.

"What are you doing? I told you to conserve your energy," Victoria shouted.

"Behind you," I yelled.

Victoria spun round and blocked an attack as I blasted the leprechaun across the room. "What did I just tell you?" she shouted.

"Look, this isn't working. Taking down the leprechaun soldiers one by one is meaningless. We need to stop Kadon. He is their leader. Without him, they won't know what to do."

"That is a good idea, Your Majesty, but how do we find him?" asked Harkura.

"I don't know. He would be leading the charge, wouldn't he? Where would be a good place to do that?" They both looked at me and shrugged. I had come here to help, but I hadn't really done anything yet.

"I know where Kadon is." My chest tightened. I turned to see Greg in the doorway. I didn't know what to say. It felt like I hadn't seen him in forever, even though it had been just over a week. "I thought that was your magic I sensed," he said.

I ran over to Greg and threw my arms around him. "I'm sorry about everything."

"Don't worry about it. There are more important things for you to do."

"But you're hurt," I said, pointing at his arm.

He shrugged. "It's just a scratch."

It really wasn't. It looked very similar to when that leprechaun stabbed me with her claws. I also remembered how much it hurt. I looked down at the floor—even more evidence that I wasn't strong.

"You said you know where Kadon is?" Victoria said.

Greg stepped around me. "Yes, Kadon has taken all the senior council members captive. He is holding them in the courtyard of the Tree of Time."

"Of course, someone like him would make an overdramatic statement like that," said Victoria.

Greg put his hand on my check, forcing me to look up from the floor. "Mellissa, you can do this."

I gave him a small smile and nodded. I wasn't as sure as he was about being able to pull this off. There was a lot at stake. I couldn't give up before I'd even tried.

"Okay, let's go guys." I walked back over to my guardians and held my hand out. Victoria and Harkura both took hold. I wasn't going to let my fear get the best of me. This was something I had to do. I looked at both my guardians. Victoria and I had spent most of the time we'd known each other at odds, but she was now one of my closest friends, and I had only just met Harkura, but I knew he would back me up no matter what. I teleported us to the Tree of Time.

For once, we landed exactly as I wanted—in the tree's

branches. I thought it would help us remain hidden, but I've never been that lucky.

"How nice of you to join us, little elf-ling, and your guardians too," Kadon said without turning to look at us. "I wasn't sure you were going to make it in time for the main event. You will have a great view in that tree to watch as I kill the council members. They all sat idly by and let my people fall into ruins. You will all fear us again soon."

Kadon had the council members bound by his shadows. The courtyard was already littered with bodies. By the looks of it, he had taken out a bunch of soldiers who'd tried to save them. They were all trained to fight. What hope did I have? Kadon was so cold. He spoke of the council ruining his people, but really, he just enjoyed causing chaos. He killed like it was his favourite sport. Kadon was a monster that need to be stopped, and it was my job to do it. Leprechaun henchmen came and surrounded the tree, waiting for us to come down.

"Which one should I dispose of first?" Kadon asked, walking up to his captives. "I think we will start with you." He pointed at Lady Gabrielle and levitated her toward him. He chuckled. "Are you trying to use your magic on me, warlock? I can't believe they let such weak creatures be senior members on this pathetic council. It sort of takes the fun out of this."

I had to do something quick. Otherwise, he was going to kill her. I looked at both Victoria and Harkura, and they both nodded at me, knowing that I was going to act. They both jumped from the tree. Victoria froze three of Kadon's soldiers, and Harkura blasted the other two across the courtyard. I teleported to Kadon and blasted him with a beam of light energy. He went flying back and hit the tree. The smile fell from his face.

"It appears your powers have grown, elf-ling. That actually hurt, but you are still no match for me," he growled, flying at me with super speed.

I teleported out of the way, but he was right there when I rematerialized, as if he knew where I was going to appear. He grabbed me and threw me across the courtyard. He blasted me with his water powers, making my impact with the ground worse. Victoria and Harkura ran to my assistance. He blasted them away with little effort, but it was enough time for me to get my act together. I blasted him with energy balls while teleporting around the courtyard, hitting him from all directions.

"Enough!" he shouted, sending out a wave of blasts, knocking me to the ground again. He bound my hands with shadows and levitated me to him. I struggled to break free. I couldn't let him defeat me so easily, not when so many lives were on the line. "You are really quite annoying. I won't let you get in the way of my revenge. I have waited so long for this. Maybe I should kill you first, and then I can finally add the Heart Crystal to my collection. I will be truly unstoppable."

He reached for the crystal around my neck, but it rejected him, emitting a massive blast of light. It sent us both flying backward. I landed with a thud while he gracefully levitated to regain his balance. The Heart Crystal glowed brightly.

I pushed myself to my feet. "Don't you know Freya bound the Heart to her bloodline? All this time, you've been trying to capture me, but the crystal will never work for you."

The crystal's glow got stronger. Seeing its light reminded me of something I had read. I shouted to Victoria and Harkura to get the council members out of there. They started to break through the shadows binding them. The vein on Kadon's forehead began to pulse as his eyes narrowed.

"I will not let you take my prize," he shouted.

He threw a shadow ball at them. I put up a light barrier, deflecting his attack. He yelled as his body became shrouded in a darkness. He blasted me away. He covered his water blasts with shadows, making them more powerful. I put up an energy shield, but he kept throwing one attack after another, and my shield cracked under pressure. I fell back. The crystal was still glowing bright. I needed just a little more time for it to build up more power. I tried to teleport again, but Kadon grabbed my leg with his shadows and dragged me toward him. I tried to dig my hands into the earth to stop him, but I ended up pulling up clumps of grass. I threw the grass at him, making it grow at the same time, but he sliced straight through it with a shadow.

"I have had enough of you, elf-ling," he shouted, wrapping another shadow round my arm. "You were amusing at first, but now, you are just a pain. I am going to do to you what I should have done to Freya."

He lifted his hand, forming a shadow sword. I tried to break free by releasing an energy blast, but it didn't work. He brought the sword down to strike me. I braced myself, but nothing happened. I looked up. In front of me was Lord Steffen, with a barrier in place. Kadon growled. The vein on his forehead looked like it was about to burst.

"I am sick of all this interference." Kadon smashed through the barrier. "I guess you are first."

He grabbed hold of Steffen's head and snapped his neck. I screamed and scurried backward, clutching my chest as his body flopped to the floor. Kadon turned to the other escaping council members and fired what looked like shards of glass at them. Victoria and Harkura both put up barriers, but Kadon's magic shot straight through them. At least three council members were hit. I wiped away my tears and clenched my fists. The ground began to shake. The grass around Kadon shot up and wrapped around him. He broke free within seconds, but I was ready. I blasted him away with as much light energy as I could summon. I had to act now. I just hoped the crystal had gathered enough energy. I ripped the Heart Crystal from around my neck and threw it in the air, then recited a spell from one of Greg's books I'd read.

"When one is no longer safe and darkness tries to take light's place, protect the caster and reject all evil from within their space."

My heart pounded in my chest. I had acted sooner than planned, but I didn't want Kadon to hurt anyone else. The crystal sent rays of light shooting all over the place, expelling leprechauns from the area. The ground continued to shake. I planted my feet and stiffened my body.

"Do you really think that weak little spell will work on me?" yelled Kadon, tearing through the light energy to reach me.

I channelled even more power into the spell. I knew it was going to take a lot of power for it to work on someone like Kadon. He pushed through the light and caught me with his claws. I yelled, taking a step back. My legs wanted to give way, but I had to stand my ground. I focused the energy from the crystal on Kadon. Pulses of light started to grab him and pull him away. He resisted, cutting the light with his shadows, but the lights just kept coming. As he fought the spell, I blasted him with an energy ball, knocking him over. This gave the spell enough time to gather around him and eject him along with all his leprechaun warriors.

The crystal fell to the ground in front of me as I collapsed to my knees. The ground stopped shaking. I was light-headed. Everything around me seemed to be moving in slow motion. I had stopped Kadon temporarily, but I knew he would be back. I felt weak after using so much power. I took slow breaths as I tried to stop myself from crying. I felt sick at the sight of the dead bodies around me. I had been powerless to save them.

Harkura came over to me and put his hand on my shoulder. "Your Majesty, you did it."

"But Lord Steffen and the others, I didn't save them." Tears streamed uncontrollably down my face.

"You did your best. That is all anyone can ask. Kadon is pure evil. More lives would have been lost if you hadn't been here."

He might've been right, but it wasn't enough. Lord Steffen had died saving me. I was a hazard to those around me. I could never make things right again. A few people came out into the courtyard to see what happened. They gasped when they saw the bodies. My heart sank as I saw Greg walk out into the courtyard. He came straight over to me.

"Mellissa, what did you do?" he asked. "All the leprechauns are gone. This warm light appeared and expelled them all."

"Greg, I'm so sorry. I couldn't stop him. I wasn't strong enough," I replied.

"What are you—" He froze when he saw his father lying

there on the ground, his neck broken. Greg's face dropped. "Dad, no!" he shouted, running over to his father's body. He knelt beside him and tried to use his healing magic.

"You can't heal the dead," Victoria said.

"He can't be dead. He just can't."

I could see the tears forming in his eyes as he tried to heal him again and again. My heart was breaking. I ran over and threw my arms around him.

"I'm so sorry. Your dad saved my life. It was because of him that I was able to expel Kadon and all the leprechauns."

I thought knowing that his dad had died fighting would help. He didn't say anything. His head fell on my shoulder, and he hugged me tighter. I could feel him taking slow breaths, his face hidden from the rest of us. I wished I could make his pain go away, but there was no magic that could fix this.

Outvoted
Gregory

Over the next few hours, Greg went around with the healers, aiding the injured. A temporary infirmary was set up to care for those who couldn't be healed quickly. The dead were taken to a makeshift morgue. The death count was currently at eighty-six and rising. Three of them were senior council members. One of which was Steffen. Greg had become a healer to save lives, but he had been unable to help his own father. Things had improved between them massively in the last week, and now he was gone. Just like that. It felt like he had an elastic band around his chest that someone kept pulling at, slowly tightening it. Greg pushed his feelings down and focused on his work. Kadon had caused a lot of damage and hurt a lot of people. He couldn't allow himself to fall apart. There were still things to be done.

The remaining council members had already sent word for more soldiers to gather at headquarters to prepare for another attack. Mellissa was hovering around. Knowing her, she would think this was her fault. People kept praising her for getting rid of all the leprechauns. He could tell by the look on her face that she didn't think she deserved the praise. Why couldn't she see what everyone else did? Without her, things would have been a lot worse. She had used their time apart well. Her abilities had grown so much in just a week. She was even stronger than the last time he'd seen her.

One of the council messengers approached him. He bowed and informed Greg that the council were waiting in the meeting room for him. Greg sighed. What did they want him for now? There was only one way to find out. He finished wrapping a bandage on his patient's arm and headed to the main hall. It appeared they also wanted to see Mellissa, as the messenger was leading her in the same direction. They both entered the hall.

"Lady Mellissa and Sir Gregory, we are so glad you could join us," Chancellor Den said.

Why had he referred to him as *sir*? Greg didn't have any sort of formal title.

"What do you require of us?" Greg asked.

"With the death of three senior council members and the remaining half in the infirmary, you and Lady Mellissa are the only senior members left of the council," Den explained. "We need you here so we can make a final decision on how to proceed."

"Since when are we members of the council, let alone seniors?" Mellissa asked.

Greg knew the answer to that question. It just hadn't dawned on him till that moment. He was his father's heir. He now inherited all his father's responsibilities.

Hogan of the Caves gave Mellissa a smile. "You are Queen of the Elves. That gives you the highest authority on the council." Hogan nodded in Greg's direction. "And since the tragic death of Lord Steffen, his son now takes his place. All the other heirs are not on-site. It is just the two of you."

Greg wasn't sure he was ready for this, but it had to be done. "Very well, what are the proposed plans?" he asked.

Den gestured for them to sit. The remaining council members couldn't agree whether to stay there and wait for Kadon to make his next move or to take the fight to him before he could attack again. The vote was tied, and they needed Greg and Mellissa to make the final decision.

Greg didn't know what to say, and it seemed Mellissa didn't either. How could they expect the two of them to make such an important decision like this? They weren't even officially council members. He may inherit his father's position, but there was usually a ceremony to induct new members. Neither of them had any experience with this sort of thing. However, Greg did understand the current situation was not good. A time like this called for proper protocol to be ignored. Greg requested that each side explain the pros of their plan. If he was going to make a decision, he was going to need more information. They spent hours listening to each side explain why their plan was best. Once they were done speaking, Greg already knew what strategy he was going to go with. There was a massive hole in one of the proposed plans.

"I'm sorry, but I was just wondering, do you guys actually know where Kadon is?" Mellissa asked. She had picked up on the same problem he had.

"Well, not exactly," Den said, "but my fastest flying fairies are currently out trying to locate his base of operations."

Mellissa shrugged. "Well, I've made my mind up. I think we stay put for now."

"I second that decision," Greg said. "We can review the plan once the fairies return with more information. Is there anything else?"

"No, sir," Den replied.

They both got up to leave. As they did, the rest of the council stood and bowed to the two of them. This would take some getting used to. Greg was usually the one doing the bowing.

Greg walked with Mellissa down the corridor. He was heading back to the infirmary, but she shouldn't. She had used up a lot of power expelling the leprechauns and needed to rest to recover her magic. She was going to have to face Kadon again at some point. However, he wasn't sure how she would respond if he suggested this. She seemed to be all right with him, but he still wasn't sure where he stood with her.

"Well, that was weird," Mellissa said.

"You will get used to it," he said, trying to reassure himself as well as her. This was all just as new to him. He'd known he would eventually have to take over for his father, but he had never expected it to happen so soon.

"Hey, are you okay?" Mellissa asked, looking up at him with big eyes. His father had told him not to hold anything back when she returned. He wanted to say that the last week without her had been the longest in his life. Mostly he just wanted to say he had missed her, but he couldn't bring himself to say anything. Now wasn't the time for that.

He pushed his fringe back. "Yeah, I'm fine. Look, I am going back to the infirmary. I think you should go check in with your guardians."

"Yeah, Victoria will want to know what's going on. I'm also pretty tired." She put her hand on her head. "Will I ever not be tired after using high levels of magic?"

"With time, your body will adjust to it."

"I'll see you later, then." She went to walk in the opposite direction but paused. She turned back to look at him. "You should really take some time. You know, to process everything."

"Don't worry about me. I'm fine," he said.

She didn't look like she believed him, but she left him to it. Greg went back to the infirmary. It was where he needed to be. He could be useful there. He was fine as long as he had something to do.

After a few hours, the same messenger returned, telling him he was needed again. It must be important. The poor warlock was out of breath from running to him. Greg made his way back to the main hall. He arrived just before Mellissa did. She didn't seem happy that Victoria had to wait outside, but it was council procedure.

"Now that everyone's here, we can start," Den said. "The squad of fairies I sent out have just returned, and they do not bring good news. They have found Kadon, and he is leading his leprechaun army to the veil. He plans on destroying the veil and enslaving the humans."

There was a chorus of gasps. Everyone started talking amongst themselves. They shouldn't have been so shocked. Kadon had simply gone back to his original plan from thousands of years ago. Greg knew this would happen. Although, this was one of those times he would've liked to have been wrong.

"Do the fairies know what part of the veil he is marching to?" asked Hogan.

"They believe he is going to destroy it at its source. The

place where the veil was first created," Den said.

"How quickly can we get our armies to Freya's old castle?" Greg asked.

"By foot, it will take at least a day, and we don't have that much time. The train service is still suspended due to the snow. The fairies said he was only an hour away from his destination when they left to fly back here," Den replied.

Greg put his hand on his chin. "How long did it take them to fly back here?"

"About an hour and a half, which means Kadon has already had half an hour attacking the veil."

"It also proves it is quicker to get there on the winds than by foot. I suggest we get the fairy warriors to fly ahead. I will also lead the changeling army ahead as well. We can all transform into fast flying birds."

"I second that idea. Everyone in favour, raise your hand," Den commanded.

Everyone raised their hand except Mellissa. Everyone looked at her. They were all probably wondering the same thing he was. His plan was sound. Why wouldn't she back it?

"I can get there the fastest," she said. "I will teleport straight to Kadon and stop him." It was a statement, not a suggestion.

"Mellissa, are you crazy?" Greg asked. "You can't go there on your own."

"I won't be on my own. Victoria and Harkura will be with me. Then the changelings and fairies will be roughly two hours behind. All in favour, raise your hand."

Again, everyone raised their hand except one person, but this time it was Greg.

"No, you can't. I am completely against this," said Greg.

"I'm sorry, you have been outvoted." Mellissa got up and left the meeting.

Greg stood up and stared at where Mellissa had just been. There was something different about her. She had changed. As a person, she was still the same. The only difference was that she was more sure of herself, which was good. To win this fight, she would need to go into it with confidence. Yet, he couldn't shake this feeling of fear. The problem wasn't her; it was him. He had also changed, and he was now scared of losing her.

The End of The Rainbow
Mellissa

I explained to Victoria what was happening. She was on board with my plan. So far, Greg was the only one that was against it. I understood why, but it was my life to risk. No one was forcing me to take this course of action. I had volunteered. I was done with waiting around to be attacked. I was sick of other people risking themselves to save me. What would be the point in surviving if I lost everyone I cared about along the way? It was time for me to step up. I was going to bring the fight to Kadon. I wasn't going to be ruled by fear anymore.

Greg ran up to us. I knew he was going to try and change my mind, but he was out of luck. I knew what I had to do. I asked Victoria to bring Harkura up to speed so we could leave as soon as possible.

"Mellissa, if you insist on this course of action, I'm coming with you," Greg said.

I shook my head. "As nice as the offer is, you can't. You have to stay here and lead the changelings and fairies to battle. Greg, I know what I'm doing. This is what you trained me for."

"No, this is not what I trained you for. I trained you to cast a sealing spell, not to go off and fight the leprechaun king on your own. Let's not forget about the army he has as well."

"I'm not alone. I have my guardians, and they are as good as an army. I also have this." I showed him the crystal. "I think I'm finally starting to understand the Heart Crystal. I have to do this. We are out of time. Don't worry. You can tell me about myself later."

I turned to go, but Greg grabbed my arm. "Mellissa, be careful."

"Aren't I always?"

"No, you're not. You are the clumsiest and most reckless person I know. You have almost gotten yourself killed at least twice since I met you. I just lost my dad. I need you to come back safe." He was being very serious now.

"I'm sorry. I will be careful. I promise I will come back." I gave Greg a hug.

He was reluctant to let go of my arm, but he had to. He knew I was the only one with any chance of stopping Kadon. I understood exactly how he felt. It was how I'd felt after losing Matt. Except I still had hope, Greg didn't. Yet he had somehow gotten himself together to assist the healers and do what was needed before getting to this point—something I hadn't been able to do. If I hadn't been too busy feeling sorry for myself, I would have been here when Kadon attacked. Maybe less people would have gotten hurt. Going to fight Kadon right now was the best decision I had made in the last few days. I was finally thinking clearly and not being selfish.

I gave Greg a smile before running to find Harkura and Victoria. I found them making their way to me. Harkura was all caught up, and they were ready to go. I grabbed hold of both of them and teleported. I didn't know where Freya's castle was, so I focused on the dark energy of Kadon. We landed face-first in a field. I got up and dusted myself off. I jumped back as a car rushed by on a nearby road. We weren't in the magic world anymore.

"Mellissa, where are we? Did you miss your target or something?" Victoria asked.

I didn't know where we were. I shut my eyes. I definitely sensed Kadon's presence here. I thought we would've materialised surrounded by a leprechaun army at an old-looking castle. However, we had somehow ended up back in the human world.

"I think we should follow the dark presence. I'm sure Kadon is here."

We ran toward the darkness. The sky grew darker, and there was an overcast of shadow. My skin began to crawl. We were getting close.

"Maybe I should have asked this before we left, but does Your Majesty have a plan to stop Kadon?" Harkura asked. "I don't mean to offend, but unfortunately, his previous prison is occupied."

"It's okay, Harkura. That's a pretty good question," I said. "I have done a lot of reading over the last week, and I realised something. Half of Kadon's abilities come from the Moon Crystal. All the water attacks he does are because of it. All we need to do is separate him and the crystal. If we do, his powers will decrease dramatically. I'm pretty sure once he is weakened, a normal prison in the magic world will hold him."

"How do you plan on doing that?" he asked.

"I didn't get quite that far, but I'll figure it out."

"Hey, is that Stonehenge?" shouted Victoria.

"I think it is." I paused, looking at the giant stones. Why would Kadon be here of all places?

Victoria's eyes lit up. "Wow, I always wanted to see Stonehenge."

I shook my head at her. Now wasn't the time to stop and admire the scenery. I ran over to the giant stones. Kadon's presence was strong here, but I couldn't see him. The area was shrouded in shadows.

Kadon landed with a boom in the centre of the stones. "I'd hoped to bring down the veil before you arrived, elf-ling. This is better though. You get to watch as I send your beloved human world into chaos. Both worlds shall bow down to me."

"I'm not going to let that happen," I shouted.

"You think you can stop me?" He snickered.

I threw energy blasts at him. He rolled his eyes, and with a flick of his fingers, he threw me against a rock and bound me to it with shadow ropes. Harkura and Victoria charged at him. He rolled his eyes again, blasting them both back, trapping them in a shadow cage.

"Did you really think you could stop me? My power is at its peak in the light of the moon. You just got lucky last time, my dear little elf. Now, you and your guardians watch while I bring down this wretched veil from its original source." He held his arms up wide as he circled us, with a smile on his face.

I wriggled, trying to escape my restraints. "I thought the veil was first created at Freya's old castle."

"Oh, you really are uneducated." He put his hand against the rock I was tied to and ran his other hand through my hair. I tried to shake him off. He smirked. "I guess I have a few spare minutes to enlighten you before enslaving mankind."

Kadon was just like all those stereotypical bad guys in the movies, who loved to chat and gloat over their enemy. He revelled in how clever he was and how dumb I—and the rest of humankind—was for not realising what Stonehenge really was. He informed us that the stones that made up Stonehenge where remains of Freya's castle, which had crossed over when she made the veil. This was the only place where the two worlds aligned perfectly, and it was the veil's weakest point. His leprechaun army was on the other side of the veil right then, at that exact spot, setting up a bunch of magical energy bombs. He pointed out the line he'd already set up in the sky. All he had to do was put the last bomb in place and make the final blow on this side, and the veil would crumble to pieces. He thought his plan was extremely clever.

"As for you"—he had his hand round my throat in a flash—"you will get to watch me kill your guardians and see this world burn."

"That is all so fascinating, but what I don't get is why you don't just kill me?" I asked. "The Heart Crystal will never work for you, and I will never stop fighting you."

He stroked the side of my face. "Oh, I will kill you, just not yet. First, you will bear my heir. Then, my son will inherit the Heart Crystal, and I will rule this world with him by my side."

I gagged. "Ew, no."

He punched the stone I was bound to. "I'm not giving you a choice."

I tilted my head and smiled at him. "Well, thanks for letting me know the details of your plan, but I will have to decline the whole producing an heir thing. Now, I'm going to stop you." I shut my eyes and engulfed my body in light, blasting myself out of my restraints. Before my feet hit the ground, I sent a beam of light, cutting though the shadow cage trapping Harkura and Victoria.

All three of us charged him at once. His plan worked in our favour. He was separated from his army, and we could combine all of our powers to stop him. We struck him with fire, ice and light. He had underestimated us. I might've still been new to magic, but I had a lot to fight for. We couldn't let him bring down the veil. Humans wouldn't be able to handle finding out about the magic world. It would be chaos—the exact thing the crystals were designed to stop. Channelling my powers through the Heart Crystal, and with Harkura and Victoria's assistance, we had Kadon on the defensive. I still didn't know how I was going to separate Kadon from the Moon Crystal, but I needed to get closer to him if I was going to try. We seemed to be overpowering him, but then his facial expression changed. He was smiling. Kadon multiplied. I spun around as copies of him started popping up all around us.

A deep laugh echoed as Kadon and his copies laughed. "It has been fun playing with you, but I'm getting bored now," came the voice of the real Kadon, but I couldn't tell which one he was.

They all moved at once, attacking us. They may have not been real, but their attacks were. We blasted our way through the duplicates. We had to find the real Kadon before he slipped away and set off the bombs. I grabbed the Heart Crystal, held it up above us and released a pulse of light energy, dispersing all the duplicates into water droplets. I looked around. All the Kadons had disappeared. So, where was the real one? Victoria pointed to the sky. Kadon was flying toward the veil. Altogether, we took aim and fired at him. He turned and redirected our attacks at the veil, then hurled the last bomb in place. All he needed was one blast to set the whole thing off.

Without thinking, I teleported and grabbed Kadon. I went to teleport away with him, but when I tried, a surge of dark power zapped through me. Kadon laughed. "Did you really think you could use that trick on me again?" He kicked me off.

I screamed as I fell toward the ground. Victoria shouted

my name. I hit ice and slid to the ground. She had created an ice slide to catch me. While Kadon was distracted by me, Harkura had used his flames to hurtle himself at the row of pulse bombs. He grabbed one from the line up, falling quickly to the ground. He called out to me, and I knew what to do. If we removed his row of pulse bombs, he wouldn't have enough magical energy to bring down the veil. I didn't know why I hadn't thought of this earlier. Victoria began freezing the bombs. I teleported as many as I could to different locations. Kadon clenched his fists and tensed his muscles. The vein on his head began to pulse. The dark shadow around him grew.

"I have had enough of you pests," he shouted, sending a wave of shadows to catch us. He got hold of Harkura and Victoria as I teleported away with another bomb. There was no way he could collect them all again easily. I went numb as a darkness grabbed me from behind. I froze on the spot.

"Did you really think I couldn't follow you, elf-ling?" Kadon snarled. He had latched on to my teleport somehow. He walked in front of me as he wrapped me in his shadows. "As soon as I realised what your abilities were, I came up with a way to counter them. I even found a way to track your teleports and follow you." He was calm again as he took back control of the situation. I tried to release a ray of light, but his darkness snuffed it out. The more I struggled, the tighter the shadows wrapped around me. He picked up the bomb I had taken and with a click of his fingers, we were back at Stonehenge.

Victoria and Harkura were both passed out trapped inside a shadow sphere. Kadon had already replaced all the bombs we'd taken. I had no idea how he'd managed it so quickly.

"Wait!" I screamed. "You can't do this. You loved Freya once. This isn't what she would have wanted. You can still turn back."

He snickered. "You sound just like her." He pulled me toward him by my hair. "Look just like her too. I will enjoy forcing you to create my heir." He licked the side of my face, and I shuddered. My stomach churned.

He flew up with the last bomb and put it in place. I had

to stop him, but the more I struggled, the tighter the shadows wrapped around me. I fell to the ground trying to break free, and I screamed for him to stop. This seemed to amuse him. Kadon blasted one of the bombs, and it exploded, setting all the others off. It was over. I had failed. The veil was disintegrating right in front of my eyes.

I stopped trying to escape my restraints and laid my head on the cold ground. It was hopeless. Kadon had won. Just as I was about to give up, I saw something that gave me hope. On the other side of the veil, the leprechaun army was battling the fairies and changelings, and the leprechauns were losing. I had to get up and fight. I wasn't going to let Kadon have his way. I shut my eyes and took a deep breath. The ground beneath me began to shake as I attempted to break out of my restraints. I was stronger than this. There was still so much I had yet to discover. It was time to stop thinking about the past and dwelling on the what-ifs. I couldn't change what had already happened, but I could do something about the present.

The crystal glowed brightly in front of me. The light dispersed the shadows that bound me and continued to shine even brighter. It was like it was trying to tell me something. I grabbed hold of it, and it surrounded me in its light. The lights filled me with a warm sensation. I finally understood what the others had meant when they said a light appeared to them and told them they were guardians. It was like the Heart Crystal had come alive, and it was telling me what to do. I held the crystal close to my chest and whispered to it to transform. The crystal emitted another bright light, and a silver staff appeared in my hand, with the Heart Crystal embedded in the top of it. I had seen a picture of this staff in one of Greg's books. I'd thought it was an old relic passed down by the crystal keepers to place the crystal in. I hadn't realised that it was a form the crystal could take on itself.

I closed my eyes and listened to the earth around me, really listening for the first time. It was like nothing I had felt before. I could feel everything that was happening in that moment—every step taken, plants growing, any move an animal made. As long as they were on the land, I could feel it.

As I exhaled, I stopped the tremors. I took a running start and launched myself off into the air by raising the ground beneath me. I knew I could do this because the Heart Crystal had told me so. I flew at high speed toward Kadon. He was too busy rejoicing in his success of destroying the veil to notice me. I twirled the staff around and fired lightning at Kadon. He was taken by surprise as he was hit by my newfound power.

"How is this possible? Freya's staff," he yelled. "Where did you get it?"

"I've always had it. I just never realised." I attacked again.

He countered my lightning with his shadows. He came at me with his shadow sword. I dodged and blasted him with light energy. I had finally fully unlocked the Heart Crystal, and it was assisting me in this fight. It was communicating with me, giving me suggestions of attack and how to counter Kadon's movements. I was overpowering him, but it wouldn't be any good if I couldn't separate him and the Moon Crystal. He was too powerful to capture while he was still fused with it. I was attacking from a distance for my own safety, but my safety didn't matter anymore. With the help of the Heart Crystal, I located the Moon Crystal inside of Kadon. I had to take the plunge. I released a ray of light and returned the Heart back to crystal form. I teleported right in front of Kadon with my arm inside his body. His eyes widened, and his jaw dropped. I had hold on the Moon Crystal inside of him.

He clutched my arm. "I won't let you take my power."

My crystal glowed brighter, and I pulled the Moon Crystal from his body. Kadon lashed out at me, stabbing me in the stomach with his shadows. We both fell out of the sky. I hit the ground hard. I lay as still as possible. A flush of pain shot through my body. I turned my head to look at the gap in the veil. It was getting bigger. I had to fix it. Harkura and Victoria must have broken free, as I could hear them shouting to me. I took slow breaths. I had both the Moon and Heart Crystals in my hands. I gasped as Kadon appeared above me. All the colour had drained from his face, and his body was shaking. He narrowed his eyes at me. I tried to get up and run, but I collapsed back to the ground.

"I should have killed you the moment I laid eyes on you," he shouted. He drew his claws and went to slash at me. I braced for impact. As he brought his arm down, his hands began to disintegrate. He looked just as shocked as I was. "No, what is happening to me?" he screamed, looking at his missing arms. His whole body started to fall apart. He screamed at the top of his voice as he turned to dust. The Moon Crystal must have been what was keeping him alive, and without it, his body crumbled.

I looked at where Kadon had just been, my mouth wide open. I shook my head. I still had work to do. The veil needed to be remade. Otherwise, the world as we knew it would end. I clambered to my knees as it was all I could manage. I put my hand over my stomach wound and winced. There was a lot of blood, but I had to finish. Grasping both crystals, I channelled all my energy into them. I could feel the magic draining from my body. I hoped I had enough power left. I focused on what I wanted to create and released a massive pulse of magical energy. The magic latched on to the disappearing veil and put it back together. I sighed with a weak smile on my face. I had done it. Both worlds were now safe from the darkness.

All of a sudden, my body went limp, and I fell face-first to the ground. I could feel myself bleeding, and my legs were numb. Footsteps came closer to me. I tried to get up, but I couldn't move. Someone grabbed hold of me and turned me over. It was Victoria. She looked panicked, and her eyes were full of tears. She was shouting at Harkura to do something. Harkura pulled off his jacket and pressed it against my stomach. I could feel myself getting weaker. I just wanted to go to sleep.

Victoria yelled at me not to close my eyes. She cried for me to keep looking at her and to focus on her voice. I tried to talk, but I couldn't. My body was cold. I couldn't keep my eyes open any longer. Victoria and Harkura were calling to me, but their voices were starting to fade. It was ironic that I was going to die the same way Queen Freya had, stopping Kadon and then creating the veil. They say your life flashes before your eyes when you die, but all I could think about was how Greg wasn't going to be happy with me for breaking my promise, and my dad. He didn't even know I had left the house. I had promised I would come back, but I wasn't going to make it. I lay on the grass, numb.

A warm feeling came over my stomach and spread over my body. A sharp pain shot through me, and I gasped for air, opening my eyes.

"She's breathing. Oh my God. You did it," Victoria said.

She was talking to Greg as he healed me. I didn't understand how he had gotten here. Why was he always turning up just when I needed him to? I rested my head on Greg's knee and shut my eyes again. I knew I was safe with him there, and so was the rest of the world.

The Keeper of the Heart
Mellissa

he castle is shaking. I wrap my little girl up in a blanket and hand her to Ivan. "Take her to safety."

He holds her to his chest. "What about you? I am your guardian. I shouldn't leave you."

"She is what is important now. If something happens to me, I need to know she is safe. I know you will protect her."

"I would give my life for her."

I stroke his cheek. "I know." There's a loud boom, and the castle shakes again. "Take care of our daughter. She will be the world's new beginning."

I press my lips to Ivan's. I don't want to let them go, but I must. "Go," I say.

He nods, pulls up his hood and runs out the back with our baby. Marissa will be safe with her father while I stand and fight, putting an end to Kadon once and for all.

"Oh my God," I yelled, sitting up.

I winced as pain shot through my body and fell back on my bed. My head was pounding. My body ached all over, and I was covered in bandages. I looked around my room. Someone had tidied it. The sun was shining in through my bedroom window. How had I gotten there? The last thing I remembered was Kadon. My heart leapt. Kadon was defeated, and I had somehow managed to survive the battle. I stood up and grimaced, sitting straight back down on my bed. Maybe standing wasn't the best idea at the moment. I picked up the

Heart Crystal from my bedside table. If I turned it back to staff form, I could use it as a walking stick. My chest tightened. Where was the Moon Crystal? I had it in my other hand when I collapsed. Why wasn't it here? I patted my bed down in search of it.

"What on earth are you doing?" asked Victoria.

I looked up to see her standing in the doorway. "I was just—"

"Get back in bed right now," she snapped, marching over to me. "I'm glad you are finally awake, but you are such an idiot. I was so worried. You're reckless."

She made me lie back down and tucked me into bed. I felt like a child being told off by their mother. "I'm sorry. I didn't mean to worry you, but what do you mean 'finally?' Have I missed a whole day again?"

"Something like that," she said, "except it was more like two days."

"What?" I exclaimed. Missing one day was bad enough. I must've been hurt pretty badly. Two days had already passed, and I still felt like I had been hit by a truck.

"You really had everyone worried."

"I really am sorry. Trust me, it wasn't part of my plan to get injured like that. It's good to see you're all right. What about Harkura? And how did I get back home?" I asked. I couldn't remember much after the battle. My memory of the events was in fragments, and they were all jumbled up.

"The fire nymph is fine. He is camping out in that silly little tent of his in your back garden. The weirdo refuses to sleep in the house. We got back here because of Greg. He appeared out of nowhere and pretty much saved the day. Well, I guess I can finally go home now that I know you're not dead. I will let the others know you're awake."

"You mean you haven't been home?" I asked.

"Of course not. What sort of guardian would I be if I left while you were still unconscious? Oh, and I hope you don't mind, but I tidied your room and reorganised your wardrobe."

She smiled at me as she swayed out of my room. She was gone just as quickly as she had appeared. I was touched by how concerned she'd been about me. She had stayed here until she knew I was all right. Our relationship had changed drastically. She was still harsh and insulted me nonstop, but I had come to realise that was just how she showed affection.

Victoria had been gone only a couple of minutes when there a knock on my door. In walked Greg. I sat up. I hadn't realised he'd actually come back with us. He said my wounds needed checking. I jokingly complained about his healing abilities not being up to scratch and that I shouldn't need so many bandages. He didn't find this funny. He then went on to tell me how reckless I was and how I had worried everyone. He sat at the end of my bed with his grumpy face on. I found myself apologising again.

"I really didn't mean to make anyone worry about me," I said.

"Mellissa, you almost died. This isn't a joke. I told you not to go on your own. If I hadn't been there to heal you, you wouldn't be here right now," Greg said, frustration in his tone. He obviously didn't think I was taking what happened seriously.

"I know, but I defeated Kadon, didn't I? Maybe I should've brought more back up, or at the very least, had you with me from the start, but there wasn't time. Is my life really more important than the rest of the world?"

"It's important to me!"

"And I said I'm sorry, but I can't change what happened. I understand that you're annoyed with me. If it was the other way around, I would be furious with you. I would have never let you leave without me."

"I don't have the luxury of being able to sense your location and teleport to follow you."

"Well, I—I don't have a comeback." I put my hand on my head. My skin was really warm.

Greg leant forward and also put his hand on my head. I think he was checking my temperature. He slouched back and sighed. "You have a fever. I can get you something for that."

He got up to leave, but I grabbed his hand. "Wait. Did you know that Ivan, Freya's guardian, was the father of her daughter?"

He sat back down. "What? All the books state she had a daughter but never mention the father. Freya never married. How do you know this?"

"Another dream. Also, Freya and Kadon dated as teenagers."

"That's why he hated you so much. Not just because Freya defeated him, but because you are the result of her falling for another man."

"So, what? He started a war because he got dumped?"

Greg shook his head. "It probably didn't help, but Kadon was still an egotistical, entitled racist." He rubbed his nose as he tried not to smile. "You know, this means the Streets are distant relatives of yours."

"They are?"

Greg nodded. "Mrs. Street told me their ancestry goes back to Ivan's sister, Isabelle."

"Huh, so Matt and Victoria are like distant cousins of mine?"

Greg wagged his finger in my face. "Don't think this interesting revelation gets you off the hook for being reckless."

I groaned. He saw right through me. I'd hoped it would work as a distraction, and he would forget he was mad at me. Although, a part of me had just missed talking to him about this sort of stuff. "Fine, this is your chance to have a go at me. Just get it all out so we can move on."

"I don't want to have a go at you. I just wish your plan hadn't involved almost dying."

"You do realise that most of the time I don't actually know what I am doing. I will admit, I was lucky you turned up when you did. How exactly did you get there, anyway?"

He shuffled farther onto the bed and sat beside me. "After you left against my advice, the rest of us followed the plan I suggested. Den and I led the fast-flying fairies and all the changelings with strong bird transformations to the ruins of Freya's castle. We found the leprechaun army there but were surprised to find you and Kadon were not. Battle commenced, and we started capturing leprechauns. It's amazing what brilliant warriors the Fay are. When they grow to their full size, their strength rivals that of the leprechauns. Then, the veil suddenly came down, and there you were, fighting with Kadon on the other side. We witnessed everything from that point. Once I saw you go down, I knew I had to help you. I managed to cross before you resealed the veil."

I took his hand. "Thanks for saving me."

"It was the least I could do. You sort of saved the world first."

My heart was pounding, and my hands were clammy. I stared at his lips, remembering what it was like to kiss him. He leant forward. I quickly turned away. "What's going to happen to the leprechauns now that Kadon's gone? And what about the Moon Crystal? Where is it?"

"Safely locked away in a council vault," Greg replied. "There is going to be a council meeting to decide on what to do with both the Moon Crystal and the leprechauns."

"Shouldn't we just give the Moon Crystal back to the mermaids?"

"Hey, don't steal my ideas. That is what I was going to suggest. Also, the correct term is merfolk or merpeople, and the mermen don't like being referred to as mermaids."

I laughed. "Sorry for my mistake. Merfolk it is."

"I think you should be the one to hand it over. After all, you are the one that retrieved it."

"It would be totally wicked to meet a mermaid—I mean, merperson. You know what I mean."

Greg stood up. "Well, you should get plenty of rest. The meeting is tomorrow morning, and you are a senior member after all."

Greg left me to rest. If I was attending a meeting with the council, I would need all my strength to deal with them. I didn't understand why or how I was suddenly a senior member of the council. It wasn't really a job I wanted. Being around the council still made me uneasy.

In the morning, Greg came in to change my bandages and get me up for the council meeting. "Why is this meeting so early in the morning?" I asked.

"Stop being lazy. Council meetings are all a part of being queen."

"I'm technically not queen of anything. I haven't officially accepted the role, and no formal ceremony has taken place."

He raised his eyebrow. "Those are all just technicalities." He left me to get dressed by myself.

I still couldn't get my head around the idea of me becoming a queen. It just seemed so unreal. I had gone from an ordinary girl to a queen almost overnight. I also didn't understand why my attendance at this meeting was so important. Surely there were older, more knowledgeable members on the council than me. Wouldn't their views on the current situation be more valid? However, I did want to know what decisions would be made. I also wanted to make sure the Moon Crystal ended up in the right hands. Maybe being on the council wasn't all bad.

I got myself washed and dressed, then went to find Greg. He was, of course, ready and waiting on me to leave. Harkura was also waiting with him. I asked if Victoria was coming. Harkura told me that she'd entrusted him with protecting me while she was at school. That's when I remembered it was a school day. I had lost track of the days after everything that had happened with Kadon. I wasn't sure how many days of school I'd missed. I was not looking forward to playing catch-up when I went back.

I couldn't worry about that now though. I had a council meeting to attend. I took hold of both their hands and teleported to the council building. It was amazing how quickly they'd rebuilt the place. Having magic on your side made jobs like this relatively simple. There were three new council members, I assumed to replace the ones that had been lost during the battle. Harkura was made to wait outside in the hall during the meeting.

The meeting went on for hours. We made a decision on

what to do with the Moon Crystal pretty quickly. It was agreed that I would hand it over to the current king of the merfolk. However, it was not so easy to decide what to do with the leprechauns. Many ideas were put forward, but no one could agree.

There was a suggestion to use the leprechauns as slaves, but that idea wasn't as bad as the councilman who wanted to kill all the leprechauns that had been captured. I knew the leprechauns had done bad things, but how could they talk about killing them so casually? They had attempted to kill me on more than one occasion, but I still didn't think genocide was a good idea. How would killing all of them or using them for slave labour be any different than what Kadon had planned for the humans? The problem was that the leprechauns hadn't had a proper leader for thousands of years. They were the only magical species living on the land that didn't have a representative on the council. When Kadon came back, they were ripe for the picking.

I suggested we help the leprechauns recreate their villages and help them form their own hierarchy of power, then give their elected leader a place on the council. They would have to live by the rules of the land, like everyone else, and those that didn't want to live in peace would stay imprisoned. My idea was rejected by many, mainly the ones who wanted to kill all the leprechauns. They were hungry for blood. The leprechauns had caused a lot of damage, and many lives had been lost.

"How does killing or enslaving all the remaining leprechauns make us any better than Kadon? What you are suggesting sounds just like the plans Kadon had," I argued.

"Says the girl that killed Kadon herself. How is you killing Kadon any different than what we want to do?" asked Sir Lee, one of the new senior council members.

"It is very different. Kadon died during battle. In addition, I had planned on capturing him, not killing him. I didn't know that separating him and the Moon Crystal would kill him. What you are suggesting is killing people while caged."

"They are not people; they are monsters. They murdered my father in cold blood. From my understanding, you were there."

My heart sank, and I felt sick as I remembered what happened that night. Kadon had killed three senior council members right in front of my face, and I had been powerless to stop him.

"My father died that day as well, Lee," said Greg, "but we can't let our decision today be based on our emotions. It was Kadon that killed the senior members of the council, not the leprechauns we have captured. They should be tried for their crimes by the rules of this land like anyone else. The leprechauns have been shunned for years. They have been treated like lesser beings. When Kadon came along and offered them revenge on the queen and the council, they jumped at it. We have to learn from our mistakes. If we go around killing them, it will just leave room for another crazy leader to move in and lead them astray."

"I agree with Gregory and Queen Mellissa." Lady Gabrielle stood up. She had been silent for a while, and everyone turned to look at her. "The leprechauns should be tried for their crimes and sentenced appropriately. We should then aid them in growing their society and educate them. If we give them some freedom to rule themselves, as well as a chance to be represented here on the council, they won't feel so separated from our society. Then, maybe they won't be so easily led down the dark path by a deranged dictator."

Once Lady Gabrielle spoke up, many council members started to come around. She had a lot of sway on the council. Not everyone was happy with the decision, but by the end of the meeting, we had the majority vote to put the leprechauns on trial. Once they'd paid for their crimes, they would be assisted in rebuilding their society. I was relieved when the meeting was over. We had been in that room for hours, and I was happy to stretch my legs.

Before heading home, I went out to the courtyard to visit the Tree of Time. I walked up to it and placed my hand on the tree trunk. It looked the same as when I'd last seen it. I could sense the great amount of magic coming from it. I activated the Heart Crystal. My powers had grown so much in the last couple of weeks. Maybe I could free Matt. I looked at the crystal glowing round my neck and asked for its assistance. I didn't get the response I had hoped for. The seal was created by the Heart Crystal and the tree. I couldn't break the spell. I sighed with a heavy heart and leant against the tree. I had managed to defeat Kadon—the most powerful leprechaun in history—and save the world, but I couldn't set my best friend free.

"I am so sorry, Matt. I promise you, I will figure something out. I will not leave you stuck in this tree." He might've been trapped in the tree, but I believed he could hear me. So, I sat and spoke to Matt, filling him in on everything that had happened. Even though I didn't get a reply, it was nice to talk to him. It helped me believe he wasn't completely lost. He was still alive, and there was still hope to free him.

"There you are," Greg said walking across the courtyard with Harkura.

"Your Majesty, I have been looking all over for you," Harkura said. "Have you been talking to the tree?"

"I haven't been talking to the tree. I've been talking to Matt," I answered.

"Matt—he was your guardian before me?" he asked.

I nodded. "Yes, he was, and now he's trapped because of me, and I can't figure out how to break the seal."

"Mellissa, we will figure something out. It will just take time," Greg said. He held his hand out to me. "Come on. Let's head back, and we can do some research."

I took his hand, and he pulled me up. Holding hands with Greg and Harkura, I teleported home.

The next few days flew by. I went back to school. Everyone was going on about the strange weather pattern that had turned the sky black and the weird mirage that appeared by Stonehenge. It had been all over the news. Whenever I heard someone talking about it, I couldn't help but smile. If only they knew what really happened. I was handed loads of homework so I could catch up on what I had missed. It was pretty lonely without Matt. Victoria had come up with a story about him getting an apprenticeship, meaning he had to leave school. I couldn't help wondering why I had put off being queen for this. I just told myself I had to finish what I'd started, and I would be done come summer. I had so much work that I didn't have any time to do more research into breaking the seal on the tree. Greg offered to help me, but I told him I had to do it myself. Otherwise, I wouldn't learn anything. Come the weekend, I was glad to be going back to the magic world.

We had arranged to meet the Sea King, Radius, and some of his subjects at the edge of the ocean. I couldn't teleport us there, as I didn't know the area, so we had to go by carriage. The trains were finally running again, but there wasn't a line that went all the way to the beach. There was still snow on the ground but not as deep as before. It was suggested that the snow had been so uncommonly bad here because of Kadon's awakening and his use of the Moon Crystal, which kind of made sense. If the balance was offset, it would affect the weather.

Lady Gabrielle had a member of her staff dress me, since what I usually wore wasn't good enough to meet with the Sea King. I had met all of them in leggings and a jumper, so why not him? They put me in a pale green dress. It fit snugly on top, and the skirt flowed loosely down to my knees. To match the dress, I wore thick, dark green tights and some fancy snow boots. My hair was braided up and around my head, with flowers weaved into it. To finish the outfit off, I wore the dark green cloak lined with faux fur.

Lady Gabrielle turned me to look in a full-length mirror. "As queen, you need to get used to looking the part." All this fancy clothing didn't feel right. Lady Gabrielle placed a silver tiara on my head and smiled behind me. "Now, you are ready."

I nodded. She was right; this was something I was going to have to get used to. She walked me out to where the others were waiting. There were two carriages to take us to the coast. I got in one with my guardians and Greg. The other carriage was already occupied by Sir Lee and his people. He had insisted someone other than Greg oversee me on this important trip. What he really meant was that he wanted to make sure I didn't screw up. He didn't seem to like me for some reason. I wasn't going to let him bother me. If I let him get in my head, then I

would mess up. It was a simple task really. As long as I stayed calm, everything would be fine.

We arrived at a beautiful, sandy beach. As I stepped out of the carriage, I was hit by the salty sea air. The wind blew my hood off. We were greeted by two women in brightly coloured summer dresses. They were barefoot, with pretty jewels around their ankles and stunning headdresses held together by seashells. It was way too cold for how they were dressed, but they didn't seem affected by it. They led us down the beach toward a marquee decorated with seashells and flower petals. I tugged at my dress and cloak. I had no idea what to do with my hands. Greg took my hand and gave me a gentle smile. I needed to stop fidgeting.

There were two more women and three men. They were also dressed in bright colours and flowing dresses. The men were dressed very similarly to the women. The only difference was that their top halves were uncovered. One of the men wore gold jewellery and had a beautiful jewel-encrusted crown upon his head. He definitely looked royal, but there wasn't a fish tail in sight. He couldn't be the Sea King, could he?

"Hey, is that King Radius?" I whispered to Greg.

"I believe so," he replied.

"But he has legs. I thought mermen had fish tails."

"It's a simple spell to allow them to walk on land, but if they stay too long, their skin will dry up."

I pouted. It appeared I wasn't going to get to see the merfolk in fish form like I'd wanted to. They looked like normal people dressed for a day at the beach, who used seashells as fashion accessories. The king was around average height and very muscular with greying dark brown hair. The tall woman with fabulously long, bright red hair appeared to be his wife. Once we reached the marquee, they all bowed to me.

The king stepped forward. "It is an honour to have the elf queen herself come to meet us." He bowed, taking my hand and kissing it.

I felt my cheeks heating. Luckily, Greg had coached me on what to do. I greeted them just as we'd practiced the night before. The king introduced his people to me. I had been right about the identity of his wife. I was surprised that the others were their children, because firstly, even with the king's greying hair, he did not seem old enough to have children their age. Secondly, they didn't look related in any way. They were all different builds and had different facial features, hair colour and eyes. They were all stunning in their own way but had no common traits in their appearances. Then again, I looked nothing like my dad.

I went through all the official ceremonial stuff the council had insisted on. Then, I finally handed over the Moon Crystal. As King Radius took hold of the Moon Crystal, it shone brighter than I had seen it before. It was as if the crystal knew it was where it was supposed to be.

"You need to bind to it," I said, "and then the Moon Crystal will find you two guardians, just as the Heart Crystal did for me."

He did as I said, then two bright lights came out of the crystal and shot off into the ocean. Two new guardians would soon be drawn to the king. We then said our formal goodbyes, and the king thanked me for everything. I was arguing with myself on whether to ask him or not, and then decided there was no harm.

"King Radius, I know this may sound odd to you, but is it all right if I wait here while you and your family go back to the ocean? The thing is, I really want to see your beautiful tails." I felt like a little kid.

He gave me a wide, toothy smile. "Of course you can. Growing up in the human world, you have probably never seen real-life merfolk. You have done so much for us all. You stopped this world from falling into chaos, and at such a young age. It is the least we could do for you."

"Thank you so much." I almost squealed with excitement. He'd said yes and didn't seem to think I was rude or some crazy freak with a tail fetish.

The royal mer-family waved goodbye and headed off to the ocean. Sir Lee narrowed his eyes at me and curled his top lip. I turned my back on him.

I grabbed Greg's arm and shook him. "I'm going to see them in mermaid form." I ran to the water's edge. Victoria followed closely. She was almost as excited as me.

"The correct term is merfolk," Greg shouted after me.

I gave him a dismissive wave over my shoulder. I looked out at the ocean. Where were they? Farther out in the ocean, they jumped up out of the water and flipped their tails in the air. Their multi- coloured scales glistened in the sunlight. It was like something out of the movies. I had the biggest smile on my face. Victoria gasped behind me. They splashed back into the water, waving before swimming off. We all waved back at them. They were truly the most beautiful creatures I had ever seen. I skipped back to the carriage, the happiest I had been in a while.

When we got back to the council building, we had to go through all the formalities of filling out paperwork, stating that our trip had been a success. It seemed a bit much to me, but I had to abide by the rules. Once I was finished, I went to find the others so we could go home. They were all in the courtyard by the Tree of Time. Of course Greg had finished before me. It was nice to see Victoria talking to the tree like I had. It made me feel less crazy.

I laughed at Greg. He had been given the official robes worn by council members. "You know, those robes look ridiculous on you."

"You realise that they have had some made for you as well," he said.

"Well, I think we should get going before they get a chance to give them to me. Are we all ready?" I asked. Harkura and Victoria both nodded. I put my arm out, and they both grabbed hold of me. I looked over at Greg. "Aren't you coming as well?"

"I can't," Greg said.

The smile fell from my face. That hadn't been the answer I was expecting. "Why not?"

Victoria grabbed Harkura, stating that she'd forgotten something and needed his help, practically dragging him away.

"Because my life is here. Now that my father is gone, I have to take on his responsibilities. I have to make arrangements for his funeral, and then there will be an official ceremony, making me an elder. I will then have to oversee Novosvillas, just like my father did."

He wasn't telling me anything I didn't know. I knew he'd had a ton of responsibility thrust upon him, just as I had. I just hadn't expected him to take on the role so quickly.

"I know. I just don't know what I'm going to do without you."

"You don't need me anymore. Your powers and knowledge have grown more quickly than anyone could have imagined."

My chest tightened. I twiddled with my fingers. "I know. It's just—I don't—I have grown accustom to having you around."

"It's not like we aren't going to see each other again." He took my hands. "There is something we should maybe talk about though."

My face heated, and I just knew I was turning red. We did not need to talk about that. I knew I had overstepped, and Victoria, who I knew was hiding somewhere, did not need to know I had kissed him and that he was now making sure I knew he wasn't interested. My hands were clammy. I pulled them out of his and wiped them on my thighs. "There's nothing to talk about. I know it was a mistake. We are better as friends. Just friends."

"Err, yeah. That's it." He turned away from me.

"I guess this is it, then," I said. "You know, till the next council meeting."

"It doesn't have to be like that. We are still friends, right?"

"Right."

"Oh, and one more thing." He handed me a map. I unfolded it. The map was of the human world. He had circled an area in Lincolnshire. He pointed at it. "That is where I discovered the elf village. I'm sure they would love to meet you, and they may have some answers for you."

I hugged him. "Thank you." I felt empty inside. Hugs are a good way to hide your face. I wasn't sure I could keep the sadness from showing on mine. It wasn't like this was the end. It was just another change, one I would get used to.

Victoria casually strolled back with Harkura behind her, acting like she had finished whatever she'd needed help with. I shook my head at her. I knew she had been just out of sight, listening to everything.

"You guys ready?" I asked.

"Yes, Your Majesty. Goodbye, Sir Gregory." Harkura bowed to Greg and then came over and took my arm opposite Victoria.

"See ya, Flopsey." Victoria waved at him as she took hold of my other arm.

I stared at him as I teleported home.

That evening, after Victoria had gone home and Harkura was back in his tent, I decided it was time to talk to my dad about my plans. After dinner, when he was sat in the living room, I told him we needed to talk and that I had something to tell him. He instantly panicked and started jumping to conclusions.

"Oh no, this can't be happening. Don't say it. You're pregnant, aren't you? I knew I should have never let that boy stay in this house. It is all my fault, and now you're not going to go to university and get a degree. Where is that boy? I notice he isn't here tonight." He spiralled into catastrophe mode. I could clearly see where I got my overthinking and worrying from.

"What? No!" I yelled over him. "Why would you think

that of all things? Jeez, Dad, let me talk instead of jumping to crazy conclusions. It's not like that at all. Just no."

"Oh, good. What do you want to tell me then?" he asked, calming down.

"I wanted to talk to you about my future. As you know, I am the heir of the elf throne." I paused to check that he was following. He nodded. "Once I finish school, I was thinking about deferring my acceptance to university and going to live in the magical world for a bit to see what's there for me. I've always felt like I didn't quite fit in here, and maybe this is why. Maybe I belong there. I owe it to myself to take a ycar to find out."

I didn't know how he was going to respond. He had always wanted me to go to university and get a degree. He'd always wanted me to be a doctor. Even though I had chosen an English literature course, he was still so happy I had been offered a place everywhere I'd applied. It felt like I was letting him down, but this was something I felt really strongly about.

"I understand. I know I have always made a big deal about you getting a degree, but that was before I knew that your big brain and beauty weren't the only things you got from your mother. Take a year off. Go discover the world of magic. If it isn't for you, come back and go to uni, but if it's truly where you belong, forget about uni and become a magical queen. I have only ever wanted the best for you."

My dad was being really understanding. I had been worried about nothing. "Thanks, Dad."

" Where is Greg? You two haven't had another fight, have you?"

"No, he had to go back home. He will be taking his dad's place as a changeling elder, so he can't be hanging around the human world anymore."

"I feel bad for him, but he seemed to be handling it well when I last saw him. What is a changeling elder exactly?"

I tried to remember what Greg had told me. I put up three fingers. "I believe there are exactly three changeling elders, and they oversee the three major changeling cities. They are also members of the council."

My dad put his hand on his chin. "He is like changeling royalty? I guess he's not so bad after all—still hasn't got anything on being elf queen though."

"It's not that impressive being queen."

" If Greg has had to go back home, does that mean the two of you have broken up, or are you trying for a long-distance relationship?"

"What? Where are these crazy ideas coming from, Dad? Greg is not my boyfriend and never has been. We are just friends."

"All right, but you can't tell me there was nothing there. Did you not see how that boy cared for you?"

"Dad, I have no idea what you are talking about. Greg's a healer. He cares for everyone."

"You really don't see it, do you?" he asked. I shook my head at him. My dad hugged me and patted my head. "Please, don't ever change."

"I have no plans to, Dad."

Greg had been nothing but a good friend to me and didn't treat me like anything more. Maybe my dad had got his wires crossed the same way I had, thinking there was something more between me and Greg. I shook my head and left him to watch television.

"You ready?" Harkura asked.

I nodded. "They are elves like me. I need to do this."

We were on the edge of a field. Harkura had travelled with me to the place on the map Greg had circled. Once we were close enough, we would set off some sort of alarm and be attacked. According to Greg, it would be plant magic—something I could easily handle.

"Let's do this." I walked across the field.

We had been walking for about half an hour when an alarm went off. The grass sprung up and surrounded us.

"Stop," I commanded. Pushing my arms out, the grass went limp.

Three men ran toward us. "Who are you?" asked the older of the three. He narrowed his eyes on me. "You are an elf."

"Yes, I am Mellissa Hail, keeper of the Heart Crystal and heir to the elf throne."

They all dropped to their knees. The older man took my hand. "Welcome home, My Queen."

Epilogue
The Queen of Darkness

The Queen of Darkness paced in her throne room. This wasn't meant to happen. Her plan had been ruined. The girl wasn't meant to defeat Kadon. He was supposed to unwillingly do her bidding and kill her. Her servant bowed at her feet. She narrowed her eyes on him. "You failed me. Now there are two new crystal keepers to stand against me."

"I am sorry, My Queen. My hands were tied. That boy got in the way. If I was allowed to kill him too—"

She slapped him across the face. "Do not make excuses. It was your idea to release the leprechaun, and what did it achieve? You wasted my power only to put me at a disadvantage. My little bird has yet to fail me like you. Until she does, the boy is under my protection."

He cowered to his knees. "But it worked, My Queen. We flushed out the last royal."

She wrapped her talons around his hair and pulled him up to eye level. "And you failed to kill her." She threw him to the ground. "The lizard prophesied the keeper of the Heart would be the one to stop the darkness and restore balance. My plan only works if the world is out of balance, you fool! I have been hunting the royals for years, and it was all for nothing."

"I know, but the girl is still young and new to magic. She will be no match for you."

She gritted her teeth. Her powers were great. The keeper of the Sun Crystal had been unable to stop her. To an ancient one like herself, the girl was nothing but a baby and untrained. She may be able to kill the keeper of the Heart, but that would be attention she isn't ready for. The world could not know her plan, not until she had all the pieces in place. The girl was meant to die while Kadon was still around, so her death could be blamed on him.

With a flick of her wrist, she produced a shadow ball. "Give me one good reason I shouldn't kill you."

He grovelled at her feet. "Please, My Queen. My family have been loyal servants for generations. I still have sway with the council and can feed you information on them."

She snarled, throwing the shadow ball just past him. He threw himself backward, wrapping his arms around himself. Pathetic, but he may still prove useful. A small orange bird glided in through the window. She put her arm out for her to land on. "What news do you bring me, Little Bird?"

Little Bird lowered its head. "My Queen, I bring wonderful news. I have located the Land Stone."

A wicked grin spread across her face. The Land Stone was the exact opposite of the Heart Crystal. The girl didn't stand a chance against it, and added to her own power, she would be unstoppable.

ABOUT THE AUTHOR

Whitney Morris has always had a passion for storytelling. Growing up she loved to escape to into the fantasy worlds of magic from her stories. She is a cat lover with one of her own, is crazy about owls, and is addicted to chocolate.

Whitney loves books, and she and her husband are raising their four children to be fellow bookworms in South Yorkshire, England.

Whitney has a degree in psychology and uses it to make her characters feel authentic. CRYSTAL HEART is her debut novel.

Find Whitney on social media

Instagram   @wrlmorris_author

Facebook,
BookBub,
Twitter &   @wrlmorris
Pinterest

www.ingramcontent.com/pod-product-compliance
Lightning Source LLC
Chambersburg PA
CBHW051008180726
48291CB00006B/2022